The Abyss line of cutting-edge psychological horror is committed to publishing the best, most innovative works of dark fiction available. Abyss is horror unlike anything you've ever read before. It's not about haunted houses or evil children or ancient Indian burial grounds. We've all read those books, and we all know their plots by heart.

Abyss is for the seeker of truth, no matter how disturbing or twisted it may be. It's about people, and the darkness we all carry within us. Abyss is the new horror from the dark frontier. And in that place, where we come face-to-face with terror, what we find is ourselves.

"Thank you for introducing me to the remarkable line of novels currently being issued under Dell's Abyss imprint. I have given a great many blurbs over the last twelve years or so, but this one marks two firsts: first *unsolicited* blurb (*I* called *you*) and the first time I have blurbed a whole *line* of books. In terms of quality, production, and plain old storytelling reliability (that's the bottom line, isn't it?), Dell's new line is amazingly satisfying . . . a rare and wonderful bargain for readers. I hope to be looking into the Abyss for a long time to come."

—Stephen King

Please turn the page for more
extraordinary acclaim . . .

PRAISE FOR ABYSS

"What *The Twilight Zone* was to TV in 1959, what *Night of the Living Dead* was to horror films in 1968, what Stephen King was to dark fiction in the mid-70s—Abyss books will be to horror in the 1990s."

—Mark Hurst, editor of *The Golden Man*

"Gorgeously macabre eye-catching packages . . . I don't think Abyss could have picked a weirder, more accomplished novel [than *The Cipher*] to demonstrate by example what the tone and level of ambition of the new line might be."

—*Locus*

"A splendid debut."

—*Rave Reviews*

"Dell is leading the way."

—*Writer's Digest*

"They are exploring new themes and dimensions in the horror field. My hat's off to Koja, Hodge, Dee and Dillard, as the others forthcoming! And hats off to Dell Abyss!"

—Gary S. Potter, author of *The Point Beyond*

"I was amazed at the high level of quality that permeates all aspects of the series. . . . It's such a pleasure to see Dell doing something original with dark fantasy/horror."
—Richard L. Cooke, Literary Editor,
Tekeli-li! Journal of Terror

"The most exciting line of horror novels to hit the field in a very long time. . . . The Abyss line will not only leave its mark on the field but may very well revitalize it."
—From the *Time Tunnel* newsletter

"The new Abyss line of horror fiction has provided some great moments in their first year."
—*Mystery Scene*

"Inaugurating Dell's new Abyss Books series, this powerful first novel, [THE CIPHER] is as thought-provoking as it is horrifying."
—*Publishers Weekly*

"Claustrophobic, paranoid . . . compelling, Dell's new horror line is definitely worth keeping an eye on."
—*Science Fiction Eye*

PRAISE FOR
THE MAKING OF A MONSTER

"The most impressive first novel I've read in some time. Petersen uses her experience as former lead singer and songwriter for the Catholic Girls to strong advantage here. Although Petersen did not invent the idea of the vampire as rock star, she makes the best and most convincing use of it ever here. Better than Anne Rice!"
—Tyson Blue, *Cemetery Dance*

THE MAKING OF A MONSTER

Gail Petersen

A DELL BOOK

Published by
Dell Publishing
a division of
Bantam Doubleday Dell Publishing Group, Inc.
1540 Broadway
New York, New York 10036

The trademarks Dell® and Abyss® are registered in the U.S. Patent and Trademark Office.

ISBN: 0-440-21389-4

Printed in the United States of America

Published simultaneously in Canada

June 1993

10 9 8 7 6 5 4 3 2 1

OPM

FOR

the Catholic Girls,
Niagara Falls,
the C.I.A.,
and all the bands
who dreamt they would live forever

Special thanks
to
the Hollywood Screenwriters Club,
Jeanne Cavelos,
Tony Gardner,
and Laurel Thomas

1
Possessed

I never knew the meaning of homesickness till I moved to Los Angeles. That feeling of yearning for everything familiar, from the way your mother's couch looks to the sun rising instead of setting over the water. A feeling that husbands and homes cannot make disappear. A feeling that makes you do desperate things.

I am thoroughly convinced that I would not be in the state I'm in now except for homesickness. After only two months in Los Angeles I was ready to run back home to New York and told Ben that. "This is the land of the friendless," I said, but he had already made friends at the computer job that brought us here, so it was not a valid point for him.

Ben made friends easily, while I was always lost on unfamiliar terrain. My husband was one of those people anyone could relate to. He knew how to tell a joke, how to give a compliment, how to put someone at ease. He was never at home with the darker side of life, had very few regrets, and could adapt to anything, even a place as foreign as Los Angeles.

"Once you start working," he said to me as we unpacked our pots and pans, "everything will be different.

Just give this town a chance, at least a year, before we give up the five thousand bucks we spent moving here." Of course, it always comes down to financial reasons. People ask why a family stays living near Three Mile Island, or any nuclear power plant for that matter. . . . The answer's always money. You can never be sure the worst is going to happen, so rather than risk losing your home or your life savings, you stay and let disaster wash over you.

I felt disaster coming, but I could not be sure whether this premonition was really a sign from God or wishful thinking on my part. Even though I barely thought about heaven or hell anymore, after twelve years of Catholic school I was still subject to a twinge of religious conscience whenever things did not go right. But because Ben believed it was all in my mind and convinced my conscious self it was, too, all those dreams of the end of the world fell on deaf ears. It was only my unconscious self that still believed, and I would wake up in the middle of the night in terror, positive that an earthquake was about to tear our house down or that World War III had just begun.

One night, fresh from a dream that left me shaking, I actually called Kevin, my older brother, back in New York. It was 3:00 A.M. L.A. time, which made it 6:00 in the morning back east, so I thought I might be able to catch him before he left for work. The phone rang and rang until finally I heard his voice, low and breathless.

"Yeah?"

"It's me, Kate."

"Kate? What's wrong?"

I heard someone whisper in the background, his wife, Maddie. There was movement and the click of a light switch. "Are you all right? Is Ben all right?"

For a moment I was speechless, not even sure why I

had called. Maybe I needed an answer only my family could provide. Maybe I just needed a connection with something familiar. But Kevin had been totally against our move to L.A. To him it was "an alien place populated by visitors from another dimension." So in the darkness of this other planet, which I now called my home, I found I could not admit defeat, not even to one of my own.

"I just miss you," I said.

Kevin laughed. "You pick a helluva time to tell me."

"Is it light there yet?"

"Almost. Are you sure you're okay?"

"I'm fine. Really. Are you okay?"

"I'm fine, too, Kate, but you did interrupt something."

"Oh, sorry." I realized my mistake. Kevin and Maddie's latest priority had been starting a family. "Well, I just wanted to say hi. I'll let you go."

"Okay. We'll be at Mom and Dad's for the ritual Sunday dinner. I'll talk to you then, Kate."

I hung up the phone and looked at Ben, whose snoring was audible even with the covers over his head. Almost sunrise in New York and still so many hours to go here before I saw the light again. Since I knew I would not fall back to sleep, I grabbed my Walkman and headed for the living room. I needed the distraction and comfort of music to separate me from the quiet menace of the night. I put the earphones on and pumped up the volume. It was the only way I could ever have it loud. After programming a computer all day, the last thing Ben wanted to hear was rock music blaring when he came home. So I confined my listening to the twilight hours when I was alone. Already the melody was soothing my nerves and relegating my nightmare to its proper place—only a dream.

But as I walked to the living room, I still checked the locks on the doors and windows. Even though I had only been dreaming, I wanted to make sure no real demons could find me before dawn.

It was at the beginning of July, our third month in L.A., that I finally started job hunting. I had made a million and one excuses before that. I didn't know the area, we still had unpacking to do, it was too hot. Finally I ran out of excuses, and the weight of boredom drove me out of the house and into an office-temps agency.

I knew how to type on a computer, and while I could not command the money Ben made with his ability to program, I was still in demand from all the businesses that needed someone to do the things no one else wanted to. The agency put me to work the next day, and that began the routine that would mark my numbered days of summer and sun in L.A. "I hate the routine of nine to five," I complained to Ben every morning as I dressed for work, although on the West Coast it was 8:00 to 5:00. I had been thunderstruck that Los Angeles did not subscribe to the thirty-five-hour work week that New York had, and felt it was just one more reason for me to long for the East Coast.

"If you hate routine so much," Ben had answered, "why don't you find a career for yourself so you won't have to go to work and just type." He had never been able to understand why a college graduate with a degree in English did not have a calling in life. For the last five years I had tried—first in advertising, then teaching, then publishing—but had gotten nowhere. With our move to L.A., I had finally given up and believed myself to be just one of the masses that made up our nondescript work force.

Being one of the masses now seems such a beautiful, peaceful thing, and the routine of the ordinary a dream to aspire to. There are still times I wish I could find the safety of that dream again, when I wish I could still wake up in the morning with Ben beside me and worry about what dress to wear to my job. Instead, in the nightmare my life is now, it's always night and nothing will ever be the same again.

As I went from one temp job to another, I ran into other people who were employed by the same agency or others just like it. Inevitably they were actors and actresses who had moved here from some other part of the country to compete in the world's hardest profession. They worked in between auditions and bit parts and always introduced themselves by their most famous role, specifying how many lines they had in their latest part and who their current agent was.

Ben thought all actors were idiots and masochists, that only a fool would want to give up every luxury in life to pay for such things as head shots and to waste valuable recreation time sitting for hours in a casting director's waiting room. In fact, he thought every aspect of the entertainment business was frivolous and inane. But as I Xeroxed and collated with them and entered data into an Apple computer next to them, I began to feel jealous of their commitment, camaraderie, and sense of purpose. They moved in a world that was larger than life. I began to envy their discussions of who was the best acting coach in town and their gossip of who was casting what and why. I became drawn into their unique world—a club, a secret society. And when I finally saw Marla, a temp from my agency with whom I had worked in several offices, starring in a Burger World commercial, I decided at that moment to give it a try. I decided I would ask Marla for a recommendation for a good acting class. At least, then I would have a purpose in life, a reason for being in sunny California.

Ben's reaction to my enrolling in Marla's acting class was predictable. He rolled his eyes in disgust but was secretly pleased I had found something to do, so I would stop complaining to him. His job had become even more demanding, and he never got home earlier than 8:00 or 9:00 at night. And once home, Ben would position himself in front of the TV and eat whatever snack food was available. I would sit across from him in the blue flowered chair and listen to him devour the corn chips one by one while the Santa Ana winds blew hot, dry air around our house and rattled our metal mailbox outside. I think it was on my first day of class that we stopped making love.

It took me an hour in traffic to reach Sandy Klein's acting workshop in West Hollywood, and I was nervous. What had possessed me to take an acting class with a bunch of strangers, I'll never know. But I had made up my mind, and there was no turning back. By the time I walked in, ten minutes late and overheated from the lack of air-conditioning in my car, Sandy was already debating the merits of The Method with his students. He brought the discussion to a halt as his tiny eyes met mine. "You must be Kate," he said, grabbing my hand and leading me to the stage. "You might as well start right now."

There were already five people in Sandy Klein's acting workshop, but he was willing to make it an even six on Marla's insistence and a check from me. I didn't want him to do me any favors, but since I had made up my mind to act, I was happy for the opportunity. Now, as I looked at Sandy's red suspenders, I wasn't so sure. I had no idea what went on in an acting class, but as with everything else in L.A., I learned the hard way.

My first lesson consisted of me telling the class about myself, with Sandy asking questions during the pauses. As I faced the darkness that hid the other four students, I found myself grateful that the fifth person seemed to be absent tonight and was missing the degradation I felt was impending. I began to compose my farewell excuses to Sandy as I spoke about myself:

"My name is Kate Davis, and I'm . . . ah, twenty-seven years old and, ah . . . I've only been in L.A. three months. I'm originally from New York and, ah . . ."

"Why did you come to L.A., Kate?"

"I, ah, I came for a job, you know. . . ."

"And why are you taking this class?"

That was a good question, but my mind was going blank. Panic was setting in. I could feel my arms held tensely against my sides and I could feel my feet aching to run. My haircut wasn't right. My clothes were too bland. Everyone in the class looked better than me. Obviously the stage would join the ranks of my failed attempts at advertising and teaching. I should have remembered how I hated to stand up in front of a class.

"Well, I thought I would like to try acting, you know, I met Marla at a job, and she was so enthusiastic, you know, I thought it would be a good thing to try."

Through all this I could hear some of my classmates sighing and yawning. I began to wish I had never even thought of acting, that I had never met Marla, that I had never come to California, that I was dead or at least unconscious for a while. I could already picture Ben asking me in a mocking tone, "So when is your next lesson?" and me having to explain I was not cut out for the exhibitionism of acting. I looked down and actually saw my toes twitching in my sneakers, moving even though I willed them to stop.

"Tell me some things you like, Kate."

"Ah, what do you mean?"

"Anything that you like, to do, to read, to own, to think about."

"Well, I like animals, and I like ice cream, and I like to

read a lot, and I like to see movies, particularly old movies, like the ones from the thirties and the forties. . . ."

"What is this, a video date?" I heard one guy mumble in the audience. That was the last straw. I calculated how many steps there were from the stage to the door. Only a few seconds in time and I could be out of there forever. I decided to make a break for it. But then the door opened, and the missing member of the class walked in and sat in the back of the darkness. I was starting to get angry now, at Sandy, at Marla, at myself, and even at the newcomer I had thought would be spared my foolish monologue.

"And I like to not have to work, and the way soda tastes when you're thirsty, and how quiet it is at three in the morning when most of the world is asleep, and I like to be alone sometimes so I can think, and I like New York during the day when everyone is rushing somewhere, and I like New York at night when everyone is still rushing somewhere but it's probably to a play or a concert or the opera. And I like *La Bohème* because the heroine dies tragically before the hero ever has a chance to fall out of love with her."

I stopped, surprised at myself, and realized the room had grown quiet. As I stared into the darkness, I thought I could see the glimmer of two eyes shining at me. I took that as a sign of encouragement.

"And what are you afraid of, Kate?"

"I'm afraid of this class."

Everyone laughed sympathetically.

"I'm afraid of spiders and rats, and I'm afraid of being alone for too long, and I'm afraid of serial killers, rapists, and the possibility of aliens. And I'm afraid of going crazy and never accomplishing anything. I'm afraid that I really do have a calling in life but will never be able to figure out what it is. And I'm afraid that there is no heaven or hell, only nothingness. And I'm afraid of dying because I know it will hurt and because there are so many things I won't have done and will never have the opportunity to do again."

"Thank you, Kate, for sharing this with us," Sandy said, smiling. "You can come down now and take a seat. Carrie and Jim, you go up on stage and do your scene from *A Thousand Clowns.* The rest of you pay attention to their technique and let them know what they're doing wrong."

For a moment I could not move. I had been so lost in my own thoughts. But it felt good to be standing up there with everyone watching and listening. Even though I wasn't acting per se, I had captured their attention. For a moment the stage had been my home. "Okay," I said, as I found my way down the stairs and into the back of the small theater.

For most of my life I had believed in nothing. I had stopped accepting Santa Claus by age seven, and as soon as I could get away with it, about age twelve, I stopped going to church. Abstract concepts like pure good and pure evil seemed ridiculous to me at that time, and the idea of God as avenger as outdated as magic. But as I took my seat in Sandy Klein's little theater, in that little place called California, I found something bigger than life sitting in the next seat, which I thought was empty. I turned my head to look into the deepest green eyes I had ever seen. They belonged to the latecomer of our little theater class. "Hi," he said, his glance never wavering for a moment. "I'm Justin." And at that moment I believed in temptation.

If I had been as enlightened as I am now, I would have started praying right then and there. Instead, I experienced with pleasure the excitement of complete and total physical attraction, the kind they call love at first sight. In the weeks to come, insult would be added to injury as obsessive mental attraction also set in and I became a woman reeling from one emotion to another. But for now, all I wanted to do was sit next to this man for hours.

Carrie and Jim had finished their scene without me even knowing it, and Sandy was giving his closing speech of the day, something about persistence or perseverance or whatever. I had not moved my eyes from Justin's, and I really didn't care if the next earthquake started right then.

I was thoroughly and completely lost. I just didn't know it was for forever.

Suddenly everyone was standing up and saying good night. "I have to meet someone in ten minutes," Justin said, "or I'd join you all for coffee. Maybe next week we could talk for a while after class. I found your thoughts very interesting."

"That would be great," I said. As he turned and left, I felt an emptiness in the space he had just occupied.

"What was going on back there?" Marla asked good-naturedly. "You give a great performance and then just sit down and stare at Justin for the rest of the class."

"I was staring?" I said, just now realizing how foolish I must have looked to him and everyone else.

"Of course you were staring. For a moment I thought you two knew each other already, like you had been lovers in a past life or something."

"Oh, no, I just . . . I don't know what I was doing."

"Well, honey," Marla said, as she propelled me out of the theater into the night, "he is something to look at, I'll give you that. But he is a strange one. Don't really know anything about him except that he's a good actor when he wants to be. Never joins us for coffee or a drink afterward, either. A real loner that one. Mr. Mystery."

"Well, he mentioned he'll join us next week," I said, not able to suppress the smirk that was building up on my face. And at that moment I felt absolutely pleased with myself.

Later, as I got into bed with Ben, who had been asleep since ten and was snoring at top volume, I was still pleased. I had not felt so energetic and excited since I went out on my first date when I was thirteen. Already I was planning what I would wear to class next week. I would have to go out and buy a whole new wardrobe. None of my clothes seemed worthy of him.

I thought of the week ahead, and six days without a glimpse of Justin seemed intolerable. How would I survive? I tossed and turned for hours that night, reconstructing with incredible delight those few moments I'd had with him. But when I finally slept, my dreams were not pleasant at all, they were nightmares. And no matter how many times Ben woke me up and told me everything was all right, I would plunge right back into the frightening world my unconscious mind had created and begin to scream again. When morning finally came, I was spared and did not remember any of the details of my nightmares or even that they were so bad.

Romantic illusions are the worst of all, and I remember my displays of obsessive behavior with an overwhelming feeling of regret. I had played it safe with men all of my life. I never took chances. My heart never ruled my head. But now I was ready to give myself over to complete abandon. I was behaving like an idiot and enjoying it. I can still recall the excitement I felt when Justin joined us for coffee that next week after class. Marla, Jim, Carrie, and Roger were there, but I barely noticed them. Everything they said was meaningless; I only wanted to hear Justin speak. I was thrilled when he gave me one tidbit of information about himself, something about a book he liked or a movie he had seen. But if I really thought about it, I would have realized he was telling me nothing. At the end of the night my coffee cup was still full and so was Justin's. I took this as another sign. I had been too excited even to drink it. Maybe he felt the same way.

I remember how as the weeks went on, I would sit at night with Ben as we watched television and think only of what Justin was doing at that point in time, what he was thinking about, and wonder if he was thinking of me. One day I would feel elated because he bought me a book on auditions he thought I would need soon. The next day I would imagine Justin with someone else, and everything about Ben would annoy me. I began to hate the way he buttered his toast, the way he drank his beer, how he parked the car, how easily he fell asleep. I wanted my husband to go away. I wished I had never been married, that I was someone else with a more interesting and intriguing life, that I was a woman of mystery.

In the back of my mind I knew I was being crazy, but my situation was so much like an episode from a Gothic novel that I could not resist feeling like the long-suffering heroine who could not be with the man she loved.

I decided that Ben did not have any of the finer points at all. He could barely get through Stephen King, let alone all of *Remembrance of Things Past* as Justin had and could quote from at a moment's notice. And then Ben was so ordinary-looking, slightly balding, with brown hair, a little extra weight, and clothes that were just there, while Justin seemed to stand out anywhere, either because he always wore black or because he had that look in his eyes of someone about to be famous. With his jet black hair and his perfect pale skin, he looked like a brooding movie star from the fifties—sensitive and a little lost, with just the right amount of forcefulness to bend me to his will. I was so obsessed that at times I even wanted to be him, so I could know him better and love him more.

Along with my obsessive thinking, I became extremely arrogant about my existence and found it unnecessary to explain to Ben why I was meeting Marla and the others after work to prepare a scene or to hang out in the local actors' bar. Sometimes Justin was there, and I felt more alive than I ever had in the five years of my marriage to Ben. I would drink just a little too much gin and forget that I had a home in Tarzana to go back to. I would talk too much. I would tell him things about myself that I had forgotten. About the diary I had written when I was nine. About the guitar I had bought when I was fifteen and how I'd wanted to be in a band, like every other teenager on earth. Or the song I had composed and thrown away.

And Justin would always listen, always know the right thing to say. He was sympathetic, understanding, and caring. I would look into his green eyes and every anxiety, every doubt I had ever felt would disappear. He knew me better than I knew myself. It seemed like magic. It seemed like a dream come true. He was the prince from a fairy tale—strong, silent, perfect. Almost too perfect to be real. But then, I wasn't interested in reality anymore. I was chasing the dream.

But when he wasn't there, the world was a lonely place. I would try to make do with the company of the other actors, but nothing could compensate my loss. I mourned him all night long, wondering why he couldn't stay.

He never gave a reason for the times when he left directly after class. And as I sat with a drink in my hand, laughing and pretending I was engrossed in the conversation, I was really on the verge of tears, believing Justin to be doing something so wonderful that he didn't care if he ever saw me again.

I even began to think of sleeping with him. By now, my

marriage had dwindled to a good-night kiss, and I played out the scene between Justin and me in a highly dramatic way. One night after class Justin would say that he had to talk to me about something. As we sat having coffee, he would look very distressed and say he could no longer hold it in. "I love you, Kate," he would blurt out. "I know it's wrong, you probably belong to someone else, but I will die if I can't have you in my life. Please come back to my apartment tonight, and I promise I won't hurt you. I only want to love you."

I, of course, after much soul-searching and the revelation that I was indeed married, would go back to his place, which would be beautiful and immaculate, and we would fall on the floor by the fireplace and make passionate love for hours. What would happen after this I didn't really want to think about, although I was already hiding away tiny bits of money just in case. As if that would solve everything. How foolish all that seems now, almost absurd. If only I had stopped for a minute and thought it through. Maybe then I would have heeded the alarm bells that were clanging inside my head or noticed my guardian angel trying to throw himself between me and evil itself. Maybe I would have prayed. Maybe someone would have listened. I should have remembered how much Ben loved me and kept on loving me even as I became a stranger to him. Maybe then I would not have had to hide under the Santa Monica pier at midnight, fearing that Justin would find me.

When I think about it now, I knew hardly anything about that man, even though I thought I knew him in my heart. I knew he was six feet tall, in perfect shape, with beautiful black hair and very, very green eyes. I knew he lived somewhere in West Los Angeles and had enough money that he did not have to have a day job. I knew he was well read, knew everything about art and music, and could play the piano perfectly. He was also incredibly witty and always knew what sarcastic remark would make me laugh.

But I did not know how old he was, where he was originally from, or why he had the money he did. I did not know if he had a girlfriend—or boyfriend, for that matter —or what he did when he was not in class or socializing afterward. He was an eternal mystery, and I found him fascinating.

"Why are you wearing clothes like that to a class?" Ben asked me the week before hell broke loose.

"I'm tired of looking like I always do—so conservative in a tee shirt and jeans. They wear a lot of short skirts out here, you should know that," I replied, gathering my script up in my arms. We were reading *Antigone* tonight, and I was prepared. Although how Sandy thought he could possibly direct a Greek tragedy, I did not know.

"Do they also wear a lot of black, and do you have to mess up your hair like that?"

Ben knew I was becoming a different person, even though he had no idea what to do about it. He was just an ordinary man doing an ordinary job. He was not equipped to deal with the supernatural. His work was exhausting him, and he barely had time to get a good night's sleep let alone worry about what state my mind was in now. If asked at the time, he probably would have been surprised to learn that we had stopped making love. I didn't care, because it gave me more time to think of Justin and a possible excuse to ask Ben for a divorce. I finally could see the real reason I had come to L.A. It was to be my destiny to find true love, the kind of emotional love I had always wanted, here on the West Coast, and what Ben thought of my clothes didn't matter anymore.

"Look, Ben—" I said, but stopped as I didn't want a

confrontation now. I opened the front door. "Well, never mind, I've got to go or I'll be late. See you later."

"Bye," he said, and the look of sadness he had on his face would come back to haunt me again and again.

Sandy's class that night was no big thrill, but then again everything took a backseat to my feelings for Justin. It was only at the end of the class when he had Justin and me read together that I felt something verging on ecstasy. I looked so deeply into his eyes that I felt I was about to fall in.

At that point Justin took my hands, and that first feeling of contact sent an electric charge through my body. I felt his fingers curl around mine and exert just the tiniest bit of pressure. His hands were cool, but they made my temperature rise to unbelievable heights. I knew I was ready to take the plunge. I no longer cared about consequences or what it would be like telling my mother that I had met a man in L.A. and was getting a divorce. Or what Ben would feel when I calmly announced my intentions to him. I was also positive that this was the night Justin would reveal his love for me. I never thought for a minute that I was assuming too much. As Sandy gave us our assignments for next week, I looked over at the man I loved with longing and smiled, but he returned my smile with a look of complete blankness. And as everyone left, so did Justin with only a brief good-bye. I stood outside, watching him disappear into the night, and I could not remember where my car was parked. I looked at my keys, unsure of what to do next. I had been completely wrong. There was nothing between us at all except in my imagination.

For a moment all I wanted to do was die. To steal a bottle of someone's sleeping pills and take them all with a glass of straight Scotch. Sandy would announce it in class next week: "I don't know how to tell you this, but our

Kate has gone and left us." And Justin would burst into tears as he realized he loved me and had just ignored me when he saw me last. Then he would be sorry and I would be dead and living in hell, the hell the nuns had taught us about in Catholic school, the one my mother still believed in—an inferno full of everlasting torment, where sinners and devils lived side by side. I stopped for a moment. Why did I say hell? That was not a romantic picture at all, and the feeling of fear it gave me took away the tears that had started to fall.

"Are you all right?" Marla asked, looking at me strangely. I had not even noticed she was standing next to me.

"I'm just overtired," I said. "I think I'll skip the coffee and go right home."

Marla did not press the issue any further, but there was sympathy on her face. "See you next week," she said, turning to join the others. And for the first time in a long time, I felt the need to be home, to be among familiar things and faces. To be somewhere safe. To have Ben put his arms around me and make me feel comfortable and warm. For the first time in weeks, I actually raced my little red Ford to get home.

But that feeling did not last, and by the next day I was convinced I was dead and living in hell. Hell being a place where I had to go to work every day and come back at night to Ben. A place where everything was mundane and repetitious and I had nothing to look forward to. Hell being a life without Justin.

I began to think seriously of going back east for a while, a visit at the very least. I was sick of the palm trees and the smog, the skateboards, the surfboards, the free-ways, the traffic, the self-serve gas stations, and the 7-Elevens. I was sick of always being warm, of the build-ings always being new, the lack of history, the lack of tradition, the lack of continuity. We had been in L.A. six months now, and it seemed a lifetime since I had seen my family. I had begun to feel a very strong need to be with my mother and father and Kevin again, as if it would be the last time I would ever see them. I didn't know how right I was about that. I only wish I had obeyed my better instincts that surfaced for those six days before the next class and taken an airplane right out of here. I never did buy my ticket, and now it's too late.

By the time the next class rolled around, I was frantic. One minute I hated Justin for ignoring me, the next I was afraid I had done something to deserve it. But he never left my mind, not even for a minute. For the last two nights I had even seen him—everywhere. In the supermarket, in the car ahead of me, outside my window. I was haunted by his image, transferring it to every stranger's face.

Ben had become a complete nonentity. He was just someone who lived in the same apartment as I did and to whom I had to speak when necessary. We moved through the rooms of our rented house without touching, discussing only the bills, the mail, the phone. His job was becoming so demanding that he usually came home just in time to sleep. I think he had given up on trying to reach me and was just waiting for the other shoe to drop.

I stood in front of the mirror, studying my black dress, trying to decide whether to attend class or not. Parting my hair first on the right side, then the left. Putting a pair of silver earrings on, then deciding gold was better.

I wasn't sure if I could face Justin again. One look into his eyes and I would probably faint dead away. But I finally opted to attend, as I did not want to look like the lovesick fool I was. He wouldn't have to feel sorry for me. I would show him. I decided to play it completely arrogant and ignore him right back. If he joined the group after class, I would say I had other plans just as he had last week. That would keep him guessing, keep him awake at night.

Unfortunately the best-laid plans are always thwarted, and my attitude of arrogance was thrown for a loop when I got to class ahead of everyone only to find Justin standing at Sandy's locked door, early as well. My composure was so shattered that for a moment I only wanted to turn and run as fast and as far as I could. Because he had already seen me, I knew this was impossible. I simply had to calm down and act completely normal. With one of Sandy's relaxation exercises, I tried to loosen the muscles in my neck, but they were locked in place and my toes were twitching again.

I never reached the door. Justin came running up to me, grabbed my hand, and said, "Kate, I've got to talk to you about something—right now. Please, could you cut class with me and go somewhere?"

I was totally shocked at hearing my own scenario a week late. "Yes," I said, because I knew this was the only response I had ever written for myself, "of course I will." And with all the beauty of temptation itself, Justin took my hand and smiled.

Somehow I must have gotten into his black Porsche with him, and somehow I must have agreed to go to his condo, although it's hard to remember. Things had started to take on a dreamlike quality, and details were getting lost. Streets were hidden in fog. The car radio made no sense.

Of course, his condo was gorgeous and immaculate, and it had a fireplace with a fire already started. It was so clean, in fact, it looked as if no one lived there. It was only later that I would remember things like that. Things like there were no photographs in his place, no mail any-

where, and when I went into the kitchen with him for a
bottle of wine, there was no food in the refrigerator, either. At the time none of this registered, only that he had
invited me into his home and that we would probably end
up in bed.

He poured the wine as we sat in front of the fireplace
and talked. "You are someone very special, Kate. Do you
know that?" I noticed he did not pour himself a glass of
wine. "You aren't like most people. You have a restless
urgency that I find unbearably attractive. It reminds me
of someone I used to know, a long time ago."

The wine was already going to my head, so I could only
nod in a knowing fashion as I felt the weight of desire
spread through my entire body. *Take me Justin,* I was
thinking. *Take me.*

"I've been debating about this for some time, Kate.
I've even come into your dreams to see what was there.
You know, you deserve better than a man like Ben, who
doesn't have a clue about your needs or the depth of your
imagination."

My dreams. I felt compelled to lay my head down. *I
must be hearing wrong. And how does he know Ben's
name? I've never mentioned it, let alone that I'm married.*

"You don't have to be afraid of death, you know. There
is a way."

I felt that I was fading fast, even after just half a glass
of wine. "Do you love me, Kate?" he asked, as he knelt
over me, his green eyes so close they didn't even seem
real. They sparkled with an unnatural light.

"Yes, Justin, I do." And as I slipped into a dream of
drunkenness, I heard his response from far away.

"Good. Then I will take you now."

In my dream I was able to fly. All I had to do was think
about it and I was in the air. I took off from L.A. at night
and headed out over the Pacific Ocean. It was beautiful

to see the lights shining below, and the air felt abnormally clear. Someone was flying beside me, but I didn't know who it was. He kept saying, "Look at me, Kate, just open your eyes and look at me." But I wouldn't. Instead, I looked down and saw the continent of Africa as if it were attached to some giant map of the world. I wondered what it would be like to live in Africa and then fly off to Paris when the mood struck me.

But then I was in bed in a strange white bedroom, making love with someone I could not recognize. I knew it wasn't Ben because everything felt too good. It was so intense that it seemed as if I was losing myself drop by drop, as if blood was draining out of my body and being replaced by a magical fluid that made every nerve ending alive with pleasure. I felt as if I couldn't stand it, but I wanted it anyway.

And then the bedroom faded away, and I was standing outside a diner looking in. In one of the booths at the window sat my grandmother, who had been dead for five years. I was so happy to see her again that I raced inside to sit across from her. "Grandma," I said, but already she was getting up and leaving. "Wait. Where are you going?"

But she shook her head. "It's too late now, Kate. I was waiting for you, but now it's too late."

And then she was gone. And I was left sitting in that diner with its white walls and white tables, crying and crying because I knew she was right.

When I woke up, the first thing I realized was that I had a hangover worse than any hangover in existence. The next thing I realized was that I was in a strange bedroom that looked vaguely familiar. Then I realized I was tied up.

Each of my hands was secured with rope to the brass headboard, and my feet were attached to the bedposts. I was completely naked. I remembered now, it was Justin's bedroom. *Oh, my God,* I thought, *he's some kind of nut—a serial killer, an ax murderer.*

Looking around wildly, I realized there were stairs leading upward. The bedroom was below the rooms I was in last night. The carpet here was the same pure white as in the living room. And even though there were no windows and the room was dark except for a very tiny night-light, I sensed it was daytime. Time had passed, and I had been conscious of nothing. A feeling of total and complete fear overcame me and scared the headache and nausea of a hangover right out of me.

I can't believe it, I thought, *I'm going to die. I went home with another man. Someone I don't even know, and now I'm going to die. And it's going to be in some horrible and disgusting manner. He'll cut me up slowly or something worse. I've got to get out of here before he comes back.*

I started struggling with the ropes, but it didn't do any good. It only increased the pain in my wrists and ankles. *Please, God, help me. I'm sorry. I'll never do it again. Just help me get away. I don't want to die like this. In fact, I don't want to die at all. Please.*

I started to cry and thought of Ben waking up this morning to find I had never come home. First, he'd be mad, but as the day wore on and he kept calling the house from work to see if I was there, he'd become worried. He would probably try to call Marla, once he found her number in my book, but she didn't know that I had tried to get to class, only that I had never gotten there. The only thing she would know was that Justin wasn't there, either. But even if she decided to tell Ben that much, no one knew Justin's last name, let alone where he lived. The only clue, parked a few blocks away from Sandy's building, would be my red Ford, which now probably had a ticket on it.

I was doomed. I would die as an adulteress and be

discovered in some empty lot days from now. Everyone would think I got what I deserved. My mother would be mortified, my father astounded, Kevin mystified. Lying there in that ridiculous position, sobbing, I realized that this kind of thinking would get me nowhere. So I made a valiant attempt to stop crying and look around at the room I was prisoner in.

Everything in it was white: the wall-to-wall carpeting, the walls themselves, on which nothing hung, the closet double doors that faced the bed, and the sheets on which I was lying. The only other object in the room besides the bed was a nightstand that held a clock. I pulled my head up as far as I could to get a look at the time. 7:00 P.M. It was almost nighttime of the next day. I could hardly believe I had slept that long. Nighttime. He would be coming back any moment now. How did I know that? I looked over at my hands and realized that my nails seemed to have grown. I also realized that I felt no sense of hunger—although I had never been a big eater—and no need to urinate at all. That was strange. And my auburn hair seemed much longer than I remembered it. It now hung down to reach my shoulders, where before it had barely touched my chin.

What was in that drink? I wondered, *some kind of weird drug?* Maybe he was planning to keep me tied up here and addicted to drugs so he could do horrible things to me. I was starting to cry again.

Maybe that was why I didn't notice Justin entering the room. All of a sudden he was sitting on the bed beside me. "How do you feel?" he asked, stroking my forehead and smiling.

"Not real well." I was afraid to look at him. His hand felt cool against my skin, almost reassuring. But then I remembered the pain in my wrists, and I raised my head as far as I could and shouted at him, "What's going on, damn it? Why did you tie me up? I need to go home!"

"You can't go home anymore, Kate," he said, withdrawing his hand.

"What do you mean?" My head fell back against the pillow as my body began to shake, and I forgot how crazy I looked tied up as if I was in a pornographic movie.

"I have to leave you like this until you are completely changed. The process is too disturbing for you to be loose right now. At least, not without me there every step of the way. It usually takes only one night, but you seem to need more time. By tomorrow evening you'll be a new woman, Kate." He began to stroke my forehead again. "And you'll feel better than you ever have, and you'll never be alone because you'll be with me." He looked at me like I was supposed to be pleased or something at this knowledge. I wasn't—I wanted to kill him.

When you watch a victim confronted by a crazed killer in a horror movie, you always wonder why they don't just play along with the madness, placate the psycho until they can escape. Instead, they always shout things like "You're insane!" or "You'll never get away with torturing me!" which, of course, drives the evil presence of the movie to prove just how insane he is and how he will get away with it by immediately chopping their heads off with a machete. If only they had pretended that the guy's deranged ideas were perfectly normal, they could have bought enough time for the hero to save them. Instead, they are left with no head and the psycho gets to perform weird sexual acts with their body.

Even though I had always been confounded by the stupidity of the movie victims, I seemed to forget all logic now and proceeded along with the predictable script.

"You're crazy, Justin," I said as loudly and as stupidly as I could. "My husband probably has the police out searching for your house right now. You'll never get away with it!"

Justin gave up stroking my head and sighed. "I thought you were smarter than that, Kate," he said. "Ben's been back and forth on the phone all day to Marla, and she still hasn't told him about me. By the time she does, it won't really matter. Besides, they haven't found me in a long time, Kate. What makes you think they'll find me now?"

He was completely crazy. A sick individual who just happened to be in the same acting class as a bored and homesick New Yorker. And he had enough money and free time to cater to his bizarre whims by holding her prisoner.

"What are you going to do with me?" I asked, but I barely got the question out before my body started convulsing in torment. The pain that had started in my wrists and ankles spread through my whole body, and it was intolerable.

Justin jumped up, greatly concerned. "What's wrong, Kate?" he asked. "This is not supposed to hurt. It's not supposed to hurt at all."

"What's not supposed to hurt?" I screamed at him through the pain. "What kind of drug did you give me? I'm allergic to all kinds of things. I can hardly take prescription drugs, let alone anything else!" Tears were pouring out of my eyes so fast that most of my hair was now wet and my body was covered with the sweat of severe pain. "What did you do to me, Justin?"

"I'm sorry, Kate," he said, trying to wipe the tears away and looking totally confused. "You must be having a bad reaction, your immune system must be very strong. But I swear to you, by tomorrow night it will all be over."

"Tomorrow night!" I yelled at him. "Tomorrow night?"

But I never heard his answer. The pain swallowed me up, and my mind became lost again in nightmares.

The nuns were always warning you about something, back in Catholic school. Especially Sister Concepta. If she wasn't cautioning you about the evils of the opposite sex, then there was always the possibility that you could be hit by a car and die before you made it to confession that week, thereby sentencing yourself to a short stay in purgatory at the very least, or hell if you had committed one of the mortal sins. When I was eight years old, I lived in fear of dying suddenly and not making it to heaven right off the bat. As a result, I said as many prayers as one little girl could manage before she fell asleep, and I always looked both ways before I crossed the street.

I had been dreaming about Sister Concepta, and it had been in black and white. Not just her habit and her rosary, but her face, her fingers, her nails.

Maybe that's why I said a quick prayer before I opened my eyes, hoping that somehow I was still eight years old, and that I still believed in God, and my mother was just about to wake me up for school. That my father had already left for work and Kevin was in the kitchen eating breakfast. That it was morning, my favorite time of day, when the sun was out and life began again. But all my praying had never done me much good. Maybe that's why I'd given it up. It didn't help this time, either. I was still in Justin's big, white bedroom and I wasn't at home and I wasn't in heaven and it was night again.

And Justin was nowhere to be seen. I had slept through another day. He had probably drugged me again last night. I remembered the pain I'd felt, and I wanted to hit him so hard he would crash through the bedroom wall and land outside. I could almost feel how good it would feel to make him pay for torturing me like this. My hand moved back involuntarily at the thought of the impact of my blow on Justin's head, and suddenly my arm broke free from the ropes.

They couldn't have been too strong, I thought. *I must have worn them away with all my struggling like they always do in the movies.* I moved my other arm, and it was free, too. I raised myself up on my elbows, completely stiff from being in one position for two nights, and untied both my ankles.

I realized that I had to think fast. Justin would probably come back any minute and make me pay for upsetting his plans. I didn't see any phone in the room or my clothes from the other night. I obviously could not call for help. I had to get out of there—and now. I stood up cautiously and went to his closet. His clothes would have to do. I opened the door and found nothing but shirts and pants in his favorite color—black. What did I expect at this point? I pulled on one of each, taking a belt to hold up the pants. I'd have to forget the underwear and shoes. As long as I was decent enough to be rescued, what did it matter? Now I had to get out.

The only exit was the staircase. Justin could be lurking right up there, but I had to take that chance. It was better than sitting and waiting for that monster to show himself again. I slowly started upward. My blood was pounding through my veins, and my legs felt weak. *Please, don't let him be there.* I stopped every few steps and listened, but there was only silence. Not even street noises reached my ears. *Please don't let him be there. . . .* And to my relief he wasn't. The stairs ended at the living room, but it was empty.

The wine bottle from two nights before was still sitting on the coffee table. *Damn him,* I thought. *He never even drank a drop.* There was no phone upstairs, either. No link to the outside world. I moved toward the front door, not believing my luck, but then I noticed the electronic security system attached to it. I had no idea how it worked. Without the code, I was trapped.

I put my hand on the doorknob, expecting nothing, but it turned freely in my hand. He hadn't even locked the door behind him. He had been so sure I could not escape, so confident I was trapped. But I was smarter and stronger than he gave me credit for. I stepped onto the sidewalk and I was out. Out of that great white tomb. Somehow, miraculously, I had escaped that bastard. I stood for a moment, unsure of what to do next, only breathing in the cool, night air. In the distance I could hear a radio playing. Frank Sinatra's voice floated on the wind.

I looked at the beautiful darkness of the night and realized I was only a few blocks from the ocean. I could see the lights from the Santa Monica pier and decided to walk toward them. I could always call for help later. It did not seem so urgent now. I was free.

When I look back on my escape from the house of horrors, it seems odd that I did not immediately search for a phone to call the police or Ben, or rush up to the first passing stranger and demand help. No, after being drugged and tied up and probably raped by a madman, I wanted to go to the beach. Somehow it seemed completely normal. Somehow I knew that I could not face Ben, that I could not go home, at least not right now. But I had to hide, that much I knew, and the most likely place seemed to be the endless dark under the pier. If I sat there very quietly, life would go on, and Justin would not find me. Of course, as usual, I was wrong.

I was also, I realize now, in a state of shock. And as I wandered zombie-like, barefoot and in black, down the two blocks to the pier, I thought about the little bits of money I had been setting aside for my escape with Justin.

Now I could use it to buy a plane ticket to escape from everyone. Where I'd go I didn't know. Maybe Florida, maybe Hawaii, maybe England. I had always wanted to go to England. No one would ever find me there.

I made it to the pier and found a path down to the beach where darkness waited. Darkness and the cool breeze of the ocean. I tasted salt in the air. There were only a few people nearby, kissing in the sand, and they did not notice me. I found a place under the pier and sat down quietly, facing the tiny lights that made up Malibu.

Over and over I cursed myself for being taken in by Justin's charm. How I had loved him or, more accurately, been obsessed by him. And all he had wanted to do was keep me a prisoner in his evil, white condo where he kept his evil, black clothing. I could smell him on his shirt even through the dry cleaning and the starch. I hated him for making a fool of me. Ben would probably feel so self-righteous about this. I got sick at the thought of having to confess. The plane ticket definitely seemed like the right idea. I could avoid telling Ben that way, avoid going home again. Everything was changed now, but I wasn't sure why.

The winds shifted slightly. Someone walked above me, sending bits of dirt blowing into my hair. I looked up, but all I saw were the soles of a pair of shoes scraping back toward town.

My attention shifted again to the waves hitting the beach. I wondered what had happened the other night in acting class. What lesson I had missed. How trivial all that seemed now—Sandy and his stupid exercises for loosening up. As if that really mattered in the scheme of things. I looked again at a couple kissing. His arm around her back, the expression on her face. They were lovers. "Oh, Justin," I said out loud, "I loved you so much."

"Can't you still love me, Kate?" he asked, and he was

sitting next to me in the sand. I hadn't even heard his approach, I had been so lost in thought.

"Get away from me!" I jumped up. "Just leave me alone." He did not move.

"I only did this for you out of love, Kate. I heard your thoughts, knew how unhappy you were, heard you call to me at night in your dreams. How could I not answer you? The only way you could be with me safely was for me to do what I did."

"Safely." I stared at him wildly, unable to run. "You call being drugged and tortured safe?"

"It's not supposed to hurt like that. I'm sorry you suffered. You have a very defensive immune system. You put up quite a fight. But the pain is over now."

"*What* isn't suppose to hurt, Justin?" I asked, the old familiar fear now returning to my brain. But it was not the fear of someone who has committed adultery and is about to be discovered, nor was it the fear of someone who's been captured by a psychotic and is about to be killed. Rather, it was the fear you feel when you wake up at three in the morning and the phone's ringing and you know for sure it's going to be real bad news. "What isn't supposed to hurt?"

"I wish you hadn't left the house, Kate. I would have liked to talk to you calmly and quietly, explained everything in as much detail as I could. And then we would have made love and gone out and enjoyed the night together. Instead, you take off without even leaving me a note, and I have to track you down to the pier, of all places. I was really starting to get worried about you."

As I looked into his eyes, and they were the most beautiful green eyes I had ever seen, and saw the look of kindness on his face, I remembered how close I had felt to him when we had talked so intensely after class. But then the memory of that pain returned and the whiteness of his bedroom walls, and I looked at him in disgust.

"Explain it to me now, God damn it. Tell me what it is you think you've done to me, and then I'll tell you in painstaking detail exactly what you did do." I was almost shouting now, and he put his finger to his lips.

"You look beautiful, Kate. If only you could see how beautiful you look now. It really does suit you." He held out a flask to me that he must have concealed under his long black jacket. "Here," he said, "you need to calm down. Have a drink."

"Why, so you can drug me again?"

"I don't have to do that anymore, Kate. I just think you need a drink. It's your first new night."

And I was suddenly, horribly thirsty. I could catch a whiff from the container he offered me, and it smelled wonderful. I had to have it—and I had to have it now. Surprised by my own sense of urgency, I grabbed the flask from him, stood up, and drank it quickly. I had never tasted anything so good. It reminded me of something in my dream last night, but I couldn't remember what.

"Explain it to me, Justin," I repeated aggressively as I stood over him, wondering what possessed me to drink anything this guy offered me. "Tell me this big secret. Am I addicted to heroin now or what? Or is it worse. . . . You don't have some horrible disease, do you?"

He laughed at that one. At least I was spared the misery of a long and sickly death.

"It's so much better than you can imagine, Kate. All the myths you have heard, movies you have seen, have distorted and confused the truth through time. Of course, you can't go out in the daylight, you sleep then. And you do need human blood to survive. Unfortunately animal blood doesn't work. It doesn't have the necessary ingredients to give us life. We need fresh human blood, but we only need it infrequently. And crosses and garlic don't do a thing."

"What are you saying, Justin? What kind of lies are you telling me now?" A trickle of fear was starting to work its way down the back of my neck.

"I'm saying that you're a vampire, Kate, just like me. I'm saying that you'll never grow old, never get sick again, and you'll never die." He looked at me with anticipation, hoping, I guess, for me to rush into his arms and thank him for making me a monster.

"Yeah, right," I said. "Vampires. You're even worse off than I thought. There are no werewolves—or gremlins or aliens or Big Foot monsters. And there certainly are no vampires. You're just a crazy man who likes to tie women up. And I'm the idiot who's still standing here talking to you."

"You know, Kate," he said, standing up, "our greatest ally has always been disbelief, an unwillingness to accept the fact that other life forms exist side by side with humanity in the darkness. Mankind has become so enlightened, so literal, that people have scientific or medical answers for everything they are afraid of. Unfortunately they are not always right. Some of the ghosts and goblins they laugh at in books or movies have sat next to them in the same movie theater and laughed just as loudly because no one would ever believe a story as fantastic as that."

Before I had a chance to react, he grabbed me around the waist and held me tight. In his free hand was a long, shiny knife. The moon illuminated it with surprising clarity.

"We could argue all night about vampires. But I'd rather save time and prove it to you. Forgive me for being melodramatic."

I should have run when I could, I thought, and he

plunged the knife into my chest. He let go of me, and I fell backward from shock onto the sand, expecting to see blood pouring out of me. It took a minute before I realized I wasn't even bleeding, let alone dying. And the knife was still there, sticking out of my chest. It had to be a trick, a sleight of hand. I pulled it out. There was no pain, and I examined the knife closely. It looked real enough. I sat up and stared at Justin in disbelief.

"What?" I said, reaching around for the flask I had dropped in all the commotion. If ever I needed a drink, it was now. Quickly I swallowed what little was left inside. It did make me feel a little calmer. "What . . . ?" I said again, but I was not really sure how to ask the question. Justin looked at me quietly and smiled.

"Come on, Kate," he said, "think about it a little. What I'm telling you is true. You are not human anymore."

I looked at the knife again. How could he be right? But there was a tear in the shirt where the weapon had been. I touched my skin tentatively through the tear. Did I really feel any different? Wasn't that my skin beneath my fingers? Wasn't I still breathing, thinking, moving? How could I be Dracula's daughter? A lost soul, damned forever. A creature forced to kill human beings and drink their blood. A certified member of hell. That was ridiculous. It was downright silly. I was letting this madman's words influence me.

I picked up the flask again and took a gulp. Several drops fell onto my hand. But they weren't the clear color of liquor; they were red and thick. I saw what my mind had refused to see just moments ago. Blood. Human blood. And I had drunk it like expensive Scotch and enjoyed it completely.

I didn't really feel like myself. I felt . . . different. What if Justin was right? What if, in these last two nights, the human Kate had died and was gone forever? What if the impossible had become possible?

Sadness overwhelmed me. Justin had taken my life away from me. And now I could never have it back. And I would never go to heaven, either. I remembered Count Dracula hurrying to his coffin before the sun rose. I would probably have to sleep in one of those, too, when it was hard enough for me to fall asleep in a normal bed. And I would never see Ben again, or my brother or my mother and father, either. I didn't belong in their world anymore. And they were not safe from me.

"I hate you!" I threw the flask to the ground. "I thought you were someone from a fairy tale, the kind of man I dreamt about, longed for, wished for—but I never dreamt about this. If you're not crazy and what you say is true, then I hate you even more. You had the nerve to change me into something else without even asking first."

Justin lowered his head and rested his hand against his chin. For a moment I thought he was about to cry, but he sighed instead. He had not anticipated a reaction like this. Surprise maybe, curiosity maybe, but never grief, never anger. He had thought it would make me happy to be something other than what I was born. He had thought I would want to live with him forever. He had tied me up, kept me a prisoner, out of love. But I despised him for it.

I knew I could never forgive him. Things had gone too far. A romantic interlude was one thing. Even a full-blown love affair I could have handled with grace. But this loss of self, this death within life, was more of a commitment than I had ever dreamt of in my wildest fantasies. All I wanted was for him to be out of my sight forever. Only days before, I could not exist without Justin; now he made me sick.

I didn't even have to say it out loud; Justin knew what I

was thinking. Disgusted, he moved to leave me. "I won't force myself on you anymore, Kate. I don't know how I could have been so wrong. I don't usually make mistakes as serious as this. I'm truly sorry, but there is no way to change you back." His eyes lingered on me. I think he could still hardly believe his great plan had failed. He had not taken the human factor into account—that we don't always want what we ask for.

Something else now materialized from his jacket: money. He held it out to me. "You'll need something to get you started. You'll need a secure place to sleep in the day. Since you won't come back with me, I can only urge you to rent something tonight. You cannot be out in the sunlight. It would destroy you."

"Maybe I should be destroyed," I said bitterly.

"No, Kate, you will want to survive. It's your instinct to go on. Suicide is an option most people cannot enjoy." He turned and looked out over the ocean. "And also, you need to know at least a few things. You should not eat or drink anything normal—it will only make you sick. But you will need human blood at times, and those times will be obvious to you. Then you will have to feed on someone. I would have liked to show you how. The first time is never easy." He touched my arm.

"Just leave me alone," I said, pulling away from him. I still did not totally believe him, but even so I didn't want him near me.

"I would have taken care of you, Kate," he said, and there was pain in his voice. "I would have loved you like you thought you wanted to be loved. But I'm a little too proud to plead. Go on and be truly alone now. Your instincts will not let you go back to your stupid little life again." He lifted his hand in exasperation. "But remember this, Kate, it's my blood you have in your veins. That will never go away. I will always be inside you."

I wanted to make him disappear. To make the last six months of my life disappear. I wanted to step off the plane at LAX and start all over. I wanted to go home. I wanted Ben. He was a good man, Ben. He was human, not like the thing that stood before me.

Justin shook his head and started to leave. As an afterthought he turned and spoke. "And don't tell anyone what you are, Kate. Humans are so jealous and petty; they'll hunt you down like an animal or run from you in fear. Believe me, I know what that's like. You can never trust them with your secret."

And then he was gone. And I was alone. It was probably at that point, I started to go a little mad. Shock was wearing off, reality was setting in, and it was all too much for this little New Yorker's brain to take. What if he really was a vampire? What if I was, too? My college education hadn't prepared me for life as a demon. I thought about praying again, but vampires didn't pray. I probably could no longer make the sign of the cross, either. Perhaps I should never have stopped praying. Never stopped going to church. Now it was too late to be saved. Because if I really had to drink someone's blood to survive, then there was no way I would be allowed to set foot in paradise.

Instead, I collapsed in the sand, the taste of blood still in my mouth. I wondered who Justin had killed to get it for me. The thought of him biting some innocent victim's neck made me choke in horror. I took the knife and stabbed it violently into my leg. Nothing, no pain, no blood. It slid in and out with ease as if I had stabbed at nothing. What was I going to do?

It's amazing how the meaning of life can become so totally clear once that life is gone. I saw for a second what could have been a happy existence if I had tried a little. But I never liked trying. I always wanted to be successful the first time out. That's why I had never found any calling in life. I had never stayed around long enough to overcome the slightest failure.

Well, now I had all the time in the world. I could find out just what it took to be a successful vampire. I started laughing at this and could not stop. There was something so incredibly funny about it. I could see myself calling up Marla and telling her what I was. Not an actress any longer, I was one of the Undead. A thing that would eventually have to kill another human being. A thing that could not be disguised by a clean and well-decorated apartment. A thing that could not be married anymore, have children, or celebrate Christmas. A thing that should only dress in black and go out at night.

It was completely hilarious. And I kept on laughing as the waves rolled up and down the Santa Monica shore. And people, real people, walked back and forth on the pier, ignoring the maniac below.

It was only when the tiny lights of Malibu seemed less and less bright and there was no one on the beach at all that I finally stopped laughing. An inner alarm clock was beginning to ring louder and louder. Something was wrong. My skin was starting to become warm and burn, and whatever was giving life to my body was slowing down.

I stood up and looked to the east, the place I used to call home, and saw the changes in the sky. There was no time now. No time at all. "I'll have to hurry," I thought, clutching Justin's money and running toward a sign that read Seaside Motel. It was almost morning.

11
Lost

I now understand how people can define their lives by what they regret. Usually there is one incident that stands out in their minds, an incident that explains why their lives were not meant to be perfect. My grandmother regretted marrying my grandfather. Kevin regretted never getting his Ph.D. My mother regretted never getting drunk and staying out too late. And Ben's father wished he had never been born.

If only. Put together they are two of the most powerful words in the human language. They can haunt us. Torment us. Drive us crazy. I should have. I could have. If only.

When I woke up that first night in the motel, I was completely disoriented. I didn't recognize the bed I lay on, the TV that faced me, or the black clothes I had been sleeping in. And there was a funny taste in my mouth, too.

I realized I was in a motel. I could see the stationery and the room-service menu with the Seaside logo lying on the night table beside me. But I wasn't on vacation, or was I? Were Mom and Dad still sleeping in the next room? Were we going to Disneyland today? No, I had just moved to Los Angeles. In fact, I was in Santa Monica right now. I remembered the acting workshop . . . and Justin. His name came into my head, and the shock of fear that ran through my body brought me back to reality.

I sat straight up in my $39-a-day bed and stared at the white walls around me. They were so much dirtier than Justin's immaculate bedroom. Yellow stains gathered at the corners of the room. I remembered the last two days with an ever-growing feeling of nausea. But memories like that couldn't be real. Some of it had to have been an hallucinogenic reaction to Justin's drugs. I felt like Olivia de Havilland in *The Snake Pit,* pleading to get out, to wake up. Nothing made sense.

But that little inner voice that I've come to know so well kept whispering, "But it is real, all of it. You're not yourself anymore. Think about it." And in a certain way I didn't feel like myself. Something was very different, although I couldn't put my finger on it.

I put my feet down on the floor and glanced at my nails, which I had been subconsciously avoiding. Something was different. They looked like talons or very long artificial nails.

I stood up and very slowly walked to the bathroom. I could feel my toenails scraping the cheap orange carpet as I moved to the mirror. Somehow I dreaded looking at the face that would greet me. But I had to look anyway. I had to know if I was still there. Maybe there would be nothing waiting for me on the other side of the looking glass. Maybe I could no longer cast a reflection. Why I even thought that, I didn't know. But I had to look.

I held on to the gold and white linoleum surrounding the sink and stared into the drain. The fluorescent light made it look cleaner than it was, and my eyes burned from the glare. The tiny window in the bathroom was closed and locked, but I could hear a woman arguing with a man who was apparently drunk in the parking lot outside.

"Damn you!"

"I only had three beers."

"Go to hell!"

"But, honey . . ."

I held my breath and raised my head. A pale face stared back at me. A face I recognized but didn't at the same time. Still the same features, but they were more focused, more refined—free of tiny imperfections. My skin was completely smooth and white, my gray-blue eyes now laced with gold, my eyelashes dark and full, and my auburn hair lustrous and long, with its red highlights even brighter and more noticeable than before.

Something was different. Very different. Something was wrong.

I looked away from the image of the creature I could not possibly be and stared down at the drain. I needed to clear my head. I probably wasn't even fully awake yet. I turned on the faucet, cupped my hands, and splashed cold water on my face. It didn't feel that refreshing. Then I raised my hands to my lips and took a drink. For a moment I could hardly believe the sensation. The taste was rancid, like Clorox mixed with vinegar. The water felt alien to my tongue, and my stomach churned with nausea. Quickly I spit it back out into the sink. Could the water have been severely polluted? But somehow I already knew the answer. Something was wrong, but it wasn't the water.

I sat back down on the bed and tentatively touched my fingers to the pulse of my left wrist. There was nothing, no heartbeat, no inner pounding of the drum. *Of course,* I thought, *why should it feel the same? I'm dead. Dead as a doornail. Or a coffin nail.*

"Stop thinking like that," I said to myself. "Don't let that crazy bastard's words influence you."

What a psycho he had turned out to be. And I was such a fool. I thought I had found romance and the perfect man, and instead, I got *The Lost Weekend.*

I reached over and picked up the phone. "Outside line, please," I said a little too loudly. The operator seemed to hesitate, but my patience was wearing thin. "Outside line," I repeated, and the dial tone came through. Quickly I dialed my own number. I would just tell Ben to drive down here and pick me up. It was that simple. But my inner voice became irritated and started shouting. I ignored the commotion and thought how good it would feel to touch Ben again, to feel his arms around me. I'd try to explain my indiscretion and the consequences later, when things were calm and I was safely in our home again. At least I would be home. Home, sweet home.

At the other end the phone began to ring. Ben was probably running across the room to answer it, but my inner voice was jumping up and down, screaming like a maniac. *Don't tell, don't tell, hang up before he hears your voice.* It rang again. *Don't tell, it would be dangerous, it would be wrong. Justin told you not to tell anyone. They'll hunt you down or run from you in fear. DON'T TELL!*

I heard the phone click, and Ben's voice came over the line, full of worry and pain. "Hello," he said. I did not speak. I was remembering the blood I had drunk last night and how good it tasted. Salty and thick. And it was blood. I had seen it with my own eyes. Even in the darkness, its deep red color showed through.

"Hello," he said again. Vampires drink blood. Vampires kill for blood. I was a vampire. *DON'T TELL!* They would kill me or I would kill them. Or I would kill Ben, for blood, to survive. Ben was shouting into the phone now. "Hello, hello, please answer. Is that you, Kate? Hello!"

I slammed the phone down, and tears poured out of my eyes without any warning. They were tears of grief. What was I thinking of? I could not tell. Something would not let me. I could never go home again. Never. And never was a long time now.

The tears would not stop. I felt so sorry for myself. So wronged. I hit my $39-a-day bed over and over again. There was no God. How could there be? To let such an evil thing happen. Or was this just divine retribution? The price I had to pay for infidelity? Was God really the vengeful figure from the Old Testament? I just didn't know. How could I know? How could anyone?

So all I could do was cry. And since I've never been that great at handling crises, I didn't deal with being dead any better, either. I kept crying and cursing and questioning for the rest of the night. Until about 4:00 A.M. when I finally stopped due to sheer exhaustion.

Out of habit I flipped on the TV set and happened upon a rerun of the *Donna Reed Show*. Everything about it was so soothing, so comforting. The nuclear family revolved in perfect order, untouched by death or despair. The biggest problem was, who would Mary go to the dance with? The dance where she was destined to sing "Johnny Angel" to an adoring public and make them wonder how lovely heaven could be.

The program was almost hypnotic in its approach, and it relaxed me as the sun began to rise and my eyes closed involuntarily. Everything was slowing down, almost stopping now. Rigor mortis was setting in. I could sleep. If that's what you called it. It was more like the beautiful repose of someone buried alive. But at least it was a break from this pain, a break from conscious thought. And tomorrow I could get up and watch TV again. It was

the easiest thing to do. Until I figured out what was next.
Where I even fit in anymore in this grand scheme of life.
My wonderful life in L.A. Kevin had been right all along.
I had crossed some kind of boundary when I entered this
desert city, and now I was truly caught in another dimen-
sion.

The motel had cable, and night after night I left the TV
on the Nickelodeon Channel where I had first found
Donna Reed.

I discovered Mr. Ed to be a very sympathetic character,
and his voice was enchanting. "Wil-bur," he would say,
and he would make me laugh and forget that no horse in
his right mind would ever come near me again, let alone
talk to me.

And then there was *My Three Sons,* which reeked of
normalcy and the contentment of being middle class. I
wanted Fred MacMurray to be my dad and come and
take me out of this hotel, out of this nightmare I was
living, and make me better and fix me dinner. I wanted to
go out on a date again and have a curfew. I knew Chip or
Robbie would never roam the streets at midnight wearing
a black shirt and a black pair of pants. Uncle Charly
would have shot them first or grounded them. I don't
think they even owned any black clothing. But their sense
of normalcy comforted me.

The manager of the motel, Mr. Chandler, a tired fifty-
year-old loser of a man with thinning hair and a suit that
didn't fit, took a dislike to me right away. He really did
not want to rent me a room that first morning, as he
could see quite easily I was no ordinary tourist. He took
off his gold-rimmed glasses, narrowed his tiny eyes, and
stared at me accusingly. But when I waved a hundred-
dollar bill in his face—Justin had given me five thousand
dollars, I'd discovered—he practically threw the keys at

me. It's amazing the power money can have, and I was desperate for a place to sleep.

It wasn't long before his dislike turned to hatred as my daily routine set in. He saw I slept all day with the shades Scotch-taped to the windows to keep even the tiniest speck of sunlight from coming in. He saw I never ordered any food and had the TV running from sundown to sunup. He probably even heard me crying but was too disgusted to ever ask why.

He saw I had no job, no visible source of income, and though I paid him every week, he knew that eventually if he was lucky, I would run out of money, and he could throw me out of his fine establishment.

I think Mr. Chandler began to live for that day. Maybe he even prayed for it. Some ignorant, pathetic little humans have nothing to show for themselves except the uncanny ability to recognize someone who is different. Then they make it their life's work to make that person pay for it, to degrade them in every way possible. To make them beg for towels or for privacy during the day.

Because I had no idea at the time just how extraordinary I had become—and the powers that went with my transformation—I was subject to Mr. Chandler's petty dictatorship, but I vowed that one day I would make him beg for something, too.

I also ran up a huge phone bill, which I'm sure Mr. Chandler noticed and probably speculated about. Maybe he even listened in. But there was nothing he could ever hear. I would dial the time or the weather or even those 976 party lines just to hear someone talking. I never spoke, but I liked to assure myself that the outside world still existed. I just wasn't ready to face it yet.

I would also call Ben from time to time, as if the first call hadn't been torture enough for him. His wife had disappeared one August night without a trace and had never been seen again. Each time the phone rang late at night, he must have hoped, prayed, that it was me or someone with some information about me. Instead, there was only silence.

"Kate?" he would finally say, and as soon as I heard my name, I'd hang up. Poor Ben. He'd never know how much I missed him. How much I longed to be back in our little rented house in Tarzana. To have boredom and homesickness as my only problems in life.

As for my family, they existed only in the past. They were not part of this current horror movie. I never for a moment thought of calling them. It was better they think of me as dead. At least I would have died a Christian and a human being. At least I would not be destined for hell.

During commercials, or even in the middle of shows, I would float back in time and look fondly at my family. There was Kevin playing with his building blocks, there was Mom talking on the phone and Dad working in the yard. It was easier to leave them there, like a wax museum I could visit from time to time. It was safer. I never thought of how hard my disappearance must have been for them, too. How they must have agonized over it, blamed Ben or even California for it. How they probably always hoped I'd turn up someday alive and well. But I was not alive, and I was certainly not well. And like anyone who suffers a severe shock and cannot cope, I had become a very selfish person.

Sometime in the middle of October, I started going out at night. It might have been just to irritate Mr. Chandler, or it might have been the noise this couple made with their headboard that drove me out, that incessant banging and the moaning in between. Or maybe it was the start of the restlessness, the need to find something or someone. A growing urgency that powered me along the beaches at night, looking, searching. I was starting to get thirsty.

Most of the time, all I did was walk, a habit I would have with me forever. I never got tired anymore. I never got dirty, either. I never needed to take a shower, although I could not break with this tradition. And my hair grew a little longer each day I slept, making me wonder if someday I'd have to buy a pair of scissors. I was surprised to find that my new life form actually had some good side effects. Human fatigue no longer plagued me. Nor did decay. I did not know it then, but I would never look any older than twenty-seven.

I had to hand it to L.A., it was beautiful down at the beaches at night. There are not too many places in this country where it's warm in October and people are out and about. If I had stopped complaining to Ben so much when I first landed here, I might have noticed. To open your eyes it often takes a tragedy, or at least a major change. I wondered how it would have felt to walk these beaches as a human in the daylight, to stop and have a hot dog and a Coke. I would never know now. I only knew that I needed something. I needed it badly. I just didn't know what.

It was eight o'clock, and there was a clothing store open on one of the main streets in Venice. I felt the money in my pocket and thought it might be a good idea to have some more clothing than the shirt on my back. I knew I didn't want shoes. For one thing, my toenails were so abnormally long that I'd need a size ten just to fit in any. For another, the very thought of shoes seemed ridiculous. My bare feet were so much better for running, for chasing. But a new pair of pants and a top seemed in order.

I walked quickly through the door, and the young blond woman behind the counter jumped. "Sorry," she said, smiling, "you scared me." She walked toward me, looking at my feet. Even in a place like Venice, where hippies still abounded, they were an unusual sight. Then she looked at my eyes and stopped smiling. "Can I help you?" she asked.

I found I was staring at her neck and forced myself to look at the racks of clothing instead. What was I thinking of? Something dark. Something warm. "I want some black clothing," I said, and then wondered why I was insisting on black. You'd think I'd be sick of the color by now. But I wanted black. I needed it.

"Black, like you've got on?" she asked with the trace of an English accent. I could tell she was starting to feel nervous. I walked over to what looked like my size and pulled out a dark pair of pants.

"These and a black shirt to go with it. And I need some underwear, too." Why underwear, I didn't know. I was doing quite well without it. But it seemed like something I should have. Old habits are hard to break, no matter how unnecessary they become.

The sales clerk ran over to the other end of the store and picked out a black turtleneck and a black cotton oxford and put them at the register. "These will work," she said, and went to one of the shelves and pulled down a box of bikini briefs. I handed her the pants and waited as she nervously totaled the bill. Her hands shook as she took my money. This seemed to strike me funny. But instead of a laugh, a low hiss came out of my throat. It did not have a happy sound.

The salesclerk almost threw the change to me, as if she did not want to touch my hand, then she backed up against the wall. She knew something was wrong. That something bad could happen, though she felt foolish for thinking that way.

She was probably praying I would leave as quickly as I

had come, before my deadly nails could find a home somewhere. The Kate of days ago began to feel sorry for her, ashamed of making someone this afraid. I remembered how many times I had felt fear looking into the eyes of some lowlife while riding the New York subways after dark. Or the creepy dread I used to feel walking home alone at night, convinced that someone was following me.

I took the package, gathered up my change, and left. I didn't want to scare her anymore. Behind me, she made the sign of the cross in the air. A black cat had crossed her path. Someone had walked over her grave. But for tonight, she was saved.

When I walked, I tended to think. A little too much, I suppose. There are so many questions that can't be answered. So many mysteries that must remain unsolved. You can go around and around in your head, wondering about something, and end up nowhere. That is the nature of the life we lead. Or even the "life" I now mimic in tone and color. There are no ultimate solutions to all of the riddles we are presented with. There are only options. Only possibilities.

My thoughts seemed to start with God, probably due to my twelve years of religious education, and end up anywhere. I could not figure out how "man" really came into existence. Evolution just did not add up. And, of course, how did vampires come into this? Were they offshoots of man? Or maybe of angels? Or fallen angels? Why did God allow them to exist? Why did he let viruses exist? Why did he let anyone invent the atomic bomb? Why? Why? Why?

And where did you go after you died? Was everything black and white, a heaven and hell? And wouldn't you be bored spending an eternity in heaven and doing nothing?

This idea had even occurred to me as a child. No, it seemed there must be another place after earth. A better one, the next step up, if you succeeded in this life.

But if that were true, what about me? I was destined to live forever. Was that good or bad? Was I really trapped in a so-so world, never able to go on to the next big thing? Or was I being spared the boredom of eternal happiness and left to roam the earth to do what I pleased?

To be able to do what I pleased. There was something very tempting in that phrase. It gave me a little thrill to say it out loud. I liked the way my tongue felt in my mouth when I said it. The possibilities were endless. I licked my lips and smiled.

But then I would think of Ben, and the pleasure would go away. I felt such profound regret about the marriage I had lost, the children I would never have. Somehow, even without anyone telling me, I knew I was sterile. Because if I wasn't, it was a prospect too horrible to even dream of, something too monstrous to endure. No, I would never be a mother and hold a baby in my arms. Of that, I was sure. I would never be able to please my mother and father. See their joy when I told them they would be grandparents. Never be able to grow old with the man I married, knowing I had done the right thing. Never be able to live the life we were put on this earth for.

I started to cry again as usual, so I raced back to my motel by the sea. I ran past Mr. Chandler's son, who was a miniature replica of his father only uglier, right back to my bed and flipped on the TV set.

The commercial for 976-STUD was on, and I watched a male model with his shirt unbuttoned to the waist announce he was "available tonight."

"Good for you," I said aloud, but the commercial gave me an idea. Why not call and really talk to someone this time? At least I'd get my money's worth. I was lonely, a human frailty that I could not shake. Even now I can't totally erase the basic desire for closeness and companionship that lives on inside me. I still needed to talk to someone. Even if it was only some fool who was paid to chitchat with women desperate enough to call a number that offered them a stud.

It was either that or Mr. Chandler's son, Jansen. And Jansen still had the remnants of acne on his square little face, so I opted for the image of the guy with the unbuttoned shirt.

"Outside line, please," I said, and I heard Jansen sigh. Unlike his father, he was out and out curious and dying to ask me if I was on the run from the law. That's about how far his mind could work.

I heard the phone ring. "Hi," a male voice said. "You've reached 976-STUD, and this is Ed. What is your name?"

I figured I'd better give an alias. "Betty," I said, almost choking on the corniness of the lie.

"Well, Betty, how are you tonight?"

"Not good," I said.

"Why's that, Betty? Things got you down? Having boyfriend trouble maybe?"

"You could say that." Ed was certainly an intuitive kind of guy.

"Why don't you tell me about it, Betty. I'd like to hear what's bothering you. You sound like a nice girl."

Nice? I thought sarcastically. "Well, Ed, I was married, you see, and I fell for another guy. Mostly because of the way he looked or seemed or something."

"And what happened, Betty?"

"Well, I left my husband, just for one night, and this guy turned out to be a lot more than I bargained for. Now my life is ruined." I choked back a sob.

Ed clucked sympathetically. "You lost your husband

over this one-night stand, and this guy didn't stick around, either?"

"Not exactly, Ed." I had gotten control of myself. "I lost my husband—and I lost my life, really—and after all that, this guy was worth nothing to me. In fact, I hated him."

"Do you want to go back to your husband, Betty? Maybe if you talked to him, he'd try again."

"Is this 976-STUD," I demanded, "or Phone Psychology 101?"

Ed was completely taken aback by this question. He stuttered on the other end of the line. "Well, ah, Betty, I was just trying to help. Ah . . . , what do you want to talk about?"

"I want to talk about your neck. What you taste like and whether you believe in vampires or not."

I felt Ed's confusion. Part of him wanted to hang up on this nutcase, and the other part of him knew the longer he kept me on the line, the more money he and his company made.

"Vampires?" he asked.

"That's right, vampires. Creatures that walk in the night. That drink your blood and never die. I'm a vampire, Ed. What do you think of that? And so was that other guy. And he tricked me and raped me, and he took away my life, and now I'm alone and I'm afraid. Afraid of the sunlight. Afraid I have nowhere to go. Afraid I'm going to hell."

I heard Ed's teeth begin to chatter, because somewhere in Ed's little "$2.00 every three minutes phone call" of a brain, he knew the truth was being spoken. His intuitive psychological self was telling him my story was real.

I started laughing at the thought of this man at the other end of the phone. An actor, no doubt, trying to make a living in between five-minute spots on sitcoms and the movie of the week. And once I started laughing, I couldn't stop. It was becoming a bad habit of mine. People could be so amusing at times.

I heard Ed slam the receiver down in fear. I didn't hang up but rolled from side to side on my cheap blue bedspread, holding my stomach. Within minutes, Jansen was pounding on the door.

"Are you all right in there? Miss, are you all right?" My voice had such an amazing ability to carry as of late.

"Yes," I said between laughs, "I'm just fine. I'm just dandy."

Jansen shuffled back down the hall, and only "Johnny Angel" was left in my head. I hummed the tune as I laughed again. And together we would see how lovely heaven could be.

I have an uncanny ability to know when something bad is going to happen. I tried to warn myself about Justin, but did I listen? You'd think I would have learned my lesson, but no, I still ignored danger signs, even when they were hitting me over the head.

I knew I shouldn't go out that night. Things did not seem right. The air had a bad smell to it. And everything about Santa Monica was suddenly creepy. Even for a vampire.

Evil was visiting the little ocean town, out on a midnight rendezvous. Evil was looking for someone to pick on, someone to terrorize. I should have known it would be me.

I sauntered past Mr. Chandler, Sr., with my eyes averted as usual. Suddenly I stopped, faced him, and gave him a great big smile. "Hi," I said enthusiastically. He stared at me in surprise, then tried to return to his newspaper. I was just in one of those moods.

Outside, the night was in full force. Stars twinkled viciously from behind the smog, and the ocean waves hit the shore with violent intent. The bums that usually littered the sidewalk were holed up somewhere because of the uncommon chill in the air.

There was an emptiness to the streets as if an earthquake had been predicted, as if everyone needed to be prepared for something. The wind blew with a low hissing sound. Unlatched doors rattled. Palm trees shook. The moon was full, and I had forgotten it was Halloween. The night when ghosts and goblins appear, when witches ride on brooms and black magic is in the air. A night for tricks and treats.

I set out in my usual direction, toward Venice, even though I felt uneasy. The cold didn't affect me anymore, but the lack of activity on a Friday night did. Main Street was usually hopping by this time, but the weekend fever seemed to have been postponed. Why it even concerned me anymore, I didn't know. I decided to ignore it and head right to the beach. Because I was preoccupied, I didn't notice that the dark figure standing in the doorway I had just passed had decided to follow me. He must have been attracted to the black.

I have never understood pure evil. Evil without thought. Without purpose. Evil whose only reason for existence is destruction. I had read about it, heard about it, seen it in the pictures of serial killers, child molesters, but I had certainly never confronted it. I had no idea how wrong it could feel. How empty. How frightening.

A shadow passed over the moon, and the water, which almost touched my feet, became one with the land. The wind blew a little harder, and I caught the smell of him behind me. Suddenly a vision of a skeleton laughing came into my head, but it was too late. He jumped on top of me, and I fell into the sand. The feeling of evil was so overpowering, I could only stare into his tiny eyes as he held a knife against my throat.

"Bitch," he said, and I could smell the liquor on his breath, the cocaine in his nose. He was probably only twenty-six, but he seemed a hundred years old. He was dirty and unshaven, and his hair hung in dark, greasy patches around his neck. I could feel his body pushing into mine. Thin, jagged bones pressing against me.

"You're gonna do it with me, bitch," he said, "or I'm going to cut you real good." He started ripping open my new black oxford and I moaned in fear. I could see the words "Halloween is spooky" on his dirty blue tee shirt. "Shut up," he said, hitting me across the face. It was only later that I realized it didn't hurt.

My shirt was open now, and he pawed at my breasts with the hand that wasn't holding the knife, and laughed. "You're gonna do me good, you slut."

I could not believe how wrong he felt. I also could not believe I was going to be raped and then possibly knifed by this filthy man. Something I had been warned about all my life. Something you had to watch out for on the streets of New York.

I tried to remember all those articles I had read about what to do if you're raped. They all seemed to contradict themselves. Some said, "Fight, scream, hit." Others said, "Don't even try to move—he will just kill you." I opted for the passive role. I was too scared to scream. And even if I did, there wasn't anyone on the beach to hear me.

By now he had my pants pulled down around my ankles and he was ready to go for it. The whole time his knife had never left my throat. I felt his hand touching me, trying to find the right place to get in. I realized his fly was open, and he was hanging out in all his glory.

Suddenly he seemed ridiculous, almost laughable. This dirty little boy was trying to rape me. How dare he? I lifted my arm out of the sand and touched his neck. It was warm and moving. Blood was running through his veins. I felt desire sweep over me. A desire I had never felt before. A desire tinged with anger.

My nails caressed the side of his neck. He stopped for a moment and looked at me curiously. "You like this, bitch, don't you? You really want it, don't you? You want it bad?"

"Yes," I said, ripping the knife out of his hand, cutting his palm wide-open, "I want it bad."

But it was not his bleeding hand that I wanted. I grabbed him by the throat and pulled him toward my mouth. I felt my new teeth emerge from their hiding place in my gums. Four long, sharp points, perfect for killing. He had a glimpse of my mouth before I bit down, and he screamed. And then my teeth tore through his skin as if it were paper. It crumbled away so his blood could pour down my open throat as he twitched and moaned above me. But I held him tight against me like a lover until I felt him go limp in every way. And I sucked as hard and as long as I could. I wanted it bad. I had wanted it for weeks but hadn't known it. Blood. Beautiful, warm, and bright red. I needed it. I desired it. I craved it. I could not live without it. It gave me strength, and this bastard was giving it to me.

I sucked him dry. Until all the veins in his body collapsed and his evil heart stopped beating. I sucked him dry because it felt good. And it was my instinct to do this to survive. And because it was Halloween. And I was a vampire. And the people locked away in their houses weren't just afraid of this rapist in their neighborhood. They lived in fear of me, too. Of things that go bump in the night.

When I finished, I pushed his dirty shell of a body off me and pulled up my pants and buttoned my shirt. I left him the way he was, exposed to the world. His fly still open in surprise. His eyes still open in disbelief.

This is what you get, I thought viciously, and kicked him once for good measure. For a moment I wondered if there was any danger of this monster becoming a vampire just from my bite. But I had a dim memory of my own transformation. It had not been a one-sided affair. Somehow I had drunk Justin's blood in return after he had taken mine. And since I was not about to give my would-be rapist the gift of eternal life, he would stay dead forever, and his blood would give me life. I could feel it flowing through me, and elation was setting in. I was getting an unbelievable high, a feeling of strength and omnipotent power. Someone had tried to hurt me, and I had hurt them back in return. All the fear and doubt that had plagued me for the last few weeks dissipated in the night air. I was alive again. I could do anything.

I danced in mock celebration along the shoreline. Nothing had ever felt this good. Nothing. Except maybe something in my dreams back in Justin's room, but I didn't want to think about that.

I went with my newfound energy. Dancing, skipping, running. This made it all worthwhile. This wonderful feeling. I was immortal. I would never die. I felt great. "Well, God," I shouted imperiously, "what do you make of this? Am I a creature fashioned in your own image? Am I still one of your children?" Who cares, though. Who cares. I could run and dance like this forever. I was already down by Hermosa Beach before I stopped. And when I stopped, reality set in.

I had killed someone. A human being. And I had done it with my teeth. And I had enjoyed it. Every bit of it. Biting down on his soft flesh until I felt the vein with my tongue. Cutting through that, too. And sucking him dry.

Shame came over me. My body still felt great. But my

mind was going fast. The truth of what I had become was
finally sinking in. I could watch TV from now until
doomsday. Hide in my hotel room. But that didn't change
the facts. I was a killer, a vampire. And even though that
guy probably did deserve it, that didn't make it any better.

A mortal sin. Thou shalt not kill. Now hell had become
part of my future, or maybe it was already all of my present. I sat down in the sand and stared at the horizon. I
was a killer, a vampire.

I could hardly believe I had done something like that.
Something so violent, so bloody. I had always been squeamish. I could never look at the disgusting parts of the
current horror flicks. I would always shut my eyes. I preferred the romantic, foggy view of the monster films of
the thirties and forties. But there was nothing romantic
about what I had done. I was a killer, a vampire. And I
would do it again. As soon as I needed blood to revive my
dead body. I would kill again.

I didn't dance my way back to the motel. I walked.
Slowly. But it was probably my slowness that saved my
life. I was dejected, ashamed. Even though my body was
screaming with life. Because I was moving so slowly, so
quietly, I heard my little voice speak as I crossed the
street. *Danger, there's danger waiting for you.* I stopped
suddenly. What other danger could there be now? And
then I saw it. Two police cars parked in the motel parking
lot. I moved cautiously around the back to see what was
going on. Guilt was pulsing through my body. Guilt and
fear.

How would I ever explain myself to them? They'd be
asking questions. Questions that I couldn't answer. Police
always did that. They must have found my victim and
were trying to find some kind of lead in the neighborhood. Even if it was some strange girl that slept all day.
Both Mr. Chandlers were probably only too eager to

point out their strange resident. Why hadn't I disposed of the body? Why didn't I think of that? A person drained of blood would make the police take notice.

I was close to the rear office window now, and I could hear voices. Jansen was speaking. "Certainly, Officer, here's the key, room thirty-two." My room. He was giving them the key to my room. That was all I had to hear.

Crazy with guilt and despair, I didn't stop to worry about the $1,000 I had left there or my brand-new black turtleneck, either. I headed out, fast and furious. The police were after me. A killer, a vampire. If they found me, they would drive a stake through my heart. And the townspeople would cheer. Thou shalt not kill.

My mind began to snap. It had only been half there before, but now it completely broke away. And I ran and I ran. I probably even flew, though I didn't know it at the time, heading east and ending up in downtown L.A., somewhere at the end of Pico Boulevard. In a self-made grave, in a deserted cellar that was buried and forgotten, camouflaged by trash and debris and the decay of things that had passed their prime. I was crazy as the day is long. A crazy, guilty, and heartbroken vampire. Heading east because it seemed familiar. Heading east, because I was probably going home.

Luckily I never made it that far. The sun rose and stopped me in my tracks. I could never go home again.

I lay on the cool, damp dirt, the new blood beating through my body, and slept. My grave. My home.

Madness is a lack of everything. Lack of meaningful thought, lack of direction, lack of stability, lack of desire. It is images, then loss of images, then images again. It all means nothing. The first month or so, I was only a little mad, a little less than human. But then I killed that man on the beach and enjoyed it every step of the way. After that, I let go and fell to where I thought it was not possible to go. Where it was always dark. Where there was no sun and nothing made sense. Where words did not connect and time was lost. I had entered the dark ages.

Without any method to my madness, but with perfect logic, I would leave my cellar at night and find myself wandering the streets of downtown Los Angeles. I became part of the group they call the homeless, but to me they were the lost souls of God's earth. If there even was a God anymore.

They moved from street to street with no purpose but with absolute anonymity. No one questioned their eccentric behavior. Why they carried millions of needless possessions around in shopping carts or plastic bags. Why they begged for money to eat and then spent it on liquor or lost it only minutes later. Why they lied about everything and everyone and remembered nothing. Why they slept in alleyways or unlocked cars or doorsteps. Or why one of them slept in the daytime and walked fearlessly through the worst part of the city at night.

I don't recall how I found that deserted cellar with no windows and an entrance so narrow only a ghost could slip through, or a vampire. I just knew that was where I had to go at sunup to be safe. Even the mentally ill want to be safe. Even if it's only from themselves.

I would lie on the cool cement floor and close my eyes and feel nothing for a while. I rarely remembered my dreams if I had any. It was probably better that way. The rats that had inhabited the place had left the minute they set eyes on me. They knew a true predator when they saw one. There was nothing but me and darkness. And right before I'd fall asleep, I'd allow myself that one thought. The single fear that had taken my reason away from me. That I had killed once and that I would have to kill again.

When I was a teenager, I thought going mad was a

glamorous thing. So many great artists had taken leave of their senses and were immortalized for it. I had thought that insanity was easy and painless. You lost your mind, and that was it. No suffering was involved, and everyone would admire the fact that you were too noble to exist in a world as imperfect as this one.

It's astounding how many stupid ideas one teenager can have in a lifetime. Madness was an ugly thing. There was nothing glamorous about it. It was not an escape at all. Instead, you were stuck inside your own insane mind, which hated you and the world you were no longer mentally—and also in my case physically—able to live in. And madness hurt a lot. And it made you cry a lot. And it made you act in an irrational manner and then know how irrationally you had just acted.

This time in my life was truly the dark ages. Great and beautiful segments of my life were lost and could not be recovered once the darkness lifted. No, even now there are still a few tiny holes in the history of my life. There are sentences that are lost forever.

My dark ages lasted about six months. They started at Halloween, when the man attacked me on the beach and the police showed up at the motel, and lasted till spring, or maybe it was the spring of the following year. I don't remember. Time really didn't mean too much to me then. It doesn't mean a lot to me now, either. I have as much time on this planet as there is available.

What I did those nights downtown is not that interesting. Mostly I walked, and since I never got tired anymore, I could walk right until the sun came out. I'd walk past junkies, muggers, insomniacs, and drifters and past the underground nightlife types who found the hidden clubs on city streets so fascinating. None of them bothered me. If they had even the tiniest speck of intelligence, they would feel a certain uneasiness when they saw me and would leave me alone. If they had not gotten out of my way so quickly, I could have knocked them into the next street with just the slightest movement of my arm. But I never had any need for theatrics. That would come later.

They would see this girl, with the piercing gold and gray eyes, the black clothing—which now included an oversize man's jacket I had found somewhere—and very dark, just slightly auburn hair that now reached my waist, and be unable to do anything but stare and then look away. I could have made them kneel if I had wanted to. But I didn't even start thinking of doing fun things like that until later.

I remember Christmas came and went. There were decorations here and there, people buying presents. But Christmas in L.A. is nothing compared to New York. There is no Rockefeller Center with its giant tree, no ice skating rink, no Saks store windows, no snow, and no ever-growing excitement as the twenty-fifth approaches. I didn't really care now anyway.

My family, who celebrated Christmas with a vengeance and in true Catholic fashion, could no longer include me at midnight Mass. And Ben, who used to love to buy me presents, could buy nothing for someone whose only need was a chance to go back in time and start over. And because I was mad, I never truly thought all of this out. I just knew I could not see any of them again, least of all at Christmas.

The dark ages continued. I spoke to no one, and no one spoke to me. In a certain way, I was afraid of human beings, afraid of what they could make me do. So I didn't dare risk contact. I had spoken to people back at the motel, but that man on the beach changed everything. There was no fooling myself after that. No pretending I could still go back. I had done the unthinkable. I had killed someone with my very own teeth. I had tasted someone's blood, and it had given me a thrill. So I walked, and after many months a little of the madness lifted and thoughts would come to me now and again. Little thoughts, like what direction I was walking in or how many jewelry shops there were on one street. Little thoughts. Sane thoughts. A few moments of clarity.

One night, around the time thought was beginning to happen again, I decided to leave my usual stomping grounds and head to Hollywood. I was actually starting to get bored, one of the first signs of an illness lifting. My mother always knew when my fever from the flu was gone, because immediately I would complain of having nothing to do.

Suddenly, just walking around town aimlessly was not enough. I felt I needed a change of scenery. I wanted to hear noise, feel activity, pretend I was alive again.

Hollywood was a bit of a hike, but I could move quickly when I wanted to. My feet would barely touch the ground, and I would almost glide along the pavement. It was an interesting trick I had learned when I had to make a fast getaway.

I moved north up Highland Avenue, passing the suburban houses with a growing feeling of longing. I used to live like that. I used to get up in the morning, leave for work, go to sleep at night. But now it seemed so long ago. It was another lifetime.

I reached Hollywood at the height of the Saturday night rush. It was 11:00 P.M., and the streets were full of every kind of person imaginable. Kids looking for fun, prostitutes selling themselves, bag people with no homes here either, rockers, pimps, gang members, and tourists with excited but horrified expressions on their faces. They were all looking for something. Most of them didn't know what, but they were quite serious about it.

I stood on the corner of Sunset and Highland and surveyed the scene. There was so much activity, so many colors and lights. It was a little overpowering at first. Someone stopped and asked for my autograph. I waved them on. What a change from the underground feel of downtown. Here everything was out in the open. I began to feel the energy emanating from the human masses roaming the streets. It was exhilarating, but I also began to feel that other urge. I could smell the man that had just passed. I knew what he would taste like, but I was determined to suppress those feelings. I wanted to put off doing that for as long as I could. Tonight I just wanted to look at Hollywood, walk on its streets, and take in its sights. I wanted to feel a little bit alive again.

I could hear music pounding from somewhere, and it made my heart beat faster and louder. I turned and headed in the direction of the sound. It took me a few blocks down the boulevard to a rock club, World War IV, where people were pouring in and out of the door. Most of them were too drunk or too stoned to know what was going on. But some of them nodded slightly as they passed by me, and some of them stepped out of my way.

I decided I wanted to go in. Unfortunately I had no money, and my bare feet presented a certain problem as did my lack of ID. I glanced at the bouncer with interest. His arms were crossed to his shoulders. His eyes were like stone. But perhaps I could make him see things my way. While I knew I couldn't hypnotize anyone, at least not yet, perhaps I could still put a little bit of the fear of God in him by the sheer force of my altered personality.

I sauntered up to the door, full of a newfound confidence. "Hi," I said, glaring through to the back of his head and thinking of what it would be like to bend his arms in the opposite direction. Slowly he looked down to my toes, and then immediately my eyes caught him again. "Hi, hon," he said, smiling an inane smile. "Go right in."

The crowd in front of me parted instantly, and I slipped into the dark environment I was so at home in. Inside, the music was even louder. A metal band was playing, and couples were dancing in a frenzied state. Twisting, turning, and sweating.

I moved into a corner where there was almost no light and leaned against the wall. I had never been to a club like this in all my life. Ben had always hated crowds, and he hated dancing to boot. If he had been here, he would have put his fingers in his ears, rolled his eyes with disgust, and demanded to leave. For a second I allowed myself a dangerous thought. I was glad he wasn't here. He'd never been very much fun. He had never liked the night.

A waitress tapped me on the shoulder. "Would you like a drink?" she asked. I looked down at her, and she quickly averted her eyes. "I'm sorry to bother you," she said, and moved away. But a few minutes later she was standing in front of me, holding out a drink as a peace offering. "It's on the house," she said, and then ran away. I took it and kept it for most of the night. It made a great prop. It gave me something to do with my hands. I curled my long fingernails around the glass and remembered how good alcohol could feel. But it was tasteless to me now.

On the other side of the dance floor, I saw a guy of about twenty-five looking at me curiously. There was something very interesting about him. Physically he was appealing. He had longish brown hair and blue eyes, and his clothes accentuated his well-kept body. But there was something else there, too. There was intelligence in those eyes. There were some great thoughts going in his mind, even though he didn't always know it.

"Come here," I mouthed to him. "Why don't you come

over here?" And he began to move across the dance floor, his feet pushing ahead of his brain. People were bumping into him on all sides, but that didn't deter him. He was on a mission, and nothing would stop him. I licked my lips in satisfaction. I hadn't made a mistake in coming out tonight. Things were going well.

He finally reached me, and he smiled warmly, letting most of his teeth show. "Hi," he said. "I'm Neil, and I just, I just have to meet you."

"I'm Kate," I said, touching his hand lightly. He felt very warm, like he was burning with a fever. And he smelled wonderful, too. A little bit like shampoo, a little bit like a man. It was a perfect combination.

When I was in high school or even in college, I was never a social butterfly, never a flirt. I never even so much as thought of chasing a boy. It seemed like the wrong thing to do. I had always dated but these were long-term relationships. I met a man, waited for him to call, and if I liked him, I stayed with him for a while. But he was always the one in pursuit. I took a passive, safe role.

I didn't like the threat of the unknown, the danger of going out with a new person every week. It was too difficult, too nerve-racking. There was nothing fun about it. In retrospect, I think that's why I married Ben. We had been seeing each other for almost two years. It was the end of college, and I was afraid. Afraid to be out on my own, afraid of trying to get a job, afraid of having to date someone outside the secure world of education, afraid of being an old maid. He proposed, and saying yes seemed like the natural thing to do. It made everything so settled, so defined. It pleased my parents, who had been expecting it. They liked Ben, and they knew he would take care of me.

But now with Neil standing so close we could almost kiss without moving, I felt the power of pursuit. I was in complete control of this man, and it was enjoyable. Why should I be threatened when I was laying down the ground rules? Now I knew why people found dating such an exciting experience. I had picked this man, made him come to me, and now I would have the pleasure of finding out how right or wrong my choice had been. It was positively stimulating. Even his breath felt warm against my face.

"Kate," he said, "would you like to dance?"

I looked at Neil's mouth and smiled. I felt as if I was coming out of a coma, waking up from the depression that had haunted my life for the last six or seven months.

"What I'd really like to do, Neil," I said, "is talk." This suggestion seemed only to make him happier.

"Well, ah, I don't know if you know this club, but there is another room that's real quiet, with tables and classical music, for when you want a break from this." He pointed to the metal band, who seemed to be getting louder.

"That would be perfect." I let him lead me to the back of the club and into a dimly lit room where various couples sat at sofas and tables scattered around the floor. Some of them were in the early stages of lovemaking. Yes, this was just perfect.

Neil and I sat in the furthest corner, and I took his hand. "Talk to me, Neil," I said. "Tell me things, things about yourself, or anything will do. I just want to hear you talk." I was so enamored of being able to speak to a human being again. I realized how very lonely I had been, spending all my nights with only my own scattered thoughts.

"Well"—he squeezed my hand—"I live not too far from here in West Hollywood, and I do drywall work for a living, you know, basically building walls and stuff. Nothing too exciting, but it pays. I like to go out on the weekends and have a good time. I sometimes go to clubs like this, or mostly I go to movies or plays. I'd love to go to a movie with you sometime. Are you an actress, Kate? You seem a little different. A little out of it, but not in a bad way. Maybe just a little removed from the ordinary. And you are absolutely beautiful."

"No." I moved closer to him. "I'm not an actress." His scent was becoming stronger and stronger. It reminded me of the way a bakery could entice me when I was younger. I felt incredibly drawn to him. I could see the little hairs standing on his neck. They were a lighter brown than the hair on his head.

"Not an actress. Well, you should be. I noticed you from way across the room. Your eyes just stand out like two electrical signs. I felt compelled to come over and meet you, and I'm not always that aggressive with women."

It made me smile to realize he thought he was the aggressor. I stretched my tongue out and licked his neck. He was so delicious. I could hardly stand it. He seemed a little surprised at my interruption, but there is hardly a man on earth who would turn down a direct pass from a woman. My touching his neck only spurred him into action. His lips, which were so close, moved in for a complete kiss. I felt his tongue moving in my mouth, and I felt his hesitation as he touched my four teeth that were becoming longer. But I didn't care. I wanted him. I broke our kiss and moved my mouth down to his neck. My tongue began to draw little circles around and around one spot on his neck. It would be so easy, and I was so thirsty and lonely—and he could fill me up. My teeth began to come down on the softness of his skin.

"Kate?" he said, and there was a touch of fear in his voice. "Kate?" And I remembered the fear in the voice and the face of the other man, when he knew he was about to die and couldn't believe it.

I pulled back from Neil suddenly, shaking in horror with the knowledge that it was about to happen again. "No," I whispered to myself. "You promised, not again, not so soon."

"Kate?" he said stupidly, his eyes blinking in confusion. "What's wrong?"

"Get away from me, Neil," I shouted, standing up and sending the table and our drinks crashing to the floor.

"I'm sorry," he said. "I wasn't going to do anything. Nothing that you didn't want me to do."

People at the other tables were staring and out of the corner of my eye, I saw a bouncer start toward us. I had to get out of there, and it had to be now.

"You should thank God I'm leaving." I turned and ran toward the door. Neil was left standing, the broken table at his feet, wondering why he'd ever come to this club tonight and cursing the fact that he didn't even know my last name.

I practically flew out of the front entrance and back onto the street. *Oh God,* I thought, *what am I going to do? I can't help myself. I can barely control it. It's coming on me again.* And with the taste of Neil still lingering in my mouth, still touching my tongue, I exercised more self-control than I knew I had and returned to my cellar, my grave, that I never should have left.

Why hadn't the nuns warned me about this? They had warned me about everything else. Especially Sister Concepta. And she had made such an impression that she still lived in my dreams, even as my humanity died. Even as I lay tied up in a stranger's bed.

She had told my sixth-grade class about all the evils there were in this world to tempt us into sin. And she had made them graphically clear by putting the fear of God into us.

There was pride, of course; that's what got Lucifer into trouble in the first place. I learned that you should never be too pleased with yourself, never revel in your accomplishments and think you're better than everyone else, especially God. In other words, no one loves an egomaniac. Pride goeth before a fall. I could definitely attest to that one now.

There was also money, something you needed in this material world but were better off having as little of as possible. Take St. Francis of Assisi. His family was loaded, but as soon as he gave his money away and went to live in the woods and talk to the animals, he became a saint. One of the best things you could be in Catholicism. All the priests and nuns took vows of poverty, too, although they always seemed well fed. Money was just not good. It could drive you to kill or steal. You should work hard, of course, but just not get paid too exorbitantly for it. If you had too much money, you could be tempting others. This I had no problem with at the moment.

But, above all, the outstanding source of evil for eleven-year-old girls, or even for a girl as old as twenty-seven, was boys. Boys were always trying to get you to do something you shouldn't. They were pushy and rough and were not able to control themselves once they started kissing. This was a major concern, for somehow, even though in sixth grade I didn't understand how, kissing inevitably led to having a baby. Something that was wonderful if you were married was a real source of shame if you weren't. Sister Concepta had me so worked up over this information that I was afraid to sit next to a boy on the school bus, for fear I would start his sexual desires going. It took me years to get over that one. I wish she had included infidelity in there somewhere. Maybe I would have been a little more leery of men with green eyes.

But the nuns never warned me about vampires. They never told me that the imaginary creatures of books and films existed in real life, let alone in California. If only someone had told me that, I might have been on the lookout for mysterious people who were never seen in the sunlight. I might have been on the lookout for Justin. But no, I didn't want to think about that bastard again. I had made up my mind to block him from my memory. I had found out awhile back that when Justin came into my thoughts, all I could see was me ripping him apart limb from limb. But I had enough bad things to think about without dwelling on him, too.

I turned my head to the side and saw a spider moving cautiously across the cellar wall. He saw me looking at him and froze in fear.

"Don't worry," I said out loud. "You don't have anything I need." He turned around full circle and scurried away. I used to be so afraid of spiders. Now they lived in terror of me. In my little kingdom of darkness, I ruled with an iron hand.

I had been lying there for weeks now. I never left, even at night. After the Hollywood experience I was too horrified to even set foot outside again. The confusion of madness had left me, never to return, and I could no longer wander the streets without a plan. I was too aware for that. Too aware of what I was capable of. And since I didn't know what to do next, I did nothing. I probably needed professional help, but no psychiatrist could talk you out of a problem like this one.

So I lay in my grave without moving, as memories floated into my head now and again. Memories of when I was alive, of my family and my friends and of Ben, too. I missed them all terribly. I wanted to call up my brother and ask him to come and take me home, to help me find some cure for the changes that had occurred in my body.

As if it were cancer or heart disease. But always there was this little voice saying, "No, this is something you cannot do." And I believed it, because everything else I used to believe in had crumbled the day I killed someone.

I had been planning to stay in that cellar forever. Since I had almost taken Neil as my next victim, it was now obvious my blood lust would never leave me. I could not stand the thought of killing again. I had stayed away from it as long as I could. But by the time I left Hollywood the desire was so overpowering, the need so great, I could not fight it anymore. I could not even be within fifty feet of a human being. It was too tempting. I thought I would just stay in my grave, buried until I died.

I had no idea, though, how painful death from starvation could be. It was no slow descent into unconsciousness. No slipping away. I was so far gone now, I was writhing in agony. The veins in my body were collapsing one by one, and it was the worst pain I had ever felt, worse than when Justin had changed me. I could not stand it. I was blind with the need for relief. A drop even. A single drop of living blood would get me through the next night or day.

I did not sleep anymore. I was always awake and aware of my predicament. When would I be released from this misery so I could not kill again?

But we all want to survive. Justin had been right. It's not an easy thing to do, to commit suicide. It hurts like hell. And I was weak. I could not fight it anymore.

"Damn it," I moaned. "And damn you, Justin. I want to live." I pulled myself to my feet and surveyed the damage. Bits of my hair lay on the ground. It had started to fall out a few days ago. And my nails were chipped and breaking, too. My skin was turning bluish gray. God knows what my face looked like now.

I would just have to do it. I didn't want to die. Whatever death there was for a vampire. It was a step into the unknown, and I wasn't ready for that again.

I would have to kill the first human being I saw. There were no ifs, ands, or buts about it. I'd try to take them as quickly as I could, so they'd feel very little pain. I was sympathetic now to that at least. I didn't want to make them suffer.

I slipped through my little crack of an entrance and stood in the evening air, my legs shaking from weakness and anticipation. I heard someone close-by draw in a hurried breath. I turned eagerly in the direction of the scent, my teeth descending at even the slightest possibility of a kill.

I turned and saw a woman, gray haired, probably seventy-three or -four, only five feet tall and lame in one leg, looking at me with outright curiosity. "Hi," she said.

Now, we all know vampires have no morals. They feel nothing for their victims, they have no regret. Dracula had no human frailties. And when he made other vampires, even if they'd been fine upstanding citizens before, they lost all their humanity and reveled in killing the innocent.

Unfortunately this was one of the myths Justin had referred to. Most of my morals were still intact, no matter how badly I behaved. I turned and saw that old woman, and was overcome with a sadness I couldn't define. I should have known that the color of her hair reminded me of my grandmother's. With a memory like that, I didn't stand a chance.

Her name was Lil, and she was hungry. That much was obvious. But what she wanted outside my hideout, I didn't know. I looked down at her and sighed heavily. "What is it?" I asked. She didn't even flinch at my appearance. Instead, she looked hopeful.

"Got any food in there?" She was gesturing at the

opening I had just slipped out of. "You've been in there for weeks and haven't budged, so I figured you had something stored away, like canned things. Maybe you wouldn't mind sharing a little bit, just for tonight?"

I sighed again. I was starving, too, and there was no dinner in sight for either of us. Isn't that always the case? You make up your mind to do something, and then someone changes the game plan. I was psyched up to kill, and someone put a hungry old lady in my way. I couldn't just ignore her. That would be too easy.

I surveyed the area around my home to see if any grocery stores were in sight. It was something I hadn't given too much thought to lately, regular food.

"Your skin tone don't look good," Lil said. "You'd think you'd look a little better having eaten all the time. I guess you just need to be out in the sunlight."

"You don't know the half of it, lady, but there's no food down there," I said, and stopped. I spotted a coffee shop closed for the evening, only a half a block away. If I could slip in and out of this cellar, I could probably gain entrance to a locked restaurant, too.

"Stay here," I said, and limped down the street toward my goal. There was something wrong with my toenails, but I didn't want to look. I guess I still commanded some authority, or maybe she had nothing better to do, but Lil stood stock-still, blinking in the darkness. She was anticipating the taste of food in her mouth.

I couldn't find a crack in the building of Ed's Luncheonette, so I stood at the door and gave the matter some thought. My little voice was speaking, but it was barely a whisper. Just the slightest effort of breath. *Just think about it, and you'll be in,* it said. Now that seemed logical. I had to get Lil some food, and I was ready to try anything.

So I thought, and I began to slip away. Little by little,

my body became nothing, until there was only my mind and that was just a bit of fog. Floating. Right through the door. Right through the keyhole. Floating. I could see the yellowed linoleum floor. I could see the coffee-stained counters. Floating. I could almost float away.

But then I remembered, and I thought myself back into my decaying body and felt the pain I had left for a few minutes come back with a vengeance. I had to make this quick so I could get on with more important things like my own survival.

I looked behind the counter and selected a loaf of bread, a fair amount of cheese, and a gallon of orange juice. It would have to do. Actually, it would probably keep her in food for a good week. So as quickly as I had gained entrance, I dematerialized again, exiting with the groceries that vanished with me.

When I got back, Lil was standing patiently, waiting for my return. I was amazed at her confidence in me. Her act of faith. I was also a little relieved to find one person who wasn't given an insight into death just by looking at me.

But that didn't matter now. My moment of weakness had passed. I dropped the food at her feet without a word and headed into the night. I was out for blood. Anybody's blood. Every fiber of my unearthly being cried out in pain. I was disintegrating before my very eyes. If I didn't hurry, I would die soon. And this time it would be another kind of death.

Down on Third Street there was little activity on a Sunday night. The Santa Ana winds were blowing warm, and everybody was probably staying near an air conditioner or some cool spot. I'd just have to walk until I found some poor unfortunate soul just begging for their life to end.

As I walked, bits of my hair broke off and fell at my feet or blew away into the night air, sweeping west and into the sea. My hands were taking on an even grayer cast, and my legs were becoming stiffer by the minute. Arteries were hardening, and my teeth felt loose. Time was running out. Somewhere in the back of my mind, a death rattle was beginning.

And then I heard it. Activity. Human activity, and nearby. Human voices, human noises, human pain. A cloud passed over the moon, blowing away the light, and I felt that my moment was at hand.

There was more than one person moving in the shadows. I could hear them speaking. I'd have to try to isolate one of them, but I couldn't do it by seduction, that was for sure. By now I was probably looking the part of the ghoul I had become.

I headed in the direction of the noise, and it led me to an alleyway. Two boys were standing over another, who was lying against several garbage cans set out by Fashions For Less. There was a trickle of blood running from his body.

I felt excitement start to build inside me. One of the other two had just knifed him, and they were gloating at their achievement.

"That's what you get, Johnny, you stupid punk," the taller one said. "You should stick to your own neighborhood." They laughed at their wit.

Johnny tried to speak, but his pain was too great. He could only choke back a reply. A reply filled with anger and fear. He tried to move, but the blood only flowed more freely.

I was only a few feet away from them now. Like a cat stalking its prey, I had been silent in my approach, but I could not contain my excitement anymore. As the scent of fresh blood reached me, my breathing became heavy and audible. It gave my intentions away.

Suddenly they turned and saw me. I had underestimated just how ghoulish my appearance had become.

Looks of pure horror came over their faces, and they began to back away.

"Hey, man," the shorter one said, "be cool. We're outta here." Their fear struck me funny, or maybe it was starvation speaking, but I let out another one of those low hissing noises, almost a growl.

That was enough for those two who'd been hell-bent on murder just a minute earlier. They were off and running before I could even take another breath.

I looked down at Johnny. He was dying, and in his altered state he saw only a person sent to save him. Someone who had frightened his attackers away. He lifted his hand in supplication, and I took it and knelt beside him. My teeth were almost bursting out of my mouth.

"I'm sorry to spoil your fantasy, but nothing in this world is ever how it seems. At least you may find peace somewhere, some answer to your pain."

He shut his eyes as if he did not want to believe what I was saying, hoping still for his guardian angel to arrive. I hesitated for just a moment. The old Kate would have been stopping the bleeding, calling for an ambulance, anything to help. But the new me, the starving me, could not let this opportunity pass.

I pulled the knife out of his chest and placed my mouth at the wound. As I sucked, the blood flowed willingly over my waiting lips and caressed my tongue, then moved lovingly down my empty throat and filled the dying shell of my body.

I felt rebirth begin. The pain that had racked my body for weeks disappeared, and life returned. Nails restored, hair growing back, skin regaining its tone and texture. Strength in everything that had become weak. I was born again. Through this boy, I was born again. And it was wonderful to be alive.

When I had finished, I licked my lips in satisfaction and felt that glorious high set in once again. It was an addictive feeling. But this time I did not revel in it at first. I decided to get right down to business. I had to dispose of the body, or what was left of it.

I looked around for a means and found it in the industrial garbage cans lying beside the boy. Inside one was a half-filled can of gasoline. I searched the ground and found a discarded matchbook. It was perfect. I would leave no evidence behind this time. The bones that would remain would give no clue to the kind of creature that had taken Johnny's life. It may have taken me a while, but slowly, very slowly, I was learning.

As I walked back to my home, I moved with the happiness of someone who had just won the lottery. The smell in the air of something burning reminded me of my sin, but I would not let it bring me down this time. He would have died anyway, even without my finishing the job. The other two had done the actual kill. And it was either me or him, and I had made my choice. I wanted to enjoy my newfound life. The need to survive can change your code of ethics real fast.

I was bounding along in a perfect mood, congratulating myself on my clearheaded thinking this time, when I almost walked straight into Lil. I was only two blocks from the crime scene, and it made me suspicious that she was there.

"You look a lot better now," Lil said. So did she, as the food I had provided had restored some color to her cheeks and some light to her eyes, too.

But I was on the defensive. What was she doing here? Following me? And if so, she must have seen. And she might tell someone. I couldn't let that happen. But I couldn't kill again. Not like this. Not when I wasn't driven by pain and desperation.

"Damn it, Lil, what the hell are you doing here? Why didn't you just take your food and go? What's wrong with you?"

I was exasperated beyond belief.

"I just wanted to know," Lil said. "I wanted to know exactly what the story was with you." She looked at me without fear and with more than a hint of being pleased with herself. She had guessed at the supernatural, and she was proven right.

"And what is my story, Lil?"

My high was definitely diminishing. The burning smell drifting over the empty streets was beginning to bother me. I thought of the look of hope that had come into the boy's eyes when I first stood over him. He had reached out to me, believed me to be his savior, and I had drunk his blood.

I felt regret beginning to seep into my mind again. I realized I still wasn't used to my new position. I wondered if I'd ever come to terms with being a vampire.

"You're just another one of those that aren't human."

I had forgotten Lil was there for a moment, but when I heard "just another," my mind snapped to attention. She knew other vampires? And they were here? In downtown L.A.? Now, that was interesting.

"You know where there are others? Others like me?"

"Well, not exactly like you, not blood-drinkers like you." She looked at me slyly. "I've seen this ghost over by Fourteenth Street a couple of times. Even spoke to her once. Her story was so sad. Killed when she was only sixteen. And then there's Henry. He says he's a werewolf. But I've only seen him as a man. And a long, long time ago, there was this gremlin that used to steal things from my mother. But that was in the twenties. Before Hollywood got L.A. so built up and drove a lot of the supernatural away. There's not a lot of places left to hide. But no one exactly like you. How long have you been stalking this area?"

I stared at Lil in complete amazement. Here was a regular if very poor human being who totally accepted unnatural life forms and didn't think badly of them, either. And she knew other nonhumans. Others who might be able to give me some clue about my current life-style. I had so many questions. This was extremely encouraging. In fact, it gave me a whole new outlook on life. It wasn't just me and that idiot, Justin, who weren't human anymore. Someone else had suffered a similar if different fate. Someone who could give me some answers.

That Henry sounded like a perfect choice. He was a werewolf, just like in the movies. I started picturing a modern day Lon Chaney, Jr. Now there was someone I could communicate with. Someone who would show me sympathy and understanding. A man I could relate to. I smiled just thinking of the bond there would be between us.

"Lil," I said, "my name is Kate, and I am really glad to meet you." Lil smiled and held out her arthritic hand for me to shake.

But unlike the boy whose blood I had just drunk, I meant to be her friend, to save her from starvation and protect her from all the junkies and hoodlums only too ready to kill an old lady for nothing. In exchange, she'd introduce me to Henry. It was a perfect arrangement. I could feel my good mood returning in leaps and bounds. Vampire or not, I was going to enjoy it this time.

It took Lil quite a while to locate Henry. He was not a man to be pinned down. In the meantime Lil became more of a friend than I ever expected. In a certain way she was almost like family. I took care of her at night, and in the day she kept an eye on my sleeping quarters.

Little by little, I told her the whole story of my transformation, right down to being tied up naked in bed. That part really perked her interest. It even made her sit up and smile.

Mine was a story she had heard many times, from many women, only this had a slightly different ending. Girl is with good guy. Girl meets bad guy and falls madly in love. Bad guy screws girl over. Girl loses good guy and pays for mistake. Most of the time the biggest payment was divorce, or in Lil's time, scandal.

Her only comment that bothered me a little was that I shouldn't have been so quick to reject Justin's offer of help after his bad deed. She thought I should have taken him for all he had, let him show me the ropes, teach me his powers, and then dump him.

If I had done that, she pointed out, I wouldn't be sleeping in some dirty, deserted cellar in downtown L.A., still recovering from a bout with madness. Instead, I would have my own coffin or whatever, in my own beautiful condo.

There was a certain logic to this way of thinking, but I doubted I ever could get over the need to punch Justin's head in for making me feel like such a fool. My pride would always be standing in the way. It was better I didn't have to look at his stupid face. I would rather figure out everything on my own. Even if it took forever. I had always been like that, and my vampirehood hadn't changed the stubborn streak I'd been born with.

Meanwhile, Lil told me her story. Her family had moved from Brooklyn to California in the twenties, and it had been beautiful back then, almost a paradise. No smog, only sunshine. No row after row of apartment buildings, only farmland and beaches. No pollution, no dirt, no grime. It filled me with longing to hear her talk of old L.A. I wished I had lived then, when life had seemed a little kinder.

And then there was the excitement of Hollywood in the nineteen forties. Lil was in her twenties when the movies were in their heyday, and she had worked as an extra for quite some time. It payed enough for her to survive, and she got a touch of glamour in return. She also got the benefit of seeing the movies in which she played a part up there on the silver screen. It was a lot more fulfilling than Sandy Klein's workshop or even a $1,000-a-day Burger World commercial. I envied Lil's brush with stardom. It made me remember how I had only just started wanting to be an actress when my life was cut short.

But it was downhill for Lil after that. In the fifties and sixties she got a regular job as a bill collector. She married one of the bad guys, who was an alcoholic, and divorced him five years later. It's so hard to find true love in this world. It seems you are either bored or alone. The fun people are always no good for you. In the end they make you miserable.

After her divorce Lil was a little sketchy about the way her life went. There were illnesses, a bout with cancer, and other things that eventually ruined her financially. Once that cycle of poverty starts, it's hard to recover. With most of her family dead and friends missing along the way, Lil ended up in the land of the lost—downtown L.A.—alone, broke, and starving, "one of the homeless again."

"Why don't you go back to him?" she asked.

We were sitting in front of King Fashions—Clothing for the Big and Tall, and night had just fallen. It was one of those beautiful evenings in L.A. when it had rained the day before and the winds had blown the smog out to sea.

All the stars were visible in the heavens. People were out and about everywhere, homeless or not, but everyone left us alone.

Besides my ability to strike fear in the heart of anyone who might bother us, I had also acquired a reputation on the streets as someone to avoid at all costs. It gave me a sense of power. And I was beginning to enjoy feeling powerful.

Most of my life, I'd always been on the shy side. I could never consciously or unconsciously intimidate someone. I was always polite, always tried to smile at the person I was speaking to. As a result, I had, from time to time, been taken advantage of or ignored. Now I didn't have to be polite. Why should I? I didn't need anything from anyone anymore, only blood, and that I could take without asking.

"Who should I go back to?" I asked. "Ben?" Someone was walking by us, a little too close, and I thought of tripping him.

"Not Ben," Lil said. "That marriage was doomed before you ever met Justin. If you had stayed with him, your life would have been one endless snooze."

She took another bite of the apple I had lifted from a closed fruit store. I was getting very good at petty theft. I had already stolen some new clothing for Lil and, of course, a very expensive black shirt and pants for myself. I still had an intense dislike for shoes. I liked to be able to flex my toenails.

"What I mean is, why not go back to Justin?" she said. "You probably still could get something out of him. Some more money at least, and maybe some answers to all those crazy questions you have about God and the after-life." Lil did not have a lot of patience for my quest for the meaning of life. To her it was as elusive as the Holy Grail and just about as pointless. Once you're dead, you're dead. No two ways about it. You were put in the ground, and you did not go on from there. I found it inconceivable that anyone could live under that assumption. If there was no heaven or hell, no divine retribution, why not just do what you pleased? "Out of honor," Lil had told me. You had to live an honorable and good life. The only one who would pass judgment on you was yourself. And to her that was enough.

As for what life meant, Lil told me, she and her best friend in high school had a running joke about that. Her friend, Jeanne, would ask her, "Do you know what the meaning of life is?" And when Lil said "What?" the answer would always be "There is none." How this constituted a joke, I didn't know. If anything, it seemed terribly sad rather than funny. None of this, though, appeared to bother Lil. She seemed at home in this lovely world of ours.

"I can't go back to him," I said, staring at the sidewalk. "I feel like such a jerk, thinking he was some kind of romantic ideal, thinking there was even such a thing as a romantic ideal. I feel cheated. Just the memory of him makes my skin crawl."

I was not totally telling the truth in this statement. Lately, though they came to mind very infrequently, I'd had a few feelings of yearning for Justin, of missing him, of wanting to lie down in bed beside him and sleep through the day together. But I had dismissed these thoughts as latent traces of my human way of thinking. It was the old Kate who always needed someone close-by, who always needed to be in a relationship. I refused to be that weak again.

A young couple on the lookout for the latest night spot caught my eye as they passed. I glared at them with conviction, and the boy took the girl's arm and hurried away.

That will teach you, I thought. *You think you can just*

waltz into downtown L.A. any time you feel like. There's danger here, more danger than you could ever know.

Lil laughed as she saw them hurry away. She was amused by my sudden displays of vindictiveness. I think she was glad I was on her side. And I was glad I wasn't thirsty enough to take one of them. I still had a month or two to go before that came on me again. Thank God, it wasn't a daily craving.

"Well, if you won't go back to him, then I guess I'll have to take you to Henry, so you'll be satisfied."

"Henry?" I jerked upright. "You found out where he is?" I had been waiting for this moment for some time.

"Yes." Lil smiled with pride. "I ran into Claire, the dealer, who said Henry was hanging around by the warehouses under the Five Freeway. He has his lair somewhere close-by. She thought we could catch him there tomorrow night. It's the first evening before the full moon."

"The full moon," I said. "That's right, that's when the werewolves change, at the full moon. And once he kills, he'll move on again, so our timing will be perfect."

I was starting to get excited already. Just one more night and I would get to meet someone else who was no longer human. I could hardly wait. At least then I would know something, something about the life or nonlife I was now leading. No matter what Lil thought, there just had to be some meaning in all of this. Maybe even some way out. There just had to be.

It's truly amazing how wrong I can be sometimes. I think Disappointment should be my middle name. Because every time I think I have the world figured out, I find out I'm mistaken again.

The next night was not quite as beautiful as the one before. The winds were still blowing warm desert air, but the sky was not as clear. The stars did not burn as brightly. And the moon, almost full, hung ominously in a red and purple sky. I usually liked the moon, but tonight I almost hated it. I wanted to erase it from the sky.

The deserted warehouses with their fading paint stood lifeless under the shadow of the freeway. No movement. No noise. There was not a soul around. Only someone without a soul. A man who would change into a werewolf tomorrow night. Henry, the Lon Chaney, Jr., of the nineties, was lurking somewhere close-by.

I could feel his presence, an animal presence, threatening. But all we could do was stand by the entrance to World Keys and wait. He would find us. He would track us down. That's how it worked.

As I waited with Lil, I thought of the scene in *The Wolfman* where Lon begs the gypsy to watch over him as she had done for her own unfortunate son. The one Lon had killed after being bitten by him. That scene had made me cry as a ten-year-old child. It had touched me somehow. I wondered if anyone watched over Henry, tried to help him with his private hell. I forgot that Lon killed the gypsy despite her help as soon as the beast took over again. Too bad I didn't remember this in time.

Lil was shifting impatiently from one foot to another when I heard a sound, footsteps, and then the breathing of someone who had been running for a long time. Heavy and winded. I smelled him then, an animal scent, full of fur and sweat and saliva. I turned and saw a very human Henry coming around the corner of the building.

He barked a familiar hello to Lil and looked at me with distrusting and slightly angry eyes. "Well," he said obnoxiously, "what do you want with me?"

In one minute my visions of a soul mate vanished. This was not the suave and troubled werewolf I had pictured. Anything but. Henry glared at me with a sneer on his acne-scarred, forty-year-old face. A major portion of his hair was missing from his forehead and I wondered if he was still as bald when he changed into a wolf. He was clean-shaven but still looked dirty somehow, in a red-plaid hunting shirt and a pair of old jeans and work boots. His breath was as bad as a mangy dog's, and I was glad I was four inches taller than him so I didn't have to greet him face-to-face. On top of this, he had about as much style and grace as a walrus, and I could picture him guzzling beer and bowling with a cap on that said, "Where's the Broads?"

I was so overwhelmed at how wrong I had been that I didn't give him an answer. He sighed in annoyance and asked me again, adding, "You're the one who's suppose to be a vampire or something, aren't you?"

I snapped myself back into reality and answered. "Yes, Henry, I'm a vampire, and I was curious to know . . ." I trailed off in confusion. Most of my questions seemed pointless now, and I was noticing the spaghetti stains that blended in with his shirt.

"Curious to know what? How I became a werewolf? What difference does it make to you?" He leaned sideways and spit on the ground. "You're the one who's got it made. You're gonna live forever and look good at the same time. Me, I'm just gonna get older and turn into a wolf at every damn full moon. And I still need to eat and have a place to sleep just like everybody else. I don't have all those great fringe benefits like you do."

"Look, Henry," Lil said, and she smacked him on the arm in exasperation, "the lady wants to know what happened to you. She's not really happy about being a vampire, and she's trying to come to terms with how the supernatural fits into God's plan for the world."

"God's plan?" Henry laughed sarcastically. "You've got to be kidding. There is no plan. No plan at all. Things just happen. Some people are lucky, and some people ain't. I'll tell you about God's plan." And he leaned against the warehouse and lifted his eyes to get a better look at the moon.

"I was doing all right for myself. I had a house in Pomona, a job with the Post Office, and a wife I liked. Then I took this hunting trip a few years ago with some of my buddies. We went up to the mountains for the weekend. Thought we'd drink a little beer, shoot some squirrels or deer, have some fun. You know, guy stuff."

I nodded as if this was perfectly understandable behavior. He leaned over and spit again with relish. This time he wiped his mouth with the back of his hand. I'm sure he knew this repulsed me and was doing it out of spite.

"Anyway, Saturday night we all had a few and were laughing up a storm. I had to take a leak so I stood up and staggered over to the nearest available tree, but I never had a chance. I never heard him coming. Never heard the branches break. Never saw the bushes part. Never even realized it was a full moon. Didn't have my rifle with me. And when this wolf came lunging at me, I didn't even have time to zip up my pants. He was on me, and he bit me good and hard on my shoulder blade. I managed to keep him off my neck. Dick, my best friend, was first up with his gun, and he shot the bastard first. Then the rest of them finished the fucker off. Or at least they thought they did. They must have fired thirty shots between them.

"I was bleeding like a son of a bitch, so they threw me in the pickup and rushed me to the hospital. They fixed me up good, and next day I was able to go home, but things were never right again.

"For one thing, the police could never find the body of the wolf my friends had shot. They found our camp, but there was nothing there. Then I started feeling funny.

Got real irritable with the wife. Even knocked her around a few times, something I had never done. Started fights at work, too. Called my boss 'a no-good fuck.' That got me suspended. And my appetite increased, especially for red meat. But I didn't like the taste of beer anymore, and that was a real shame.

"I was a man out of sorts, and everyone turned on me. My wife moved in with a girlfriend. Dick and the guys stopped calling. I couldn't sleep at night. I started to smell bad, and in general everything just went to hell. And sure enough, as soon as the next full moon appeared, it happened like clockwork."

"You changed," I said, giving Lil a look of disgust.

"That's right, honey. I changed. Right into a big, bad wolf. Right in my own living room. I became an animal, and thinking just like an animal, I tore through my screen door and set out to kill the first person I could find. I was driven to draw blood.

"Unlike you, I don't need to drink it. I just have to see it splattered all over the place. Nothing dainty about me. Unfortunately the first person I found that very first time was none other than a cute little ten-year-old girl who was sitting innocently on her front porch. I came right up, out of nowhere, probably looked like an insane German shepherd to her, and ripped her throat apart.

"I can still hear her mother screaming and screaming. I may not know what I'm doing at the time, but I certainly remember it afterward. It is televised over and over in my dreams."

Henry closed his eyes for a moment as if trying to change the channel.

"Nowadays I move around a lot and try to take to the hills when the full moon is due. But I always kill someone, I just can't help myself. But sometimes when I'm lucky, I actually have a little control over my destiny. I can pick and choose my next victim, single them out in a crowd, mark them for death. This way I get the fun of the hunt along with the down and dirty of the kill."

There was a catch in his voice, but the look of stupidity on his face was hard to ignore. He could see the disapproval in my eyes.

"But not like you, sister, Miss High and Mighty, all dressed up and looking like you just came from a beauty parlor. You don't have to worry about anybody shooting you with a silver bullet. You can't die. Unless somebody gets you with a stake through the heart while you're sleeping.

"And you always know what you're doing, don't you? Even when you kill. You think you got it over everybody. And you want to ask me about God's plan. That's a laugh. If there's a grand scheme to life, nobody's cued me in. I'm just a poor working stiff who went on one hunting trip too many."

He turned and started to walk away. I really did not want to hear one more word out of his mouth anyway. Talking to Henry or having him talk at me had been as useful as trying to get a dog or cockroach to tell me something I didn't already know. Even if I'd still been human, I would have brushed him away. How could I feel any connection, any sympathy for a man whose jeans hadn't been washed in years?

"I gotta get going anyway," he said without turning around. "Tomorrow night's the full moon, you know, my time to howl. It was a real pleasure meeting you, vampire."

And then he was gone. An animal running from himself, chasing his tail in circles until he died. A real jerk.

"Well, Lil"—I patted her on the arm—"that was a thrill a minute."

"I never said he was a professor from UCLA or something," she said defensively. "Anyway, you did learn one thing."

"What's that?" I asked, as we started to walk back to our own turf. Another night of watching the world go by. Of walking and talking and thinking and of sometimes scaring a passerby.

"Things could always be worse. That's what you learned from poor, old Henry. Things could always be worse."

I started laughing at this, my sense of humor returning. Lil certainly had a point. At least I wasn't wearing a red-plaid shirt and work boots. Things could always be worse. And as usual, as soon as I started laughing, I couldn't stop.

So I laughed and hissed like the creature I was all the way back home. And Lil laughed right along with me, as I repeated over and over again till it hurt, "Things could always be worse."

And things got worse. The very next night. Like clockwork. When the moon was full and Lil was nowhere to be found. As I walked alone past building after building littered with sleeping refugees, I thought I heard him howling. I should have listened harder, I know that now. But hindsight is always twenty-twenty.

The next day I dreamt for the first time since I had changed. I had forgotten how real a dream can be. I was sitting alone at a bar in a nightclub. I knew it was the nineteen forties by the way people dressed and their hairstyles. Some men were in uniform, so I suppose World War II was in progress.

I was wearing my usual black outfit, unlike all the other women, who had on dresses. Women only wore pants in the factories then, so everyone was giving me embarrassed, sidelong looks.

I wondered why I hadn't made the effort to blend in. I took a sip of my gin and tonic and almost choked. For a moment I had forgotten I was a vampire. Alcohol was not the drink for me.

I swiveled around in my seat to look at the dance floor. A big band was playing and there were probably fifteen couples dancing to "Someone to Watch over Me." Most of them looked like they were in love or wanted to be.

A man in a black suit seemed vaguely familiar. He was dancing with a woman in a blue dress with dark brown hair who looked like a movie star. He held his arm tightly around her waist, and he was whispering in her ear. I could almost hear what he was saying. "I love you, I really do love you, but . . ."

And then I realized who the man was. It was Justin, and to my surprise, seeing him with another woman gave me an unreasonable surge of jealousy.

I felt my hands shake and my head begin to pound. I wanted to do something about it, but I didn't know what. I stood up in a rage, and the overabundance of anger in my body started my transformation. My teeth grew long and hung below my lips in a grotesque pantomime of attack. My nails seemed to gleam in the spotlights, and I realized I was hissing, low in the back of my throat.

By now everyone in the nightclub was staring at me openly and in fear. Justin dropped his arm from the woman's waist and turned toward me. The woman started crying. I could see her eyes were as green as his.

"What are you doing here?" Justin shouted at me, as he took a few steps in my direction. "I don't even know you yet."

The directness of his question took a lot of the steam out of my anger. What was I doing here? Why was I so mad? I felt my teeth retracting as I calmed down.

"You didn't want me," Justin continued. "I tried to

give you everything, but you couldn't be bothered. How dare you come here now when you haven't even been made yet?"

I looked at him, speechless. I just didn't know. "Justin?" I said hesitantly, but there was no stopping him.

"Get out of here, Kate. You don't belong here. You have no right to intrude on my past. Go back to whatever it is you're doing now."

I started to walk to the door. The woman was crying even harder now. "Justin," she said, "please let's dance. Come back and dance with me before it's too late." The band had started playing again, and the nightclub was returning to normal.

Suddenly I felt even more alone. All these people dancing and having fun, and all I had was a hole in the wall where I slept all day. I turned to say something to him, to ask him something important—I think it was "Why?"—but Justin had already become one with the crowd.

When I woke, I felt incredibly sad. Dream or not, it left a lasting impression. I was alone except for Lil. And I desperately needed to talk to her that night. I needed her calming stories, her sense of humor. She was my family now.

I walked outside my cellar and looked into the darkness. But as on the night before, Lil was not in her usual position near my resting place. I walked for a little while, looking for her, but eventually inertia set in and I returned to my cellar. My dream, plus the sense of doom that had pervaded my waking hours since the previous night, combined to make me realize I had nowhere to go. I was no different than all the other homeless humans who had no future. Lil's absence only drove the point home.

I slumped against the brick of the building that housed my grave and waited. Something bad was coming. I could feel it. Just like I had felt it back when I was human and didn't know I was in love with a monster. At least this time my eyes were wide-open and I was ready for almost anything. So I waited. It didn't take that long.

It was almost daylight when Claire, the dealer, came by. She had been looking for me all night, calling my name. I had no idea that she even knew my name, let alone where I could be found. You just never know how famous you are sometimes. As soon as I saw her, though, I knew she had come for me.

"Claire." I stood up to meet her frightened face. "What is it?"

She took a few steps back, then swallowed hard. Although the thought of confronting a possible demon was making her nervous, she had dealt with enough threatening figures in the drug world to be able to maintain a semblance of bravery. She had come here to tell me something, and she was damned if she was going to leave without doing it.

"It's Lil," she said in a voice that began to waver. "She's been killed."

"Killed?" I had expected something bad but nothing like this. Suddenly I felt weak and drained and lost. A tear appeared in my left eye and trickled down my cheek. The last tear I would shed for a long time. And the part of me that still called itself human shouted out Lil's name. As if words on air could bring her back and have her talk to me again. But she was lost, too, and I was alone again. My one tear became a pain that became anger, an easier emotion to withstand, so I held on to it. I began to see quite clearly who the murderer must be.

I could visualize his ugly face even as it turned into an animal's. That bastard. He'd said sometimes he could choose his victim. And he had chosen Lil. It was personal this time, I was sure of it. He had done it just to get to me. Why, I didn't know. But it was definitely a message for me.

"How?" I said quietly, but I was already plotting Henry's death in glorious detail. He didn't know what he was doing, going up against me. I wanted to take his dirty work boots and shove them down his throat.

"She was attacked by some kind of wild animal. The police found her late last night, and they've been asking questions all day long. They say they've never seen an animal do something like this, not even a pit bull." Claire backed up a few more steps and looked at me hesitantly. She knew my reputation and was afraid I would take out my anger on her. But she had liked Lil, too, so she continued. "You know, I suppose, that it has to have been Henry, don't you?"

Hearing his name spoken out loud made me so grief-stricken, I began to lose all control, just as in my dream. I felt the tingling in my gums that signaled my teeth were starting to grow. At that point I wanted to kill someone, anyone. No one was safe in my presence.

"Leave," I said to her in a low growl, moving a few steps toward her. "Just get away from me—now. . . . I'll take care of Henry. Don't you worry about that."

Claire didn't say another word. She knew a threat when she heard one. She was already halfway down the street before I was coherent enough to realize her absence.

"Where?" I shouted after her. "Where was she killed?"

"About three blocks from the warehouses by the Five," Claire yelled without turning around, and then she was out of sight.

Near the 5 Freeway, where Henry and I had met. He had killed her right there. Then that's where I would start. I would track Henry down from there, by the scent of blood that would still linger on the ground and cling to his body. That I could always smell a mile away. This time it was the blood of someone I had cared for. "Watch out, Henry," I said under my breath. "I'm coming for you."

But it was already too late. The first ray of sun was rising in the east. It hit my left hand, and I felt a strange burning sensation that extended through my arm. Day was coming. I'd have to postpone my manhunt until tomorrow night.

I retreated into my cellar as sleep came over me like a coma. I had only a minute before unconsciousness, and I thought of what Lil must have felt when she saw the monster that Henry had become, charging at her. There was nothing she could have done to protect herself. If only I had been there. Why hadn't Lil come to find me as usual the other night? That was another mystery that would never be solved. And even worse, what would I do without her? She had been my only friend, the only human being who knew what I was and accepted it, the only one that ever would. I missed her already, the sound of her voice, her presence sitting next to me, keeping me company through the night.

My final thought before the nothing of sleep was that at least I had the ability to make Henry pay for his sins. It was small compensation, but I could make him pay. The old Kate would have been as helpless as Lil. At least I had the power. The power to do what needed to be done.

But it would be a long time before I got to use it on Henry. And it would be a long time before I realized that any power, even mine, can have its limits.

I would spend the following weeks trying to find him. Searching through every warehouse, every empty building, looking for paw prints or footprints, traces of his fur or skin. But I secretly hoped to find him in human form.

So he would know exactly what I was doing when I tore him limb from limb, and why. I could make him pay, and I wouldn't need a silver bullet to finish the job.

But Henry is a hard one to find when he doesn't want to be found. And I'm sure he expected me to be out for revenge. He was long gone after the kill. Probably headed for the hills or desert.

It took me years of developing my powers before I found him again, and then it was quite by accident, just a chance meeting in the dark. I'll never forget his face when I started by tearing his ears from his head. "This is for Lil," I said first, and his eyes froze in fear at the memory of what he had done and the knowledge of what I could do to him. Ultimately it gave me very little satisfaction, even when he lay there crying and begging. By then Lil was just a memory, and many other people had filled up the space where my heart was supposed to be.

I stood in front of his door, suddenly unsure. What if he slammed it in my face? What if Lil was wrong? In death, her words had come to haunt me. I could see her face, hear her voice. "Why not go back to him?" They had rung in my ears for weeks, until I felt an overwhelming desire to please her. But now I wondered if I shouldn't have stayed in my hole in the ground. At least I was used to that way of life and knew what to expect. I barely knew Justin, and here I was asking him for help. The very idea of having to ask for something made me nervous. It made me feel weak.

I had finally given up on my quest for Henry. It was getting me nowhere and starting to drive me crazy. I was almost sure he had left L.A. Not even his shadow remained. I could not hear him howling, could not feel any of his animal thoughts. I needed to go on, to give up that obsession or at least postpone it for the future. If I didn't,

I would descend into madness again, and once there I did not think I could dig myself out. I was afraid of losing my mind entirely. That would be a dangerous thing, to myself and everyone in my path. Everyone in the world.

So I listened to Lil, instead, and headed west, leaving my memories of downtown behind. Maybe I could get a fresh start from Justin. I would not lie to him or take everything I could from him. I'd simply ask him for help. A little money perhaps and some ideas on how to fit into society, to pass for normal.

Little did I know how easy it would become for me to take or make money. But I was still operating within the confines of human morality where money was something you had to earn or be given.

I reached up and knocked on his white door. Even though I could slip through the opening if I had to, I felt I needed to be conventional.

I waited, but no sound came from his house. I tried again but there was no response. Standing on his doorstep, I could see the ocean rolling in against the shore. I had forgotten how reassuring the sea could be. I almost felt as if I had come home.

And if this was home, maybe I could just let myself in. He was probably out for the evening and would return as soon as daylight was imminent. If I had to, I could always sleep there.

Suddenly I felt slightly embarrassed. I wasn't even sure what our relationship had been. What exactly he had done with me. Or I with him. And what if he brought another girl home with him tonight?

My dream came back in full force, and I almost started to run away. But then the sea calmed me down and made me think rationally. If that were the case, I would just have to be gracious. Make an appointment to see him at another time, then scurry back to my cellar. What did I have to lose anymore, except my pride?

I melted into fog, slipped under the door, and reappeared inside. Everything was still so white and clean, immaculate in appearance. I walked into the living room and stared at the scene of the crime. This is where it had begun, that night I was drunk with desire.

The wineglasses were still on the table almost two years later, and the fireplace was full of burnt cinders. I also noticed things I had not seen before. One of the walls of the living room was a gigantic bookcase, housing thousands of books that looked to be first editions. And on the walls were paintings that I knew had to be originals: Renoir, Matisse, Gaugin.

The kitchen was even more sterile in appearance. No food was eaten here. I opened the refrigerator door and saw the half-filled bottle of wine. I touched a drop of the liquid to my lips and made a face. It was wine all right, but it was laced with blood. Blood that was almost two years old, and its staleness made it bitter.

So that's what he had given me. Maybe it was his own. At the time I had thought it was an expensive French burgundy. Which shows you how much I know about wine.

I debated about going down to the bedroom. That might be too much. A tiny thread of anxiety began in my neck. But curiosity drove me on, and I wanted to face the room that had frightened me so much for two days and nights.

Down in the whiteness of where I had been captive, things hadn't changed, either. Ropes were still attached to bedposts, sheets were still in disarray. Nothing had been disturbed since I had broken free that night. Even the closet door was still open, just as I had left it when I took Justin's clothes, and I could see his black shirts hanging neatly in rows on white plastic hangers.

The reality of the scene hit me hard, and suddenly I knew what had happened. Justin had never come back here that night. When he left me on the beach, he had left Santa Monica for good. His house was still intact, but he would never return. My chance to ask him anything was gone the moment I told him to leave me alone. Now I was alone, and it didn't feel very good. The joke was certainly on me. All this time I had thought he was leading the high life in his sparkling clean condo while I suffered downtown like the martyr I felt I was. But he had left without even packing his things, without even a note in case I came back. My decision was final to him, and it had driven him away. He didn't need to be told twice that he wasn't wanted.

I sat down on the bed and stared at the empty white wall in front of me. In minutes my entire plan for reshaping my life had fallen through. I was at a complete loss, and it made me feel incredibly sorry for myself. I always seemed to be losing people just around the time I began to take their presence for granted. Ben, I could never go back to, Lil was dead, and Justin was missing off the face of the earth. Why was I always in the wrong place at the wrong time, doing the wrong thing? When would I ever get things straight?

But I hadn't asked to be a vampire. Justin had decided that for me. So why was I feeling sad about him? If he wasn't here, why shouldn't I take up residence in his condo? He owed me that much. Lil would approve. She'd say I was getting something out of him at last for what he had done to me. And I couldn't go back to my cellar anymore. At the very least I needed a change of scenery, but more importantly, I needed to make some kind of life for myself.

I looked a little harder at the wall in front of me. Something was bothering me about it. There was a certain part of it that was just slightly darker than the rest. If I looked long enough, it took the shape of a door.

I got up and walked over to it. It was strange that no furniture, no picture graced this wall. It was completely empty. *Yes,* my inner voice said, *there's something there.* I reached out to a spot that looked inviting and touched it tentatively. There was only the slightest noise, the smoothest movement, and the "door" receded into the rest of the wall, leaving an opening for me to walk through.

On the other side was another room as dark as the bedroom was white. The walls were painted a deep scarlet, and the carpet was a rich burgundy. More priceless works of art hung haphazardly throughout the room, and on one side was a huge video screen, with shelves and shelves of videos in alphabetical order, all of which were old movies from the thirties and forties.

And in the center of the room, mounted on a platform, was the finishing touch. A coffin, ornately carved and opened to reveal a purple-velvet lining. For a moment I was afraid there was someone inside, but it was as empty as the house.

So this is where he slept. I walked over and touched the velvet. It was definitely better than a dirt cellar floor, but very melodramatic. Justin certainly took his death seriously.

As I moved my hand along the lining, I touched something. I reached in and picked up a square box made of gold, and I debated about opening it. This looked like something personal. But I was determined to get some information no matter how thirdhand it was, and there was no one to tell me any different.

Inside, I found what could only be called a collection of

mementos. There was a silver ring with the initials *J.M.A.* on it; three pictures yellowed with age; a small gold key and two larger metal ones; a green hair ribbon; an old hardbound copy of *Frankenstein*, with the inscription: "To my beloved, I am with you always, Nicholas"; a newer version of Wallace Stevens's poems; a white business card with the name blacked out, leaving only an address: 253 W62nd Street, New York, N.Y.; and $10,000 in cash.

I took a closer look at the photos. One was of an older-looking house that reminded me of the ones I had seen when I vacationed one summer on Cape Cod. It was a two-story, gray-shingled model with a porch that ran from the front to the sides of the house. In the distance you could see the ocean and a small dock with a rowboat tied to it.

The other two pictures were of women. The first was a black and white photo of a young woman and a little girl, both with dark-colored hair, and they were sitting in an art-deco-style parlor. On the back was written: "Elizabeth with Adele, age six."

The other was a publicity photo of a beautiful woman who bore a striking resemblance to the actress Hedy Lamarr and seemed to belong to that same period. On the bottom her name was scratched out, but her agent's remained: Max Weinfield, 6507 Sunset Boulevard, Suite 6, Hollywood.

I felt a sickening pull in my stomach as I realized that this looked like the woman Justin had been dancing with in my dream. I didn't even want to think what that meant, so I put the picture and everything except the cash back in the box and sighed.

It was obvious that Justin had been around a lot longer than I had, but his treasured possessions meant nothing to a vampire of the nineties. Only the money mattered to me now.

I wondered when he had been born and in what time period he had changed and who had done it to him. I would probably never know the answer to those questions, either. I left Justin's private room, closing the door behind me. It was not a place I wanted to be. I had no use for coffins. Instead, I fixed the sheet on his double bed and untied the ropes from the brass posts.

Even though there were no windows in the bedroom, I could feel morning coming, and I had to get ready. It always inspired a sense of dread in the very core of my being. But from now on this would be my bed until the owner showed up to throw me out. I had been killed here or born here, so to speak, so I saw it as my legal right. What I'd do from there I wasn't sure, but I had a million tomorrows to plan.

And plan I would. No more aimless nights for me. No more pointless walks, no more prayers to God, no more questions. I was tired of doing nothing, of feeling sorry for myself. Lil's death had broken the spell of defeat. It gave me anger, and that gave me energy. I was now free to do whatever I wanted. I was twenty-seven years old, and I always would be. The gift of eternal life would make sure of that. I was a vampire, and I was going to have fun.

I lay down on the white cotton sheets that had seemed so monstrous to me almost two years ago, and smiled. Even though I didn't need creature comforts to survive, I enjoyed them when they were there. The bed was soft, there were no bugs or rats for me to scare away, and I had a closet full of black clothes to wear and $10,000 to spend. Yes, I was beginning to feel better already.

III

Music

Vampires need goals like anyone else. Just finding your next victim and drinking him dry is not enough. I needed a sense of purpose, a place or a reason to belong.

The glimmer of hope that acting had offered me died the day I could no longer face the sun. I needed something to replace it, a reason to go on. Something as driving and life-giving as the theater. Something as exciting as the stage.

There is always a single moment of inspiration. Even if it takes days or weeks or years for the idea to become whole, to become completely fleshed out. The cartoon of the light bulb flicking on over someone's head is totally accurate.

The idea of being a musician, of being part of a band, struck me that way. Divine intervention hit like a bolt from the blue, and suddenly I knew. I opened my eyes, and I knew. I saw my goal, and I was inspired.

Before my moment of inspiration arrived, I spent many months in Santa Monica adjusting to my new existence. I decided to call Justin's condo my home, but it always felt temporary to me. His scent, his being was everywhere.

The whiteness stared back at me when I lay in bed. His TV talked to me late into the night when I had nothing to do and nowhere to go. His clothes caressed my skin, his couch cradled me, and his balcony showed me the beauty of the night. And his coffin filled the secret room I made a point of avoiding. That felt too intimate, a little too much like trespassing.

Sometimes I wondered why there was no phone or mail, how the bills were paid, how the electricity still ran, and why no one foreclosed on the condo for taxes. I also wondered where Justin had fled to and whether he ever thought of me anymore. But most of the time I thought of nothing except how to make my existence more pleasant, more tolerable, more acceptable to myself.

I woke. I slept. I took up TV again. Sometimes I walked. In three months' time when I needed blood again, I killed, and it was easier this time, with just a hint of regret. I was still in training to be a vampire, and bits and pieces of my humanity still dragged me down.

Every night I made a greater effort not to dwell on the past as I had for the last two years, to exorcise all ghosts from my mind, and most of all not to worry about hell and damnation anymore. The depression that had claimed me for so long when I lived in the cellar was too frightening to ever contemplate again. And every night I became a little stronger, a little less of a human being. A little more of a thing that lives in darkness and likes it.

For a long time I knew I could fly, I just didn't know how. And why shouldn't the dead have wings? Why shouldn't they be able to rise above a world they are no longer part of and drift like a bit of vapor through the cool night air? Even if they can never reach heaven, they can be closer to the stars. I found the way three months after I made Justin's condo my home. I was sitting on his balcony railing watching the stars and the planes and the helicopters that filled the sky at night. Justin's building, which had one other empty townhouse attached to its left, was only two stories high, but there was a definite decline from the balcony down the mountain cliff to the houses fifty feet below. If there was ever a major mudslide in Santa Monica, I would probably lose my new home to the ravages of nature. But rain was usually not a problem in Los Angeles, so I had nothing to fear.

I dangled my legs over the iron railing and felt the ocean breeze blow around me. So cool, so calm, so perfect. Suddenly I wondered what it would be like to let the night air carry me away. To be able to fly. Justin had hinted at things he could teach me. Maybe that's what he meant. But my mentor was nowhere to be seen and if I wanted to learn to fly, I'd have to figure it out for myself.

I stood up on the railing, curled my toes, and maintained my balance. Though I had never been one for gymnastics, I suddenly felt very agile, graceful, and natural. I was poised and ready for flight. And if I could float like fog, why couldn't I fly, too? Why couldn't I? But if I jumped into the night and fell the fifty feet below, what did it matter? I wouldn't die anyway. If a knife in the chest didn't kill me, why should a nasty fall? It was worth a shot to find out. Besides, I was restless and bored.

The sky looked like a blue-black ocean, and the air currents felt like waves that could support my form the way a swimmer is supported by water. So simple really. Why hadn't I seen it before?

I relaxed completely and let my body dissolve until it was nothing and my mind was one with the wind. Then I drifted off the balcony and found myself floating free above the Santa Monica community. I looked at the roofs of the houses below, with their sharp points of red tile and jagged edges of stucco, and hesitated. What if I fell now and found myself impaled on someone's fence or TV antenna? What if vampires really could die from a stake in the heart? For a moment I lost my confidence, and as I did, my body began to take form, accumulate weight, and fall.

Damn it, I thought. *Damn it! Relax!* The houses came closer as I tumbled through the night. *Relax!* I braced my arms out as if I could break my fall. *Relax!* At the last second, instinct finally kicked in, and I dissolved in a rush and blew out toward the ocean. Another second and I would have probably landed in someone's bedroom, really making a spectacle of myself. But I had conquered my fear, and from then on it was easy.

Of course, originally I was afraid I would turn into a bat and go chirping off, looking as ugly as possible. Maybe that's why I waited so long to try my wings. Luckily this was as meaningless as crosses and garlic. Instead, the freedom of flight was one of the benefits I inherited along with never getting dirty and never getting old.

The first night I found my wings, I soared above the Pacific Ocean for hours, reveling in my newfound ability. No wonder Wendy was so entranced with Peter Pan. No wonder Superman could command such fame. "Look at me," I whispered to the birds below. "I'm flying."

I decided to head down to the water and follow the Pacific Coast Highway as it made its way to San Diego. It was a beautiful night. I flew above the natural wildlife and below the unnatural life of metal and steel cutting its patterns around the lights of LAX. I wondered if I'd ever get tired. I wondered if I could make it to New York as long as I got there before the sun. Maybe some other time, I'd try. It sure beat standing in line at the ticket window of TWA.

I wondered why I hadn't discovered this talent before, during my long days in downtown. But maybe flight was a skill you developed as your body matured within your new state of being. Maybe there were other powers I would discover as time went on. Either way I was delighted. At last I had found something that gave me pleasure again.

As I looked down at the tiny cars racing along the curves of the highway, I realized I would never have to worry about traffic again. Never have to sit on the 405 and ponder the meaning of the accident some five miles ahead that was making life a misery for everyone else, only to find out at last that it was not a ten-car collision but just some poor fool changing his tire or looking in his trunk for something unimportant. For some unknown reason these activities fascinated California drivers so much, they felt compelled to slow down to ten miles an hour so they could observe a tire change in action.

Now I was above all of this, both literally and figuratively. It's a bird, it's a plane. I could fly. Just like the angels, I had been given wings.

I alighted at the seaside town of Carlsbad. My landing was as simple and graceful as my takeoff. I merely thought myself lower until I reached the sand, and then I regained my body, as a cloud passed over the moon and its shadows hid my transformation.

I was whole again, and I had accomplished a two-hour drive in thirty minutes and without even trying to make good time. Later I would find that by working a little harder and by keeping my mind on movement and not the sights below, I could be in Vegas in less than an hour, one sixth of the usual time. It would still be a while, though, before I made that long journey east to the place I used to think of as home. New York was still a memory I couldn't confront. I wasn't strong enough physically or mentally to face my human origins. I had not been dead long enough yet.

I sat down on the beach and rested for a while, surprised to feel fatigue for the first time since my change. Flying took a lot out of me; it drained my energy away. It made me weak in an anemic sort of way, but somehow I knew blood was not the answer this time, only rest.

It was only midnight, so I had plenty of time to refuel my spirit before flying home. If home is what you could call it. I still never said the word out loud. But always, before sunrise, I'd return to that same white room, hang my black clothes on the white hangers in the closet, lie down on the white sheets that were always clean and pressed, and I'd be safe.

A late-night jogger came running along the shore and paused as he saw me sitting quietly in the sand. "Are you all right?" he asked in a concerned voice, his silhouette illuminated in the glow of the half moon.

"Yes." I looked up at his troubled face. "I had to rest a bit, but I'm all right now."

He could barely see me in the darkness. He squinted at me anxiously as he stretched his legs. "It's not good for a woman to sit out here alone. It's not really safe." He didn't know he was addressing a species other than his own, but something didn't feel quite right to him. Taking his own advice, he turned around and jogged back in the direction he had come from. The territory he had just passed seemed safer than the unknown stretch of beach that lay before him.

I had killed only a week ago, so he held no fascination for me. He represented nothing more than what a chicken or pig means to humans when they are not desperately hungry. He was a harmless, cute little animal that one day could mean a potential source of nutrition, but for now was just something to be played with, tolerated, or ignored.

And like any other animal, he didn't know his days were numbered, that he had narrowly escaped the hand of slaughter. He only jogged a little faster, convinced somehow that neither the woman on the beach nor he would ever be safe again.

My moment of inspiration, when I saw what I could do with my life, or unlife, came the fourth time I visited Las Vegas, a city that was even more perfect than L.A. for unnatural life forms. The town is alive twenty-four hours, but nighttime is its time to shine.

Someone who sleeps during the day is never frowned upon there. The best gamblers and drunkards live that way. And Vegas is full of transients, thieves, and weirdos. People using phony names and credit cards, people hiding from someone, running from someone, people who have either just won or just lost and have no regard for personal safety.

In a normal town, most of the citizens would be wary of a stranger, would question why you were there, what you wanted. But in Vegas, I could have picked them off like flies if I had wanted to. The little luggage they had could disappear with them, and no one would ask twice. Just another loser skipping out on his bill. Of course, when it's that easy, you can become careless; you can believe that you are greater than you are. I was a little guilty of that in Vegas, but it was in Los Angeles that I finally made my biggest mistake.

The only ones I had to watch out for were the casino owners and the pit bosses. They didn't like it if you won too much, too fast, and were obviously arrogant about it. But I played their game well. Even though I had now won $100,000 to date, I had done it quietly, over a period of time and never in one casino. I always acted surprised when I won, marveling at how Lady Luck had blessed me at that moment. But I'd also make a point of losing in the same casino where I had won. I needed to reassure them that I wasn't infallible at roulette. But I was.

It was the TV that led me to Vegas in the first place. I was watching a rerun of *Dallas* one night when I decided that what I really needed was money, a lot of it. This way, if I somehow lost the use of the condo, I could buy myself someplace to hide out in, even if it was a castle in Transylvania.

J.R. had bet another Texas millionaire that he could drink him under the table. The stakes were high: each other's businesses. The winner, of course, was J.R., and he had used a little cheating to his advantage. Why couldn't I?

Gambling seemed like a perfect way to make money quickly, cleanly, and tax-free. Why couldn't a college graduate like myself, who also just happened to be a vampire, make the system work for her? Vegas was just a hop, skip, and a jump away for someone who could become a bit of fog and fly through the air at about 150 miles an hour. Why not start there?

First, I had to learn to alter my appearance. The bare feet had to go, and I had to file my toenails and fingernails way down and keep an emery board with me at all times. I refused to give up wearing black, but I bought clothes that looked a little more feminine. Sometimes I'd even wear a black dress and black sheer stockings. Heels were out of the question, though, as I needed to feel my feet as close to the floor as possible. I cut my hair to shoulder length each night, and I combed it into a semblance of the current style. I also started wearing a little makeup again. My eyes were so golden, my skin so perfectly white, that I had an unnatural look to my face, as if I wasn't of this world. A little dark shadow near my eyes toned them down, and a dark blush made my skin tone appear a little uneven.

Despite my efforts, I was constantly mistaken for someone very famous or very rich. No one, though, ever suspected I was a vampire, because no one believed anything like that could exist.

My first assignment, with the few dollars I still had left from Justin's money, was to buy a few books on gambling to acquaint myself with the rudiments of the game. Needless to say, I had never gambled in my life. It was something gangsters or lowlifes did, or at least men. Ladies had to confine themselves to the church's bingo halls, where the stakes weren't very high. And Lotto was one of those games no one you knew ever won, so even though it was legal, Ben and I had never bought a ticket.

"It's just a waste of another dollar," Ben would say, laughing at the lines in the 7-Eleven. And for him Vegas was just as laughable. He left that to the Elvis impersonators and professional racketeers. I wonder if he'll ever know what he missed.

I acquired a basic knowledge of roulette and then spent some time actually watching people play—how they reacted, how they bet. The dealer would spin the wheel, roll a little ball onto it, and it would stop on a number with the color red or black. You could bet on a specific number, on the even or odd numbers, or on a color. Sometimes a combination of numbers or colors. I chose to be on black. It was, after all, my lucky color.

I started off slow, winning a little, losing a little, but in general keeping a low profile. After I was up about fifty dollars with no help from the supernatural, I decided to use my influence to motivate the ball onto the black. I concentrated on the little devil, made friends with it, and convinced it to land on my color as long as I was betting high. It was just a matter of communication. Even inanimate objects liked a little attention sometimes. When I bet low, the ball would be allowed to choose red. In two hours I had won three thousand dollars and the admiration of everyone at the table.

I allowed myself to lose a hundred, then said good-bye to the ball, and moved on to another casino. By the end of the night I had accumulated twenty-thousand dollars and packed it in for the day at Caesars Palace. The ornate Roman statues in front of the casino had struck me so humorously that I knew I had to sleep there. It was glitzy, it was entertaining, it was fun. With a little extra tipping on my part, I was able to get the darkest room in the house and a Do Not Disturb sign that lasted until the sun went down again.

My visits continued like that until my fourth trip. I had just won nine thousand dollars at the Golden Nugget, and I was getting bored. I felt that I needed a little company, or a little conversation at least. You can communicate with a roulette ball for only so long. I needed something warm and alive.

I decided to make an appearance at Circus Circus, one of the gaudier casinos with the big top as its motif. I sat down at one of its many bars, pretended to drink the gin and tonic in front of me, and watched the world of people desperately trying to make money. It wasn't long before someone sat down next to me, and I thought I would amuse myself for a while at his expense.

He was in his early thirties, very thin, with his long dark hair tied into a ponytail so he could appear as hip as possible. He could have been attractive—his eyes were big and hazel—but his mouth had a funny twist to it, giving him a perpetual sneer. He was one of those men that you didn't trust the minute you met them, and in my human days I would have run from him immediately. Instead, I waited for him to speak.

"Can I buy you a drink, babe?" He raised his hand to the bartender before I had a chance to answer. "Another one for the beautiful lady and a Scotch straight up for me."

With the drinks ordered, he turned his complete attention on me. "So, has anyone ever told you that you have the most photogenic eyes I've ever seen?"

My immediate response was a sarcastic one, but I decided to bite my tongue and play the innocent he believed me to be. I could tell by the glint in his eyes that he intended to get me severely drunk and up to his room for the night.

"Why, no"—I smiled at him—"but that's very flattering to hear."

"Well, I know what I'm talking about," he said, warming to the subject. "I'm a film director—my name is David, by the way—and I can spot someone who should be in the movies from fifty yards away."

I couldn't control myself at this point, and a little laugh escaped me. I had never believed anyone like this could live and really survive in the world. All of his actions, all of his words were a cliché.

"What's so funny?" he asked. The bartender delivered the drinks.

"Oh, it's not funny." I was desperately suppressing my laughter at this point. "I'm just so happy to actually meet a real director. My name is Kate, and you'll never believe this, but I'm an aspiring actress. I live in L.A. and take classes with Sandy Klein. I only came to Vegas with some friends for the weekend and thought maybe I could win some money."

"Really," he said, not believing his luck, and I could

almost hear him thinking, *This is going to be easy.* He licked his lips and settled back in his chair.

We talked for a half hour more, through several drinks that he did not notice I was spilling on the carpet. I pretended to get high while he informed me that he had directed *The Cheerleaders in Moscow* and *Houston's Candystrippers.* Amazingly, this information was true. He quickly assured me that no nudity was involved, at least most of the time.

Before long he got around to asking me up to his room so he could take some Polaroids as a pre-screen test. If they came out well, he would set me up in L.A. with an agent friend of his and probably get me a small part in his next film, *The Women of Canyon Country.* I told him it sounded too good to be true. Of course, it was.

Once we were up in his room and he had locked the door, David dropped a little of his polite attitude and came on much stronger.

"Where's your camera?" I asked sweetly, but he motioned to me to have a seat on the bed next to him. I pretended to be shocked at his insinuation, but too drunk to really act on my outrage.

"Ah, come on, honey," he said, grinning. "Show me a little consideration, and I'll definitely get you in my next movie."

I thought for a moment about actually going to bed with him. It had been a long time since I'd had sex, and there was a part of me that missed it dearly. But this guy was too much of a clown to be even slightly intimate with. Besides, his ponytail was starting to get on my nerves, and it was becoming progressively more dangerous to get on my nerves.

But there was another part of me that wanted to play it out a little further, maybe scare him a bit. Teach him that his pathetic little lines belonged in the movies he made. I sat down on the bed and let him put his arm around me.

"That's better, honey." He put his free hand on my breast. "I want to get to know you so I can cast you in a part that suits you. Besides, you're not a little girl anymore. You know what this world is about."

He pulled me back so we were lying on the bed, and he began to unbutton my blouse.

"I wish you wouldn't do that," I said, trying to sound like I was pleading.

"But I want to." David unzipped my pants while moving his hand around in an attempt to be erotic. "And your body looks really great."

I know I should have stopped him at this point. I could have knocked him off the bed with just a flick of my hand, like a fly that had become too annoying. Then I could have left with very little turmoil, very little mess. But as my new policy was to have fun, I let myself feel the urge that wasn't due for at least another month. I let my teeth come out with their little sharp points, and I directed my attention to his neck.

"If you think my body looks good," I said, exchanging pleading for outright aggression, "you should see my teeth."

He was a little surprised by the change of tone in my voice, and he looked up casually to notice the difference in my mouth. What he saw, he could not believe, and he sat straight up on the bed.

"What is that?" David asked, trying not to scream, "some kind of phony Halloween shit?"

"Halloween, yes." I sat up, too, and grabbed his arm— the very one that had been stroking me moments before. "Phony, no."

He tried to run then, but I wouldn't let him leave the bed. The place where I held his arm started to bleed.

"Oh, God," he cried. "What's going on?" He was sweating now and talking more to himself than to me. "She's crazy. This bitch is absolutely crazy. I gotta get out of here."

"You know what your problem is, David?" I released his arm and smiled. "You've made too many porno films and not enough vampire films."

Free from my grip, he raced to the door. But I was faster than him. I was waiting when he reached his destination. I grabbed his other arm and threw him across the room and back onto the bed.

"I thought you wanted to get to know me, David," I said, walking toward him. "As you can see, I'm not a little girl anymore."

"Please." He tried to run to the window this time. But I caught him again and cast him back onto the bed. This time he rolled over to the night table and pulled out a .38.

"Leave me alone, or I'll have to use this," he shouted.

"Go ahead." I moved toward him. "It might be an interesting experience."

He squeezed the trigger at the same time he peed in his pants, and the bullet veered left, passed by my shoulder, and lodged in the wall behind me. He was not a good shot.

Lucky for me, the silencer disguised the sound of gunfire. All I heard was a pop. He never got to shoot again. I jumped on the bed and ripped the gun from his hand. Then I dropped my full weight upon him and held him captive between my knees.

"I wish I had seen *Cheerleaders in Moscow*," I said, and leaned down and bit through his artery, hard. Then I pulled back to catch his reaction. Shocked by the sight of his own blood, he began to cry and babble incoherently. There was nothing left for me to do but finish the job. I put my mouth to his neck and sucked him into oblivion.

In seconds his crying stopped. He moaned for a moment in pleasure. Then he and his entire career as a film director were gone.

I rolled over onto the bed and enjoyed the moment. I felt stronger than ever, and I had put this little person in his place, too. But the bed was spotted with blood and the only wounds on David were the tears I had made in his arm and the four tiny ones on his neck.

With my nails hard and still ready, I extended the cut my teeth had made all the way around his neck as if someone had slit his throat over and over again. I had to fake an explanation for his great loss of blood, and this would at least seem plausible.

I then ransacked the room to make it appear that his killer was looking for something that David was hiding. Maybe drugs. What else would a porno king have? I picked up the gun and pocketed it for fun, just to confuse the police a little when they found the bullet in the wall. But no matter what theories they came up with to explain this homicide, they would never in their wildest dreams pin it on a vampire.

With my work done, I listened at the door for the sound of footsteps but there were none. The night was young and the casino was still going strong. And all the hookers and their paying customers were locked tight in their rooms, unaware that death was just around the corner.

I left with the taste of blood in my mouth, confident that no one could trace the kill to me. Convinced that no one believed in vampires. But at the time I was only thinking of the police. I stepped into the elevator feeling satisfied with my handiwork.

But killing without any great need still made me feel a little uneasy. As I rode the elevator down, an uncomfortable image came into my head. I remembered the time I was walking on campus with Ben, and we heard a funny noise coming from under the porch of the biology building. We looked underneath to see a cat playing with a half-dead mouse. The cat would allow the mouse an inch of freedom and then secure it with its claws again. The mouse was terrified beyond belief, but the cat was enjoying the game to the fullest extent.

I gave Ben a look of revulsion and asked him if there wasn't something we could do for the poor mouse. Ben shook his head. It was something he had seen many times, adding that cats often played with their prey. It was a little bit of sadism the animal acted on naturally.

As I reached the lobby floor, I felt a lot like a cat. A little too much for my own sanity. I had just barely gotten over taking someone's life to save my own, and here I was killing for fun. I was so unnerved, I left Circus Circus and headed back to the Golden Nugget where I had intended to sleep in the day. It was still only 1:00 A.M., and I had hours to go before the sun forced me to bed.

I heard the music coming from the lounge. A Top 40 all-girl band was playing rock 'n' roll, and I found myself led to a seat by the interesting beat of the bass guitar. Inspiration, being true to form, was sudden and swift. Here I was amassing lots of money but still as aimless as ever. I couldn't be an actress because auditions and shootings were done in the daytime. But a musician's life was a different story. It took place at night, revolving around the bar scene. If I couldn't be on stage as an actress, I could be as a musician. Even the devil was allowed the luxury of playing a violin as he served his sentence in hell.

Suddenly it was clear to me. Here was something I could do with my life. Now that I had degenerated into killing people for amusement, I knew I needed a reason to act like a human being. I needed a goal in front of me. Music. Why hadn't I thought of it before?

I had forgotten how much I loved music. I think Ben had turned me against it for a while. He didn't like the stereo loud, he didn't like the car radio loud. At thirty he was already drifting into an easy-listening state of mind that was making me feel old way ahead of my time.

In those days I didn't have the energy to fight for what could make me happy. I became apathetic, and I gave in. Until those acting lessons, until Justin.

Hardly anyone was paying attention to the band. They were just background music to most of the patrons of the Golden Nugget. But they had given me the answer of a lifetime, so when they finished their set, I felt compelled to buy them a round of drinks. They had no idea why I was being so friendly, but hardly anyone will turn down a free drink, so we sat together at one of the larger tables and I listened to their road stories.

They made everything sound like fun, and they all had such a sense of belonging, some of the same aspects that had enticed me into Marla's acting workshop back when I was still human. As a vampire, I hadn't belonged to anyone or anything for such a long time. Lil had filled that space in my heart, but then Henry took her away and left me cold and dead with no one to hold on to. Now I could see a way to become alive again. I knew right then and there that this was something I could do. I now had the money to buy a decent bass and amp and pay for as many lessons as I needed, and I had all the time in the world to concentrate on something important. No distractions like husbands or jobs here. I was free to do whatever I wanted.

But it wasn't Top 40 with its incessant need to make small money and copy the popular tunes on the radio that

I really wanted. I decided to go for the higher stakes, original music, a band with a future, maybe even a record contract, if I could work the minor confines of my night-time existence around it. If only I could.

The girls in the band suggested we go to another casino, one where they knew the action was, as their gig was over for the night. But it was a little too close to daylight for my comfort, and I declined, wishing them good luck. Even inside the Golden Nugget, where day blended into night, I felt that familiar uneasy feeling creep down my neck just knowing the sun was only an hour away.

The band left in a blur of spandex and sparkles, with the smell of hairspray lingering in the bar behind them. I turned my attention back to the casino, where the sound of clicking slot machines, the sound of money, never stopped. Sometimes a bell went off indicating success, but more often you heard the cursing and groaning of people as they lost bits and pieces of their paychecks, or worse, their life savings.

And for some reason none of them knew how to dress. They all wore flowered prints or polyester pants from the seventies or mismatched colors that gave me eyestrain just passing them by. The smell of sweat and desperation began to overwhelm the residue of the band's perfume, and I knew it was time for me to leave. I was tempting the fates by staying just a little too long in the vicinity of a crime scene. I had enough money for now, and I could get more whenever I desired it. I could get almost any-thing I desired except love, and that I had sworn off the first night I had awakened in a motel alone and no longer human. I could live without life. I would survive without love.

Life was hard, but life after death was even harder, and I had to take pleasure wherever I could find it. The dice had been rolled and had come up music. From now on I was a musician. I was somebody.

Rock 'n' roll. How could I have existed so long without it? When I was younger, I had played a little guitar, but like all teenage whims, I had given it up when the season changed. Maybe I wasn't encouraged enough to really pursue it, or maybe at that time it just seemed like something only boys did. But nowadays women lived the rock life as much as men did, and being a vampire only increased my willpower and my stamina.

And it was a perfect life for a vampire. One that took place only after dark and in crowded bars, where eccentric behavior and bizarre appearance were not only tolerated but expected, and where potential blood donors would be easy to find.

After my revelation at Vegas, my nights began to take form. I was filled with a purpose, a holy mission.

I spent almost a year learning the intricacies of the bass guitar. I hired an instructor to come to the condo twice a week to teach me how to keep a beat and how to find the right notes on the guitar's neck. It was a lot of work, and I had to pay extra to keep my teacher from feeling too spooked by my presence, but my change in life gave me the time, the determination, and, of course, the money to achieve my goal. I found I had a natural ability. Music came easier to me than I had ever expected, like a second language. And it filled my nights with a driving energy that broke my link with a past that still tried to haunt me in my waking hours.

I also became familiar with the L.A. music scene. I frequented the rock clubs, watching other musicians play, and I learned from that, too. I felt at home in the smoky darkness of the clubs. With all my nails cut short (something I had to do every night as they grew back) and my hair shoulder length and tamed into a style appropriate for rock 'n' roll, I could pass for human. The only other thing I needed was a little makeup to hide the perfect pale quality of my skin. I could fit in much better than I had in my homeless days, but I still caused a fair amount of commotion when I walked into a room, because without a mask I could not conceal the striking outworldliness of my appearance.

At first I had been embarrassed by the seductiveness of my new look and felt self-conscious when I wasn't alone in the condo. Kate, the old conservative, was not used to so much attention. But after a while I found out how much fun it could be to use sex for personal gain, and I decided to relax and go with the gift I was given.

At the end of a year I felt I was finally ready to find a band of my own to perform with. I took my time, studying various possibilities, until one night I came upon The Uninvited. They were a band that had everything I was looking for. The Uninvited were young, energetic, and ambitious, and they were on their way up. Everyone said it, and you could see it in the way they played on stage. They had the look of a group that had been hungry for a long time, but now knew how to get exactly what they wanted. And they dressed in black, which fell in nicely with my sense of fashion.

The style of music they played was alternative rock— driving, danceable, a little left of center. It was commercial enough to sell but not so commercial that it was sickening. They had a mighty rhythm section, a killer guitar player, and an unbelievably charismatic lead singer. Their fans were devoted to him. They hung on his every sung word. "Drew!" they would scream, and he would smile at them and throw back his head of perfectly straight, long, blond hair.

Drew was the perfect front man for a rock band. He

was strong and virile-looking, totally in command of the stage and of the audience filled with ladies-in-waiting. But he had the slightest hint of sensitivity lurking in the depths of his pale blue eyes, a sensitivity that rarely showed itself to strangers but gave him the emotion to feel the words of the songs he sang and partially wrote. And there was something about the way his body moved that could drive a crowd into a frenzy. He could make grown men and women lose their cool, throw their drinks in the air, and dance with abandon. Drew knew what he had and used it to his advantage. I could admire that in a human. Here was a band that could give me what I wanted. I only needed the opportunity to join.

I stood one night in RiffRaff, an up-and-coming Hollywood bar, and watched them roll through their set, upstaging the other two bands before them. I made my decision that night, as I fought off every pickup in the book with a "bad" look I had developed for such occasions. I didn't want to be bothered with these mortals searching for only one thing. I wanted to hear the band.

They were playing as a unit unto themselves, through crashing guitars and haunting melodies, losing themselves in their dream, in the creation of the moment. In that moment they seemed even more supernatural than I was, as if they knew something that no one else did. As if they had all the answers.

I decided that all The Uninvited needed was me: a touch of immortality. Their bass player was good, but I was better. Since he didn't seem to have any intentions of leaving the band on his own, I would have to create the vacancy myself. I wanted to take his place, and I had the perfect solution.

I held my glass of gin and tonic, which as usual I would eventually discard, and thought about my plan of action. Picking Mitchell up seemed the logical thing to do. But I would have to use a little finesse approaching him. Instead of acting like just another star-struck fan, I decided to also be sympathetic to his artistic angst.

I felt someone brush up against me, and I turned around. "Excuse me," a tall guy with glasses said. "Don't you play Melissa in *Another World*?" He stood over me and smiled.

The idea of me as a soap opera star struck me as mildly amusing, and I laughed quietly. "No way, pal," I said, and he slowly backed away. Even though I had worked very hard to tone down the threatening side of my appearance, it still had an unsettling effect when I was off my guard or when I laughed. It was something that I perfected only with time. As long as I was in control of myself, I was just a charismatic and seductive human, who sometimes struck a chord of uneasiness in a person's soul. It would be this gift of seduction I would use to make Mitchell want to take me home with him tonight and give me his blood without question or even a struggle.

I would have to be cautious about it, though, because I did not want the rest of the band to be too familiar with my face yet. I didn't want them to actually meet me until I auditioned for them. I'd have to trap Mitchell when he was packing his equipment in the car and had had a few drinks to ease his suspicions away.

I reached into my pocket and fingered the gun it held. It was the memento I had picked up in Vegas and I might need it tonight to cover up my kill. These days, I was always prepared, something I had learned the hard way.

The band's set was over, and they were finishing their encore. It was almost 2:00 A.M., and I knew they would have to stop by then. Los Angeles was such an early town compared to New York City. Back east the show would have extended until four in the morning or beyond, which was a much more civilized hour for a vampire. If it wasn't for my fear of running into my family or friends, I would have moved back east a long time ago. But L.A. was now my hometown so to speak. I would have to make my fame and fortune here in my private little cemetery away from the glare of my past.

Nathan, the drummer, and his current leather-clad girlfriend were packing up his equipment side by side. I could see by the way they were kissing that they planned to spend the night together in bed. Drew was standing near the dressing room, accepting compliments and phone numbers. As he casually touched the golden hair of one girl in particular, I wondered if he had already decided to go home with her. It gave me a sudden feeling of longing, but I pushed it away. The last thing on earth I needed was to be involved with a human. A little sex, a little fun, maybe—but certainly not with someone in the band. It was too dangerous for them and me, and no one could ever know my secret. Charly, the guitarist with his reddish hair and his perpetual annoyed look, was complaining bitterly that Mitchell had lost the groove more than once that night. Once he kicked the wall with his steel-toed, leather boot. It left a black mark.

"How can I play a brilliant lead when you're dropping beats all over the place?" Charly grumbled. "It's a wonder Nathan can keep time at all with backup like that."

Mitch looked at the floor and shrugged his shoulders. "Come on, Charly," he said to the guitar player, who was two inches taller and thirty pounds heavier. "I can't always be perfect."

"You need to get a lot closer to perfect than tonight," Charly said, his voice rising, "if you expect to get anywhere in this world. This band will make it to the top with or without you, if you know what I mean. So get it together before your number is up!"

"I know what you mean." Mitch picked up his bass and started for the parking lot. As he walked to his car, he looked like he was about to cry. In a matter of minutes his ego had been totally deflated, depression had set in, and he was probably contemplating the easiest way to commit suicide, if only to make Charly sorry for what he had said. But some people yearn to be dead without knowing just what they're asking for, and Mitch would find his answer tonight.

"Hey." I ran up to him as he opened the hatch of his blue Toyota. "You guys were just great tonight!"

Mitchell turned around to see me smiling at him with the most open and winning look I could muster. He was not an unattractive man, about twenty-six years old, with brown hair and eyes, but he lacked the vitality that turns most women on. He never stopped slumping and his pants were a little too loose in the back. Nothing about him was strong or noble. And he needed a better haircut.

"Thanks," he said, as he threw his bass in the car, "but I must have been a little off tonight."

"You, off?" I said in disbelief. "I thought you had every note nailed." I moved a little closer to him, my breath warming the coolness of his face, and he took a step to meet me, our bodies almost touching. He had a sweet scent to him of limes and nutmeg, and I could feel my tongue working in my mouth. I did not want to jump too soon, though, and take him down right in the parking lot. I had to make it all look natural, so I stepped back a little and tried some psychology.

"You seem awfully down tonight, Mitch. Is there something I could do to help? I hate to see a great musician like yourself so depressed, although I know it's only the greats that get that way."

That little statement did the trick. Mitch smiled at the realization that at last he had found someone who appreciated his dark moods. Someone who would listen to him complain. Someone who would understand his side.

"You're right, I am depressed, and I really don't want to be alone right now. Would you like to go somewhere and talk?"

I smiled again, as softly as possible. "Yes," I said as he opened the passenger door to let me in. "That's exactly what I wanted you to say." He leaned over, turned on the radio, and kissed me on the lips. I knew right then it was going to be easy.

Mitchell's apartment looked like every other mid-sized apartment building in Los Angeles. It was part of a yellow stucco motel-like structure that encircled a tiny pool. Inside, his furnishings were minimal: a tiny unmade bed and a brown plastic dinette set with an opened box of Cheerios sitting in plain view. A couple of posters of Sting and James Dean were hung on the dirty, off-white walls, along with various flyers of The Uninvited playing history.

In the far corner of the room were the only things of value: four bass guitars, two of which were vintage, and an amplification system and a stereo. Guitar picks littered the floor, and I stepped on several of them as I made my way to one of the dinette seats. I pushed the box of Cheerios to the side. Somehow the sight of them made me ill.

Mitch sat across from me with two glasses of straight vodka. "I've got a headache," he said, as he popped two aspirin in his mouth, followed with a gulp of liquor. "The volume we play at is not only making me deaf but blowing my brain out, too. But aspirin is a lifesaver. A regular miracle drug, and combined with this"—he started to roll a joint and smiled—"I'm in heaven."

I had never liked marijuana before, and I couldn't be

bothered with it now. It's sickeningly sweet smell reminded me of embalming fluid or overripe fruit. But since Mitch thought this was all part of being a musician, I only declined politely when he offered me some and left him to his outdated fantasy.

"I'm very depressed, you know," he said, coughing slightly.

"Yes," I said, "I could see that in your eyes when you were on stage."

"I don't know why exactly. I mean, the band is doing okay. It's just Charly is always on me about something, and Drew and I used to be great friends, but now that seems gone. Almost like I'm not worth his time."

He put his mouth on the reefer, breathed in deeply, then held for a five count. When he exhaled, smoke hung over the dinette set, some of it drifting into the open box of Cheerios, negating its nutritional effect. I was beginning to get bored already.

Mitch was the first person I had decided to take in a calculating manner, and it was for personal gain. I wanted to get into the band, and this was the fastest way. Besides, I was thirsty again, and someone had to provide the next meal, the next transfusion for my survival. Why not the bass player whose position I coveted?

I still felt twinges of guilt about my bloodsucking ways. Sometimes as I fell asleep, I would remember a victim's face or the color shirt he was wearing, but the image would quickly melt away.

My initial horror at killing a human being became less important, less earth-shattering, less real with every passing night. I had reasons for doing what I did. Justifiable reasons. Remorse became a twinge of conscience. I needed to survive. The voice of my conscience became matter-of-fact. Everything is easier the second, third, tenth time around. Adaptation is the key to life. I was a vampire, and there was nothing I could do about it except crawl in a hole and die. Since I had tried that already and failed miserably, I decided to relax, to go with the flow.

How was I any different from a human that slaughtered an intelligent animal for food? The farmer's little girl, whose pet turkey was sacrificed for Thanksgiving dinner? Ultimately it was just one endless food chain, with me right at the top as far as I could tell. Why should I feel guilty anymore about survival?

"Sometimes," Mitch said, "I feel like James Dean. Like I'm destined to die young in a car crash or something. I know I don't want to get old and live in suburbia like my parents. Maybe I should just OD like Jimi Hendrix and become a legend forever."

I picked up my vodka-filled glass and fingered the K mart sticker still attached. The price was 79 cents.

"I could help you with that," I said, pouring my vodka into his empty glass.

"Help me with what?" Mitch asked, and I knew he thought I was referring to sex in some backhanded way.

"If you're really into dying, I could help you die right now. No waiting. No questions asked. A one-way ticket to the grave before you're a minute older than twenty-six."

Mitch looked at me curiously, not sure if I was kidding and a little too stoned to be frightened.

"Have you got some heavy-duty stuff? I like a girl who carries her own supplies."

"No," I said matter-of-factly, "I'm not talking about drugs, I'm talking about blood. I'm a vampire, and that's what I need."

Mitch started laughing at this, and he got up and flipped on the stereo. The Uninvited's tape of their live show just happened to be ready to go, and between giggles he pointed out what bass lines he had written himself.

"Who writes the songs?" I asked, because that was
what really counted in the music business.

"Well, Drew and Charly write about seventy percent of
them. The rest of the band contributes some of the melodies and some lines here and there. I wrote most of the
music to 'Gotta Go.'" He sat down on his tiny bed and
motioned for me to join him. "You wanna just go to sleep
together?" he asked. "This pot is really making me tired,
and I'm not up to much else. Or are you going to suck my
blood or something?" He smiled at me with clouded eyes.

"As a matter of fact, Mitch, that's exactly what I'm
going to do." I sat down next to him. "It's not really that
painful; in fact, it's a little bit like lovemaking, a kind of
release for you."

"You can't suck my blood. I'm wearing a cross," he said
stupidly, "and I had pasta with garlic for dinner."

"Old wives' tales. Why don't you just lie back and relax."

Mitch did as he was told, folding himself up like a baby
on the crumpled pale blue sheets. He was too stoned to
argue and, of course, he didn't believe that I could do
him any harm. I lay down beside him and began to stroke
his hair, my nails moving like the teeth of a comb.

"Forget about the band," I said. "Forget about everything that ever was and everything that ever could be.
. . . I'd tell you a fairy tale, but I really can't remember
one at the moment. . . ."

I felt my teeth move down into place, clicking softly as
they brushed my lips. "See," I said, turning his head toward me, "I wasn't lying."

Mitch stared at me in disbelief, unsure if he was caught
in a hallucinogenic dream. But then his body started to
shake from instinct, and he knew it wasn't the drugs.
Even animals can sense when they're being stalked as
prey.

"Hey, this isn't funny anymore." He looked toward the door, but he couldn't move. Fear can be a wonderful paralyzer. "I don't really want to die. I mean, not this minute. I was just talking."

"I want you, Mitch." I opened the collar on his shirt. "I want your blood, and I want your position in the band. You serve two purposes, you know. You're the perfect victim."

"Wait," he moaned. "What are you talking about? Vampires aren't musicians. That's the craziest thing I've ever heard of. They don't kill to get into groups. They kill only for blood. They're monsters. They're murderers." He took another look into my eyes, and now he knew for sure. "Oh, God. . . . Just like you."

"Gotta Go" was the next song up on the cassette, and I hesitated for just a moment. But the moment was lost like everything else. A bunch of rowdy drunks passed by his window. The Cheerios box stood unaffected on the table. I remembered eating breakfast with Ben, somewhere else in another lifetime.

"Next stop, heaven," I said, and bit down hard and quickly.

"God," he said, and that was all.

Sometime after Mitch's death but before I became part of the band, I was uncontrollably tempted to look on the face of the past. I wasn't really thinking of Ben; I wasn't really thinking of anything. Maybe I was only feeling, and that can always get you into trouble.

I found myself heading toward the Valley, a place I had avoided even cruising by like the plague. It represented in my mind everything I was trying to replace: a home, a husband, a living situation, a day job—everything good and normal and unattainable to me now. Maybe Mitch's death affected me more than I wanted to admit to myself. Maybe it was the fact that I never even got to cover it up.

Someone had been banging at the door just seconds after Mitchell breathed his last. I felt warm and fulfilled at a death well taken.

"Mitch," the visitor yelled, and I recognized Charly's voice. Charly had probably forgotten to tell him some other flaw he'd found in Mitch's bass playing that night.

I barely had time to rip The Uninvited's demo tape from the machine for future reference before I heard a key turn in the door. Suddenly I realized my mistake. Charly must sometimes crash here when he needed a place to stay. He was knocking in case Mitch's ship had finally come in and he had a girl inside with him.

When Mitch didn't answer, Charly thought it safe to let himself in. He had no idea just how unsafe it was. I was so flustered by this turn of events, I didn't even try to make Mitch's death look like anything normal. Escape was the only thing on my mind. I actually felt desperate, and my ability to reason was cut short, propelling me to become a bit of nothing and ease out the window just as Charly opened the door.

I was still hovering above the complex when I heard Charly scream, and then I heard him vomit. He must have been horrified by the sight of Mitch's shrunken body. Depleted of blood, Mitch looked like a white-faced rag doll with just four tiny puncture marks on his neck, showing where the damage had started.

I had planned to burn Mitch's body or at least bury it. This way it would have seemed like he had disappeared one night after a gig that had been particularly bad for him. Now it looked like something from hell had gotten him when he was stoned and trying to mind his own business.

I refused to let all of this put a stop to my musical

plans. No one could ever trace it to me, and no one, least of all the L.A. Police Department, would ever believe in vampires. At worst they would think that some weird Ted Bundy-like character had followed Mitch home and killed him for pleasure in some kind of bloodletting ritual. Nevertheless, it had unnerved me. I was not omnipotent yet, and the best-laid plans of mice and men still applied to me.

For days I had not played my bass, nor did I move out of the security of the condo. I watched TV again, instead, focusing particularly on *David Letterman* and every stupid pet trick he could muster.

And now I found myself suspended above that little rented house in Tarzana that had been such a source of discomfort for me in the past. The lights were on, and I wondered if anyone was home, particularly anyone that used to be my husband and who used to love me when I still ate cereal and hamburgers to survive.

I let myself materialize at the mailbox and checked that out first. His name was still there after all these years. Davis. I ran my nails along the letters, but it did not belong to me anymore. I probably should have taken Justin's last name. I was related more to him than anyone else at this point in time. But aside from the initials I had seen on his ring, I had no clues as to what his last name might be. I couldn't go back to my maiden name again, either. My family didn't deserve that claim to fame. Instead, I was just Kate. I didn't belong to anyone, and no one belonged to me. It would probably be that way forever.

With a quiet only great predators can achieve, I walked up to the living room window and carefully peered in. There was Ben on the very same brown sofa, his head a little balder, his feet up on the coffee table.

And sitting next to him was a woman, about thirty-five,

pretty in a pleasing sort of way and about five pounds
short of being thin. Her light brown hair was curly and
hung just to her shoulders, and as I watched, Ben moved
his arm around her and played with one of those curls.
He did not look unhappy at all; he looked like a man who
had just recently fallen in love again.

I don't know what I thought I would accomplish by this
visit. Whether I had hoped to see Ben still in the throes
of despair or not. Whether I thought he would be gone
from this house, which had been the scene of so much
grief, or still be here waiting. Maybe that was it—I
wanted him to be waiting. Something constant in this
ever-shifting, monstrous world of mine.

But people can get over anything, so they say. Time
helps you forget, and time with another person helps you
along even faster. When it was three o'clock in the morning and Ben woke up from a nightmare, he might still call
my name; he might still wonder if, somewhere in this
world, I was alive and well. He might even cry sometimes,
thinking there was something he could have done. That
he should have stopped me from going to that acting
class, that one night in particular.

But most of the time he probably got on with his life,
because that's all you can really do. And when someone
came along who offered a little comfort, he took what
was offered, maybe eventually realizing that our marriage
had been far from perfect, and that this curly-haired
woman was the one who was really meant to share his
name and his life.

Being this philosophical did not exempt me from feeling sad with a little anger thrown in for good measure.
Even if I were dead and safely in heaven, he should still
be searching every corner of the globe for my where-
abouts. He was the idiot who dragged me out to L.A. in
the first place—that land of sunshine I could never see

anymore, anyway. He was the reason I was suckered in by Justin's mystery-man technique. He was the reason I had to kill a bass player to get into a band.

With all the fury of a spoiled child, I ran back to the front of the house and kicked over his aluminum mailbox in one fell swoop. It broke at the base and went crashing down onto the sidewalk.

I heard Ben and his new love come rushing out the door as I sauntered down his street, pleased with myself and hidden to the naked eye by the absence of street-lights.

It was only later, when I really thought hard and long about it, that I realized he had said my name. Just once. "Kate?" echoing in the freedom of the darkness. But then she took his hand, telling him it was probably just kids wreaking havoc, and led him back into the light.

We are led to believe that suffering makes us stronger. A long illness, endless bad luck, financial ruin is what makes a man, sets him apart, gives him something to struggle against and overcome. What they don't tell us is how it changes that man or woman. Breaks him down and puts him back together a different way. Stronger, maybe, but harder, too. If you want to make your dreams come true, you have to be powerful. And to be powerful, you have to have the killer instinct. No one can stand in your way. This is the lesson we learn, through the long, dark nights of suffering. You must kill to survive.

It took The Uninvited only one month to get over Mitch's death, and then the ad appeared in the local music paper. They were holding auditions at a high-class studio in Hollywood known for catering to the pros. The Uninvited wanted to appear famous even before they were, and they weren't about to let Mitchell's departure from the world slow them down, either. I gave them credit for that. They had the killer instinct. They were destined to survive.

In my former life I would have been terrified of an audition. Butterflies would have attacked me and probably kept me from going to Studio B to try out as the new bass player for the band. But after being a member of the Undead for some time now, nothing seemed very terrifying anymore. I knew what I wanted, and now I knew how to get it.

It was night, as it always is. I was waiting on a bench just outside the studio, listening to the adequate playing of the person auditioning before me. A foolish man, who thought all there was to music was money. No dreams, no drive, just dollars, every time he played. A man who thought he was a professional just because he always got paid and would not give up any of his free time for the possibility of a greater achievement than a paycheck. He had told me all of this while we sat together listening to someone else's audition. And I had only shaken my head in reply. If I had needed blood, I would have gladly made him my next victim. Gotten his address and taken him in his sleep one night. But I still had months to go, so everyone was safe for a little while.

I was prepared for the audition. I knew their songs like the back of my hand from the tape I had stolen from Mitch, and I had altered my looks somewhat with the help of a little more makeup. Blush on my cheeks and lipstick on my lips, so I did not seem like a ghost come back from the grave to play with them. Certainly not the thing that had left Mitch drained and bloodless. I was getting better at deception all the time.

Rather, I looked like the answer to their prayers in a short leather dress and sheer black stockings, with Justin's tuxedo jacket thrown on for good measure. I had left off the shoes because I wanted to feel exactly right, and since I had become a vampire, I never felt right with my feet encased in anything. Only my eyes betrayed me, told the world I was something different, something strange. But I was learning to use that as an advantage, to make it work for me.

I startled them when I first walked in; they had not heard me enter. But then they were a little jumpy, too, whether from the wind that was knocking at the windows or the memory of Mitch that entered the room from time to time. I thought of Mitch's apartment—dark and dreary and full of stale smoke—but I pushed the thought away. Someone else was probably living there now. Life goes on. I had only taken what I wanted, what I needed to survive.

Drew recovered first and came over to greet me. He was wearing a white tee shirt and tight, faded jeans that clung to his body. As he came close, I smelled the enticing scent of his cologne—light and spicy and tinged with salt. For a moment neither of us spoke, we only smiled. I could see myself reflected in his eyes, and I knew he had already made up his mind who would be their next bass player. I toyed with him for a moment, wondering what it would be like to be held in this man's arms after being on stage together, then dismissed the thought. It was a dangerous one. I would be playing with fire. How long would it be before I wanted to sink my teeth into his neck, or he discovered what kind of creature was actually sleeping in his bed? I needed to keep my distance. So I made things simple and shook hands with him, telling him I was ready to set up my Fender to play.

The audition went as well as I had expected, as I had planned. Nathan and I fell into sync immediately on a musical level. My bass and his drums matched perfectly. He was young and sandy-haired and could barely keep a thought in his head. At twenty-four years old he still talked seventeen, but he played well and that's what mattered at the moment. If he surfed in his free time, it didn't concern me.

Drew was already sold, and I felt at home backing him up as he sang. Like most lead singers, he seemed in control as the front person of the band, even a little arrogant. I watched his hand caress the microphone, and I admired his blond good looks. Before long, we were casting little side glances at each other as if to be sure the other was still there. I felt a brief moment of pleasure in flirting, as if for that point in time I were part of the human race again. As long as that was all it ever came to, I could enjoy the game.

Only Charly was a little bit distant. His brush with death had taken some of his momentum away, made him question things a little more, doubt everyone a little more. It made him now sleep with a night-light when he had never been afraid of the dark before. I smiled at him, but his mind was far away.

Everything was going well, the band was packing up, and I was sitting with Drew explaining how I was busy during the day and could only rehearse at night. It was something he could understand, as most musicians had to have a day job to pay their rent while they pursued their love at night. Suddenly there was a knock on the studio door, and I felt colder than usual. I wanted to tell them not to answer it, but I didn't know why. Something felt wrong, as if daylight was coming, but my watch only showed midnight. Nathan opened the door, then turned around in disgust. "Hey, guys," he said, "it's Detective Warren for the one hundredth time with his same old set of questions."

"Damn," Drew muttered next to me, "will this never be over?"

A man in his late thirties entered the room, then made himself at home in one of the chairs. He even seemed like a detective from the movies: dark looks, the requisite trench coat, a day's growth of beard. Only his Reebok sneakers with their red pinstripes marred the traditional image. He took out a cigarette, lit it, then pointed to me. "Who's this?" he asked, then settled back for an answer. He was a man not used to being in the dark.

"She's our new bass player," Drew said defensively. "Do you mind?" Then he turned apologetically to me. "I didn't want to mention this to you yet, but our former bass player was murdered, it seems, and the detective and the whole L.A. Police can't figure it out, so they keep bothering us about it. As if we haven't gone through enough already."

"He wasn't just murdered," Warren said. "His body was completely drained of blood." He took a puff of his cigarette and watched the smoke advance in our direction.

"Jesus Christ," Charly turned and shouted at him, "do you have to keep saying that? I've told you everything I know, everything I can remember. I don't have any clues. I can't even believe it happened." Charly was close to tears, and I noticed for the first time a streak of white in his reddish hair.

"Look," Warren said, "I'm not out to harass you guys. I keep hoping someone will remember something. Maybe some weird religious cult took a dislike to your band, maybe someone here dabbled in Satanism. Do you believe in Satan, Miss ah . . ." He was looking directly at me.

"Kate, my name's Kate."

"Miss . . . Kate, do you believe in Satan?"

"Well," I stammered, "I don't know. I haven't really thought about it lately."

"Did you know any of the band members before-hand?"

"No, I just answered an ad for a bass player." I shifted uncomfortably next to Drew. "I had no idea that's how you lost your last bassist," I said to him irritably. "Maybe I should be leaving."

"Don't go." Drew subtly pressured me back into a seat. I liked the feeling of warmth against my arm.

"Look, Detective," Nathan said, "we don't know any-thing, and Kate just met us. Don't make us lose another bass player by scaring her to death."

"All right, all right," he said, getting up to leave, "but it still bothers me. Your friend Mitch had to have known, or at least didn't fear, his killer. There were two empty glasses of vodka on the table and no sign of a struggle. I can't believe none of you saw him leave the gig, and none of you is concerned enough about not knowing anything for my taste."

He threw his cigarette on the floor and stamped it out in frustration. Some of the ashes clung to his Reeboks. A residue of smoke circled his hair. He coughed, and I thought of Mitch breathing his last.

"And another thing," Warren said, before he opened the door and left, "whoever was there took a tape. His cassette machine was hanging open with the power on. I'm sure they had been playing music, but there was no cassette inside."

I felt myself freeze in place as if one more move would reveal my true nature to everyone in the room. I cursed Charly silently for showing up when he did. I had needed the time to hide my kill. Instead, I left a grisly scenario for the police to play with for the rest of their days. Of course, they couldn't trace it to me. Why I was even slightly worried, I didn't know.

But I did not want Mitch's ghost haunting me as I

found salvation in my new career as a musician. I was hoping that with time, the problem would fade away, and I could assume a human identity without any repercussions. That people like Detective Warren would eventually give up, and life, such as it was, would go on.

But death has a life of its own, and ghosts can follow us anywhere. And eventually everything catches up with everybody.

I heard Warren slam the door, and the band breathed a sigh of relief. With the detective out of the picture for the moment, even I relaxed visibly. "Sorry about that," Drew said, touching my hand lightly. "He's something of a fanatic, it seems. And there's nothing worse in this world than a fanatic. We're all sorry about Mitch, but his death had nothing to do with the band. You don't have anything to worry about, believe me."

I looked into his cool blue eyes, and I did believe him. I felt that if I kept on looking long enough, things would be all right, and I could never have to worry again.

"Saturday, then," I said, shaking his hand again. He held on for just a touch too long. It was tempting, but I had to break his hold. Then Nathan was beside me, telling me how happy he was to have me in the band. And Charly was speculating that we could play out in only a few weeks since I could pick up their songs so fast. They looked like happy children who had found a new playmate, and I felt happy, too.

Mission accomplished. I was in, a band member, soon to be performing on stage. A far cry from the human that could barely speak in front of a tiny acting class. A far cry from the human who could never find her dream in life and whose husband was only too quick to point it out.

Instead, I had found my dream in death and the death of others. I was a vampire and getting to be proud of it.

* * *

For the first time in a very long while, I was truly enjoying myself. I barely watched TV anymore, I was much too busy. We had band practice almost every night and the novelty of it never wore off. I loved being part of a group, having a goal, working at something.

It was incredibly interesting to see the progress of a new song, from its tiny inception as a melody and lyrics to a completed piece with three neatly orchestrated parts. I was pleased to find I had a natural ability to come up with the perfect bass part. Before long I had replaced most of Mitch's parts for the old songs with my own ideas—deep, dark, melodic low notes that lit a fire to the back beat—and the new songs had my touch on them right away. They seemed to come alive beneath my hands.

On the home front, I installed a phone and purchased some new white sheets and an entire new wardrobe of black clothing. I let one of my nails stay long and painted it red for fun. I bought a pure-gold cross on a chain and wore it always for spite. Since crosses couldn't affect vampires, why shouldn't I wear one again just as I had in Catholic school?

The band members became my friends, the way Lil had been my friend, but without knowing my secret. I hung out with them after practice, discussing everything from music to relationships, but I remained aloof and mysterious enough that I never had to explain my reasons for a strictly nighttime existence. They appreciated my eagerness, my enthusiasm, my drive, and in the excitement of preparing for our first gig, they never once questioned anything about me.

They could respect a touch of eccentricity when they saw it, and they accepted it for the time being as my style. I was just Kate, who lived somewhere in Santa Monica, worked at some kind of job during the day, and played a mean bass. That was all they needed to know.

But when they weren't looking, when they weren't knowing, I was something else—and that could be fun, too. I could fly to any part of L.A. I wanted at a moment's notice. I would walk the streets at all hours, knowing I was more powerful than any insignificant human who might bother me. If I wanted to, I could throw a man twice my size clear across the street before he realized what was happening. And if I needed to, I could pin a man twice my size against a wall, hold him still with my eyes, and drink his blood before he even knew he was going to die.

The first gig was not the spectacular success everyone anticipated. The band was a little awkward, the turnout was sparse, Charly broke a string, Nathan dropped a beat, and I stood stock-still through the set, unsure how to move now that I was actually on stage. Drew, always the trooper, carried his end of the show, but on the whole, the performance was not ready even for a tiny club in Hollywood.

Everyone was depressed about it for days, except me. Having never been on stage before, I was happy just to get through it alive. Besides, I found I truly loved the feel of performing, the look of the lights, the musical intimacy with strangers, the hunger, and the fulfillment. And I was confident things would come together. And they did. With time and practice, we worked out the kinks in our show and I loosened up so much, Sandy would have been proud of me.

Within three months we were a tightly knit working unit, and one night we hit the first high point of our career. The owner of the club came back after our show and actually asked us to appear again in two weeks without us having to beg and plead. It was cause for celebration.

Tom, a friend of Nathan's who'd been to a majority of our gigs, decided to throw a party on the spot. Although he had a tendency to look conservative with his dark brown hair always neatly combed and his shirts always ironed and ready for a day's work, Tom had a wild and energetic side that could get him in trouble. I watched as he enthusiastically organized forty people for a night of fun, and I thought that without the pinstriped shirt, he could be very attractive.

It was going to be a gala event. The night was young, the world was mine, and the band was a success. So why did I feel uneasy about attending a party thrown partially in my honor? Perhaps I was just reliving my human days, when social events could throw me into a trauma of shyness. When I would stand flattened against a wall, sipping a drink and praying no one would notice me. When all I could think about was escape.

Perhaps it reminded me of that first night at Sandy's acting workshop, when I felt mortified to be standing before a group of strangers, giving away secrets about myself. A night when I wanted to run and never made it to the door. A night that changed my life forever.

But all the shyness was behind me now. I had entered a new existence where shyness and weakness were a thing of the past. Besides being an integral part of a respected band, I was not only more than human, I was on the road to fame and fortune.

So when my fellow musicians shouted for me to follow them to Tom's house, I smiled a smile of genuine delight and started my car, never once thinking how much I needed blood again.

Tom and his two roommates lived in a small, weathered house in Venice only steps away from the beach. By the time I arrived, the party was in full swing. The stereo was so loud, you could hear it three blocks away, and the house so full, people were dancing in the sand just outside the front door.

Tom's neighbors were benevolent people, and they had joined in as soon as the party started, bringing several cases of beer with them. With no fear of the police ever showing up, the guests had thrown all caution to the wind, and their inhibitions were left at the door.

I walked in to see a guy with orange-and-black-streaked hair dancing on the coffee table without his pants. Seated below him were three people arranging lines of cocaine, while on an ugly green couch an older man and woman were making love frantically.

I was searching the room for someone familiar when Tom appeared out of nowhere and hugged me so hard and so unexpectedly, I almost lost my balance. "The Barefoot Contessa!" he screamed in my ear, then shoved a drink into my hand without ever letting go of me. I gave him my most dazzling smile.

"Where's the rest of the band?" I asked.

"I love you, too," he said, misunderstanding my question, "and you're one beautiful bass player!"

He led me over to the only available seat and pulled me on his lap. The bald-headed man in blue who was sitting on the floor beside us looked up from his bottle of Johnny Walker and smiled. "Great show," he said enthusiastically, then turned his attention back to his scotch.

"See," Tom said, "you're already a star." I laughed, but in a way he was right. If nothing else, I did have my place in the sky.

And Tom could barely take his eyes off me, as if I lit up the world around him. As if nothing else mattered but having me in sight. He was as lost as I had been when I first met Justin a long time ago. Ready to abandon everything and everyone for a stranger. He was possessed. He was fragile. He was human. But I wasn't, anymore.

From Tom's lap I spotted Charly staring out the front window as if he were waiting for something to show itself. "Look," I said, "there's my favorite guitar player." And I used it as an excuse to escape from Tom's clutches. I didn't need to be reminded of my past indiscretions, to see my former human self reflected in someone else's shadow. My host voiced disappointment, but I was much too quick for him.

I joined Charly at the window. "Who are all these people?"

But he was looking beyond the people dancing outside to where the ocean met the sky. "Sometimes I hate the darkness," he said. "You never know what's out there waiting."

"It's just the beach," I said lightheartedly, but I knew what he meant. Charly turned and looked directly into my eyes.

"If only I hadn't seen Mitch's face, so white, so bloodless, but still smiling. If only I had just gone home, instead. You have no idea, Kate, what death can look like. And it's still out there, waiting. I know it is. I can feel it. Somewhere in the darkness, it's waiting."

I looked down on the dancers jumping and hopping ecstatically to an old Motown tune. I recognized Drew in the thin glow of the spring moon, dancing with Carla, a blonde who was one of the band's followers. I felt a twinge of longing, then let it go.

"What's waiting, Charly"—I turned my attention back to his troubled face—"besides the cover of *Rolling Stone*?"

Charly brushed a loose piece of hair from his forehead. Since I first saw the band, he had lost almost twenty pounds and was looking fairly handsome. Mitch's death had eaten away at him, made him fearful and anxious, but it had done wonders for his sex appeal. I smiled at him, trying to break his mood, even as my mind wandered back again to Drew.

"Some kind of monster," he said flatly, "somewhere out there, still waiting."

I opened my mouth to answer, but no words were there. I looked at the tired lines on his face and noticed that freckles had appeared as the result of some recent suntanning. It had been so long since I had seen the sun.

"And I'm afraid he's coming for me."

At that moment Charly brushed his hand along the open window in frustration, then pulled back quickly with a little yelp. A piece of broken glass had cut his middle finger, and blood was oozing out into his hand.

"Shit." He searched his pockets for a handkerchief.

But I barely heard him. All I could see. All I could feel. All I could smell was blood. I wanted to take his finger into my mouth and suck it until it came off. Then I could work my way up to his wrist, which was already covered with that beautiful liquid, and bite down on that one essential artery while Charly fell to his knees in submission. I didn't care who was looking. I didn't care about being a bass player anymore. I didn't even care if everyone knew I wasn't the human I pretended to be.

I wanted him now. I could feel the slow aching in my gums as my teeth started their long descent. Only seconds away, the life force that I needed, that I had almost forgotten about in my pursuit of music. It would soon be on my tongue again.

But suddenly Drew was beside me with Carla, and it was she who grabbed Charly's hand and wrapped it in an embroidered handkerchief, licking the lingering drops of blood away with her lips. I wanted to kill her for taking those drops away from me, but Drew's voice brought me back to reality.

"Hey," he said, "we came in to see what you guys were doing, and we find Charly practically bleeding to death."

Charly laughed self-consciously. "It was just a piece of glass." He wrapped the cloth around his hand even tighter.

I felt my teeth go back into their hiding place. How could I have let myself come so close to losing control?

"Lucky for Charly," Carla said, licking her lips. "I've always wanted to be a vampire."

I looked at her for a moment in horror, then realized she was joking.

"I used to always lick my little brother's cuts and scratches, too, and my mom used to hate it," she said. "I guess old habits die hard."

The bleeding in Charly's hand had stopped, but he was still a little shaken. "I'm going home," he said. "I've about had it."

"Oh, come on," Drew said. "Why don't we all go outside and dance? We're supposed to be celebrating tonight, no need to get morbid on us, Charly."

But I felt almost as morbid as my guitar player. I needed to make a kill, and I needed to make it now. I had gone too long on pure adrenaline, swept away by the excitement of being on stage. But as my reaction to Charly's cut showed, I was long overdue. If I couldn't find my victims in a quiet and controlled way, then I could never hope to keep up this human facade. And if that slipped away, then I might as well resign myself to a life of endless loneliness in a condo I didn't even own.

"Let's dance." Carla pulled Charly away from the window, where he had started to stare again into the shadows. "Don't you know, I vant to drink your blood."

Charly let himself be led outside where the crowd

seemed to have doubled its size. A number of people were in various stages of undress, and a few of them, stripped to their underwear, were heading for the water. A song I had never heard before blasted over the speakers, and Drew looked at me and sang the words:

> "What I want is a heart that won't break,
> What I want is a life with no mistakes,
> And what I want is you.
> Why can't I have what I want?"

I smiled at him and decided to act normal at least for a little while. Maybe I could break my own mood, too.

We ran out together to join the others, and I lost myself in the grinding and twisting of the song. Why can't I have what I want? I tried to put the picture of Charly's finger oozing blood out of my mind. I danced in the moonlight. But the image refused to leave. I looked at Drew's face and could see he was well on his way to being drunk. He lifted his bottle of beer and guzzled what was left, then threw it away in the sand. He laughed and I laughed with him. He danced and I danced with him. But all the time I was thinking. Licking my lips and thinking. *Oh, baby, why can't I have what I want?*

The music changed. Something fast. Something pounding. Carla appeared and pulled Drew away. I wanted to reach out and drag him back, but I had to let him go. Charly was leaving, too. I saw him wave. I saw his hand, his finger. Why should I wait? My blood was pounding. These were just people at a party. Somewhere in hell. I was so much more than they were. I could fly. I could kill. I would never die. *Why can't I have what I want?*

It was a party for the band, to promote our success, to celebrate. Why should I wait? Why shouldn't I have what I wanted now? I moved to the music, lost in the crowd.

They were all smiling at me, looking up to me, the bass player in the band. I felt a little drunk myself, as if their condition was catching.

And I thought to myself, *Even if they knew, would they hate me? Would they really blame me?* I was the next stage of evolution, only steps from being an angel. I had a right to my existence and a right to sustain it. Why, they would probably adore me for it.

Moving to the music and drunk with desire, I looked to the window and saw Tom standing there, beer in hand, smiling to himself. He was possessed. And I needed someone now.

Come to me, I thought. *My little human, come to me.* The music continued and shook the sand. *Do you wanna dance?* And he was there. His arms around me.

"Tell me," Tom said, "can a beautiful and mysterious musician find love in the arms of an ordinary accountant?"

A couple on our right, exhausted and stoned, fell face first onto the ground. I laughed out loud. They were having fun. I wanted to have some, too.

"Why don't we find out?" I took Tom's hand. His face filled with pleasure. Why should I wait? It was my right. I was sure of it now. I did not obey mere human laws anymore. I was steps from being an angel. Even if it was only an angel of death.

I led Tom away from the lights of the party. I cornered him alone. There was a secluded part of the beach where even the moonlight could not totally get in. Very dark. Only a quarter of a mile away. And I liked the darkness. We sat down on the sand, our backs against the rocks, and looked out at the sea.

"I'm sorry," Tom said, "but I'm a little high. I've been attracted to you for a long time. I hope I'm not rushing you." He touched my face with his fingers. "I've been hoping we could get to know each other, but I've been a little afraid of you up till now. I guess the beer has made me strong."

I turned toward him, and he kissed me lightly on the mouth. "It's all right, Tom," I said. "Everything is going to be all right now." I looked directly into his eyes and lulled him halfway to sleep. I could hear the water hitting the rocks, rhythmically, like the music. *Why can't I have what I want?*

Gently I turned his head to the side. I brushed his hair from his neck. My tongue moved with the water, up and down, around and around. He tasted good. Like salt. His breathing was relaxed and far away.

I found the spot, the perfect spot, and bit down quickly and cleanly. Tom moaned in his sleep as I took what belonged to him and made it part of me. For the first time there was no violence, no fear. I held him tight against me and stroked his hair as I drank all the blood from his body. His heartbeat became as distant as the music of the party until finally I was full and the beat died away. I loosened my grip, and Tom's body, robbed of life, slumped over into the sand.

For a long time I sat there thinking of Tom and how good he had been. Watching the water roll back and forth. Counting the waves as they broke again and again. And then I took the matches that I now always carried out of my pocket, found some dry wood, and burned his remains on a tiny funeral pyre.

When the fire was over, I took the bones that were left and crushed them into tiny pieces beneath my feet. I had the strength to pulverize them completely. Then I scattered some of the remains into the water, buried some in the sand, and let the wind blow the rest of them away. Until there was nothing left but me and the moonlight.

To anyone looking from a distance, the fire had just

been another barbecue. And being a fun-loving vampire
and full of life again, I went back to join the party, as
there were still three hours before dawn.

No one had noticed, no one had cared. And no one
would ever suspect me. Not even the next day when people discovered Tom was missing and searched frantically
for him along the shore. Not even a week later, when they
finally decided Tom must have drowned and been washed
out to sea. He had been very drunk, after all. No one
noticed, no one remembered him leaving the party with
me. They had all been too concerned with themselves.

Only Charly was sure what had happened, and no one
believed his ramblings anymore. The monster he had
been waiting for had finally shown up, and unable to locate Charly, had chosen Tom, instead. A lucky break, a
blessing from God, that Charly had gone home early,
avoiding death by mere minutes. Leaving him to wonder,
when would the monster strike again?

I knew it was only a dream, but the suggestion of reality was overpowering. I was standing in what seemed to
be an underground room. There were no windows, and
the only light came from a few burning candles. The
room smelled of torture and death and little bit like dirt
mixed with roots.

As my eyes focused, I saw what looked like a separate
cage or prison in the far corner. Behind the bars was a
beautifully decorated bedroom with a dresser, a chest of
drawers, a four-poster bed of carved, dark wood, and a
rocking chair that was empty but still moving. There were
no mirrors, no pictures on the walls, but on the floor was
a hardbound copy of *Frankenstein* that looked familiar.

As I moved closer to the prison, I saw there was someone lying face down on the bed, half covered by the white
sheets. The man's back, which was uncovered, was

bruised and bleeding, and the blood was changing the sheet from white to red. The man turned his head slightly in my direction, and as soon as I saw the glint of green from his eyes, I knew who it was.

"Justin," I said in surprise, but he did not seem to recognize me. Only sensing there was someone present, he opened his mouth to speak, and the word came out in a choked whisper.

"Run," he said.

For some reason I took him at his word. I did not ask him why, I did not try to help him. I thought only of myself. I ran. Farther and farther. Beyond the dark cellar until I was running on the sand and I could hear the ocean rolling only steps away. But I knew it wasn't the Pacific. There was moisture in the air and the water smelled green instead of blue.

Run. So I kept on running until there was no more sand and I felt myself enclosed in something. Something dark and purple. I opened my mouth to scream, afraid that no one would hear me before I died. Then realized I was already dead and screamed even louder. In the darkness I hit my foot against something, and my eyes opened suddenly as at last I woke up.

"Damn." I pushed open the coffin cover that had somehow closed when I was sleeping. "I'll never try that again."

What had possessed me to take my daytime rest in Justin's coffin, I'll never know. I had done it on a whim, as a joke, and in return I'd had a dream for the first time since I had slept in my downtown hiding spot. I was starting to hate dreams. From now on, I was sticking to the bed. There were too many ghosts or memories or magic in that coffin.

I kicked Justin's gold box to the side and sprang out and onto the floor. Evening had fallen, and as long as I could keep that dream out of my mind, I was feeling young and strong and fine. And, of course, immortal.

I had a few hours to go before practice, and as I did not want to think about anything, I decided to wing my way up to Tower Records. This was a store known for having everything in music, and they prided themselves on their late-night musician hours. There I could pick up a few new tapes to listen to so I could keep up with the latest developments and maybe learn something, too.

The night was clear for a change, and my visibility was perfect. I let myself drift slowly from Santa Monica to West Hollywood, surveying the cars and people scurrying from place to place below me. I enjoyed the feel of the wind lifting me and wafting my vision gently through the night air. I felt so comfortable in the sky, so relaxed. If I didn't have the band, I would have spent even more time flying, as the experience never lost its charm.

Tower Records was fairly empty even for a Thursday night. The fluorescent lights inside were a little too bright for my taste, and I squinted as I walked in past the cashier, who was combing his heavy head of black hair and chewing bubble gum. He smiled faintly.

I headed to the latest releases, barely noticing the five other people shopping at various points in the store. In fact, it was only later that I realized there had been five, one of them a TV star. Other people's fame meant nothing to me now.

They say that cities like L.A. attract all the weirdos, and I suppose this is true. Even though smaller towns have their share of bizarre killings, a lot of them get buried in the news, and no one ever hears about them. But in Los Angeles, the entertainment capital of the world, celebrity killings, no matter how minor, become just another piece of publicity to be brought into the light. Something everyone should know.

I did not see him enter because I was absorbed in reading the production credits on the CD I had just picked up. But I heard the cashier scream, and then I heard the gunshots. "Karen," he was shouting, "I love you." And at the end of the aisle I was standing in, a woman gasped in horror and hit the floor, ripping her black-seamed stockings in the bargain. I realized she had to be Karen.

From a few aisles over, I could hear the labored breathing of someone in pain, and I stood stock-still for a moment in complete confusion, trying to remember if there was a back door. "Karen," he called again, "I saw you come in here. Where are you?" I heard the click of his shoes, and then a minute later he stood above her, his gun pointed at her head.

"Oh, my God," she said, looking at me—and the panic in her eyes held me in place.

"I love you," he said, "and you never even give me the time of day." He adjusted the black sunglasses, which had slid down his nose, and noticed me. "What are you looking at?" he asked. And because there is no one right answer to a question like that, he shot me, instead. Once —directly in the chest.

Still confused and suffering from temporary amnesia, I reacted, even though I felt nothing, and fell to the linoleum floor. I heard him laugh, and without knowing why, felt the bullet pass out of my body again.

Karen gave a strangled scream. "I love you," he said again and turned the gun on her, firing the remaining three bullets into her waiting body. Karen felt all three, and Karen bled. Some of the blood splattered on the floor near my leg, and I stared at it, believing for the moment it was mine.

Maybe it was the police sirens, maybe it was all that blood, but at last my memory kicked in. I remembered the knife that could not hurt me, and I was angry again.

"You jerk." I half-rose and grabbed the bottom of his blue jeans as he passed. Taken completely off guard, he lost his balance and tumbled to the ground. The gun went sliding along the floor as I held him in place. He turned and looked at me in utter disbelief.

"Surprise, jackass," I said. "You can't kill a ghost."

He screamed and laughed at the same time, struggling to get away from my grasp. You would think that after seeing all those movies where the person you just killed comes back to life again and again, he would have been prepared for a moment such as this. But in real life we are hardly ever prepared.

I raised my hand and smashed his face directly into the floor. I heard the crack of bones breaking, and I sighed in satisfaction. I let go of his ankle just seconds before the police ran in, and I managed to resume a cowering and frightened attitude in time for their arrival.

I hope they'll believe he fell, I thought, and curled up into a fetal position, pulling my jacket tight to hide the hole the bullet had made in my shirt. Hoping for the best, I began to make myself shake.

Now you would also think that Los Angeles was a big enough town that the chances of running into anyone familiar at this point in time were nil. But again I was wrong. I heard several cops enter the building. I heard the ambulance's siren. I heard them put the cashier on a stretcher. I heard them find Karen's body.

Still I didn't look up. Not until they were handcuffing the killer, who had very little face left. Someone gently touched my shoulder, and I opened my eyes. I made sure my face was contorted in an expression of shock, then turned my head to look right into the eyes of none other than Detective Warren.

"Miss, ah, miss, ah . . . Kate, isn't it?" he said in surprise.

Upon hearing my name out loud, the killer, who was being dragged roughly down the aisle, turned and shouted, "She's a ghost, God damn it. I shot her, the bullet went right through her. She's a ghost, I'm telling you."

"Shut up, you stupid fuck," the arresting officer said, and pushed him even harder toward the door.

"Are you all right?" Detective Warren asked, still a little distracted from this latest outburst. I couldn't help but notice his Reeboks again. He was helping me into a sitting position and making sure I was unharmed. I pulled my jacket even tighter, wishing he wouldn't look too closely.

"I think so," I said. "What happened?"

"That asshole—excuse my language—came in here with a gun looking for Karen Winters, and shot and wounded the cashier and a customer and then killed his beloved television idol. Following this activity and being swift on his feet, he fell facedown on the floor. Apparently he took a shot at you, too, and missed. You must have dropped to the floor in the nick of time."

I brushed my hair out of my face and shook my head. "Oh, God," I said, "I can't believe it. I only came in here to buy some CDs."

The detective lifted me up to my feet and led me over to a chair someone had pulled out from the back room. The other two customers who were not injured were sitting down also, and both of them were saying they had seen nothing, that they had only heard the shots and someone yelling.

"How about you?" Detective Warren asked me hopefully.

"Well," I said, "I don't remember much. I heard the gunshots, and I guess I became paralyzed. I think he was yelling her name. She was on the floor, and he came around and pointed the gun at me. I think I must have blacked out after that. The next thing I remember is you being there." I put my face in my hands for effect, hoping I could get out of there soon. "Can I go home now?" I asked. I was tired of playing the wimp, and something about Detective Warren made me a little nervous.

"Sure," he said. "I don't think we'll need you anymore. Just tell me your address in case we have any more questions."

Damn, I thought, then realized I would have to give in to avoid any further suspicion. I rattled off Justin's address and started to leave. The detective turned around suddenly.

"You're with that band, right?" he asked. "The one with the murdered bass player?"

"Yes," I said carefully, "but that was before my time."

"That's right," he said. "You had just gotten the audition for his position when I met you." He shook his head slightly. "It's amazing how you guys always seem to be in the vicinity of strange and violent events."

I studied his face, unsure of what he was getting at. I could not read the movements in his eyes. "How do you mean?" I asked, starting to feel that things were no longer going well.

"Oh, you know." He followed me to the door. "Another detective, a friend of mine, was investigating this missing-person case last seen at a party in Venice. Last week I happened to find out that it was a party thrown in your band's honor after a show."

"That's right," I said, trying to cut the conversation short and get out of the store. "Tom Hyden, he's a friend of our drummer's, threw the party and then disappeared afterward. It was real strange." I tried to look as confused as possible, wishing at the same time I had taken more acting classes.

"Hmmmmm," the detective said. His face registered nothing. "Do you need a ride home or anything?"

"No, no," I said, "I'm fine." I took the final steps across the threshold and felt the night air and freedom greet me.

Detective Warren stood in the doorway and watched me walk away. I turned and waved, but he did not move.

Oh, well, I thought, *what does that all mean anyway? What can he prove?*

But I kept walking down Sunset Boulevard for a while. Afraid to take to the skies. Afraid that somehow, someway, Detective Warren was still standing behind me in the darkness, trying to put two and two together. Standing in the darkness and watching.

Later, at practice, when I told the band the story of the shooting, they marveled at my calmness and that I still had the composure to play. Drew kept asking me if I was all right, while Charly mumbled something about death being everywhere.

They were even more surprised to hear that Detective Warren had been there. They had all come to dislike him after his grand interrogation of Mitch's death. They clucked sympathetically when I said he had detained me with stupid questions and I still had to be bothered with the Mitch thing. But they were all happy that no harm had come to their new bass player, that God had spared me from a maniac's bullet.

We rehearsed the set with even more energy, even more urgency that night. Everything sounded great and on the money. I could really see my new life and my career starting to fall into place. Only once, between songs, when I let down my guard, I could still see Detective Warren watching in the shadows, and I could still hear Justin whisper, *Run.*

* * *

I had a band, I had money, I had an attitude. Things
had never been better. I began to contemplate buying my
own condo, but the whole process seemed so complicated
and legal that I decided to wait awhile. Since no one was
charging me rent and the electricity never went off, I decided to leave well enough alone. Instead, I went out and
bought a high-priced answering machine to accept my
daytime calls, and the most beautiful and expensive pair
of black boots I had ever seen.

I also bought a full-blown audio system so I could blast
the roof off the place when I was in the mood. I particularly enjoyed playing the tape of our last gig at top volume. There is nothing like hearing yourself perform to
get your blood pumping. Rock 'n' roll made me feel good.
It made me feel alive and in control. If I played just right,
I could manipulate and move every member of the audience staring up at the band. And I had come to love the
feeling of control. As a human, I had never dreamt of
power, and during my early days as a vampire I could
barely control myself, but now on stage I could have the
audience within my grasp, tightening my hold on them
with the very look in my eye. It was driving, intoxicating,
and it was sexual.

Music gave me the strength of purpose that acting
could never have supplied. It was not just an art, it was a
way of life. A life I needed, to give me a reason to go on
anymore. Because every day I felt less and less a part of
the human race I had been born into. Less able to remember why I cared about anyone or even why I should.

But there were still times, though very few, when I
missed the feel of life, the presence of a heart beating.
That sense of urgency that is distinctly human, dictated
by the knowledge that you are merely mortal.

I even missed the experience of time passing, of seeing

my body change and age. Most of the time I reveled in not being confined to human parameters, answering to no one, living outside the law. But there were still a few nights when memory would hit me hard and I would stumble in the darkness and fall, forgetting I had ever learned to fly.

It was one of those nights, and in the back of my mind, I knew who had thrown my emotions into reverse. When I was rehearsing or doing a gig or blasting the stereo, sadness could not be heard over the music. But it was Monday, a quiet night, and everyone I knew was busy doing something, taking care of the things the living need to do. So I went out into the night and found a place that had just the right atmosphere for my state of mind.

I was sitting now with my back against the tombstone of Errol J. Garrett, 1925–1976, in a tiny forgotten graveyard off North Avenue. The moon was only a crescent peeking through the darkened sky, but I could still see clearly the rows of marble squares designating all the people who had gone before me.

Intermixed with the plain, generic tombstones were a few ornate ones from earlier times. A little to my right was a beautiful carving of an angel staring serenely into the distance while keeping guard over Constance Chambers's (1902–1912) remains. The angel appeared to be almost smiling, as if he knew some secret. Perhaps that heaven was just a moment away. Maybe that's what he saw in the distance beyond the valley of death. Maybe that's why he feared no evil.

Directly in front of me, though several feet away, stood another angel, but he was a far more aggressive one than my friend on the right. With his eyes narrowed and his sword in hand, he was an avenging angel, one of those destined to appear at the end of the world. No choir practice for this fellow; he was on the warpath.

He did not seem to like me, either. If his form could have taken life, he would have leaped off his pedestal and run me through. But he had been turned to stone, and all he could do was give me dirty looks when he thought I didn't see him.

The angels could not speak to me, and there was no other sound in this land of the dead. I was too far from the road to be disturbed by cars, and no animal life had chosen to make this lifeless place their home.

People are always afraid of graveyards at night. Afraid that ghosts will rise from the earth and chase them for no reason whatsoever. But the dead are smarter than that. They need their rest. They've seen enough of this world to know there's little to be gained from scaring fools and half-wits—a fact I had yet to learn.

But still I felt close to these unmoving bodies. These were my people here, my kin. I really belonged under the ground with them, hopefully with an angel to guard me, too. Someone to watch over me. Only an unnatural act caused me now to walk, to talk, to think.

And I was different for it. Even Lazarus, after Christ had rolled away the stone, was never the same. He lived, he breathed, but death had touched him, had held him in its arms. Somewhere in his mind were memories too terrible to remember, even as he rejoiced with his sisters at the miracle of resurrection.

I raised my hand and ran it along the smooth curve of marble. "Where are you now, Errol?" I asked softly. "Do you know I'm sitting on your grave?" But no one answered. I was talking to a stone.

I had spoken to Drew only a few hours ago on the phone, as I lay in bed and studied the ceiling. At the time I had an overwhelming urge to beg him not to go to his parents' house but to meet me somewhere, instead. "There are monsters out there," I wanted to say, "and I need to be with someone tonight."

But cooler heads prevailed. I did not want to seem the fool, especially after I had worked so hard to appear the always confident, always strong bass player extraordinaire. Besides, I had my nonhuman existence under control now and working well. I did not need to press my luck with any signs of human weakness.

The relationship between Drew and me had changed a bit since the party. After the initial shock of Tom's disappearance had faded away, the band seemed almost closer because of it. As if another friend gone bound us together. And what had been mostly innocuous flirting between Drew and myself developed into endless and sometimes heartfelt conversations on the phone and in many of the dressing rooms of the clubs we played. We would get into discussions about everything from music to the way the sky looked at night, and I found myself more and more drawn to him.

At first I had been attracted to the image he projected on stage, the image the public expected of a rock singer. A persona that was sexy, confident, defiant, and ready to bring any woman to her knees. It was a myth he had to live up to, one that had been acted out by every other lead singer that had gone before him. It sold records. It got good press. It made money.

But as I got to know him better, it was the human side of Drew that appealed to me more and more. I enjoyed his sense of humor, his individual way of looking at life, his concern for my well-being, even his little weaknesses the few times they showed up when he was tired or caught a cold. He was still sexy but in a warmer, more human way, and I began to wish it would be Drew when I heard the phone ring and was always disappointed when it wasn't.

But fortunately we were still only friends and colleagues, and I was not in a hurry to push the point. I didn't need to start trusting someone again, especially with a secret as earth-shattering as mine. Lil had known and understood, but I wasn't sure anyone else could be that open-minded.

Besides, for the most part, I was enjoying my existence as a single, fun-loving vampire in the entertainment world. Just two nights ago we had played one of our best gigs. It was the first time I had been able to lose myself completely on stage. It was an indescribable feeling, one that I could become addicted to, a lot like the release flying gave me.

On stage you were out of your body and into the music. The beat became everything. Without even thinking, my fingers moved to the places they were supposed to be, intertwining, counterpointing, and keeping time with Nathan's back-beat. Somewhere Drew was singing, and certain notes gave me chills inside. I felt even closer to him as his voice rose and fell. Even Charly's guitar solos were inspiring. Lately his melancholy feelings had put a certain bite into his music, and that night he sounded like he was playing for his life. When he stepped up for his encore lead, I moved till my shoulder touched his, and we leaned for a moment back to back. The crowd reacted appropriately, and I could see what a wonderful game this was all going to be. Music and the joy of performing went beyond my wildest acting fantasies, and more importantly they were keeping me sane.

As Charly completed his run, Drew pulled his mike over to us and leaned right alongside me to finish the song. I looked into those blue eyes and thought, *Do you want to kiss?* and the answer came back plain and simple.

Yes. Everything about him said yes. I smiled to myself, satisfied for now in knowing he was there for the taking, and then turned that confidence and sensuality back to the crowd. I could feel the heat radiate from the band to every person in the audience. Somehow, no matter what they did, no matter who they were, no matter why they came out that night, for that moment all they thought of was sex.

When it was over, we rushed back into the dressing room to achieve some distance from our fans. In the last week we had acquired a roadie, so we didn't have to worry about packing our equipment anymore. We threw ourselves down on the chairs and took in the afterglow.

Drew was laughing and shaking his head. "Damn," he said. "It's never been this good."

"Yeah," Nathan answered. "I think we've got the band right here. I hate to say it, but Mitch's departure has been a blessing in disguise. If we keep going like this, we're bound to get some record company interest."

Charly wiped his face with a towel and looked at me. "You know, Kate, I never understand how you can play for an hour and never sweat."

Everyone else was dripping wet, their hair hanging limply in spite of the hair spray they had used, their wet shirts clinging to their backs. But I looked exactly as I had when the show started.

I smiled at Charly. "Just lucky, I guess."

"Who cares whether she sweats or not," Drew said. "She played great . . . and she looks good, too."

As if on cue, Max, the club owner, came bounding in, his hair sticking up in a perfect triangle. "You guys were fantastic. When can we do the next date?"

Max was feeling very warm toward us as our name was now drawing larger and larger crowds, which meant bigger receipts for him. Three months ago, when we first started playing out, we practically had to beg him for a gig. At that time the band had to call up every friend they knew to prove to Max that we had a following. But little by little our local fame grew. We had a few tiny write-ups in the smaller music papers, and word of mouth in the street began to build. We signed up people for our mailing list at our gigs and sent out an announcement to them each time we played, all of us chipping in for postage and the price of an ad in the *L.A. Weekly*. Now people came from just seeing our name in the paper, and life had become easier overnight.

"Well, Max," Charly said, brightening visibly, "why don't we go into your office and chat." Charly was the unofficial booker of the band's dates, and it made him feel happy about one thing in life, as if he had some control over something at last.

"Right," Max said, and he turned to smile at me. "You, darling, are so good, the devil must have taught you how to play." He winked at me flirtatiously as he ushered Charly out the door.

"Not far from the truth," I mumbled, but Max was already out of earshot.

Jeff, a blond-haired nineteen-year-old with a fake ID, came in and handed me my Fender guitar to put away. He was our roadie, who now did all the dirty work of packing and unpacking equipment. "Hey, Nathan," he said, "there's a couple of girls out there who want to dance with you, and they look hot." Nathan needed no further encouragement. He bounded out of the dressing room with Jeff close behind him.

As I closed my case, I looked up to see Drew staring at me intently. "You know, Kate, you are definitely one of a kind."

"Is that good or bad?" I asked, straightening up.

"Oh, good, as far as I'm concerned, but I bet you scare a lot of guys." And he smiled.

I thought about an answer to that, but all of the ones I had were morbid.

"But I do love talking to you, Kate. I don't think I've ever told anyone half the things I tell you. I'll bet we spend more time on the phone than most band members. If I don't speak to you at least once a day, I don't feel right anymore." He looked at me, hoping for an answer.

"Yes." I took a deep breath. "I don't feel right, either."

We sat in silence for a few minutes, pondering this mutual revelation. There was something very frightening about it. I had been intent on keeping my distance, but that distance was beginning to decay. For a moment I thought I heard my little voice but it was only someone yelling on the dance floor. I stared at my guitar case awkwardly. All of my bravado had gone right out the window. I was completely tongue-tied.

"Do you want to get your stuff, and you and I go have something to eat somewhere?" he asked.

It was the first time Drew had ever mentioned us doing anything without the rest of the band. I was sorely tempted, although food was totally out of the question—I couldn't even fake a glass of water. I remembered my question on stage and his answer. What would it be like to actually kiss someone again without taking his life? But that last thought, the taking of life, sobered me right up. How could I get close to anyone again, especially one of the band? It was too dangerous for them—and even more dangerous for me. Justin had said, "Never tell," and on that I believed him.

I looked at Drew's pale blue eyes and the way his shoulders looked square and strong, and I sighed my usual heavy sigh. "I have to meet someone," I lied blatantly. I could see the disappointment rise in those eyes, and he settled back in his chair.

"Sure," Drew leaned over and picked up his jeans jacket. "No big deal. I saw some friends of mine outside. They'll probably want to hit one of the late-night clubs after this, anyway." He looked down at a napkin he was holding in his hand. "Maybe I'll ask Marissa and Kristen to join us. They were in the audience again tonight. I'll catch you Tuesday at rehearsal."

And then he was gone. Nothing like rejection to change a man's attitude completely, to make him start thinking of someone else. I picked up my Fender and started for the door myself. Jeff came running up with my amp in tow, eager to help me to my car.

As we walked out to the parking lot, I looked up at the stars visible through the minimal smog that night. *That's where I'm going,* I thought, as there were still four hours before dawn. I would rise up into the stars, where regret couldn't touch me. Where humans could never go.

With all my equipment packed securely in the Porsche, I tore out of the parking lot at about 60 miles an hour in an attempt to get away. I opened up all the windows and cranked up the radio. But Drew would not leave my mind. He was there, whether I liked it or not, and I could see it was going to be a long, hard battle with my self-control. Drew was tempting, but I was strong. If I just kept running, he would never catch me. And with the wings I now possessed he would never have the chance.

Still, it was I who'd called him earlier this evening on the pretext of asking what time practice was, as if I didn't know. He was decidedly cool, but I ignored the urge to confront him. I hung up with a lot of words left to say, all of them filling up my mouth and making me uncomfortable. I felt weighed down. So, instead of flying, I walked the streets hoping something or someone would distract me from my dark mood, but nothing seemed to capture my attention.

Until the dead caught my eye, hidden away from the lives they once led. Errol J. Garrett had probably walked on North Avenue, too, but tonight he moved quietly underground. And I sat above him, wondering what it was like down there.

Suddenly I heard voices—human voices, teenagers. They were setting up camp not far from Errol's gravesite. Two boys, two girls, and three six-packs. They were giggling in the darkness, pleased they had found such a secluded party spot but still a little afraid of their own shadows.

"Hey, guys," an orange-haired girl said, "think we'll see any ghosts here tonight?"

"I thought I saw something moving over there," said one of the boys. He was pointing in my direction.

Damn, I thought, *I didn't think they could even see me.* And I began to drift out of the form that was me and into nothing again.

"Where?" shouted the girls in frightened unison. But the boy only laughed.

"Come on," he said. "Shit like that only happens in the movies. I was just kidding. There's no one here but us and a bunch of dead and decaying bodies, and they're not going anywhere fast."

I thought of showing them just how fast the dead could move when they were properly motivated, but I didn't have it in me tonight. I hovered in the sky and watched as the practical joker used his advantage and put his arm protectively around the orange-haired girl. She leaned her head on his shoulder, and he bent over and kissed the top of her hair. It was a surprisingly romantic gesture and only drove home the point of what I was missing. What I thought I could live without.

In a rush of air and darkness that none of them noticed, I left the graveyard behind me. I knew where I was
going, I only wondered if he'd be home.

Drew's apartment was not that far. In a way I guess I
was always heading there. Within minutes I alighted in
front of his white stucco building at the edge of Hollywood, unsure of what to do next. A couple of bums
passed by, but I showed them my teeth and they left me
alone.

I looked at the mail directory for a moment, trying to
remember Drew's apartment number, but it didn't matter. As I raised my head to look at the third floor, there
was one window that attracted me above the rest, as if it
had a neon sign flashing his name.

With a tiny jump I was up there, and just barely fitting
on the window sill, I peered in. It was his bedroom—
messy, small, but comfortable. I knew it even before I saw
him sleeping in his bed. I was glad he was alone that
night. With his eyes closed in peace, he looked like an
angel, maybe the one I needed to watch over me.

I thought about going through the window and lying
down next to him for the night. What would it be like to
sleep with someone again? Just sleep, nothing more. So
close that when you turned over, you would always brush
up against another body. You would always know someone was there.

But I was afraid, and I did not move. And just like the
person who whistles in the dark to counteract their fear, I
started to hum to myself the words I could not sing:

> "What I want is a heart that won't break,
> What I want is a life with no mistakes,
> And what I want is you.
> Why can't I have what I want?"

And I sat on the windowsill and looked at him sleeping, watching him turn occasionally and whisper words in his dreams. Until dawn was close, and I could feel the tinge of fire on my skin, warning me as always that I had to hurry home.

History repeats itself, but I never really believed it. Or maybe I just thought I was beyond it. That all the mistakes I could possibly make had been made and then some. That I was now infallible the way the pope was supposed to be, or at least worldly-wise enough to avoid having a tragic flaw.

But look at King Lear. He never knew who was on his side and who wasn't until it was too late, and he was God knows how old and how experienced. Why should I be any smarter than him? Why should I live forever?

After that night on the windowsill of Drew's apartment, I acted cooler toward him. As if Drew knew I had been there and done nothing about it. In some ways I was almost rude to him. I couldn't bear to admit I needed someone again. It was so much like something from my past, so needful, so human. In a way, almost degrading. I wanted to be above that now.

When he called, I barely stayed on the phone five minutes. "I'm real busy," I would lie, and then hang up, feeling justified. At practice I would talk to everyone but him unless necessary. Afterward, instead of socializing, I would leave immediately. "I have to meet someone," I'd say, and Nathan would wink at me.

"He must be pretty special," he would say, as I was leaving, and I'd nod in a knowing way.

I saw this was having a bad effect on Drew and was counterproductive to the band's morale, but I couldn't help myself. I had been foolish that one night, in front of no one except myself, but I couldn't live it down. Now I was hell-bent on proving there were no feelings for him on my part.

Of course, scenarios like this usually lead to an explosion. You can only keep up a facade for so long. It happened at a gig that was to prove momentous for more reasons than one.

That was the beginning of the end of a lot of things, but I didn't realize that until it was too late. When a bomb goes off, all you hear is the noise.

There was a crowd outside the Crime Club waiting to get in. Many of them dressed in black. All of them dressed to kill: lots of hair, earrings dangling, tight pants, short skirts, boots, and high heels. They carried with them the scent of perfume, smoke, liquor, and leather. Some of them were together, had slept together, were going to sleep together. Some of them were alone. But all of them loved music and were here to see one of the most popular bands in L.A. On the local scene we had "arrived."

The parking lot was full, and I cursed silently as I hunted for a space to park the Porsche. It was going to have to be the streets—unsafe for any car, let alone this one. "God damn it," I said, as the only available spot was a good three blocks away. Then I saw Nathan and Drew standing at the back entrance, their mouths closed tight and hard.

"Over here," Nathan shouted, pointing to the alleyway where I saw Drew's white Honda. With a screech of rubber, I pulled in behind his car, almost hitting the bumper. I was still reacting to Drew's shortness with me at our eight o'clock sound check. It was one of the few times I had ever hit a wrong note, a glaring B instead of a C. I heard Drew falter as he sang. The automatic feel of his voice had been thrown by a wrong note, twisting it out of harmony. Usually we try to cover mistakes like this by ignoring a bad note and going on to the next one. Within seconds everything usually rights itself, and the song goes back to harmonic perfection. Instead, Drew had stopped the entire band with a wave of exasperation.

"How can I sing with nothing but bad notes?" he had shouted in the silence, while everyone stared at the floor, confused by his behavior. Then, with an exasperated glance at me, he had started the song again. I continued playing, but I wouldn't look at him for the rest of sound check, not even saying good-bye when we left the club to go our separate directions on break.

Now it was 11:45 on a Saturday night, and we were due on at midnight. I was late, the moon was full, and no one was in a good mood.

Nathan rushed up to my door as I opened it, and grabbed my Fender out of my hands. "For Christ's sake, Kate," he said, "where have you been?"

"Don't even bother asking her," Drew commented, as he stood there smugly with his arms crossed. "This is Kate, our good friend, who won't even give anyone her address, let alone any other pertinent information."

I opened my mouth to say something cutting, then thought better of it. There were enough bad feelings already. Besides, what could I say? That I was upset at our sound check and decided to go flying? That I lost track of the time, sunup being the only hour significant to me anymore? That I couldn't tell them where I lived, because the condo belonged to the vampire that broke up my marriage?

Instead, I walked quietly past Drew, turning only to Nathan to say, "I'm sorry. I had some problems, but I can be ready in five minutes." And I was.

The crowd was now inside, filling every inch of the floor from the stage to the bar. Drinks in hand, sweating in the dark, they waited expectantly for the band to appear. We stood backstage, guitars in hand, makeup on, checking one more time that we were ready.

The band was a little tense. When I hadn't arrived an hour before show time as we always did, they had started to worry. Charly with his usual bleak attitude feared some harm had come to me. When 11:30 rolled around, worry became anger. This was an important gig. There were rumors that several record companies were coming to check us out. What if I didn't appear? Even worse, what if Charly was right and some evil genius had stolen my soul? The possibilities were endless.

But now that everyone could see I was safe, if not truly sound, Nathan and Charly were trying to put away their anger so we could have a good show. Only Drew was distant, his eyes focusing everywhere but on my face. And I did nothing to bridge the gap between us. *He'll never get my address,* I thought, as Drew slipped into automatic.

"Okay, guys," he said, "let's go out there and blow them away."

We hit the stage to loud applause, then barreled into our opening song, "Take Care." By the second verse I had forgotten my war with Drew. There was only the crowd. Swaying, jumping, living to the music. I felt them reach out to me, and I touched back. I felt the approval, the warmth, the desire—but there was something else. Something that had never been there before.

Something wrong. Someone was out there. I tried to look beyond the stage lights but I couldn't see. *Who are you?* I thought. But only my little voice answered. *Something's wrong.*

There was a pause between the second and third songs where Drew spoke to the audience. A crowd of girls in the front whistled and called his name. I moved to the far right of the stage, searching for the presence I had detected. I turned my head and saw Charly looking in the same direction. He had sensed it too. *Who are you?*

The next song began. I heard the count, four drumstick clicks, then lost it as a series of unwanted images came into my mind. A skeleton lying on a table. A fetus wrapped in a plastic bag. An orange held in a dead man's hand. *Who are you?*

Then it was winter. In New York. A young man lying crumpled against a brown and white building. The final drops of blood oozing from his neck. He had something in his hand. I couldn't see what it was. The snow began to fall. It turned his hair white and washed the blood away. A skeleton came walking down the street. He sat down next to the dead man, took the orange from his hand, and rested the lifeless head on his bony shoulder.

"Kate," Charly whispered. I shook in surprise. The last notes of "Changed" were fading. We were already on our seventh song. "Are you all right?" He searched my face, but I stared at him blankly. The snow. From the other end of the stage, Drew gave me a quizzical look. He was wondering whether to start the next song.

"There's someone out there," I said to Charly, as if emerging from a deep trance.

"I know," he said. "I feel it, too. It's just like Tom's party."

But it wasn't like the party at all. This time I felt threatened. "Let's just get through the last song," Charly said, and he touched me lightly on the arm. His touch broke the sorcerer's spell, and I looked across the stage at Drew as if I couldn't imagine what he was waiting for.

"I'm all right," I said to Charly, and he nodded to Nathan to start the last song. I heard the count of the sticks and forcefully shut out the right side of the room. I would deal with my enemies, if any, later.

Right now I needed to worry about the music business

because, as the song began, I realized there really were
record people in the audience. I could tell by the way they
were dressed and by the way they watched both us and
the crowd. Knowing that helped me shake off my feeling
of dread.

Drew sang the words that Charly had written only last
week.

> "If there were angels,
> I wouldn't need you.
> I'd have heaven
> to help me through.
>
> "If there were angels,
> It would be all right.
> I would never be afraid
> of the dark of the night."

The crowd stood frozen in fascination. The melody and
the words had hooked them into zombielike obedience.
The skeleton bit into the orange, but I refused to look.
"Think records," I said to myself and played my bass even
harder. *Are any of you the one?* someone asked, but I
refused to answer. "If there were angels." Drew's voice
verged on perfection as it led into the solo.

Charly played his guitar, moving quickly back to the
left side of the stage as if he was retreating from an attack. I decided to join him. Things definitely felt better
over there. Safer. The floor felt stronger. It would not
cave in.

The song was almost over. *Are any of you the one? I've
tracked you here. From New York to Florida to Vegas.* Juice
was running down the skeleton's chin, but I stood my
ground. "If there were angels." And I wished one was
here now, instead of the demon that was out there asking

questions. Concentrate. I had to keep time. No matter how cold it got. No matter how hard the snow fell. Concentrate.

The music built to its climax. The crowd moved closer as Drew commanded them. I locked eyes with one of the record people and would not let him go. My fingers pulled harder and harder on the strings. There was a drumroll, the crowd moaned in surprise, and then it was over as we crashed down on our final chord and heard the thunderous applause.

Released at last, the band rushed back to the dressing room, never considering an encore, even though the crowd outside was shouting for more. Charly placed his guitar down, then bolted the door.

"No one's getting in for a little while," he said, and we began to hear people pounding.

And suddenly I was afraid that they were not people at all but an army of dead men. Skeletons wanting to get in. Their tiny bony hands cracking against the door.

"What's the matter?" Drew asked, sweat pouring down his face. "I turned around for the encore, and the entire band was gone."

I looked at him in surprise. He had felt nothing.

Nathan shook his head. "There was something wrong. I don't know what exactly. For a little while there, I felt uneasy, but I thought it was just my nerves."

Charly looked at me but said nothing.

"Well, anyway," Drew said, "we gave a great performance. If anyone was here from a record company, they had to be impressed."

As if on cue, the pounding stopped, and we heard Greta, the club's manager, say, "Hey, guys, will you open up for CMD Records?"

We stood for a moment in shock. CMD Records—she might as well have said God, for a record company did hold the power of the almighty in its hands. They decided who would live and who would die in the music business. Without a record contract a band was doomed to the living death of playing forever in the local bars for no money and no chance of success. But one good word, one signature on a piece of paper could mean your picture on the cover of *Rolling Stone,* your name on the marquee of Madison Square Garden, and heavy rotation on MTV.

Drew raced to the door, almost knocking Charly over, and unbolted the lock. Nathan and I waited, a prayer forming on my lips as if I was still seven years old and still believed that God was a kindly grandfather figure who sat in an easy chair in heaven and controlled our destinies. The excitement had made me revert to my childhood fantasies. I had forgotten that I was no longer allowed to pray. For a moment I believed I was perfectly normal, a human who still needed a little help from heaven.

The door opened, and two fairly unassuming men walked in. I noticed the taller one's teeth were capped, and he was wearing a Led Zeppelin tee shirt. His sandy brown hair was long and carefully placed behind his ears to reveal a single diamond earring. "Hi," he said. "I'm Matt Wilson, VP of A and R for CMD, and this is Ronny from Promotion." Ronny smiled the smooth smile of a salesman, and I could picture him running his hand along his dark oily hair as he sold some sucker a lemon. We all beamed back at them. Even Charly was willing to be optimistic for the moment.

"Mind if we talk to you for a few minutes?" Matt asked. His brown eyes lingered for a moment on me, and I realized he was the one I had been staring at during our performance. I guessed him to be about thirty-five.

"Of course not," Drew answered. "Have a seat."

They found an empty spot between my bass and the cases for the drums. Ronny lit a cigarette.

"You're a good band," Matt said, "and you've got a big following and some good songs. I particularly liked that last one." Charly smiled warmly, as we all waited on the edge of our seats.

"You just don't have a hit in any of them yet," Ronny added, and everyone's face fell. We had been expecting something more magical than that.

"Every band needs that one song that will be a breakthrough for them on the radio," Matt continued. "That's the most important thing: air-play. That's what sells records. A band can be popular in their own town, have stage presence and musicianship, but without the song, they ain't gonna make any money for us."

He looked at the disappointment in our eyes and smiled. "But we didn't come backstage to make you feel bad. Ronny and I think you've got it as a band. What we'd like to do is put you in the studio to cut a demo at a fairly low cost to us. Say in about a month or so. Till then, do some more writing. Think commercial. Think hooky. Think new and different."

I looked at Matt in confusion. It seemed to me he was already contradicting himself.

"Then we'll go in and record four songs, get some pictures taken, and present it to everyone at CMD. We'll see what the general consensus is and take it from there."

"Well," Drew said, recovering his momentum, "that sounds great."

We all smiled in acknowledgment. They did want us, it just wasn't going to happen overnight. But still, I let my imagination work a little overtime. I could see the record in the stores. My picture on the cover, my name on the credits. It didn't occur to me there could be a problem with that, considering everyone I had known in my past life thought I was dead or at least missing in action. All I was thinking about was the high of the moment, and everyone around me was thinking the same thing.

Drew could hardly control his exuberance as Matt handed him his card. "Call me next week, and we'll set up a meeting to talk about the studio and set you guys up on a strict rehearsal schedule. Meanwhile, write me that hit song."

He breezed out of the room with Ronny in tow, and we barely waited for the door to close before we let out a scream.

"I can't believe it!" Nathan cried, dancing around the room. "MTV, here we come."

Drew and I looked at each other, smiling, then avoided each other's eyes. "I hope your invisible boyfriend won't mind you being famous," he muttered. But before I could reply, Charly broke in with his usual dark sensibilities.

"Hey, guys, we aren't actually signed yet. Till then, they can always say no. And even after you are signed, they can throw you off the label at a moment's notice."

"Oh, Charly," Nathan said, slowing his steps. "Can't you ever be happy anymore? Does every event in life have to have a shade of despair to it?"

"Yeah, buddy." Drew turned his attention away from me. "When we started this band two years ago, you partied harder than any of us. You always believed we'd make it big. It's still this Mitch thing, isn't it? You're letting it drive you crazy. You did nothing but complain about his playing, and now you're letting his death turn you into Mr. Charly 'We're all going to die' Turner."

Drew sighed in exasperation while Charly shook his head. "You just don't get it, do you? There was nothing normal about Mitch's death. And then Tom disappeared. And now tonight . . ." He trailed off, unsure of what he was even thinking, let alone what he wanted to say.

"Tonight what?" Drew asked and then proceeded without waiting for an answer. "Tonight you decide something bad is going to happen again, and you go and spook Kate so much she practically has to stop playing. . . . Well, Charly, I didn't see any would-be chain-saw murderers in the audience, nor did I see any ghosts, ghouls, or the Frankenstein monster. In fact, all I saw were a lot of happy fans and two pretty happy record company people."

"Yeah"—Charly's voice rose—"well, Kate felt it, too." He turned toward me looking for support, but Drew didn't let me answer.

"Oh, really, Kate," he said. "I guess the fucking goblins got a hold of you and made you late, too!"

"Hey," Nathan interrupted. "I thought we were going to try to get past what happened to Mitch. I know you still feel bad about it, Charly, since you were going over to his apartment to apologize for chewing him out again about his playing, and you had to be the first to find him, but you've got to let it go sometime."

"It's not just Mitch," Charly shouted. "There was someone out there. Waiting. I could feel it. I think he's after all of us." He picked up his brown leather jacket and guitar. "And sooner or later," he said, moving toward the door, "he's going to kill us all. Just like Mitch. Not a drop of blood left in him." The door slammed behind him.

"I suppose you think Ted Bundy was out in the audience tonight, too," Drew said, turning his anger on me. "Or maybe it's Count Dracula returned from the grave, wanting to drink somebody's blood. Maybe there's a bat still flying around the club somewhere."

"Don't be an asshole, Drew." Nathan turned to see the door open. "Now you're getting as weird as Charly."

Jeff, the roadie, came in to let us know the drums were packed up and ready to go.

"Great," Nathan said to him. "How about you and I find a couple of girls and go have a drink somewhere. Maybe my apartment. I'm sick of all this bullshit. All this arguing. I want to celebrate for a change."

"Sounds like a plan," Jeff said, as they left the dressing room together. He knew better than to ask what was going on.

Drew continued glaring at me. "How about you? Is the love of your life waiting for you at home in front of the fireplace? Or do you have a date with Satan?"

I leaned against the wall and watched him rant and rave and thought of how he had looked sleeping in his bed.

"Maybe Satan can't figure out where you live. Maybe that's the problem. Or maybe I'm the one who's crazy? Two guys from a record label say they're interested, and I'm the only one who's happy about it. Everybody else is worried about ghosts or devils hiding in the audience. Well, I'm sick of that shit. I don't believe in any of it. All I believe in is fate. And it's our fate to be famous. I can feel it."

He slammed his fist into the wall next to my head. I didn't flinch. I met his eyes head-on.

"And damn it, Kate, I'm sick of your attitude. I'm sick of you avoiding me. Of never staying on the phone anymore. What did I do? I'm sick of it. I want to know your address, right now. I want to know it, now! Where the hell do you live?"

He stood only inches away from me. I could see the little beads of sweat still lingering on his eyelids. The tiny hairs he had missed when shaving. And I thought, *I could kill this man before he even took his next breath.* But I didn't want to kill him. He moved a little closer. Our toes were touching.

"Ask me again," I whispered, and then our lips met.

"Tell me where you live. . . ."

And as I felt his body lean into mine, I was grateful that for once, I was close to someone and didn't want to sink my teeth into his neck and taste his blood on my tongue.

I felt my body twitch as if an alarm clock had sounded. I sat up quickly and checked the color of the sky through the window. There was not much time left. I would have to go.

I looked at Drew dreaming helplessly beside me. I did not want to wake him; he was enjoying himself too much. His breath was flowing peacefully in and out of his body. I was happy to see he did not snore.

I had thought it might be strange, making love again after such a long time. But it was easy, natural. My body worked the same as always, only better. And I realized it was something I had been missing for a long time. Something I had tried to deny but still needed. And Drew had wanted it, too. He told me in between kisses. He just hadn't known how to ask. How to tell me he loved me.

"We are the perfect couple," he had said, smiling as we lay down in his bed. "We make music together, we go to bed together, and soon we'll be famous together. For you I would give up all the other girls in the world. I'd be monogamous for once in my life, as long as you gave up all the other guys."

"No problem," I said, admiring Drew's body and the way he seemed at home in bed. Not like Ben, always pulling the covers over us as if we had something to hide, always self-conscious and uncomfortable. Drew was sure of what he wanted and why.

Everything had been perfect between us except for once, when I lost myself in the darkness. I started to whisper another's name. *Justin,* I almost said, then stopped myself cold. Why was that man always haunting me, driving me crazy?

Drew didn't notice the slip of my tongue, only that I spoke and he thought it was to him. What was it Justin had said? "It's my blood running through your veins." Well, so what? I had found the perfect partner, and it was not another vampire. He was a warm and vital human being. He loved me, and maybe what I felt was love, too. Either way, it definitely felt good. And as long as I concentrated, I could keep my mind off his neck, where I could see an artery just waiting to be torn in two.

We could have a life together. Drew and I. I wouldn't have to be alone anymore. We could make a record together, make love together. As long as I concentrated, tried to remember, what it really felt like to be human.

I leaned over and kissed his forehead. "Kate?" he said hopefully, then drifted back to sleep.

I got up and looked at the black figure on his brown carpet—my clothes that Drew had thrown on the floor earlier. And I thought about the Porsche still parked behind the club. I'd have to leave it there till night fell again.

Making sure Drew was still asleep, I lifted the window and stared at the grayness outside. I would blend easily with the fog drifting over Los Angeles.

"You're mine now," I said to Drew, and then I flew away.

IV
Madness

The most insidious thing about radiation is its invisibility. After the bomb goes off and everything appears to be safe, it's not. The radiation is there waiting in every shadow, every breath of air. And slowly, very slowly, it takes away the life you have rebuilt for yourself and replaces it with an empty and decaying shell.

I thought I was safe. Locked in the condo by day. Pretending to be human by night. I forgot about the skeletons. I forgot about the snow. I forgot about blood and desire. I was immune to death and destruction, or so I thought.

But Drew still didn't know where I lived.

"Where are you from?" Drew asked. "I mean, I never even asked you that." It was weeks since we had spent our first night together. But there had been a lot of nights since then.

My face remained impassive as I thought of the many answers to a question like that. Why people always needed to hear little details like this, I didn't know. It was as if by possessing information, they could possess you, too.

"If you won't give me your address, you could at least tell me where you're from." A note of irritation was creeping into his voice. "Or what you do for a living. I don't know that, either, what kind of job you have during the day."

Drew leaned on his arm and looked out his bedroom window as I opened my mouth, but no words came to mind.

"You know," he said, "I've made love to a lot of girls, especially since I've been in this band. And they would ask me a lot of questions, and I always tried to avoid giving any answers. Now I'm on the receiving end, and I don't like it much. Maybe I should go back to being the mysterious one in the relationship. Maybe I should take up my old life-style."

"Somewhere else," I said. "That's where I'm from." And I watched as his face went from frustration to benign amusement. Even Drew could see the humor in the situation.

"Where is somewhere else?" He pulled me back down on the bed, and I moved my hand down along his chest. Then I buried my face against his neck.

"Not here."

I had been surprised at how easily Drew had given up his former life-style. How he changed from the rock singer girls chased after every gig and who went home with at least one of them a night to the rock singer girls chased but who went home with his one and only girl-friend each night.

Maybe it was because the boys chased me, too, and it reminded him of what could happen. Maybe it was because the single way of life can get old and dangerous very fast. Or maybe it was because Drew had finally found the right person, someone he could relate to, and suddenly no one else was that tempting anymore.

I found it very flattering, and I was used to monogamy, so it didn't seem that strange. I thought I was in control of the situation, that I had gotten what I wanted, that I had everything figured out. But as time went on, I found our relationship cramped the new "life" I was leading, and all I could do was keep avoiding the answers.

"Let's write a song together," Drew said.

It was Wednesday night, and the band wasn't playing. I was watching the movie *D.O.A.* on TV, and Drew was cooking in the kitchen. There was something slightly nauseating about the smell of eggs combined with grease in a frying pan. I found myself pressing my wrist against my nose to disguise the odor.

"What?"

"A song, you know those things I sing on stage." He smiled a little. "I can't write with Charly anymore. As a matter of fact, I can't even talk to Charly anymore." He had finished the omelette he was making, and he put it on a plate and sat at his kitchen table. His knife made a squeaking noise as it cut across the eggs, like chalk on a blackboard. "I don't know why you always have to be on such a strict diet. You're in perfect shape."

"That's why," I said from the floor. "So I can stay that way." But I winced at the smell of the butter he was putting on his toast.

"Let me give you a tape of a melody I have. All you have to do is put words to it. Just give it a try, that's all I ask." He put the last of the omelette in his mouth. "I know you can do it, Kate. And since Charly is out in never-never land, and Nathan can barely form sentences, you're the only hope I have."

So I took the tape. I played it in the car. I played it in the condo. I liked the melody, but no words came.

Why, I thought, *am I even trying? I'm not a songwriter.* But I hadn't been a musician before, either. Or a vampire.

But then the phrase came, as I woke up one night, stretched, and went upstairs. As I checked the elaborate alarm system for any daytime defects. As I looked out the window to the sea drifting along the coast. A phrase. "Without a country." Only a phrase. But it was a start.

I could hear Drew talking on the phone.

"You're kidding, Nathan, I don't believe it. . . . You saw him where? . . . And the older guy had his arm around him? . . . Well, that doesn't mean anything. . . . Jesus Christ! . . . Did he see you? . . . Well, we're still starting in the studio tomorrow. . . . It's now eight o'clock, not nine. . . . You call Charly and tell him. . . . After all this, I don't even want to talk to him. . . . Yeah. . . . See you tomorrow."

Drew appeared in the living room again. He threw himself down on the couch and sighed.

"What's the matter?" I said, looking up from the floor.

"Oh, it's nothing . . . nothing worth talking about anyway. Hey." He propped himself up on his arm. "I told Nathan we were together now. You know, he thought it was great. He said he had seen it coming a long time ago. But I'm not going to tell Charly."

"Why?" I asked.

"Because he's completely nuts, that's why. If we weren't going to start our demo right now, I'd look for a new guitar player. But I don't want to give Matt the idea that anything's wrong. Maybe Charly will get back to normal one of these days. But let's forget about him. Come on, show me those lyrics." Drew picked up his acoustic guitar. "I can't wait any longer."

I handed him the piece of paper I had written the song lyrics on. It had started with a phrase, that became a title, that became a chorus.

" 'Without a Country,' " he said, and then he sang the song.

"You said you loved me, so I moved to Germany,
Then I worked in a factory in Switzerland.
Came out of Scotland, it's not like England,
So we ran away again, to Canada.
Why are all the homes we built always built on sand?

I remember the Empire State—when will I see it
   again?
One more time without a country, I'm one of the
   homeless again.

Went down to India, then to Arabia.
Stopped once in Africa to feel the rain.
I dreamt in Russian, then spoke in Latin,
So we caught a plane to paint in Paris.
All across the continent, all the way to Greenland.

I remember the Empire State—when will I see it
   again?
One more time without a country, I'm one of the
   homeless again.

We fought in Ireland, then escaped to Sweden.
Someone said there were jobs in Japan.
I lost a friend in Mexico—it doesn't matter where
   you go.
I slept real close to you at the border of Spain.
Is this the way we make a world without end?

I remember New York City—when will I see it
   again?
One more time without a country, I'm one of the
   homeless again.

"It's beautiful, Kate," he said, looking at me. "You
never cease to amaze me."

It had amazed me, too, to hear him sing it. I loved
hearing my words over his melody. It was something that
bound us together.

"Play it again," I said, and by the time the night was
over, he had played it one hundred times.

When I was young, Halloween was a wonderful holiday. You got to dress up as anything you wanted to be—
someone on TV, an animal, a cartoon, something scary.
And you got free candy. People gave it to you just for
knocking on their door. If you were really industrious,
you could amass quantities large enough to satisfy your
sweet tooth until Thanksgiving. Kevin and I would sit on
the floor and pour out our bags and decide who had gotten the most and the best stuff, counting the M&M's,
arranging the red and black licorice.

Only once was Halloween not a happy time for me as a
child. It was the year Kevin decided to dress up as Frankenstein, and I was almost afraid to go trick or treating
with him. He looked a little too much like a monster for
me. His skin really seemed green; those two little pins on
the side of his neck looked real. He had even gotten Boris
Karloff's voice down perfect and had the little kids of the
neighborhood running from him in terror.

I had to keep checking every so often that it was still
Kevin under all that makeup, and that some supernatural
transformation had not stolen my brother from me.

That night I had a dream that I was strapped on the

operating table and Dr. Frankenstein was about to shoot an electric charge right through my neck. I woke up screaming for my mother, and Kevin never wore that costume again.

And Halloween went back to the fun day it was meant to be for children. Where I traded Kevin two of my Snickers for one of his Milk Duds, while we watched *Abbott and Costello Meet Frankenstein* on TV.

But there was nothing childlike about Halloween anymore. I had made my first kill on the beach on that holiday, and I was very close to killing again. And candy didn't taste good to me anymore.

It was that time again. I could feel the ache everywhere, the longing. Even as I drove past trick-or-treaters on my way to the studio, I was fighting it. As I saw little tigers and ghosts, Batmen and cowboys. I bit my lip and thought, *Not now.*

We were recording tonight and then going to an "invitation only" party at The TrapDoor. I'd have to deny my need for at least one more night. I sucked on my finger in an attempt to distract myself. We were going to lay the guitar solo down for "Without a Country" this evening, and Matt and Ronny would be there to supervise.

But then I thought of Kevin in his Frankenstein suit, and I was afraid again. Only this time my reasons were different. I knew it wasn't only a movie.

"How old are you?" Charly asked, staring up at Drew. It was our third week in the studio, and it was the twelfth time we had run the tape, but Charly kept missing notes for his solo. Almost everyone sighed in unison as Ronny threw a newspaper he was reading on the floor. He wasn't smiling as much as he used to.

"How old am I?" Drew repeated, not believing the question. "What does that have to do with anything?"

"How old are you?"

"You know how old I am, for Christ's sake. I'm twenty-six and one-half years old. You've known that since I first met you. What do you mean how old am I?"

"Have you ever been to Vegas?"

Drew looked like he was about to explode.

"Vegas!" he said. "You idiot, I went to Vegas one time with you. Don't you remember? What does that have to do with your solo and the price of tea in China?"

"What about Florida?"

At that point Matt interceded. "Look, we're not getting anywhere tonight. How about we stop and go for the solo on Tuesday night? You guys got a party to go to, I'm in need of a little sleep . . . we'll pick it up next time."

The engineer running the sound board didn't even wait for an answer. He was already closing down the equipment. Nathan jumped up and ran to the bathroom to change. He was going to the party as Harpo Marx. Drew was already dressed as the devil, and I had broken with all tradition and was wearing white with a little halo suspended over my head.

Only Charly was not going to attend. "I have a meeting," he said mysteriously, "with someone important." It was all very vague, and without knowing why, I didn't like the sound of it.

Matt and Ronny had moved outside to have a private conversation. I was not meant to overhear, but I needed a little air and had followed quietly behind. Something about Charly mentioning Vegas was bothering me, and I wanted to clear my head. Because I could hear as well as any predator in the jungle, I caught their conversation from several yards away.

"I don't know, Matt, I just don't know."

"I think they're really doing well. I really like that 'Without a Country.' "

"It's a good song, but I don't know if it's for radio. It's not commercial enough."

"You really don't think so, Ronny? You're the one who's going to be pitching it to the stations."

"No, Matt, I don't. It's not for Contemporary Hit Radio. It's not Album Oriented Rock. The most I could do is throw it out there to the alternative stations and hope it sticks to the wall. But even if it does, we're still not talking profit." Ronny was starting to look less like a salesman and more like a weasel in a jogging suit. His nose seemed to have grown longer and his eyes smaller. "I think you should stop it right now. We haven't spent that much. I think we should quit while we're ahead." Ronny blew smoke into the night air. I could see his gold chain with the letter *R* around his neck.

"But I'm not sure you're right. I have a feeling about this band." If Ronny was a weasel, then Matt had the look of an overgrown puppy dog in a green tropical shirt and black jeans shorts. Loyal, protective, and in perfect L.A. style. "I like them, and I think they can really get somewhere."

"Think about it, Matt, just think about it over the weekend. Let's talk Monday. I believe you'll come to the same conclusion." Ronny patted Matt on the back, as if he had just closed a sales pitch. "C'mon, I'll buy you a beer. It's Halloween."

God damn it, I thought. *Things seemed to be going well till Charly had to pull twenty questions with Drew.* We couldn't stop now. The music was sounding too good. We'd just have to convince Matt that Ronny was wrong. I'd have to think about how to do it. For now, though, I had to slip back in before they noticed me.

I found myself starting to dematerialize before I even

realized what I was doing. It was becoming natural to me, like breathing. But I caught myself before anyone saw my body turn from flesh to smoke.

"How about New York?" Charly was still bothering Drew as he packed up his guitars.

"I've never been there. I've never been out of California, except for our Vegas trip, for that matter."

"Can you make the sign of the cross?"

I felt myself stiffen at that last question. Why was he asking Drew something like that?

"That's it. That's your last question. No, Charly, I'm the devil. Can't you see that? I can't make the sign of the cross. I'm not saved. I'm going straight to hell. Does that satisfy you? And hell is probably somewhere in Florida or New York, so I'll be seeing one of those states soon."

Drew moved over to me and grabbed my hand. "Come on, Kate, we have a party to go to. Why don't you work on your solo, Charly, and not spend so much time reading horror novels and thinking of stupid questions to ask me?"

As we ran out the door, Drew turned around and did make the sign of the cross. I felt a chill creep down the back of my neck, but it wasn't because ancient rituals like that were really a threat to a vampire. It was because I caught a glimpse of something in Charly's mind. For a moment I saw Mitch lying bloodless on his bed, and then his skin melted away and I was staring into the empty eye sockets of a skeleton.

"Have a good time," Charly said, but I knew he didn't mean it.

My halo was giving me a lot of trouble. It kept sliding off my head and down over my eyes. Drew and I were kissing in the corner when it fell down again and knocked into his horns.

"Why don't you just take it off?" He laughed and adjusted his costume.

"I can't," I said, licking his lips with my tongue. "It's Halloween. And I'm in disguise."

Around us the party raged. There was no band tonight, only a DJ playing records, but the crowd was dancing frantically. I wondered if they'd play the tape of our song. I wanted to dance, too.

There were so many people here tonight, living, breathing people, all of them in costume. I saw an alligator and a cowgirl dance by. They smelled tantalizing. I licked Drew again, then pulled him onto the dance floor. I wanted to keep my mind off the thing I needed.

We danced slowly while couples rocketed past us, many of them smiling hello in recognition. Suddenly Nathan appeared with a short, dark-haired girl in tow. She was wearing a low-cut black dress.

"Hey, guys," he yelled. "Marsha here is a witch, a real one."

Drew smiled at him, as if he were referring to her costume.

"No, really she is, a real, live witch. She just read my tarot cards, and it was great. I'm going to be successful. She saw it right in the cards. The Wheel of Fortune showed up. Right in my cards. The band's gonna be famous!"

I looked at Marsha, whose lipstick was a little too red, and she was staring at me strangely. I wondered if she really was a witch, descended from a long line of witches direct from Salem. Maybe her great-grandmother had been burned at the stake for dancing naked in the cornfields under a full moon. Or maybe she was just a girl who called herself a witch for lack of a better name to make herself important, never really knowing that something supernatural could exist. Never knowing that vampires could dance, and werewolves could dream of getting even.

"You're no angel," she said under her breath, and Drew laughed.

"How about she reads your cards, too?" Nathan said excitedly. "Right now. What do you say, Kate?"

"Why not?" Drew said. "I've always wanted to know the future."

And before I could even think of a way to protest, we were sitting across the table from Marsha and Nathan.

"Are you a good witch or a bad witch?" I asked, as she placed Drew's cards face down in front of her.

"Oh, I'm a good one." She was unable to meet my eyes. "I only do spells to help people. People who are ill or who have a broken heart."

"How about someone with a broken brain?" Drew said, referring to Charly, and Nathan laughed.

"No," she said. "Once someone's mind is gone, it's hard to bring it back, and once their soul has left, it's lost forever."

"All right," Drew said, "I'll be serious, just tell me what's in my future. Am I going to be a star or what?"

She lifted the first card and frowned. "The Lovers, this is your present position. In your case, it refers to temptation, rather than harmony and love."

Drew shifted in his seat. "Well, it's love to me, and very tempting."

"Try to control yourself," I said, and laughed.

Marsha ignored him and turned over the next card. "Your immediate influence, the Queen of Swords. Possible sadness, loneliness." She looked at me for a second, then looked down again.

"Third card, the Sun, your destiny—success, triumph, happiness."

"Well, it's about time," Drew said. "I don't like all

these sad cards. I don't feel lonely at all." He squeezed my hand.

Marsha was not interested in Drew's comments. "Strength, your distant-past card, determination, action, confidence. This is the foundation that will help you achieve your goal. Recent-past card . . ." She turned over another and bit her lip. "The Death Card, not always physical death. It can mean change or a loss. But . . . in your case . . . I believe someone near you died not too long ago. In fact, someone else will die soon."

Nathan picked up his drink and quickly swallowed what was left of it. "Mitch died only six months ago," he said, and then as an afterthought, "I hope Charly's all right tonight. We don't even know where he's going."

Drew sighed. "I don't like this. I thought this was going to be fun. Why don't we forget the whole thing, huh, Kate?"

But I was fascinated in a perverse way. "Go on," I said slowly to Marsha, and she obeyed.

"Number six, your future influence . . . the Four of Cups. Aversion, disgust, disappointment. This is coming soon. You must pass this stage before you reach the Sun."

Nathan waved for the waitress. He needed another drink.

"The Fool, this is you right now, someone who is careless and thoughtless. Who is engaged in some kind of folly. Someone who will fall off the cliff very soon. Do you understand how that might be happening in your life, how you're being foolish?"

"Of course not," Drew said. "I took a vow never to be foolish, isn't that right, Nathan? Waitress, I'll have another vodka and tonic; Kate, you don't drink; Nathan, another Seven and Seven; Marsha, anything for you?"

"No," she said, not taking her eyes off the cards. "The eighth card, influences around you or your influence on others close to you . . . the Five of Swords. Destruction, degradation, dishonor."

"Dishonor and destruction!" Nathan shouted, standing up and downing his drink, which had just arrived.

"And don't forget degradation," Drew said, sarcastically. "I've always fantasized about being degraded."

"How come my reading was so good?" Nathan sat down. "We're in the same damned band. I had material attainment or whatever in this position."

"Everyone is on their own path, even if they are together," Marsha said, then turned over the next card. "The Seven of Cups, your inner emotions, what you're feeling now: daydreams, foolish whims, weakness. You're living in a fool's paradise. But the final result, your last card . . ." She hesitated, almost afraid to turn it over. "It is the Tower." She breathed a sigh of relief. "Deception, disruption . . . that will lead to something new. A change, a good thing. You will fall off the cliff, but you will see the Sun. You will find happiness in the light." She looked up at Drew and smiled. "It will be all right, in the end it will be all right."

"Great," Drew said. "I've never been happier. It's Halloween. I wanted to drink and dance—and instead, it turns out I'm a fool who's cruising toward destruction and death."

"No, no," Marsha said. "It will be all right. After the dishonor, it will all work out." She picked up the cards and shuffled them again.

Drew started to leave, but I grabbed his hand. "Fair is fair," I said. "It's my turn now."

"Fine," he collapsed back in the chair. "Read Kate's cards, and get it over with. I'm sure she won't get the Fool one, at least."

Marsha dealt the cards, and her hands were shaking, just slightly. Her eyes moved back and forth under her dark lashes. "What do you want to know?" she asked, finally meeting my eyes head-on.

"Everything," I said, and picked up the first card myself. Of course, it was Death. The atmosphere surrounding me right now. "Not physical, of course," I said.

"Of course," she answered hurriedly, and turned over the second card. "Immediate influence. The Magician, a man who is masterful, confident, and full of deception. Someone strong, an enemy. He carries death with him."

"Not me," Drew said, ordering another drink. "I'm too foolish and weak for that."

"The third card, hmmm, interesting." Marsha ran her hand along the face on the card. "The Knight of Swords, your goal or destiny. That's not what I expected. Hmmm. Someone brave, who will come charging into your life to try and save you. A strong man. Not an enemy."

"Probably me," Drew said. "After I fall off the cliff, I'll rise like the Phoenix and rescue Kate from the Magician."

"That's it," Nathan said. "You're a gallant knight." Marsha shook her head slightly, but only I noticed.

"Your distant past that influences you even now. The Empress, a marriage card, a wife."

"Were you ever married?" Drew asked. "Not that you'd tell me anyway. You never give me any information." He was starting to slur his words. He was on his fifth vodka and tonic.

"And your recent past card, the Hermit. . . . It means withdrawal, caution, solitude, fear of discovery." Marsha looked up suddenly. " 'Oh,' " she said, " 'it's dark all the time and the cellar's damp, but it doesn't matter—I've scared the rats away.' "

"What?" Nathan regarded her apprehensively. "Are you getting drunk, too? And without even drinking a drop?"

"Sometimes," she said, "I see things. . . . I don't know . . . I don't know what they mean." She shook herself as if she felt very cold. " 'It's hard to only live at night. . . .' "

"Hard to what?" Drew said. "For Christ's sake, get it together, Marsha. I need another drink. Waitress! . . . Finish Kate's cards so we can go home to bed. How about it, Kate? Waitress!"

"Sixth card," she said quietly. "The Hanged Man . . . your future. . . . Oh . . . where can you go? Where can you hide? I see sacrifice . . . surrender . . . abandonment . . . the Magician."

"You've already said that card once," Drew yelled, paying the waitress for another round. "This is getting boring!"

"Go on." I adjusted my halo. "I want to know everything. Forget about the cellar, forget about the night."

"Oh, shit." Nathan leaned sideways in his chair and passed out, his Harpo hat falling off his head. Drew laughed and gulped down the rest of his drink.

"Go on."

"The seventh card, what you're feeling now. . . . The Chariot. War . . . vengeance . . . indecision . . . triumph and failure . . . chaos . . . fleeing from reality. Oh, Kate, who are you?"

"That's what I'd like to know," Drew said, grinding an ice cube with his teeth. "Does anyone realize I've never been to Florida?"

"Go on."

"The eighth card, your influence on other people and theirs on you." She turned over the card. "The Devil!"

"That's me," Drew said, "red hot." He gave a short gasp. "Watch me make the sign of the cross." He raised his hand to his forehead, then collapsed against me, and fell asleep instantly on my shoulder.

"I said go on!"

"I don't like this. I've never seen a reading this bad. I don't feel right. I feel cold. I feel the snow."

"What about the snow?" I leaned across the table until I was only inches away from her face. "What about the snow?"

Marsha turned and stared vacantly at the dance floor.

"He's looking for you, Kate. Everywhere. Time is running out. He's been tracking someone. Not you. But someone like you. He was attracted to your band by the death of the bass player before you. The loss of blood. Who are you, Kate? What are you?"

"You don't want to know," I said, settling back in my chair. "If you can't tell me about the snow, then tell me what the Devil means."

"Influences, they're not good. Violence, black magic, bondage, a downfall. . . . I don't want to see anymore. I'm cold." She was holding her shoulders and shaking. "He carries a black bag."

"Who is he?"

"I don't know. Someone bad. What are you, Kate?"

"I told you, you don't want to know. Go on."

Drew stirred for a moment on my shoulder and attempted to lift his head. "Let's go to bed," he mumbled, and passed out again.

"Number nine, your inner emotions." Marsha turned over the card, and tears came into her eyes. "The Ten of Swords. Affliction, sorrow, trouble, remorse, absence—none of it good. Kate, what has happened to you? I see death everywhere in this reading. It's standing over you, even now, as I speak. It's kissing the top of your head." She looked at me, and I saw fear in her eyes. "You're not alive, are you?"

I tore my halo off and threw it on the floor.

"Just finish reading my cards," I hissed at her. "What

about the last one?" I wanted to know who this mysterious magician was and if it even mattered to me. But I was losing patience fast.

I grabbed her wrist and pulled her toward me. A tiny stream of blood started from where my thumbnail had made contact. I watched the flow with fascination and felt the pain of emptiness awaken in my body with a vengeance.

"Please," she whispered, and with her free hand she turned over the last card, never taking her eyes off my face. She held it up for me to see. "The Moon." Tears were pouring down her face. "You're hurting me." The blood had reached her elbow.

"Finish reading my cards. What does the Moon mean?"

"The final result: danger, error, insincerity, deception. Use caution, the cards are warning you. Go away, Kate, while there's still time. There's danger here, something very bad, something worse than you. . . . Something bad."

I let go of her wrist, and she fell back in the chair, knocking Nathan onto the floor. He moaned once, but he never woke up. It was his destiny to sleep it off on the dirty floor of the club.

Marsha looked at me as if she had just awakened. She spotted Nathan on the floor and checked to see if he was all right. Then she saw the blood on her arm.

"What . . . what happened?"

"He's drunk," I said. "You know how that is." With my hand I knocked the evidence of the cards off the table. "And you're no witch—believe me, I know. You can't even foretell the future."

"I don't remember," she said, staring at the Death card on the floor.

I rose out of my chair and picked up the sleeping Drew

and hoisted him on my shoulder. Several people stared, but most were too busy or too drunk to notice. I had to get him home, and I had to get some blood. Eventually I had to get some blood. But it wasn't going to be anybody here.

"Why am I so cold?" Marsha said to no one in particular. And no one answered her.

I left her picking up her precious cards and muttering in the darkness. "I'm a good witch. Really I am. A good witch. I never hurt anyone. I am . . ."

And Nathan slept through it all and didn't remember, either.

I pulled up to Drew's apartment and scanned the area. No one was around. It was already three o'clock in the morning. All the good souls were asleep.

I picked him up and threw him over my shoulder. It was as if he weighed nothing. He was my baby. And because he was barely conscious, he couldn't be surprised by my strength or embarrassed by it, either.

"Kate," he muttered. "Where's Kate?"

"It's all right," I said, and proceeded to his apartment. I had a set of keys, so it was easy. I laid him down on the bed and then rested beside him.

"Drew," I said, unbuttoning his shirt. I couldn't let him sleep in his clothes. "I wish I could tell you something."

"Really," he said. "I wish you could tell me something." His eyes rolled back in his head for a second, then opened again. "I love you, Kate. That's something, isn't it?"

"Yes," I said, "love is always something. Even in the darkness it's still something." I put my head on his chest and his arm circled around me. "I'm from New York."

"What?"

"Originally, that's where I'm from . . . New York."

"I love you, Kate. Where's New York?"

"It's very far away. Very far."

"That was something . . . wasn't it? You told me something."

"Yes, that was something."

And as he rolled over and got sick on the floor beside the bed, I held his head and thought, *I wish I could tell you.* But there was nothing I could say.

"I'm so sick," Drew said. "I feel like I'm dying." He had left ten messages on my answering machine, and I had returned his calls as soon as I woke that next night.

"My head is splitting, my stomach's upset. If I don't die soon, I might just kill myself."

"You were pretty drunk," I said. "It's no wonder your hangover's so bad."

"I'm dying, Kate, really." But Drew didn't have a clue about what it felt like to die, let alone be dead and need blood. Even as I spoke to him on the phone, the color red was flashing in my mind.

"I talked to Nathan, and he's dying, too. Only Charly hasn't checked in. Maybe he's still at his mysterious meeting." His voice got softer for a moment. "Hey, Kate. . . . You told me where you're from. I remember that much, at least."

"Yeah, I told you where I'm from."

"Everything else is blank. Did that Marsha finish reading your cards?"

"Yeah, but she told me nothing. She wasn't a witch at all. She's a fake."

I thought of how bleak my future looked to Marsha and of the dark stranger with the black bag who was out to get me, but what could you do with information like that anyway? It's like having a blood test and worrying all week for the results to come in. The worrying doesn't help anything, eventually you find out anyway. Besides, I wasn't leaving. Not Drew, not the band, not this town. Even if a snowstorm hit L.A. and buried it completely, I was sticking it out. Even if there was something worse than me.

"I didn't go to work," Drew said, "and I don't think I can even get out of bed. I'm dying."

"That's okay," I said. "Why don't we just get together tomorrow?" I had an important mission anyway. I had planned it carefully in my mind. I knew who my next victim should be, and it was going to happen tonight.

"I don't know why you don't just move in with me. It would make our lives easier."

I didn't answer Drew. It was something that had come up before, and I was running out of excuses.

"Or I could move in with you . . . if you'll ever give me your address."

"Let's talk about it in person," I said. "Why don't you take some aspirin and go back to sleep?"

"All right, Kate, if that's what you think. But promise me you'll be over tomorrow night, if I'm not dead from alcohol poisoning."

"If you're not dead, I'll be there," I said, and I hung up the phone with a smile. I did love him. I was sure of it now. Maybe things could work out somehow. Maybe I could have a relationship with a human being after all, as long as I was careful.

But my smile soon faded. All the veins in my body were aching, calling for blood. I checked the phone book and found his address: the Hollywood Hills, not too far away. I put on my black jeans and my black tee shirt, and then I was out the window, flying east and then north.

He had a beautiful home; I had to give him that. It was a classic piece of California architecture, in the Holly-

wood Hills, overlooking the lights of L.A. He had a pool
and a tennis court and a garage with a Jaguar in it. I
walked around the grounds for a while, just to make sure
no one else was there. But Ronny lived alone.

I slipped through an open window and blew up the
stairs to where I imagined his bedroom to be. It was only
nine o'clock on a Friday night, but he was sitting in bed,
reading Lawrence Sanders, turning the pages slowly to
make sure he had understood every last word.

"Which 'Deadly Sin' is it?" I asked, materializing at the
foot of his waterbed.

"Shit," he yelled. "You scared the hell out of me. How
did you get in here?"

"How do you think?"

"Well, what are you doing here? What do you want?
You should have called first."

"Why?" I said. "So you could tell me that you had
convinced Matt to stop our recording?"

"How do you know that? Did you talk to Matt?"

"No, Ronny, I just hear real well."

"Oh, you heard us outside the studio, huh? Well, it
doesn't matter. Matt may have signing power, but I'm the
one who calls the shots. I'm the one who gets it on the
radio. Without air-play, it doesn't matter how good your
record is, you'll fail anyway. Unless you came here to
offer me something. Your services maybe, then I might
reconsider. Is that why you came here, Kate? Is that what
you want?"

"I want to drink your blood." I walked over to the
window. "You know that's what vampires do."

"Cute, honey, real cute." I heard him throw his book
down, as he looked for his bathrobe. "By the way, how
did you get in here?"

"I flew in."

"Hey," he said to the back of my head, "enough of this bullshit. Either put out or get out."

But then I turned around, and there I was, looking scarier than any of the characters in Lawrence Sanders's books.

"Shit, Kate, you are absolutely crazy. What the hell is this? Do you still think it's Halloween? Are you trick or treating or what?"

"Kneel," I said.

"Fuck you. You're the one who should do the kneeling."

"Kneel, right now." I walked over to him, grabbed him by his arms, and dragged him down. Ronny looked at me in disbelief.

"God, are you strong!" He attempted to rise, but I held him in place, my hand fastened on his skull.

"Look, you stupid bitch, what is this?" He tried to twist his head, but my nails began to dig in.

"It's not like I haven't done this thing before," I said, "making one of my victims a business move also."

"Wait," he cried. Blood was beginning to drip into his eyes. "Please, wait. . . . What do you want?"

"I don't know, Ronny, what do you have to offer?"

"Let me go," he cried. "We'll talk, anything. Oh, God, are you really a vampire? Just let me go."

I released his head for a moment and laughed.

"Please, Kate, just wait a second." He brought his hand up to his head, and when he pulled it back and saw the extent of the bleeding, he almost screamed. Then he tried to stand again.

"I didn't say you could get up!" I shouted at him and latched on to his head again.

"God, Kate, please . . . stop. I'll do whatever you want. I'll give the band all the help I can. I'm sorry I tried to interfere, please. My head, you're killing me."

"Not really," I said, "but I'm just about to."

"Please, Kate, I'm sorry . . ."

With my free hand I grabbed his neck, and his eyes bulged from the pressure. Blood was soaking his bathrobe.

"I don't hear you making me any good offers, Ronny. Can you get us major radio air-play?"

"Yes. Yes." His arms were jerking at his side.

"How about MTV?"

"Yes, anything. Please . . . my head."

"Well," I said, pulling his neck toward my teeth. "Somehow, I don't really think you're sincere, and besides that, I never really liked you, and most importantly, I need to drink someone's blood right now, and as you're available, I might as well dig in."

Ronny screamed something. It was probably "please" again. And then I bit down on the artery pulsating in his neck. There was nothing seductive about it. His body convulsed for a moment, and then he caved in, as vein after vein was drunk dry, collapsing into flat blue lines on his wasted body. There would be no more cocaine for air-play, no more prostitutes or cars, no more bribes to be on the video channels.

What a fool, I thought. Then Ronny was gone, and he couldn't take our record contract away anymore. He was somewhere else, where record contracts meant nothing, and where I could never go. I wondered if he'd run into Mitch.

Ronny disappeared over the weekend. I was too smart and too quick to leave evidence behind anymore. His Jaguar disappeared from his house, too. They found it the next day crashed into one of the *O*s of the Hollywood sign. But his body was never found. He was just gone. Another record executive over the hill, missing but not remembered. And Matt forgot why Ronny was so against

The Uninvited and decided to keep working with us anyway.

Afterward, I crept back to Drew's apartment. It was late, he had been sleeping, but he was glad to see me anyway.

"Hold me," I said. "That's all, just hold me."

And he did, as we lay in bed.

"I didn't die," he said, touching my face.

"No, you didn't." And I wondered briefly if I had made a mistake this time, striking so close to home. The Hollywood Hills were just a step away.

"Kate," Drew said, "why don't we just get a new apartment and move in together, in a place that's all ours? One we pick out together. I could get a paper tomorrow . . . look at the ads?"

"Wait," I said. "Wait a little longer. I need more time."

Drew sighed impatiently. "Why?"

"Oh, I don't know, I just need more time."

"I thought you said you loved me," he said, looking at me closely.

"Yes . . . I . . . I love you." I closed my eyes for a moment and tried to think of something to say.

Instead, I thought of a graveyard, cold, hard, stones in the moonlight. Snow falling and covering the dirt that buried the dead. Flowers, frozen under someone's name. In a certain way I always felt cold. I pulled Drew's blue bedspread tight around my body.

"Okay," I said. "Go ahead and get a paper. We'll start looking."

Drew held me even tighter.

"Great," he said. "Why don't you think about where we should live? Maybe you'd like to stay in the West L.A. area?"

"Sure. Maybe that's where I'd like to stay."

I looked at the shadows on the wall, changing shape with every flicker of Drew's ten-dollar lamp. And I tried to remember what it was like to be married, to have to explain everything, account for every action.

But I couldn't even recall Ben's face. His features blurred and became one with the shadows moving across the room toward morning. How long had it been since I had seen the light of day? Since I had woken up with the sun in my face and seen my husband lying beside me?

I tried very hard, but I couldn't remember. There was only a wall there, where the sun used to rise. A wall that rose up cool as metal and shut out the memory of a human life. But still somewhere, in the back of my mind, a moment of mortality lingered, and made me warm as Drew pressed against me the way humans always do, trying to become one within the boundaries of separateness.

"Forever is a long time," Charly said, looking at Drew. He had been acting strange all through sound check, actually for the entire last week. At our recording session on Tuesday he barely said a word except "Oh, really?" when Matt mentioned that Ronny was missing. He'd left as soon as he'd finished his guitar solo. He had a meeting just as mysterious as the one the Thursday before, and no one knew where he was going or where he had been.

Now it was Saturday night, several hours before a major show, and though it was cloudy and a tiny bit of rain permeated this dry desert of a city, I knew behind the apparition of smog and darkness, a full moon was waiting.

"He's losing it," Drew muttered to me under his breath as we moved our things off stage for the opening act to set up. "I don't know if I can take him much longer, especially with a record contract at stake. He's a mental case."

"He'll snap out of it," I said, but I wasn't sure. And with our demo almost finished, now was not the time for one of the band's members to start acting strange. Nor was it the time to lose a member, either.

"Get a life," Nathan yelled at Charly as he threw his drumsticks in his case. But Charly had already wandered off. Since Halloween, Nathan had lost all patience with our guitar player's bizarre questions. His casual California attitude was now tinged with irritation.

"There's a guy who wants to talk to you," one of the waitresses said, coming over to me. Drew looked up. "And he's really cute, too." She winked slyly.

I turned my eyes in the direction she was pointing and saw, seated at one of the booths, the back of a man with long black hair. It was too early for any fans to be here yet, and I wondered who it was that demanded my attention.

"Do you want me to set him straight?" Drew asked, moving toward the table. But I stopped him with a wave of my hand. Something about the man's back looked familiar.

"It's okay," I said, walking away. "I'll be right back."

You may believe that you have wiped someone entirely out of your mind. Obliterated memories like dust in a hurricane. But somehow the picture remains, needing only a tiny current of power to illuminate again the face you have fought to forget.

I saw the curve of his shoulders, and I said his name. "Justin, what a surprise seeing you again."

"Hi," he said, and I sat down in the seat opposite him.

"What happened to your hair?"

"I wasn't in the mood to cut it when I woke up this evening." He smiled slightly.

"Well, what brings you back to town?" I said. "To my sound check, to be exact?"

"My financial manager told me someone was living in the Santa Monica condo. I assumed it was you, but I wanted to be sure."

"I can move out any time you want," I said defensively. He looked down at the drink I knew he could never swallow.

"I have a lot of houses, Kate. I don't need that one in particular. I just had to know . . . how you were doing."

"It took you three years to wonder how I was doing?" I said. "Well, I'm doing fine. As a matter of fact, I'm doing real fine."

"Doing this," he said, and he gestured toward the stage he had his back to. "Playing rock 'n' roll with a bunch of teenagers—you know you're asking for trouble."

"Hey," I said, "all of the guys are in their twenties, and even if they don't behave like it all the time, it's still better than you hanging around acting classes, looking for some fool you can turn into a vampire as soon as they fall for you."

"I'm sorry about that, Kate. Really I am. I guess it's been so long . . . I had forgotten. I didn't really think it through. I've been alone so long. I suppose I was just being selfish."

"You could at least have asked me," I said. "You didn't even give me a choice. You just assumed I would want to be dead and have to drink people's blood to survive. I can't believe I was ever attracted to you."

Justin pushed his glass to the side and leaned across the table.

"I've admitted I was wrong, Kate. I can't do much else. I can only say I'm sorry so many times. But playing in a rock band, being in the public eye, being interviewed by strangers—it's too much of a risk. What are you thinking of?"

"I'm thinking I can do whatever I damn well please—

and you've got nothing to say about it. I've found something I enjoy, and I've found someone I can be with, too."

Justin turned his eyes to Drew and back again. I smiled triumphantly.

"Maybe you'd rather I was still tied up in your stupid bed, helpless and afraid, instead of on stage and in control of my life."

Justin shook his head and rested back against the booth.

"You know," he said, "I hated the sixties and the seventies, and the eighties were just passable, and now it looks like the nineties aren't going to be much better. Keep the condo for as long as you want. Just remember what I told you: Don't reveal to anyone what you are."

"Right." I got up and moved toward Drew, who was giving me quizzical looks from a distance. "Or the villagers will rise up and drive a stake through my heart and burn your precious condo to the ground. Don't worry about me, Justin. Since you've left, I've learned how to take care of myself. Why don't you just go back to the coffin you crawled out of?"

I stormed across the length of the club, never looking back.

"Who the hell was that?" Drew asked. "One of your old boyfriends or what?"

"What makes you say that?" I tried to lead him to the door, but he stopped and looked back toward the table.

"The way you look at him," Drew said. "Like you've told him things you won't tell me."

"That's ridiculous. I haven't told him anything. That man is a complete idiot. I can't stand him."

"Kate?" I heard suddenly from behind me, and Justin was touching my shoulder. "There's one more thing I have to say."

"Look, buddy"—Drew tried to push his arm away—
"the lady has better things to do than talk to you."

Justin turned quietly and looked Drew directly in the
face. The green in his eyes burned.

"You've got to be kidding," he said, and smiled.

And Drew, without knowing why, moved back a few
paces. "It's all right," I said to him, but Drew stood for a
moment transfixed by something in Justin's smile. Something that froze all thoughts of action and left him waiting.

Finally he said, "As long as you're all right," and went
over to join Nathan, who was getting ready to leave for
dinner.

"Well," I said, "what other news flash do you have for
me, Justin? Are you going to warn me about the sunlight
again? Just how many other women have you changed
into vampires and then left to fend for themselves a few
hours before dawn with just a couple of bucks for a hotel?"

"None," he said. And I found myself studying the
curves of his face. "There was only you, Kate."

I sighed in exasperation. How could I have loved that
face?

"And who made you, Justin? Transformed you into the
being you are today? Or were you created on the seventh
night by the devil himself?"

"It might as well have been the devil, Kate, but you
don't really want to know."

"Well, what is it you do want me to know? What ancient secrets are you going to give away? What mysteries
of the Undead are you going to reveal?"

I looked at him impatiently. There had been so many
things I had wanted to ask, but none of them really mattered anymore. And Drew was starting to make his way
back to me.

"Forget it," Justin said, and started to walk toward the door.

"Hey," I said to his back, "don't cause a commotion when you leave by turning into a bat and flying away."

I had just motioned to Drew that I was coming, when suddenly I felt myself backed against the wall with Justin holding my arms.

"I came here to tell you something"—I could feel his nails through my shirt—"so listen for a change. Have you become so hard that I can't even talk to you anymore, Kate?"

I was so surprised at his anger and the tiny bit of pain I felt in my arms, I could only stare at him as Drew and Nathan began to rush to my side. I had been so sure that being immortal also meant being free from pain. Apparently someone could still make me know the meaning of being hurt.

Justin loosened his grip a little, but his body still pressed against mine.

"Forget the jokes, Kate, forget what you think of me now or what I think of you. Forget about condos and coffins and bats and stakes through the heart. Forget about all the thoughts we've shared, all the times I've watched you dream, all the reasons you had for coming back with me to my house. And forget about the moon that's full tonight. Forget about everything, but remember this. If you need me, no matter what, I'll be there. From now on, I'll be there. You may be able to take care of yourself now—or you may not. But if you need me, I'll be there."

He let go of me as Nathan and Drew reached me, and before they could shout out a protest, he was gone. And no one, not even I, saw him leave.

* * *

I had come to hate restaurants, diners, and coffee shops. The way bits of food and grease clung to the walls and the tables, the sleeves of waitresses' uniforms, the plastic liners of worn-out menus. I hated the names of dishes: teriyaki chicken, double beefburger, grilled ham, Polish sausage.

I had decided that cooking was not an art but a disguise, an invention on man's part to cover up the fact that all he was really doing when he broiled and marinated, spiced and flavored, was killing animals and eating their bodies. This was really the main thing that distinguished man from any other species. Not that he could build hotels, produce television shows, laugh at his own jokes. Rather, that man was always trying to pretend that his food was something other than dead meat.

I sat in the red booth of the diner with Drew and Nathan, playing with a salad I would never eat and wishing I had gotten in one good shot to Justin's face. Just one. It was something I had been dying to do for years. Something I should have done that night on the beach. Instead, he got the last word as usual and then vanished without a trace.

I wondered how long it would really be before he demanded his condo back. Before he needed to use his coffin again. Before I was forced to find another retreat, when this had been my white, clean home for almost forever. Had I really ever lived in Tarzana?

And Drew was still pressuring me to take an apartment with him. To share pots and pans, sheets and towels, records and TVs. To sleep together. To wake up together. There was the problem. Waking up together. When I slept a sleep that would probably look like death to him. Frozen. Immobile. Mostly dreamless and maybe defenseless.

I poked at a piece of tomato and sighed. It would be

easier to share an album together than a mailbox. It was easier to play music together than play house.

I decided to think about Matt and CMD and the real possibility of us getting signed, instead. And the band and its fans and its followers. And the way it felt to play bass against Drew's voice, and not how it felt to lie next to him. The distraction, the momentum of the record deal would have to be enough intimacy for Drew and me for now. Hopefully it would be enough to make Drew forget about apartments.

Music had been the force that once led me out of a life of endless darkness. It would have to save me again. I belonged on stage; it was where I wanted to be. And no one even knew my last name. Or where I lived. Or how I lived.

And Justin could just go from one acting class to another or one house to another and imagine he was so much safer in his pursuit of trying to find a place in this world.

Still, I wished I had been able to hit him hard. Right in the middle of those bright green eyes that sparkled even in the dim light of the club.

"Kate," Drew said. "Earth to Kate. I'm talking to you."

"What?"

"I said, if I ever see that guy again, I'll punch his lights out. You know, your wonderful friend in the black leather jacket. Hell, I don't care what you think, Kate, I'm not going to stand around while someone pins you up against a wall. No matter who they are. And since you won't tell me, next time, I'll ask him his name before I kill him."

"Does Charly realize when the show starts?" Nathan asked, trying to get us onto another topic. "He's behaving so weirdly, I'm afraid of what he'll do next."

Nathan was pouring ketchup on his french fries. I watched as some of it dripped onto the table.

"And that guy better not come back to hear us play, either," Drew continued, "because if I see his face in the crowd, I'll tell one of the bouncers to throw him out. I'm not going to put up with this."

"Please," I said, "let's forget it."

"I was asking about Charly," Nathan said again.

"Yes, he knows what time the show is," Drew said. "He's known it for weeks. Even though he's barely communicating with me. In fact, he won't even stand near me anymore." He turned to face me in the seat. "Is that guy a musician or what? Do you know him from another band?"

"He's not a musician," I said, moving the tomato from one side of the plate to another. "He's an actor."

"Well, he'd better go act in another part of the world, 'cause if I see him again, I'll tear his heart out."

"All right, Drew," I said. "If he ever shows his face again, you can tear his heart out. Now can we drop it?"

I put my hand on his, and he softened.

"Okay," he said, "we can drop it. Let's talk about more interesting things, like the record contract that's almost in the bag, or our demo that will be finished right before Christmas, or Nathan's latest girlfriend. How about it, Nathan, are you and Sherrie thinking of moving in together, too?"

And as Drew ate his hamburger and Nathan finished off the rest of his fries, and they talked of other, more interesting things, I turned one piece of lettuce over and over again on my fork, and looked out the window at night closing in.

For fifty minutes time was suspended. The world stood still. The moon lost its power and was replaced by a spotlight, illuminating the way in the darkness. Heads were turned in one direction. Bodies pointing north. Hands were raised. Faces visible for tiny moments. And the stars, swirling outside in the night air, gave up the fight and listened to the music that made every pain of ordinary existence worth enduring for this hour in time.

On stage, you can truly forget all the evils and demons and disasters that plague you in every other place in this world. All the bills you have to pay. All the lovers you need to leave. All the words you forgot to say.

I looked at Drew, I felt my fingers on my bass, and nothing else mattered. Not the tarot cards, not the snow, not green eyes or blue, not the tiny memories of childhood I had lost somehow in a dark cellar, a long time ago. Being onstage was the only time in my life, or my afterlife, when I ever truly felt free.

"I have to talk to you, Kate," Charly said, grabbing my arm. "Before the crowd gets to us, before Matt and the rest of the people from CMD pounce, and we don't have a minute alone."

I had stopped from the pressure of his hand just as we were running off stage after our third encore. Drew and Nathan were already safely inside the dressing room and I could see the mass of people beginning to move in our direction.

"What is it, Charly?" I had been wondering about him all night. Even though he had played well—no one could ever accuse him of not doing his part during a show—mentally he was not on stage with us. Even in the pleasure of performing, I could still feel the weight of his absence. A tiny hole that left us incomplete. The person that had been Charly was gone, and the ghost he left behind did not remember who his friends were or even what a record contract meant.

"What is it?" I said again, but he never got to answer. Matt came running up and kissed me on the cheek. He was wearing a sports jacket over his tee shirt for a change, but like a true Californian, he was still wearing cut-off shorts.

"Quick," he said, "you guys pack up your stuff. I'm taking you to Le Bonheur for some food, drinks, and celebration. The show was great. I've got Lisa, the new head of promotion with me, and she thinks you're wonderful, too. So grab the guys, and let's go party!"

The rest of the crowd had now reached us, and Charly only had time to say "Later" before we were pushed inside the dressing room.

In the resulting confusion, with everyone talking at once and no one making sense, I found I had said "thank you" almost fifty times before I finally handed my bass to Jeff, our roadie. I grabbed my black leather jacket, ready to leave. Then I noticed Drew on the other side of the room, talking to Lisa. She looked to be about thirty and was dressed in black leggings and a low-cut red jacket that revealed a little too much. Her black-dyed hair was permed tight and teased to create an illusion of fullness and style. I motioned to Drew that I would meet him outside the dressing room, and he smiled and rolled his eyes. I could see he was a little worn out from the show, but Matt's offer was one we could hardly refuse.

As I finally reached the door, I started thinking about what Charly could possibly have to say that was so important. He and Nathan had already left for Le Bonheur. I would have to ask him again when I got there. Though I was afraid it was something I really didn't want to hear.

As I stepped outside, someone opened a bottle of champagne, and the popping sound made me jump and drop my car keys at my feet.

"It sounds a lot like a gun, doesn't it?" someone said, as he reached down to pick up the keys for me.

"Yes," I said absently, and turned to see what was keeping Drew.

"It sounds so much like a gun that I'm surprised you didn't drop to the floor like you did in Tower Records, rather than just dropping your keys, miss, ah, Kate. That's it—Kate. I've always liked that name."

As I took the keys from him, I looked directly into Detective Warren's eyes.

"Thanks," I said. "I didn't know you liked rock music, Detective."

"Not usually, but you guys put on a great show. Your reputation is well deserved. I've been wanting to see what it is about this band that's causing all the commotion, all the buzz."

"So you came just to hear us play?"

I looked at Detective Warren and thought, *If I have to, I can always kill him.* He was starting to show up a little too often for my taste.

"I came to hear you play and to satisfy my curiosity. Something I keep wondering about over and over again. Maybe it's the way your band's name keeps coming up at the station. First in one death, then a disappearance, now another person who was connected to you guys is missing and presumed dead. It makes me wonder. Is there any meaning to all this, or is it just one of nature's little coincidences. What do you think, Kate? Is there any meaning?"

"I don't know." I turned to see Drew still talking to Lisa. She was carefully wiping the sweat off his forehead with a tissue. "I don't know if there's any meaning to anything."

"Well, what did you think of this person, Ronny? Was he a nice guy? Did he have any enemies that you know of?"

"I didn't really know him. We only saw him a few times. He and another guy from CMD Records were helping our band."

Detective Warren pulled out a cigarette and lit it with a match. The smoke circled his hand for a moment, then blew away. And he took the used match and stuffed it into the pocket of his trench coat, as if neatness really counted.

"What about the other guys in your band, Kate? Does anything seem, ah, strange about them? Do any of them seem capable of violence?"

"Violence? Not at all. They're great guys. They'd never hurt anyone."

"Even this Charly character, the one who found his friend Mitchell's body?"

"Yes," I said, "even Charly. They're all perfectly normal."

"Okay," the detective said, finally taking a puff of his cigarette, "I guess you're as tired as I am. You probably don't need to stand here and chat with me all night. Let me just give you my card." He placed it in my hand.

"If you ever feel you need to talk to someone about anything. If you're ever afraid. If anyone threatens you. Call me. I will be glad to help you all I can." He smiled. "If it's an emergency and I'm not there, just tell the officer on the phone, and he'll get a hold of me. Any time of the day or night. I can be reached. If you need me, I'll be there."

"Thanks," I said, forcing a smile, and then he turned and left, and I watched the trail of smoke he left behind. Suddenly I felt Drew behind me. He kissed the back of my neck.

"Is this perfect or what?" he said, smiling. "You know, they love us. If this demo turns out the way it's supposed to, I don't think we'll have any trouble getting signed to the record label. And after that, you and I are going to have it all. The life we want—everything. Now let's go party for a while at CMD's expense, and then go home and have our own private party, okay?"

I took his hand, and we walked out to the parking lot. The tiny bit of rain that had fallen had cleared the air and left the night pure and perfect. And because all of our best dreams are only dreamt in the dark, I could not remember what I had ever found attractive about a sunlit sky.

"I guess you think I've been acting a little strange," Charly said.

We were sitting together at one of the back tables at Le Bonheur. I had listened for more than an hour to Matt's theory of why "Without a Country" could be an AOR hit and Lisa's theory of why Ronny had disappeared.

"He was abducted and probably killed because of the drug thing he was involved in," she confided to me. Her long gold earrings shaped like dollar signs got caught in her hair every time she moved her head. "Dealing is always dangerous and not too smart. Everybody knew he was doing it. It was only a matter of time before someone got him."

When Matt ordered the third round of drinks and chocolate mousse for everyone, Charly leaned across the round wooden table and asked if we could talk privately. Nathan, Sherrie, and Drew were involved in a discussion of drum fills, and no one else was clearheaded enough to even wonder where we were going.

"I guess you could call it strange," I said tentatively.

Charly took another sip of wine.

"You know," he said, "I used to think I had a firm grip on life. I knew what I believed in and what I didn't believe in. Things weren't always black or white, but the gray areas were few and far between. Now it seems like I took a wrong turn somewhere. Like I stumbled into the

Phantom Zone. You know, the one in the *Superman* comics. And now reality seems to be fantasy, and what's even worse, everything that was fantasy is becoming real." He gulped down the rest of his wine, then looked around the room to make sure no one was listening.

"And I'm afraid most of the time. Of shadows that stalk my room. Of phones that ring in the night. Of gremlins and ghosts and especially things that fly. And now, Kate, I'm afraid for you."

"Me?" I almost laughed. "Why me?"

Charly leaned back in his chair. "I want a record deal as much as everyone else, Kate. It's not that I want to blow it. I keep trying to make my mind focus on it, but I can't do it all the time. Not when there are other things at stake. Not when there is a matter of life or death. . . . And after all, who's to say that a record contract is any less of an illusion than everything else." He turned to look at the party that was still going on without us.

"I have to be sure first, you know. And it's all so tricky. What if I'm wrong?"

"Wrong about what?" I wondered what Charly was getting at now.

"About Drew. And then I ruin the record deal for all of us. Or just for myself, if everyone thinks I'm nuts. But if I'm right . . . and I wait? . . ." He leaned in toward me. "Kate, I didn't know you were going with Drew. Not until I saw you two kissing before the show. If I'm right about him, he could do something to you before I have a chance to stop him."

"Stop him from what, Charly?"

"From hurting you, or even worse, subjecting you to a fate worse than death. I couldn't live with myself if that happened, and I could have prevented it."

"I don't know what you're talking about," I said, but

that little voice I tended to ignore nowadays said I did, and it gave me a chill.

"I have a friend. He's a doctor, really. He's helped me face my fears. He's shown me how to deal with them. The same thing happened to him almost twenty-five years ago. He lost his brother the same way. Just like Mitch." Charly's face was flushed with excitement. "He's been tracking the killer all his life, and now he thinks he's found another one, not the original, but a creature just like him, right in our band. He picked up on this killer in Vegas, and when he learned the details of Mitch's death, he immediately flew to L.A. He knew it had to be some-one close to our band. Actually, someone right in our band."

The word *Vegas* gave me a sharp jolt as if someone had just walked on my grave. I shuddered, but Charly didn't notice.

"He's made it his life's work to hunt down these crea-tures and destroy them. All of their kind. I didn't believe him at first. But he took me to these meetings. This club. Where others believe. He made me see. Now I just have to be sure."

"Look, Charly," I said, "you're not making any sense. What did he make you see that others believe? What club? What doctor? What the hell are you talking about?"

"He was a coroner, really—you know, he examined dead bodies, determined the cause of death. He's retired now. He devotes his life exclusively to hunting them down and wiping them off the face of the earth."

"Off the face of the earth?" I said, wondering exactly what that statement really meant.

"Yes, Kate, though he's not really sure what works. He hasn't really come face-to-face with one of them since his brother's death. So there's always a question about what renders them powerless. Maybe holy water, maybe a stake through the heart."

Stake through the heart? Now there was a threatening thought. I felt my teeth ache to reveal themselves, but I calmed myself down and tried to make sense of Charly's melodramatic rambling.

"Maybe this miracle drug would work. I don't know. So I guess I'll have to wait. At least until we're signed. Then if I'm wrong . . . no one will suffer. I just wanted to warn you, Kate. I know I can't make you see right away. Just watch him. See what he does. Don't let him touch you, especially not your neck."

"Charly"—I leaned in toward him—"what are you accusing Drew of?"

He looked down at the table and thought for a moment, debating about what word to use. What noun would best describe a thing that could fly.

"I guess what I think he might be, Kate, is a vampire. A being that lives on the blood of others. A being that isn't human, at least not anymore."

"Wait a minute, Charly," I said, trying to suppress a smile. "You're trying to tell me that Drew's not human?"

The growing sense of dread that had been building up in me evaporated in a moment. Suddenly I had an image of Drew, complete with fangs and a black and red cape, rising out of a coffin to hunt down another beer and a few potato chips.

"Yeah, definitely not human. It's nothing to laugh about. I don't know when it happened to Drew. Sometime before you joined the band. It may even be a gradual process—we don't know. We also don't know if they really only live at night. If they sleep all day like the ancient myths or what. The doctor says he does know that they don't have to kill every night. More like every month or every two or three months. And they can decide who they want to feed on. It's not like they're totally out of control."

We're never out of control, Charly, I thought but, instead, said out loud, "Go on." I had to hear the rest.

"So maybe Drew won't harm you. Maybe you're safe. Maybe he just wants to be with you and not drink your blood. Maybe vampires want relationships as much as everyone else. Although why a member of the Undead needs a record contract, I'll never know. He could have anything he wants . . . anything. Well, I just wanted to warn you. . . . Please, whatever you do, don't let him know you're aware of his secret. It could be dangerous. Just keep your distance. Be careful, Kate. Once we're signed, I'll make my move."

I stared at Charly, completely fascinated. "And what move is that?"

"The doctor and I will determine if he's the genuine thing, and then we'll render him powerless."

"You mean you'll kill him?"

"If we have to. Or if the Doctor does perfect this drug, we'll try to change him back. Make him mortal once more. That's if he even wants to join the human race again."

I thought for a minute what it would be like to become mortal again. What if there were a way? Would I even want to take it anymore? But then, Charly's doctor was probably as much of a vampire curer as Drew was a vampire.

Charly stopped and studied me. "You think I'm crazy, don't you? You're just like everyone else. You think finding Mitch's body put me over the edge, and I'm not coming back, don't you?"

"Well"—I tried to placate him—"this stuff about vampires is a little hard to swallow. . . ."

Charly shook his head. "Why don't you come with me

to this club, sometime? You should listen to what they have to say. It's a club for people who believe in the supernatural, who accept the fact that vampires and ghosts exist, and who want to share information. Or just talk to the doctor. I want you to keep an open mind, Kate. This world is not what it seems."

"I wish someone had told me that a few years ago," I said, and smiled. "Okay, Charly, I'll be careful; it never hurts to watch your back. But I do love Drew, and I think you're way out of line, accusing him of being a vampire of all things. Life is too short for you to go alienating your friends. I think all you're doing is creating a bogeyman to explain away a murder that can't be solved."

I got up to join the party again, but Charly was still in his chair, staring at the water stains on the table. I reached down and lightly touched his shoulder.

"Why don't you calm down, Charly? Get a little more sleep. Stop looking for monsters in the dark, and start acting normal so we can finish this demo and get a record deal. You know as well as I do that Drew is as human as the rest of us. Start listening to your friends again, instead of this doctor."

Charly sighed and stood up to join me. I noticed his clothes seemed loose. He had lost even more weight, probably another ten pounds. He seemed to be fading away. I could probably knock him through the wall with just the touch of my little finger.

"You know, Kate," he said, as we walked across the room, "sometimes I wish I had never met the doctor, that I had been able to forget Mitch's death, that you had fallen in love with me instead of Drew." I looked at him in surprise.

"My life would have been very different. Now we've all made our choices, and all that wishing is a little too late.

Just be careful, Kate. That's all I ask. I don't want anything bad to happen to you."

I looked at Charly for what seemed like the first time. He seemed more like a child than a man. And suddenly I wanted to be able to lead him out of the Phantom Zone. To bring him back into the life we had been brought up to believe existed. He was, after all, my friend. I wanted to make him safe. But how could I? I was only a fantasy, something dreamt of in horror tales, and I had no power to take away his fear anymore.

"More chocolate mousse!" Matt screamed, as we reached the table, and I looked at Drew, still smiling as I sat down next to him.

"Did you talk some sense into Charly?" he asked hopefully. "It better have worked, because Matt just told me that if Charly doesn't shape up and start acting like a person, he's going to find us a new guitar player. And despite how irritated I've been at Charly lately, I'd hate to see that happen. It would set the rest of us back, too. We'd have to teach someone else all the songs and then wait for our showcase gig for CMD till the new guitarist was ready."

"I tried," I said. But Charly was staring out the window again, and I could see by the five plates of uneaten chocolate mousse in front of him and the frozen look in his eyes that he was lost in the Phantom Zone again.

I was meeting Drew at ten for a movie in Westwood, but the church was on the way. I saw its steeple first, pointing toward heaven in the first glow of the moonlight, and I followed it like a beacon.

Churches had always fascinated me when I was a little girl. White and solid on the outside, dark and brooding inside. Where statues dressed in purple and dark red stared at you with haunted and hungry eyes. Where stained-glass visions and stations of the cross lined the walls. Where God hid inside a tiny tabernacle, locked up and unreachable.

I did not even try the door. I knew it would not open. Instead, I dissolved into dust and floated through the keyhole, finding my body again on the other side in the dark. As I materialized in the center of the church, I felt a twinge of fear.

It was like going back in time. Even the smell was the same. The odor of incense, palm leaves, and Communion wafers. A few of the votive candles flickered and went out, and for a moment, I wondered if God would vaporize me for entering a church when I had probably lost my soul.

I stood quietly, waiting for the worst. But lightning did not strike. The sky did not fall. Just as our prayers are never answered, neither were my fears.

I turned slowly in a circle, surveying my surroundings. The red glow of the candles gave me enough light to see: the dark wooden pews, the ornate altar, a statue of Saint Sebastian, and a choir loft above. Finally my eyes rested on what I was searching for. It looked like a cement birdbath in the far corner, with a picture of the Sacred Heart presiding over it. The container that held the holy water.

I heard a little noise, and I whirled around, afraid that I was not alone, that some other angel or devil was in town for the night. But the church was empty till morning. The only movement was the flicker of another red candle as it struggled and died.

I walked over to the font at the back of the church and looked in, debating what action to take.

While I knew Charly was as helpless as a kitten and this doctor about as threatening as a dishrag, it still made me wonder. What if this man who imagined himself to be a modern-day Van Helsing had stumbled upon one of the ancient myths that was true? What if sunlight wasn't my only curse?

Even if he was stupid enough to decide Drew was one of the Undead and would never suspect me, I still thought it better to check his theory out. In case I needed to be prepared. Every once in a while a fool gets lucky and then proceeds to do foolish things.

Water stagnated in the basin. For all intents and purposes, it appeared as if it came out of the tap. But supposedly it had been blessed. That's what they taught us in Catholic school. That's what I used to believe. What if touching it burned my skin? What if I melted away? I hesitated for a moment. What if it hurt? Still, I had to know.

I raised the tip of my pinky finger and dipped it in. There was no smoke. There was no pain. I lowered the rest of my finger. Nothing. No reaction. Finally I reverted to my final test.

Touching my forehead first, then my chest, left shoulder, then right, I made the sign of the cross, dropping the holy water at each place.

I waited, but God did not strike me down. No burning bush. No voice from above. Holy water was as useless as the rosary beads I'd carried as a child. It was a lie like everything else.

"A lie," I said out loud, and with my left hand, I lifted the concrete font off its stand and threw it to the ground. It broke into several large pieces. The holy water leaked through the hardwood floor into oblivion.

"Like everything else."

I heard a noise again.

This time it was more distinctly human, the sound of a shoe scraping, of someone getting ready to run. And I lifted my eyes from the broken birdbath to look into the frightened face of a young priest only several feet away.

"What are you?" he whispered, and I knew by the expression in his eyes, he had seen my grand entrance and my display of strength.

"I'm a little bit of hell," I said, "who's going to be late for the movies. Unless, of course, you'd like to hear my confession?"

He began to back away, sure he had seen the devil incarnate, intent on damaging church property just to be a pain in the neck.

"Bless me, Father, for I have sinned. . . ."

He made the sign of the cross. He shook his head.

"It's been a lifetime since my last confession."

He turned in the direction of the altar.

"Father, I've killed a man—several, as a matter of fact. By now the body count is probably ten or twelve. But I don't think it's a mortal sin. Do you, Father? Not when you aren't human anymore?"

At that point he began to move faster, and even though I had better things to do, I ran after him.

I should have just disappeared. Who would ever believe his tale? A figure dressed in black materialized in his church and proceeded to knock over the holy water font in one of the ultimate acts of defiance against God.

Still, I couldn't just let him go. And there was something about someone running that made me want to join in the chase.

"Wait, you haven't heard the best part. I went through twelve years of Catholic school, and I have the teeth to prove it."

He reached the altar and stopped to stare at me. I stood before him, my fangs gleaming in what seemed like the red glow of hell that had opened for a moment to release one of its own.

He held out the cross he was wearing around his neck. "Satan, leave this place."

"Wrong again, Jack. That stuff doesn't work. You might as well throw it away. All that junk you learned in the seminary is about as useful as sacrificing dead goat heads. You'd better get hip. There are vampires out there. And they drive Porsches and take acting classes, and they even own condos in Santa Monica."

I laughed, and he gasped a little in fear. But he didn't drop his cross. He didn't believe me. And that made me angry. I wanted to show him that everything we had been taught to believe was wrong. Dead wrong.

"But you still haven't answered me, Father. Do any of these killings count? When I do them to survive?" I raised my hand toward heaven. "Will God forgive me if I say one Our Father and two Hail Marys? Does God even know that I'm no longer alive?"

"God?" he repeated after me. "God? . . ."

And then he backed up a little too quickly and tumbled over the last step before the tabernacle. He swung his arms in the air for a moment and then fell flat onto the floor.

I heard the crack as his head hit the stone. His eyes were open but sightless, staring up at a heaven he hoped was still there.

I walked over and sat down next to him, surprised that he had died as easily as people in murder mysteries do. And I noticed the pool of blood that was gathering by his head. All that warmth running out of him.

And with the same finger that had touched the holy water, I reached over and dipped it into his blood and brought it to my lips for a taste, still delicious, after the first touch of death.

And then I lay down next to him, moving his head to the side, and began to lick up all the blood that would have gone to waste on the altar. I cleaned up every drop with my tongue until I left God's house as immaculate as I had found it.

But I did not leave a mark on the man. I had no need to take anything left inside. I merely closed his eyes and told him one more time. "It's a lie, like everything else."

"I'm sorry I was late, Drew," I said again. "You know how traffic is in L.A." I had missed the movie by twenty minutes, and it was the last showing of the night.

He looked at me from across the table as the waitress set down another beer. "It's not just the movie, Kate," he said irritably, "it's everything."

"Everything?" I asked.

"Well, actually, it's this apartment thing. You find something wrong with every one we look at. And if we lived together in the same God damn place, we wouldn't have to meet for a movie, we could drive there together. And it would be so much easier. Especially when we start to make the record. Then you wouldn't have to work at that stupid accounting job or whatever you do all day, and I could quit selling shoes, and we would both be in the same place all the time. Sleep—and I really mean sleep—together. Make love. Write songs. . . . I'm tired of you always running home right before dawn. It's getting ridiculous. Why do you have to fight me every inch of the way? I thought you wanted to live with me."

"I do." Outside the window, people were milling by. Mostly tourists and students of UCLA. "We'll find the right place soon, Drew." And I reached under the table and rubbed his leg, my hand moving smoothly over his jeans. "Soon," I said again.

He brought his hand down and grabbed mine. "You always know how to distract me." He turned to the waitress who was passing. "Check, please. Okay, Kate, let's go home—at least it's my home, anyway."

I smiled at him, knowing I had bought a little time again. But I was starting to take that time for granted.

Sleep, when it came over me, was sudden and swift. There was no time for preparations. Dawn approached, and I knew it was only a matter of time before I was robbed of all mobility, all signs of life. I lay down on the white sheets of Justin's bed. The sun rose. My breathing stopped. And I was gone.

Until night again.

But sometimes I missed those precious moments before sleep. The interim that marked the space between conscious thought and dreams. The time when you could let your mind wander over the day's events or the days before. The time to recall memories and bring meaning to them. The time to create fantasies and let them run.

I missed those moments because they were gone.

It was 5:35, fifteen minutes before dawn. I turned my head and looked at Justin's closet, trying to recall my mother's maiden name. It was something they asked on every application for insurance or for employment. It started with a D. Or was it a C? I went through the alphabet, searching phonetically, but it would not come to mind.

I could see my mother standing on our porch and her mother standing beside her, but I couldn't connect. Another memory gone. Another line broken. And they break as easily as dead leaves off a plant you've been trying to save. Brown and cracked. Returning to dust and blowing away. My mother's name. I had forgotten it as easily as a stranger's. Something you hear once then let go of as soon as you can.

And as I waited for the signs of rigidity, which I always felt first in my little toe, I realized there is a moment when the unnatural becomes natural. And that's when you start to take it for granted.

"Look at this one," Nathan said, pointing to himself in the photograph. His eyes were closed again. "I do that almost every time I see the flash."

"But you look so cute," Sherrie said, smiling at him.

"Well, I know I'm cute, but we've got to settle on one publicity picture where everyone looks human. Kate and Drew look perfect in every picture. Charly always looks depressed, so it's hopeless there. But I don't want to come off as a drunken, drug-crazed drummer, so I guess it's between these three."

He handed the proofs back to Drew, who was lying on his sofa with his head in my lap.

"Okay, Nathan," he said. "I can live with any of these three. What do you think, Kate? If they're all right with you, and we don't care what Charly thinks, we'll leave the final selection to the man in the know, Matt."

"No problem," I said, studying the proofs again. I was still amazed to see myself captured on film.

The night before the publicity pictures were to be taken, I had run out to the nearest department store and bought a camera that developed pictures instantly. Even though I had been able to see my reflection in the mirror, there was always the possibility that Kodak wouldn't be able to capture a vampire's image. I loaded the film, pointed it at my face, and winced when the flash hit my eyes.

When the picture popped out, I was almost afraid to look. What if there was nothing there? The image of a ghost cannot be copied. Isn't that what the legends said? How would I explain to the band that I couldn't be photographed? What excuse could I give Drew?

But the holy water hadn't worked, and the mirror had

reflected my face, so why should any other half-forgotten myth be true? And when I examined the photo, it was nothing more than me, my eyes wide and golden, staring at the blaze of an artificial sun. Me but not me. Someone like me. Someone I had never seen before on film.

"Hey, guys?" Nathan said. "What are you two doing for Thanksgiving? Now that Sherrie and I are living together, rock 'n' roller or not, I've got to bring her to my parents' house for turkey."

"That reminds me," Drew said, sitting up, "I've already said yes to my mom about us coming over next Thursday. I didn't think you'd mind since your folks aren't around. Why not spend it with my family?"

"What?" I said softly.

"Well, where else would you be going, Kate? You'll love my parents, and you can break your diet for once and try some of my mother's famous pumpkin pie."

"Pie," I said, starting to feel ill. "Pie?"

"Is there some kind of problem with my mother's pie or Thanksgiving in general?"

"No," I said, "it's just—"

"It's just what?"

"Oh, I'd, ah, rather be alone, I think."

"Oh, really." He stood up and walked to the kitchen for another beer. I heard the refrigerator door open and the click of an aluminum tab.

"Uh oh," Nathan said. "I think that's our cue to leave."

"No," Drew said. "Why go now? Why don't we all hear why Kate wants to be alone? Not only on Thanksgiving but every other day of the week. At least, she doesn't want to be with me. What is it, Kate? Have you got some other guy stashed away in this condo I never get to see? Maybe it's that jerk friend of yours with the leather jacket. The one that looks like he buys all his clothing in the same store you do. And that's another thing—"

"Drew," I said, cutting him off, "calm down. I didn't really say no."

"I really think we've got to get home." Nathan edged toward the door. "Isn't that right, Sherrie?"

"Oh, I see." Drew stormed around the living room. "You didn't really say no *yet*. You want to drag it on till I get tired of asking. Just like the apartment thing. You put me off and put me off. Hoping I'll forget. Well, I'm not letting this one drop. I want to know, Kate. Are you coming with me to my parents' house for Thanksgiving or not? Yes or no?"

Nathan and Sherrie were poised at the door, afraid to make another move. Drew stood over me while I stared at the food stains on his rug. They had formed some amazing patterns.

"Yes or no?"

I wondered how I would deal with the turkey. How I would deal with the pie. Not only could I no longer put food near my lips, I could barely watch humans when they ate. But most of all how I would ever get around the problem of daylight. Still, sometimes you have to be brave.

"Yes." I remembered how difficult Thanksgiving could be without all these nonhuman problems.

"Good." Drew sat down on the sofa again with a satisfied expression on his face. "And for this one time, I really think you should wear some clothes that aren't black."

When it came right down to it, black was the only color I could wear.

I tried. I really did. I went from one fitting room to another, blinking my eyes against the fluorescent lighting I had come to hate, and stared at someone I hardly recognized anymore. Someone who could no longer wear blue or brown or God forbid, red. Even gray seemed inappropriate.

It was like dressing a corpse in fuchsia for a wake. It was wrong. Totally and completely wrong.

Once upon a time Kate was at home in cool, muted tones. The colors of spring. Or was it summer? I couldn't remember. What did it matter when the seasons never changed?

I turned sideways in the mirror, viewing another pastel dress, the fifth one for the night, and felt as if I were wearing a neon sign that flashed: Look at Me—I'm Dead! I heard the voices of women, laughing about what didn't fit, telling their children what they couldn't afford. They echoed through the dressing-room walls.

Without any effort or another thought I brought my hand up and smashed the mirror into pieces. Glittering, tiny pieces that could no longer cast my complete reflection.

The laughter stopped. I heard the women gasp and wonder, but no one actually came out to look. Ultimately they were only interested in what color looked right on them. How many bargains they could find in the short time left to them.

While I had forever. And forever is a long time to waste shopping.

I thought of Thanksgiving decorations. The ones we used in grade school. Cardboard cutouts of Pilgrims and turkeys. Pilgrim's hats with buckles. Bunches of corn that were brown instead of yellow.

And we drew pictures of the *Mayflower* landing. And Plymouth Rock. The Indians shaking hands and sitting down with the white men to eat, teaching us the value of maize.

We hung them on the school windows and on the bulle-

tin boards to celebrate this historic event, this day of giving thanks. But everyone knew what it really meant—
there was only a month to go before Christmas.

"I absolutely cannot eat," I said to Drew, as we drove
to Ventura. "I told you what the doctor said."

"Oh, come on, Kate, a little turkey is not going to hurt
a stomach virus. Besides, you don't look sick to me. You
look great, as a matter of fact. I just wish you had canned
the black clothes for once. We don't have to live our rock
star image every minute. My mother's going to think it's
weird. To say nothing of the fact that I told them we
couldn't be there before eight. Thanksgiving is an after-
noon kind of holiday. How could you have been so sick
only six hours ago that you could not even come to the
phone and now you're sitting here with me? Of course, I
threatened to come over and drag you out of the house,
once I found it, which is enough to make anyone instantly
recover."

I looked at a sign that said Camarillo, two miles.

"I'll be fine. . . . I just can't eat."

Drew's parents lived at the end of a cul-de-sac in a red
ranch house, with white wooden ducks surrounding the
rose garden.

I had expected a quiet family dinner. Drew's mother
eyeing my black clothing as I sat in front of an empty
plate, feigning illness. His father wondering about my
background, asking accounting questions I could not answer. And his younger brother, Joe, finding ways to trick
me, to get me to tell something revealing about my nighttime existence.

Instead, it was a mob scene. Aunts and uncles, cousins
and friends, all bearing foods too numerous to mention.
Too numerous for anyone to notice who had eaten and

who had not and how much. There was no set schedule, the turkey was on the table until the last bone was gone, plates strewn everywhere, laughter, talking, fun. In the background the stereo shouted, and the TV and the kitchen radio.

Downstairs Drew and Joe played pool in between turkey legs and biscuits. Opening a beer to wash it down. Telling each other private jokes, then explaining them to me. While Uncle Ed kept score, Aunt Martha offered everyone advice on how to beat the flu. Children chased each other. A baby cried. I smiled. I remembered. This is what it was like to have a family. This is what it was like to belong again. I had forgotten how comfortable it could feel.

I felt a tug on my arm, and Drew's mother pulled me into the living room. "I wanted to show you these," she said, displaying a box of photos.

I sat on the couch and watched as Drew's life unfolded. An infant in a bunny suit, a fair-haired toddler, a child reaching for a toy, his first school picture, graduation, his first band.

"Mom!" Drew cried, sitting down next to me. "Don't show her these."

I brushed a bit of stuffing from his face.

"You know," Mrs. Andersen said, "Drew's father and I met through music also—actually it was the high school band. He played drums. I played the clarinet. He always marched in back of me, and I guess that's what did it."

Drew put his arm around me and held me close. But outside, the wind had started to blow. Even in California the November air was turning cold. Tomorrow morning there would be frost on the wooden ducks' wings. And somewhere inside me, I could feel the chill.

His mother shivered and went to shut a window. I touched the picture of Drew as a baby. Smiling, years ago. Someday he would grow old while I would stay the same. He would get sick. He would die. "Look," his mother said, "it's already after midnight." And she went off to look for his father, who had fallen asleep after his third helping of pumpkin pie.

"I don't know why we didn't just stay over," Drew said, as I flipped through the car radio, looking for something interesting. "I know she would have made us sleep in separate rooms, but that's nothing new for us. Why do you have this obsession with sleeping in your own house? I think my mother was a little insulted. Neither of us have work tomorrow, and there's no band practice."

I paused for a moment on a song by the Stones, listening to the guitar work.

"And you could have eaten a little something, some turkey at least. And Aunt Mary thought you were going to a funeral. I asked you to wear a different color, but apparently my opinion counts for nothing. And I don't see why you can never have a beer with me, cut loose a little. . . . I thought—"

"Look," I said, snapping off the radio, "if I had known this was a test, I never would have gone." I was thinking of Drew as a baby in a bunny suit. He would grow old. He would die.

"What's that supposed to mean?" Drew's hands tightened around the steering wheel.

"I mean if you had wanted someone to fit the approved guidelines for girlfriend, you never should have hooked up with me."

"What do you mean?" he asked. "You know I love you."

"I mean you should love me as I am. Do you want a rock 'n' roller, nightlifer, song partner, or do you want someone like Joe's girlfriend, Tammy, who studies prelaw just like him, lives two blocks away, wears a dress, and thinks music means the stuff they pipe into elevators? You'd better get your priorities straight, Drew. Are you a musician or a yuppie?"

"I thought Tammy was nice."

"Fine."

"Yeah, fine."

I turned the radio on for a second, then turned it off again.

"If you wanted to marry someone just like 'dear old Dad' did, you picked the wrong girl."

Drew turned to look at me; then his eyes found the road again.

"Maybe I do want to get married someday, Kate, once the music gets settled and makes us rich. What's so bad about that?"

"It's so typically middle class." So typically human.

"Oh, so that's what you think of my family? They're too middle class for you? Well, maybe I'm too middle class for you, too. Maybe I think it's a little weird that you never sleep over at my apartment. Maybe I think it's weird I still don't know your address, exactly what you do all day, or anything about this family of yours that lives a mysterious existence somewhere on the East Coast. . . . Maybe I am too middle class for someone who seems to be hatched right out of an egg!"

"An egg?" I said. "An egg?"

"That's right, an egg. Maybe what you need is a boyfriend who treats you bad, cheats on you, sees you when he feels like it, destroys property, drinks, and takes drugs. Maybe a lowlife bastard is more your style. Maybe it would have been easier if we had just stayed friends, members of the same band, that's all."

"Is that what you want, Drew?" I shouted at him. "Because I'm sick of you always asking me a lot of stupid, personal questions. I have no intention of answering to anyone, least of all you. As far as I'm concerned, we can go right back to being colleagues—and I wouldn't blink an eye."

"Fine," he said, "then that's what it will be. We'll go back to the way it was. No questions. No nothing. We'll keep the band together because that's still good. But you can go your way, and I'll go mine. No more questions, Kate, and no one will ever know where you live."

"That suits me just fine," I said.

And the only sound the rest of the way home was the wind that rose up out of the desert, cold and cruel. Battering the car. Shaking the windows. Sending static through the airwaves. Blowing us away.

I was better off without him. I was sure of it.

It had started as an easygoing, rock 'n' rolling kind of affair and had turned into the relationship from hell. I didn't need it. I had enough problems just trying to decide if hell really existed, let alone living in it on a full-time basis.

If I had wanted a demanding and predictable life, I could have run right back to Ben and let him badger me with questions and insinuations about my new style of existence. Let him tell me how to dress and why. I could have been pressured by my own family instead of someone else's. I could have confessed to old and familiar faces. Confided my blood lust to people who had known me as a normal person for years. Had loved me as a child.

I had thought Drew was an ideal human companion for me—independent, fun, and sexy. But I was wrong. I thought I loved him, enjoyed him, but he needed too much. I thought he would be happy just to play music with me and have me in his bed. I thought I could be a vampire, and he'd never know. That he'd never ask so many questions. I had forgotten how demanding humans could be. But I had given up all my ties to humanity. Renounced my name. And I was sure as hell not ready to take on someone else's again.

I decided it was about time I played the field. I had been married to Ben for five long years, spent two forgettable nights with Justin, and then had gone right back to a monogamous relationship with Drew that had started to border on courtship.

What I needed to do was go out and have a good time. No ties involved. No one to answer to. Men with no names. Only faces and bodies. And L.A. was certainly the town to do it in. Why had I ever wasted so much time feeling sorry for myself in that abandoned cellar?

I was twenty-seven, and I always would be. I looked great, played music with a hip band, and was soon to have the world at my feet. Why whittle away the hours with a man who claimed black was his favorite color and then was embarrassed when I wore it to his parents' house? As if we were going to church or the school prom. A man whose happiness depended on me drinking beer with him and waking up with him in the morning. A man who was getting a little too close for comfort.

At rehearsal the week after Thanksgiving, Drew was cool and distant, I cold and detached, Nathan nervous, and Charly surprised and a little suspicious. Only Matt with his usual lack of observation noticed nothing, or perhaps he just didn't care about the personal side of the band.

Despite our differences, Drew and I still performed up to par, and our tape was only two weeks away from completion. We were taking those weeks off to give our ears a rest. When you spend hour after hour in a studio trying to get each part right, finding the perfect sound for that part, and then recording it perfectly, you need to take a

break before you do a final mix. Before you take the
twenty-four tracks of music and vocals and combine them
into a two-track stereo master tape. We would do the mix
three days before Christmas. Then Matt would present it
to CMD the first week of the new year, and they would
decide whether we were signed to the label or not. A lot
was riding on this tape, the very future of the band, but
we all felt confident that things would turn out right. Everything was going according to plan. It was meant to be.
It was in the cards.

It was the fifth night of vacation, and I was enjoying my
independence. I woke up feeling rested and ready to
party. I had slept in Justin's coffin again for fun, and it
had felt good. I understood now why he found it so comfortable, so secure. There was something very natural
about being enclosed. It was dark and safe. No light could
ever penetrate. No one could ever find me there. And
dreams of Justin no longer haunted me when I slept in his
resting place.

I pushed open the lid and looked at the dark red walls
and smiled. I had been limiting myself, sticking to my old,
very human, way of thinking. Tonight I was going to do
what I pleased. I was going to get dressed, and I was
going out on the town.

The Fox and the Hound was the place to go in Hollywood. Nathan had recommended it as the place to pick
up people of the opposite sex. As a matter of fact, he had
met Sherrie there. So I fired up the Porsche, blasted the
radio, and headed east, my hair blowing up toward
heaven as I opened the sunroof and took in the night.

It had rained earlier, and the air smelled of wet wood
and saturated cement. The smell reminded me of home.
But now, instead of feeling sad, I realized home was just a

memory and relegated it to its proper place. Not forgotten but definitely replaced.

It was 11:00 P.M., and the club was just beginning to get crowded. Its main bar was inside, but there were also two outside bars on a large patio complete with metal chairs and tables.

I sat down at one of the tables and ran my finger along the residue of moisture that was waiting to evaporate in tomorrow's sunlight. "Gin and tonic," I said to the waitress, and watched as she scurried through the maze of orange lights leading to the bar. In between the orange lights were men, mostly unattached, all with different names and faces.

I looked them over and wondered, but I decided to take my time. To wait until the right face appeared. The right one for tonight. But before the waitress even returned with my drink, someone decided for me. Without even making eye contact, he walked toward me, pulled a chair over, and sat down.

"You look lonely." He pushed up the sleeves of his brown leather jacket. His hair was the color of his jacket, and his eyes were dark. "Well, maybe lonely isn't what you are. Maybe *detached* is the right word. Aloof. Unattainable. Removed from the rest of us peasants. An observer in the game of life."

I touched the sleeve of his jacket to see how soft the leather felt.

"Still, I'm not afraid of you. I know you for what you are. You're just as scared and terrified as the rest of us. You put up this cool facade to protect yourself, but I'm just the kind of guy you need to tear it down. I'm really good at handling women who think they're better than everyone else."

"Really?" I said. "You figured this out all by yourself?"

"That's right, baby." And he let his arm drape around

the back of my chair. I wondered if he used this technique with every girl he wanted to meet. The waitress returned with my drink and another for him.

"Let me," he said, handing her the money, and she disappeared again into the orange lights. "Did you ever hear of the band The Immaculate Destruction?"

I nodded slightly. I had seen their name at some of the smaller clubs in town.

"Well, I'm the band's lead player. Do you like metal, baby? Hard-rocking, hard-driving metal, with a little leather thrown in for good measure?"

"I suppose you could talk me into it," I said absently, as I looked around the patio again. It was almost time to lose this guy.

My gaze stopped at a table in the back that I hadn't noticed before. A man was sitting by himself, reading what looked to be a script. I took a quick breath in disbelief. "God damn it," I whispered out loud, "this had better be a coincidence, or I will punch him right between the eyes for sure."

"Hey, baby, don't get violent on me so quickly. It's too early for any of that. Whose eyes are you talking about anyway?"

I looked at Justin's hair, which was back to normal, and the precise line on his neck where it reached his shoulders. I watched his hands caress the script, his nails a little longer than a normal man's. He closed his eyes for a moment, and I forgot what it was about them that had inspired me to such heights of hatred. All I could remember was how green they really were.

"Excuse me, baby, but I don't pay for your drink and then let you look at some other man like you mean business. You are mine for tonight, and my women know how to behave. Pay attention, or you are outta here."

"You're the one's that out of here," I said, standing up and leaving the gin and tonic behind. "I like your jacket, but that's about it for me."

With my right foot I kicked the chair out from under him, and he went sprawling, long hair and all, into another table of heavy metalers, who decided to take vengeance on his leather jacket. I heard his screams as I walked over to Justin, determined to be nice for a change.

"Hi," I said, looking down on him.

He looked up, smiling, then stopped abruptly. "Kate?"

"Hi," I said again, debating about whether to sit down.

"If you're going to lecture me again about how much I've ruined your life, I really don't want to hear it. I've told you I'm sorry. I can't be any sorrier or any guiltier. And there doesn't seem to be anything I can do to make it up to you."

"No." I lowered myself onto the seat. "I don't need to go over ancient history again."

He put the script on the table and turned to look at a couple passing by. "Where is that blond boyfriend of yours tonight?"

"He's home," I said. "I go out alone sometimes. I like to be alone when I'm in the mood for it."

"You never used to, Kate. You used to be afraid of being alone."

"Did I?" I said. "I don't remember."

His eyes flickered past me, looking out at the night shifting just beyond the patio lights.

"Why, Justin?" I said, catching his eyes.

"Why what?"

I extended my hand a little as if to touch him. "Why did you change me, make me like you? Why me? I still wake up every night and wonder, why me?"

"Because you said my name."

"What?"

"In your sleep. You said my name. I sat at the edge of your bed and watched you for several nights in a row. I saw your husband snoring on the other side of the bed, his back toward you, his hands pressed against himself. And I saw you, crying in your sleep, reaching out to someone who wasn't there . . . and then you said my name. Not once, not twice, but three times. Justin. You said my name. And that's when I knew I loved you. When I heard you call out to me in the darkness, afraid you were alone. I knew I loved you. And I wanted to make sure you were never alone again."

I looked down at the table, unable to think of anything to say. Why hadn't I felt him at my side, reaching through my dreams? If only I had known.

"But I was wrong, Kate. And if there was a way I could reverse the process, I would risk everything to change you back. I would give you back to that man still snoring somewhere in Tarzana, and I wouldn't have to keep telling you how sorry I am. At least you can't say you're bored like you were when I met you. As you told me at your sound check, you're in love and you're playing music, something you enjoy. . . ."

"Justin," I said, but I was interrupted by the arrival of a petite, curly-haired blonde. Her blue dress shone in the moonlight.

"Justin," she said, "I'm sorry I'm late, but rehearsal ran overtime again."

She looked down at me in surprise, but I didn't relinquish my seat.

"Denise, this is Kate. Kate, Denise."

"Are you an actress, too?" she asked, as Justin got up and offered his seat to her. She laid her purse on the table and smoothed the fabric of her dress.

"Definitely not," I said, wondering how anyone's hair could be that curly. She looked up at Justin and smiled.

"Isn't that just the perfect part for me?" She pointed to the script still lying on the table. "I can't wait for you to read with me."

Justin started to speak, but I cut him off.

"Don't rehearse any scenes with him alone," I said, "unless you want to wake up one night tied up with your clothes missing off the face of the earth."

"Excuse me?" she said, staring at me as if for the first time.

"And in the name of God, do not, under any circumstances, drink any red wine he offers you." I smiled a little. "Do you know, Denise, that he sleeps in a coffin?"

She turned to Justin in confusion.

"Kate was just leaving." He pulled my arm slightly.

"That's right. I'm leaving. But seriously, Denise, ask yourself this. Have you ever, under any conditions, seen this man in the daylight? Think about it. Think about it hard. Have you ever seen him during the day?"

At that point Justin pulled me out of my seat. I could feel his nails through my shirt. "Damn it, Kate," he whispered, "stop."

I pulled back my head and shook my finger at him. "Oh, I've forgotten the golden rule: Don't ever tell."

"My ex," he said apologetically to Denise. "You know how it is. She got the Porsche. She got the condo on the west side—but it just isn't enough, is it, Kate?"

He pulled me out into the circle of orange lights. "Let's not fight," he said softly. "I'm still a lot older and a lot stronger than you, and definitely a lot wiser."

"Okay, okay," I said a little too loudly, "I'm going. But think about it, Denise. Have you ever seen this man with a tan?"

I stormed off to the inside bar, but I heard a few of their final words.

"Drunk?"

"Again."

There was a blond-haired man sitting at the bar. His haircut was perfect and I liked the fact that he was wearing a white tee shirt and black jeans. I touched him on the shoulder as if I knew him, and he turned and smiled.

"You're not an actor," I said, smiling back at him.

"Definitely not," he said, and that was enough.

When we left, it was only midnight, and Justin was bent over the script, his hand touching one of those tiny yellow curls. And I wondered if it was true. Had I ever been afraid to be alone?

"What are you thinking of?" Tim asked, running his hand along my back.

"Nothing."

He held out his finger, and I bit it again. With my regular teeth. And sucked a few drops of his blood. His eyes rolled back into his head while I sucked. A fetish was all he thought it was. And I let him think. But it gave me very little pleasure. In the end it just wasn't enough.

Back home, I took Tim's number and threw it on the floor. I wouldn't throw it away. But I wouldn't exactly save it, either.

I looked at the videos Justin thought worth saving— *Casablanca, The Ghost and Mrs. Muir, Portrait of Jenny.* He really was a romantic at heart. He had watched me sleep, and I never knew it. A long time ago. And now I lay down in his coffin as if it was something I was supposed to do. Something all monsters do when they go to sleep. And I pulled the lid shut and waited. As all the little lights, the little energy centers, went out in my body, one by one. And I drifted into unconsciousness, which was always somehow better than any thinking state I had ever known.

The phone rang. I heard it as consciousness gripped me and released me to the night again. I pushed open the lid of the coffin and moved out into the bedroom. Still stiff from sleep, I sat down on the bed and grabbed the receiver.

"Kate?" Charly's voice said. "Kate?"

"Yes," I said, unsure of where I was for the moment.

"I wanted to check, to make absolutely sure, you're not seeing Drew anymore, are you?"

"No, Charly."

"And there's no chance you'll be going over to his apartment tonight?"

"No, I have no intention of . . . Why?"

"Because I've decided, Kate, I shouldn't wait. I know the demo's almost finished, but I just can't wait. I had a dream last night that you were in a coffin and then a priest appeared and told me. I have to act before it's too late."

"Wait," I said, now fully awake. Charly's dream was a little too close for comfort. "Wait a minute, Charly. Before you do anything drastic and completely alienate Drew." I had this image of Charly trying to drive a stake through Drew's heart and succeeding. And with Drew dead and Charly in prison, our chance of musical success would be over in a flash. I was mad at Drew, but not that mad. "Wait," I said again. "I think we should talk about this. Maybe you should let this doctor friend of yours try to convince me that Drew is some kind of vampire or whatever. If he can do it, then I'll give you my blessing, and you can proceed according to plan." I was starting to see the value in meeting this mysterious doctor, in learn-

ing how much he really knew and then setting him
straight and out of Charly's life forever.

Charly sighed into the receiver. "He's out of town."

"Who is?"

"The doctor, he's out of town. He went back to New
York for a while. Someone gave him a new lead, a trail
that is fresh. I don't know when he'll be back, so I have to
take matters into my own hands before it's too late."

"Charly," I said patiently, "listen to me. I'm coming
over, to your house, right now. I want to talk to you in
person. Do you understand? Don't make a move till I get
there."

Charly was silent for a moment. I could hear him
breathing softly into the phone.

"You're coming over here to my apartment?"

"Yes, as soon as I get an address and some directions. I
think we should talk about this seriously face to face."

"Okay," Charly said. "I'd like that, Kate. I'd feel a lot
better if you were on my side. I wouldn't want you to hate
me for jeopardizing the band. I want you to understand. I
don't care what the others think, but you I want to understand. I'll see you soon." And he gave me the directions
and hung up.

I sat up and looked at the white walls surrounding me
and listened to the wail of the wind that was just starting
to blow again, making another December night in L.A.
unnaturally cold. And I wondered if it came right down to
it, whether I could really put an end to Charly's life.

"Look," Charly said from the sofa, "this is where the
monster destroys the bathysphere."

I was sitting on the matching love seat, watching *The
Beast from 20,000 Fathoms*. I looked at Cecil Calloway
trying to describe the prehistoric nightmare he was wit-
nessing before being eaten away. In a certain respect, I

was now rooting for the beast. "It's structure is cantileveric," Cecil said, and then he was gone, eaten by the monster.

I turned to study the volumes in Charly's bookcase for a moment. From *The Alexandria Quartet* to the Bible to a collection of vampire tales to a how-to book for coroners. Coroners, people who are professionals in death. Doctors who feel the cold touch of the dead and look inside their bodies to see why they died. It seemed like just another crazy obsession on Charly's part.

"I didn't know you were such an avid reader," I said, watching the ship's crew reel the cable up only to find the bathysphere missing.

"There's a lot of things you don't know about me, Kate." He muted the volume of the TV. "And I guess you'll never know."

With the beast no longer audible, the sound of the wind took over, hissing and clawing outside. Charly got up and walked to the window. His eyes rested on my Porsche parked on the street.

"I hate the wind," he said, "almost as much as I hate the dark. You never know what it will do next." He shivered slightly. "It's blowing so hard, I could almost imagine it picking up your car and throwing it away."

I wondered what it would be like to fly in a wind that strong, but I would have to wait till another night. Instead, I looked around in amazement at Charly's more than comfortable two-bedroom apartment in Brentwood.

I had been surprised to find him not living in the starving-artist type of apartment that Nathan and Drew and, of course, Mitch had inhabited. I had marveled at his computer and his collection of vintage guitars. At his neutral furniture that all matched and Charly's own private eight-track recording studio, which he had rigged up in his second bedroom. There was a lot I would never know.

"I'm not waiting for music to give me everything I want," Charly had said, when I stared in surprise at the collection of high-tech gadgets he had in his kitchen. Everything from a microwave to an espresso maker to a Cuisinart.

"I may play rock 'n' roll at night, but during the day I hold down a decent job at the post office with benefits and a 401K savings plan. The same way you plan for the future by being an accountant. Nathan and Drew may think it's cool to live like slobs, but I want more out of life while I'm waiting to be famous."

Now I looked at the beast, crushing a city beneath its feet, and wondered how I would talk Charly out of trying to murder the man who sold shoes by day but by night was the pivotal person in the band that would soon make us all rich.

"Charly, what about this whole vampire thing? Don't you think you're letting someone else influence you a lot, someone who may not have both oars in the water? Someone who's not playing with a full deck? You've known Drew for years. How can you possibly think he's some kind of supernatural creature? A mental case from New York comes to our gig one night with his hare-brained story, and you buy into it so completely, you're ready to risk killing a friend just to prove a point. Doesn't that seem a little weird to you?"

It seemed more than a little weird to me. It seemed downright frightening that a stranger could come out of nowhere and control someone with just the right play of words and images, hope and fear. The doctor was becoming more of a threat with every passing night.

"If you'd heard the doctor speak, you'd understand the way I do," Charly said. "I always felt there was something strange about Mitch's death. That it was not an ordinary killing. That there was something inherently evil about it, and it plagued me constantly. Then the doctor came into town. He was following the lead from Vegas to another murder in Redondo Beach. He heard about Mitch's death and put two and two together. He came to hear us play and immediately knew it was someone in the band. He felt the presence of something inhuman."

Charly touched his finger against the window, as if testing how cold it really was outside. "The snow," he said, pulling back and rubbing his hands together.

"I told you how his brother died, didn't I? Murdered by a creature just like Drew. He was found on Wall Street one morning completely drained of blood. The doctor said that in all his practice he had never seen a face look quite that white in death. And it's the image of his brother's face that haunts him, forces him to go on. To find the vampire that killed him or any other vampire that may plague our world.

"When the doctor told me it was someone in the band, I knew it had to be Drew. Do you know, he never really liked Mitch? I'll bet he never told you that. I was always yelling at Mitch for screwing up his bass parts, but I wanted him to stay in the band. But Drew was planning to fire him before the next rehearsal. I guess he didn't want to wait that long. Or he needed blood and decided to combine business with pleasure. Either way, I know I'll never forget the look on Mitch's face the night I found him. I have a feeling I only missed his killing by minutes. If only I had been a little faster with my apology."

"Wanting to fire someone does not prove Drew is a vampire, Charly," I said, but he was looking out the window again.

"You never know what's out there, hiding in the wind. I used to worry about my car being stolen. Now I know there's a lot more important things that can be taken away."

Charly closed his eyes for a moment and sighed. "Drew has changed, Kate. Believe me, I know. He's not the man I met five years ago. Now all he thinks about is his music, not the people who play with him, or anyone else, either. He didn't give a shit that Tom disappeared. In fact, I think he may have killed Tom, too, and disposed of his body. A number of people told me Drew was the last person who was with Tom. Think about it, Kate. It makes sense."

The beast was dying a slow death on screen, unable to triumph over a couple of people and some guns. He screamed out his rage in the lights of a crumbling amusement park.

"It doesn't make any sense. He's as human as the rest of us. I should know. I can't believe you're taking the ranting of this maniac doctor seriously. Please, Charly, just drop it. Leave Drew alone."

"And that's another thing," Charly said. "There's you. Look at Drew's effect on you. You joined the band, and a month later he claimed you as his own. You can't tell me it wasn't supernatural the way you went from an independent and strong-willed woman to his slave, who races to his apartment to be at his beck and call.

"For Christ's sake, Kate, he won't even drive over to your place to pick you up. You always have to go to him. And then from what Nathan has told me, he throws you out as soon as it gets close to dawn. Open your eyes, Kate. Don't you see? He's more than human. He's not like you and me."

"More than human?" I lifted my hand in exasperation, but there was no stopping Charly.

"And now you've had some kind of fight. Maybe you've asked more of him than he can ever give you. Maybe you've made a simple, human demand like the need for security, the need to be loved. You want to share an apartment with him, just like Nathan and Sherrie do, just like he's been claiming he wants . . . but he can never give it to you. Because he's a monster, Kate. Someone who lives on blood. Someone who flies. Someone who looks like a man but no longer has the heart or soul of a man. Every minute he's awake, he's only pretending he's human. He can't live with you because he's not alive."

Charly pulled the blinds shut abruptly and came over to sit down next to me on the love seat.

"I have to act now, Kate, while there's a break in his power over you. Please"—he took my hand—"say you understand."

"Charly." I shook my head. "Charly." But I was only buying time, desperately trying to think of a way to prove him wrong. If only I could hypnotize him and make him forget. Ease his memories of Mitch and the doctor away. But even though I could influence people to some degree by the sheer force of my personality, I was still not a magician. If modern-day vampires could hypnotize like Bela Lugosi, then I still had a long way to go. Of course, I could always remove Charly from the land of the living, but it would be such an inconvenience to kill him now and possibly bring the doctor back from New York with a fresh disappearance. Or give Detective Warren one too many coincidences.

I leaned forward and listened to the wind surrounding us outside. It seemed as if everything in the apartment moved with it. Charly's glass coffee table inched closer toward me as Charly gripped my hand tighter.

"What is it that kills vampires?" I sat back, suddenly inspired. I would use the myths to my advantage and make all of this madness go away. "Didn't you tell me one possibility was holy water?"

"Yes," Charly said excitedly. "That's right. The doctor is almost sure that would do it. It's supposed to burn a demon's skin on contact. As a matter of fact, I have a jar of holy water I've been keeping in the house for protection along with some fresh garlic and a crucifix that's been blessed by the pope."

"Good." I smiled at him. "Take all those things with you when you go to Drew's tonight."

"Tonight?" Charly's eyes lit up. "Then you want me to go tonight?"

"Yes, absolutely. I'll wait in the hall while you knock on Drew's door. When he answers, throw the holy water and garlic in his face and say the Lord's Prayer. If his skin burns, or he screams in pain, or if the door to hell opens wide for a moment, I'll be behind you one hundred percent, and you can drive ten stakes through Drew's heart tomorrow morning."

Charly was nodding eagerly. His face was alive with religious fervor as if he were about to enter Frankenstein's castle and emerge the hero of a B movie. If only life were really that black and white. But at least it was a plan I hoped would cure him forever, so I wouldn't have to worry about Drew's fate or my own.

"But if nothing happens, and Drew is only left irritated and wet, then you have to promise me that you will drop the whole thing once and for all. That you'll tell this doctor not to bother coming back, and we'll all be friends again and go on to make our record without the shadow of monsters in the background."

"All right," Charly said, releasing my hand. "For you, I promise. If I throw the holy water in Drew's face and nothing happens, I will never mention vampires or werewolves or anything like that again.

"But, Kate, if you're the one proven wrong, I hope you're prepared to face the consequences. To realize that life is not what it seems and that there is a devil and that he has power in this world. And God help me, Kate, if you're proven wrong, I can't wait for the doctor to return with some experimental drug that may or may not change Drew back into a human being. I can't wait. Drew will have to be destroyed."

The wind shook the apartment one last time, sweeping cold air through every crack in the walls. A window shattered. Bits of glass flew everywhere, the outside air storming in. The climate of the room changed immediately.

"See," Charly said, "it's starting already."

And he jumped up to look for something to tape over the open window. But it was only a temporary measure, as the cold was already inside.

I hadn't been to Drew's apartment in two and a half weeks, but I automatically reached for the keys as Charly and I rounded the stairs to the third floor. I was already halfway down the hall when I remembered I wasn't going in.

Charly had called Drew first to make sure he was going to be home, explaining that he wanted to come over to talk about the final mix of the demo next week. Drew was hesitant but finally gave in when Charly insisted this meeting could not wait.

I could imagine how disgusted Drew must have been at the thought of having to listen to the ravings of a madman right in his own apartment. But if this all worked out the way it was supposed to, Charly would be cured of his psychosis overnight. He would face his fears and find them without substance.

Unlike a majority of L.A. apartment complexes, this one was mostly enclosed, but the wind still found ways to get in. It blew my hair into my eyes as I shook Charly's hand and wished him good luck, as if he were going off to fight the next world war. I assured him that even if Drew did turn out to be the Count Dracula of the nineties, he would not attempt to kill Charly right then and there with me and most of the tenants as witnesses.

Charly smiled grimly, not really believing me, but knowing he had to do the right thing. And I stayed behind the way women used to do at wartime, safely hidden again in the stairwell.

Charly walked up to Drew's door, armed with a crucifix in one hand and a container of holy water and some garlic in the other. He closed his eyes for a moment, summoning up the courage it would take to face the wrath of hell itself.

I could see by the movement of his lips that he was praying. I tried to remember the way it felt to still have faith in something, but all I could think of was how little effect Charly's prayers would really have on someone like me.

Charly opened his eyes, filled with determination. He lifted the top of the crucifix and knocked on Drew's door. I waited in silent fascination.

I could almost hear Drew sigh in annoyance. Then the door opened, and Charly faced his nemesis. There stood the "deadly Drew" in a white muscle shirt and cut-off jeans, looking more like he was about to go surfing than bloodsucking.

"What the fuck?" Drew said, staring at the crucifix Charly was holding and the garlic Charly had already dropped at his feet. Before he could utter another word, Charly threw the container of holy water directly in his face.

"Our Father, who art in heaven," Charly said, waiting for Drew's skin to melt.

But Drew showed no signs of melting away. Instead, he looked like a candidate for the next wet-tee-shirt contest. He reached up tentatively and touched his hair, not believing he was soaked through and through. His hand stayed raised as fury replaced disbelief.

"You are fucking insane," Drew shouted, and his voice echoed through the hallway.

"Hallowed be thy name . . . ," Charly trailed off. He realized that the holy water wasn't burning Drew's flesh. He started to smile with relief, but Drew was too wet and too angry to even notice. I had never seen a funnier sight in all of my existence, especially the way Drew's perfectly styled blond hair was now hanging in wet patches on the sides of his head, but I never got to laugh. Drew aimed his fist and punched Charly right smack in the middle of his forehead. I could hear the slap of bone against bone, and then Charly collapsed on the green outdoor carpet in the hallway, his arms outstretched in a mock crucifixion.

There was a rustle of tenants against their peepholes, but no one made a move. I wondered if anyone would call the police.

"Shit," Drew yelled, looking down at the unconscious body of Charly. "What the hell is wrong with you?" He rubbed a trickle of water off his forehead, then realized Charly wasn't getting up. He wasn't even moving.

"Charly?" Drew knelt down beside him. "Charly. Hey, man, are you all right? Speak to me, Charly. Shit, are you still breathing, man?"

But Charly lay rigid, his crucifix halfway down the hall.

God damn it, Drew, I thought, *you've gone and killed him.* And I came out of hiding and hurried to Charly's side. I knelt down beside him and carefully felt for his pulse. I sighed in relief; it was still beating. Drew had only knocked him out.

"Kate?" Drew stared at me in astonishment. "What are you doing here? What the hell is going on?"

"Let's get him inside." I stood up to help Drew carry

him, but Drew had already grabbed Charly's feet and was dragging him into the living room like a dead body.

"Do you have any smelling salts or ammonia or anything?"

"I guess," Drew said. "I think I have some Windex. That might do the trick. There's ammonia in that stuff, isn't there?" Drew turned to go to the kitchen and stopped. "You didn't come here with this fucking pea brain, did you?" He pointed to Charly on the floor.

"As a matter of fact, I did."

"Oh, I see. Maybe it was your idea to have him throw a glass of water in my face, just so you could see me get all wet."

"It was my idea, Drew, but that wasn't ordinary water, it was blessed, you know, holy water. I wanted Charly to get over his strange ideas about you once and for all. He promised me if he threw it at you and nothing happened, he'd stop accusing you of being a vampire and start acting like a normal human being."

"Wait," Drew walked over to his front door and kicked it shut. "Am I hearing right? That's what was bothering Charly? He thought I was a vampire? You've got to be kidding. That is the stupidest thing I ever heard. A vampire? Like Christopher Lee with the big teeth. Sleeping in graveyards. Biting people's necks. Drinking blood?" Drew opened his mouth in a gruesome parody of attack. "Take a look. See any fangs in there? How could he possibly think something as laughable as that even existed, let alone that I was one?" Drew shook his head and looked down at Charly again. "Oh, I know. It was because of Mitch, wasn't it? He hasn't been right since then." Drew's face softened. "Always looking for some kind of explanation, someone to accuse and to put on trial. But why me? We've been friends for years."

"He's had a hard time coping with finding Mitch's

body," I said. "And then some jackass doctor from nowhere comes up to him at one of our gigs and convinces Charly that not only did a vampire kill Mitch, but that somebody in the band is this very same vampire. Since Nathan is always happy and I'm a girl, that only leaves you."

Drew started to smile slightly. "The poor jerk. He's been driving himself crazy with this bullshit horror crap, imagining God knows what. Why didn't he just talk to me? We could have cleared this up a long, time ago."

"He was afraid," I said, "and fear makes you do strange things. It makes you hate your friends, trust your enemies, hurt your lover, and pray to God that someone will save you in the end."

Charly moaned a little, and his eyelids began to flutter. We both looked at him, suddenly aware we hadn't even moved him to the couch.

"I have to go." I felt self-conscious about being in Drew's apartment again. "Can you take care of him? Put an ice pack on his head. Talk to him when he comes to. Maybe work out your differences so we can do a good mix-down of our tape on Wednesday?"

"Sure." Drew picked up a comb from the floor and ran it through his hair. Water dripped down the sides of his head.

"And dry yourself off while you're at it," I said, smiling a little. "You should have seen your face when Charly threw the water at you."

Drew laughed. "I'll bet it was a sight to see." He dropped the comb back on the floor. It landed between his mail and an empty beer can. "Do you have to leave right now?" He moved a little closer. "You know, Kate, I've . . . I've missed you."

"You have?"

"Yes, I have."

I felt the wetness of his tee shirt against my face, and then I lifted my head and he kissed me.

"I've missed you, too, Drew," I said, and we kissed again.

We both looked down at Charly.

"What about him?" Drew said. Charly's eyes opened in confusion, and he began to rub the area just above his eye, which was already starting to darken.

"He needs a little medical attention," I said, heading to the kitchen to get some ice, but Drew ran up behind me and grabbed me around the waist.

"The hell with him," he said, pulling me toward the bedroom so fast I almost lost my balance. "He can get his own ice."

Drew dragged me through the door and onto the bed. I buried my head in his pillow as Drew fumbled with the lights.

"If you want to watch TV, Charly," he yelled, "the remote is hiding in the sofa somewhere and there's plenty of ice in the refrigerator. Just make yourself comfortable. I have a feeling this isn't going to take too long."

Drew tore off his wet tee shirt and jumped in bed beside me. As he fought to get my black turtleneck over my head, he laughed and said, "A vampire. Of all things. Leave it to an idiot like Charly to believe in vampires." Drew lowered his voice a little. "Damn, I hope he didn't hear me."

And then he ripped off the rest of our clothes, and I heard the TV set click on, the opening music for the *Tonight* show covering all the noises Drew didn't want Charly to hear.

Later we lay in bed, still holding each other tight and wondering why Charly didn't leave. His ice pack had to have melted and the only thing left on TV was the late, late show.

"I guess we shouldn't have done it twice," Drew said, "but two and a half weeks is way too long for me to be without you."

He began to rub my leg again in earnest.

I felt the warning fear of dawn approaching. "I really need to go."

"What we really need to do is talk," Drew said. "You know we haven't worked out any of our differences."

"I know."

"I need more from you than this coming over just for the night stuff."

"I know, Drew. We will talk. Right after we finish the mix. We'll sit down and talk quietly and calmly. No more fighting. And we'll see if we can work this out."

"I love you, Kate."

"I love you, too." And at that moment in time I really believed it. I believed we could still find a way to be together. Maybe what Drew needed wasn't so bad, after all. Maybe vampires needed it, too—someone else's touch in the darkness.

We got up without turning on a light, and I struggled to find my clothes, as Drew got dry ones for himself from his closet. Then we stopped and listened at the bedroom door. Perhaps Charly had left without turning off the TV. Whatever was now on sounded vaguely familiar. We decided to be brave and opened the door and walked into the living room.

All the lights were turned off, but there was still enough illumination, coming from the refrigerator door that had been left open, for us to see. Charly was lying on the sofa, a wet dishrag on his head and eight empty beer cans at his feet.

"Drew, old buddy," he said happily, "I'm so sorry I ever thought you were one of those goddamn, fucking, bloodsucking bat-head things. Can you ever forgive me?"

"Sure," Drew said. *Bat-head things?* he mouthed to me.

"And, Kate, I love you. Really I do. You made me see the light. You released me from my prison of hatred. For that I owe you my life. God, I feel great! I am really having a wonderful life! I just needed someone to show me."

"All right, Charly," I smiled at him and moved toward the front door. I didn't have much time left before the sun rose. "You owe me." I turned the doorknob and walked into the hallway. I could tell by the way the shadows were rimmed in blue that dawn was only thirty minutes away. I would have to speed all the way home.

"Let's spend the next few days thinking." Drew kissed me good-bye. "But while you're thinking, remember this: I love you, Kate. All I want is for us to have a life together. We won't be young forever. Someday the music will be over, and then we'll really need each other."

"I know." I turned and walked down the hallway. Water stains still showed on the green carpet, the only evidence of the fight that had taken place. I knew Drew was watching me, but I did not turn around. And from a distance I heard Charly shout:

"Hey, Drew, my main man, come on back in here. Let's have another beer. My favorite movie is on again. *The Beast from 20,000 Fathoms.* And you've got to see this monster to believe it!"

I woke up. Dreamless again. Almost forgetting what a dream felt like. Opening my eyes. Stretching my toes. I pushed open the lid of the coffin and took my first breath of air. It was a deep breath, and it filled my lungs to capacity and started all the systems on their way.

Moving. Imitating. Life.

I walked to the closet and selected a black shirt, different from the night before. And a pair of black jeans. I turned on the TV and watched the seven o'clock news and the weather. It was cold again, they said. But to me it didn't matter. The temperature of the night air always felt the same. Smooth. Cool.

I pushed the code to disarm the electronic alarm system and the security release to lift the solid metal gratings off the windows to reveal the stars almost touching the dark water below.

Then I walked out onto the patio, closing and locking the door behind me. I looked up at the stars, plotted my course, and dissolved matter into nothing until it mattered again.

Floating. Flying. Moving with the night.

I could fly to San Francisco and back in only an hour. Even when I followed the shoreline. I had gotten faster with time and practice. I was perfecting my skill.

As I looked down, I could see the red and white lights of the cars pushing their way along the Pacific Coast Highway. The waves cresting out beyond the sand. Tiny homes and stores and gas stations.

I could go as high as a plane but no higher. As if an invisible wall kept me from leaving the atmosphere. This was my world without end. Forever. And I was still bound by its limitations. Everything has limitations. Even something that's not human. Even God, I was beginning to suspect. Everything.

I had ended my run to San Francisco and moved a little east to Brentwood. I found his apartment easily from memory. Blowing through the window he still hadn't fixed, I materialized in the darkness of Charly's living room. The TV was still on. A Bette Davis movie. But Charly was sound asleep on the sofa. He was holding a blanket against his chest. The bruise on his forehead was now completely black and blue.

I sat down on his love seat, just as I had done two

nights ago, and looked at his sleeping form. His body rose and fell. His eyes moved back and forth under his lids. His hand twitched, and he turned over slightly. He was dreaming a peaceful dream. His face showed no signs of distress. He murmured a little. A sigh, and then he brushed a piece of hair from his forehead.

"I'm so glad I convinced you, Charly," I said softly. "Because you can see how easy it is. I can watch you sleep, or I can kill you. Right in the middle of a dream. In between breaths. Or when you wake for a moment wondering why the TV's still on. One minute you're breathing, the next minute you're not. You can see how easy it is. We are never more vulnerable than when we're asleep."

And with the flick of my hand, I turned off the TV, ripped the newspaper away from the window, and stole his copy of *Ethan Frome*. I did it because I could. Because I wasn't human, only pretending to be. And even though Charly was my friend and I was his, there was no guarantee it would stay that way. Unless Charly and the rest of humanity were kept in the dark about my existence forever. So I kissed him lightly on the neck, and then I left.

Later, I took the book and added it to Justin's collection, in between *Summer* and *The House of Mirth*. Then I lowered the metal gratings and secured the alarm system. Checking every lock to make sure I was safe.

I would have to do something about Drew. It had felt so good to be held by him again, but I'd have to find a new excuse about why I needed to be alone. Something to buy me time. Until Drew forgot to ask anymore. But I would worry about that tomorrow. There was always tomorrow.

So I shut the coffin lid as the sun rose outside the condo's walls. And lay down to sleep. Dreamless again.

* * *

It was beginning to look a lot like Christmas. Even if there was no snow. Even if nothing was white. There was still red and green. Christmas lights strung up on palm trees. Santa standing on the beach. The Three Kings wearing sunglasses.

Only in the mall was the atmosphere identical to the East. Longer shopping hours. Wallets and ties and earrings featured on little tables throughout the store. Twenty-five percent off. Fifty percent off. Free gift wrapping with reindeer and elves. Extra sales personnel reaching out to help you buy. Reminding you of someone you might have forgotten on your Christmas list.

I had not intended to buy anything for anyone. The last time I had celebrated Christmas was four years ago, only months before I was to leave for L.A. and end up as one of the living dead. Since then, I had not really taken an interest in celebrating the birth of Christ. It seemed like a contradiction in terms.

But at the last minute, on my way to the studio for the final mix, with only two shopping days till Christmas, I had stopped at the Beverly Center to buy a present for Drew. It was the decoration of Rudolph hanging over Third Street that did it. The song came into my head. I remembered how Rudolph was an outcast in the reindeer world until his nose proved useful, and I was lost.

With only twenty minutes to spare, I parked the Porsche and rushed up the escalator, trying to think of what Drew would like. I could have bought him a car with the money I still had left over from Vegas, but that would take too much explaining. I would have to find something more worthy of an accountant's salary.

I walked into one of the more elite men's shops, blinking erratically from the fluorescent lights, and tried to visualize the perfect gift.

One of the salesmen ran over, then stopped short when I shielded my eyes.

"Can you lower the lights?" I said.

"What?" he stammered, confused but still eager to please. It was obvious he worked on commission.

"Can you lower the lights for a minute so I can think? I need to buy a gift right now, tonight, and it has to be . . . the most perfect and probably most expensive black shirt in existence. So as a favor to a paying customer who is ready to use force to get her way, please lower the lights, before it gets bloody in here."

The salesman ran to obey me. All the fluorescent lights were turned off except one, and he returned in less than a minute with three black possibilities.

I settled on the button-down china silk, an Italian import. It was cut beautifully and would conform to Drew's body like magic. They gift-wrapped it in silver foil for free, and at four hundred dollars it was worth it.

I hid it under the seat of the Porsche, wondering when it was I intended to give it to Drew, when I hadn't even thought of how to handle Christmas yet. And Thanksgiving's problems were still lurking ominously in the shadows, waiting to be talked about. And I was running out of tomorrows.

I had not expected the final mix to go smoothly. It usually doesn't. I had read so many articles about bands that had come to blows over the mix-down. Of a famous English rock star who almost strangled his lead player when he insisted on mostly guitar in the mix. It is a touchy time, when frustration and ego run very high. You have to take twenty-four individual tracks of music and vocals and combine them together to make one. Needless to say, it's a very subjective thing. Each band member has their own opinion as to how they and the rest of the band should sound. One minute the drums are too loud. The next minute you can't hear the vocals. And then there were Matt and Lisa's ideas, and it was their company that was paying for it so we had to placate them, too. Not to mention the engineer, who always has something to say, and he's the one who has his hands on all the controls.

Maybe the Christmas spirit was hovering around L.A., or maybe we were all in the same state of mind at the same time, but a miracle did happen, and the mix was completed in only six hours—by 2:30 A.M.—with minimal disagreement and to everyone's satisfaction. No one had fought or sulked or threatened to get their way. Instead, everyone treated the mix as the important business venture it was and cooperated to make it a success.

"A masterpiece" is what Matt called it. "A definite hit. All the songs have melodic hooks for people to remember. Once they hear them, they will never get them out of their heads. And I will make sure there's just enough bribery and favoritism showed to insure that people get to hear your record once it's made."

"You can count on it," Lisa agreed, unbuttoning the top button of her blouse as Drew and I sat with the two of them at the control board after listening to our tape for the third time.

Behind us Charly was dancing a rumba and singing "Rudolph the Red-Nosed Reindeer," while Nathan acted out all the parts. Nathan was using a cherry from Drew's fruit salad to play the lead character. Their voices were rising to a fever pitch.

"I think I liked Charly better in his early depressive stage," Matt said, shaking his head. He was wearing his varsity jacket that had the CMD logo in orange and black on the back.

Drew and I looked at each other and smiled. It was a secret smile, full of memories. Memories of another night. I could still remember how Drew looked wearing a wet tee shirt. Delicious.

"Yeah." Lisa moved a little closer to Drew. "All of a sudden he's gone from Mr. Doom and Gloom to one of the elves in Santa's workshop. By the way, how do you look in a wet tee shirt? Is it better than none at all?"

I saw her casually touch Drew's leg, and for a moment it made me wonder. What did she mean by "none at all"?

"I guess you could say a glass of water changed him," Drew moved his leg away and smiled at me again.

"That's right," Charly yelled, hearing their conversation. "I've been an asshole from outer space for way too long. All it took was a little H-two-O to bring me back down to earth. Now look at me. I've been saved. I'm not afraid of the dark anymore, and all of the reindeer love me." He began to sing again.

Drew put his hands over his ears and shook his head.

"Speaking of history," Matt said, "I'm going to present this to CMD on December twenty-six*th* and by the time you do your next gig, you will be signed. I might even have you announce your record deal right on stage. But right now, kiddies, I think we all need to go home and get our beauty rest. Christmas is right around the bend."

"Oh, shit," Charly moaned, and stopped dancing. "Only one more shopping day and I haven't bought a God damn thing. I've been too fucked up with the bullshit side of life to celebrate the holiday. I'm going to have to spend all of tomorrow at the mall. Oh, well, it will still be the best Christmas ever."

"I'll say." Nathan laughed. "I've already bought Sherrie about twenty presents. I guess I'll have to buy a few more. Mind if I join you, Charly? Maybe we can check out the lingerie department one last time."

And they began to sing "Rudolph" again, this time in harmony.

"How about you?" Lisa touched Drew. "Is this Christmas special for you, too?"

Matt had packed up the tape that held our mix, and we were heading for the door.

"I agree with Charly," Drew said. "With a little help from CMD and the god of romance, this will be the best Christmas ever."

"Well, then how about toasting your success with a quick nightcap?" Lisa said. We had reached the outside steps. Nathan and Charly were still inside, but now they were singing "O Holy Night." "I know how much you like nightcaps. Or maybe we could have another wet-tee-shirt contest of our own?" I looked at Drew in surprise.

" 'Long lay the world in sin and error pining.' " Charly was veering off key. " 'Till He appeared, and the soul felt its worth.' "

"I'd like to, Lisa," Drew said, "but my car is at Kate's, so I have to go there first, and it's a little late, too."

I opened my mouth but said nothing.

"Some other time." Lisa touched his arm, turned, and walked to her car with Matt. They laughed as she unlocked the door. I thought I heard her mention Drew's name.

"Well," Drew said to me quietly, "let's go."

"Where?" I was still wondering about Lisa.

"To your place, Kate. I want to go to your place. Nathan gave me a lift here. My car's still at my apartment. But for once we're going to your place."

"We can't," I stammered. "It's—it's not really clean. I'm not prepared."

"Look, Kate," Drew said, "this is the way it is. Either we go to your place right now and work out our differences, or we drop the whole thing and I go out with Lisa for a drink. If you love me the way you keep telling me you do, then you'll trust me and let me into your home, just this one time. So what's it going to be?"

At that moment Charly and Nathan tumbled out the door.

" 'Fall on your knees, O hear the angel voices.' "

Charly knelt down on the steps, his hands raised in supplication.

"Come on, you two lovebirds, stop squabbling."

Nathan joined him in mock prayer.

From a distance, I saw Lisa sitting in her car and staring. Wondering. Waiting.

"Take me home, Kate," Drew said again, his eyes catching Lisa's for a moment. "It's now or never."

"Now or never!" Nathan and Charly said together.

Now or never.

"All right, Drew," I said, giving in, imagining the way his new black shirt would fit his body. And I did not want to think about Lisa touching Drew's leg again. "I'll take you home."

Now, you would think that after all this time, I would see disaster coming when it was only inches away. That I would recognize catastrophe when it looked me in the face and smiled. But it was Christmas. And I had fallen on my knees. "O night divine."

"I can't believe this is where you live," Drew said, staring at the whiteness that was everywhere. "Why in God's name have we been spending our nights at my place?"

"It's not really my condo," I said, checking the living room for any telltale evidence. "I sublease it from someone. In exchange for house-sitting, I get a break on the rent."

"Still," Drew said, "this is magnificent. The artwork in here alone must be worth a fortune. And everything's so clean. It's as if no one lives here. Nothing's out of place. There's not a crumb on the floor. And look at that fireplace. How can you stand to spend one minute in the clutter of my bedroom?"

"I have to keep it this clean, this perfect. It's part of the bargain."

"We'll talk about this bargain of yours later. Where's the bedroom? Downstairs?" Drew pulled me in the right direction. "I can't wait to get a look at where you sleep."

"Wait," I said, suddenly remembering I had left the secret door open and the coffin was in full view. "I mean, I can't wait. Not that long. Not down all those stairs. I have to have you now." And I pulled Drew to his knees and kissed him so hard we both fell backward.

"Okay, Kate." His arms circled my waist. "We can talk later. There's just one thing I need to explain first."

"Explain later." I leaned down and kissed him again. His blond hair blended perfectly with the soft white carpet. He smiled.

"Later." Drew pulled me flat against him and rolled over until he was on top of me. He bit my neck softly while he struggled with the buttons on my shirt. "Kate, do you know how much I love you? I want to be with you forever."

And then I forgot about everything, including the time.

It took me a minute to realize what was wrong. I felt too warm. I smelled smoke. Something was burning. I must have left the oven on or turned the heater too high. But then I realized I never used the oven anymore or the heater either. And it was the tip of my toe that was on fire. And it was me that was starting to burn.

"Oh, God," I screamed from the lethargy of sleep that was starting to drag me under. "It's dawn!"

I hadn't lowered the metal coverings for the windows, and the sun was sneaking in. How could I have forgotten?

"What's wrong, Kate?" Drew said, sitting up sleepily. "Did you have a nightmare?"

He reached around to reassure me, but I was already dragging myself to the control box on the other side of the room. Desperately trying to ignore the horrible pain in my toe and the smell of something burning. Like a barbecue gone wrong.

"What's on fire?" Drew asked, turning to look for me, and then he saw the flame singing my skin. "Jesus Christ!" he screamed, grabbing his shirt. And he ran to my side and threw it on my foot, trying to smother the flames.

As my finger closed on the switch, the grates came down over the windows, blocking out the light. Darkness descended into a room that had just been lit by the morning.

"Are you all right?" Drew asked, holding me. "What the hell is going on? How's your foot?" He pulled his shirt away to see half of my toe blackened and eaten away.

"Oh, my God," he said. "How could something like this have happened? We have to get you to a hospital! Your toe was on fire. It was actually burning."

"No," I said. "Drew, please, just go. Now, please. Get out of here."

It was an effort just to form the words. The sun was rising, and I would have to get downstairs soon, where it was safe and even darker. I had to sleep.

"Leave?" Drew said in disbelief. "What, are you nuts? Your toe catches fire spontaneously, and I'm just supposed to leave? On top of that you don't look right, in general. Your skin feels funny. You feel cold. I'm getting some clothes on both of us, and I'm getting you to a hospital."

He moved to find my shirt and pants, and I moaned a little in pain. But most of the sensation was gone. Gone to wherever those sensations go when I'm asleep. Wherever dreams run away and disappear. Wherever the dead live by day.

"Your eyes look weird, too. Like you have a fever or something."

But I was crawling to the stairs. I hit the alarm for the door as I passed it. No one would be able to get in or out. But it didn't matter. I only knew I had to sleep. Someplace safe.

"I've never seen anything like it, Kate. It was like someone took a match to your toe. It was like a fucking nuclear chain reaction. I'm not sure which hospital is closer. We better hurry. I wonder if there's something weird in the air? It stopped when you closed those God damn windows. I've never seen windows like that. God, Kate, I hope you'll be all right. Your toe . . ."

Drew turned around in mid-sentence to find me gone. He stood up and stared into the darkness in confusion.

"Where the hell are you?"

He ran down the stairs, with only his shirt on, banging against the wall. "Kate? Kate? Come on, we've got to get to a hospital. What are you doing, Kate?"

I never made it to the coffin but I did reach the bed. My body began to stiffen, as I fought to remain conscious one more second.

I saw Drew stop at the bottom of the stairs, lost in the confusion of the white bedclothes, the white walls, and the charred, black remains of my toe. Finally he turned to see the last wall, which opened into a dark room that held a coffin, raised on a platform like a throne.

"I'm sorry, Drew," I said, with my last breath, and with

my last ounce of strength, I reached down and tore out the phone cord so I could be sure he would stay alone until night brought me back again.

I woke up with a vague memory of sadness. I had lost something. In a fire. A long time ago.

I opened my eyes and looked down at my toe. The blackness had disappeared and so had the pain, but the part that had held my toe nail was gone. Eaten away by the sun.

I heard someone breathing and turned my head to see Drew, sitting on the floor next to the bed. I could see by the swelling of his eyes, he had been crying.

"You have teeth," he said, not looking at me.

I sat up in bed and reached down to touch his hair. He pulled away from my touch but otherwise did not move.

"At first, I thought you were dying, Kate, really dying. I did everything I could to break out of this nightmare of a condo so I could get you a doctor's help. But it's a fortress in here, isn't it, Kate? No one can get in, and no one can get out, without your permission. What an asshole I am!"

He closed his eyes for a moment.

"Then I thought you were dead, and I just about died myself. I blamed myself for not being able to save you. For ever suggesting we come here. I thought I had lost you. That something had burned away through your toe and had reached your heart. I couldn't hear it beating. Couldn't feel you breathing. And then something strange began to happen. I saw your nails begin to grow. Longer and longer. And your hair, too. And then I saw your teeth. Four tiny points, barely visible under your lips. The lips I've kissed."

He raised his fist and hit the floor. The sound echoed through the bedroom.

"And, of course, you had disconnected the phone, so what could I do? Maybe try on the coffin you have in your secret chamber for size? Is that where you really sleep?"

I tried to touch him again but he moved away this time.

"So what is it, Kate? Has Charly been right all along? Should I have put a stake through your heart while you slept? Are you going to drink my blood now? Maybe give me eternal life?"

"I would never hurt you, Drew." I got up and went to the closet to put on some clothes. If I was going to have to explain, then at least I could be dressed. But as I walked I felt the absence in my toe. And I stumbled a little on the white carpet.

"You fucking lied to me, Kate. I held you in my arms. Told you about my dreams. Took you to my parents' house. But everything between us has been a lie, hasn't it? What are you exactly? Is vampire the correct word for it? Is that what I've been making love to all this time? A real live—or should I say dead—vampire?"

With my clothes on, I went over and sat down beside Drew. He looked older from crying, and his hair was matted flat against his head. He had put on his jeans, but only remembered to put on one sock, and his shirt was buttoned all wrong.

"Yes," I said softly, "I'm a vampire, but it's not what you think, Drew."

"You're a vampire, but it's not what I think?" he said. "I can't believe this. I can't fucking believe this."

"Listen," I said, "all those myths, that stuff in the movies and on TV is wrong. I can't go out in the daylight. I have to sleep then. And the sun hurts me, obviously. But that's it. Holy water and crucifixes don't affect me any more than they do you. And neither does garlic. And I have never been, nor do I have any intention of becom-

ing, a bat. And I swear to you"—mentally, I crossed my
fingers—"I absolutely do not drink blood."

"Well, what do you drink? When I think about it, I
realize I've never seen you eat or drink anything. And
I've fallen for that bullshit line that you're dieting. What
do you drink?"

"Nothing," I said. "I don't need to eat or drink anything."

"Well, if you don't drink blood, why do you have those
teeth, huh? And besides that, you're supposed to be
dead, aren't you? I didn't hear any heartbeat in there.
You may be breathing and talking now, but an hour ago
you were as cold and hard as any stiff. And I've seen a
couple when I worked one time in a hospital."

"We've been in bed together, Drew. Do I really seem
dead to you?"

He lifted his head and looked at me.

"God, Kate, what is going on here? I feel like I'm in
the middle of a nightmare, and I want to wake up. First,
your toe lights on fire. Then, I find out you're a vampire.
How did this happen to you, Kate? As far as I know, no
one's born a vampire, are they? So I guess some bastard
must have turned you into one somehow, right?"

"Yes, Drew," I said. "Someone did this to me. Without
my permission. Against my will. He changed my life. Took
my family away from me. Took the daylight away from
me." I smiled inwardly at my own inspiration. "Don't you
see, Drew, that's what the teeth are for, to change someone else into a vampire. Even though I have no idea how
to accomplish such a thing, nor would I ever want to."

He shook his head back and forth. "And what about
living forever? Are you immortal? Except for the fucking
sun?"

"I don't know," I said. "Maybe. Guns and knives don't
work, at least."

"Oh, great," Drew said. "So you probably won't die, and on top of that you'll never age, while everyone around you marches to the grave looking progressively more like shit with each passing day. I can just picture me trying to explain to my mother: 'I know Kate's fifty years old but those new skin creams can work wonders.'"

"So I'm a little different. So what. I'm not hurting anybody. You're a rock musician. You're supposed to live on the edge. To be flexible. To be open to new life forms when you encounter them, the way they did on *Star Trek.* You'd never survive a day on the U.S.S. *Enterprise.* You'd be horrified every time they landed on a new planet. Can't you just think of me like that? An alien life form. Different from you but the same in all the important ways. Captain Kirk was always falling in love with alien women as long as they looked human."

Drew lifted his hand and touched me tentatively.

"But those teeth."

"They're meaningless, Drew. A relic of another time. Kind of like an appendix. It's a handicap that I'm stuck with. But people learn to live with handicaps all the time."

"What about Mitch, then? What about all that shit Charly said about Mitch?"

"Drew, I swear to you, on a stack of Bibles, I had nothing to do with Mitch's death. It must have been some weird religious cult or something, like that Detective Warren said. You've got to believe me. I really don't drink blood. Just the sight of it makes me sick. I'm really squeamish."

Drew looked over to the right, at the coffin in full view.

"What about that?" he asked.

"It belongs to someone else. The vampire that made me. And when I cursed him for making me, he took off and left this condo and all of its contents to me. You know, I was alone for a long time. I didn't know what to do. I didn't fit in anywhere anymore. I couldn't go home again. I was alone and afraid. And then I found the band, and then I found you. Please, Drew, I don't want to be alone again. . . ."

I touched his face, and he didn't resist.

"I don't know, Kate, I don't know. It's all so weird."

"I love you, Drew, I really do."

He put his arm around me, but he didn't hold me tight.

"I want to be like Captain Kirk, really I do. But I'm not sure I can handle it. The real world is not like a TV show, you know. I have to think. I have to be alone, be by myself for a while. You really scared me, Kate, with spontaneously combusting and then with not breathing. I even tried mouth-to-mouth resuscitation, but your lips were ice-cold and your teeth got in my way. . . . I've never been more scared in my whole life. You could have prepared me for this, you could have talked to me about this. You could have trusted me."

"I was afraid you wouldn't understand. That you'd be disgusted by me. The way people are disgusted when they find out someone's sick."

"I'm not disgusted, Kate. As long as you don't drink blood, I'm not disgusted. I'm just a little shocked, and my entire set of beliefs are shot to hell, but I guess ultimately everyone can adjust to anything given time. . . ."

Drew looked at his watch, as if suddenly the time mattered.

"You know," he said, "it's Christmas Eve. I was due at my parents' house tonight. I'm supposed to bring you, but I don't think my brain can deal with it at the moment. I need time to adjust. I'll have to talk myself into being flexible. Into accepting a girlfriend who won't grow old while I get bald."

He laughed a little.

"At least you didn't die. I was so afraid you were dying. How could someone dare do this to you without your permission? What kind of monster was he?"

"The worst kind," I said. "The kind you fall in love with. But there's nothing I can do about that now."

"Well, we'll talk about that another time. I don't think I can handle that story at this point. Right now, I have to go home, take a shower, and head to my parents without any sleep. They've probably called my apartment about twenty times by now, wondering where I am. Don't worry about driving me to my apartment, I'll catch the bus." He lifted his hand as if he meant to protect himself from something—an invisible evil that neither of us could see. But somehow I knew it was directed at me. "We have a gig to do in a week. Give me that much time to sort out all this new information. To let it compute. I don't feel too well right now." He stared down at his shirt, the way it was buttoned.

"Drew," I said, "you realize you can't tell anyone about this. I don't want anyone else to know. Especially not Charly and Nathan. They wouldn't understand. And it would ruin everything with the band."

"I know that, Kate. I may be easily fooled, but I'm not stupid. God, I can't believe just last week I was laughing about vampires. The next thing I'll find out is, Charly is a leprechaun, Nathan is a ghost, and Matt is an alien from outer space, who really has nothing to do with CMD Records. If the woman I love is alive only at night, then maybe nothing else in this world is the way I think it is, either." He stood up and started to fix the buttons on his shirt.

"That coffin in there has gotta go if you expect me to ever come over here again. It gives me the creeps. What did the jerk who owns that do, lie in there and watch old movies about Dracula?"

I got up and walked to the wall and pressed the right point so the wall would close. "There," I said, "it's gone."

I went back to Drew and put my arms around his waist, but somehow he didn't feel the same. "What's that in your back pocket?"

"Oh, that," he said. "That's a good one. My Christmas present to you."

He reached into his pocket and took the tiny package out. It was wrapped in silver with a tiny black bow.

"I don't know if this makes sense anymore," he said. "I don't know if anything makes sense. But I bought it, so you might as well take it."

He handed it to me, and I rested it on the palm of my hand.

"Go ahead, open it."

I pulled at the silver wrapping. Since I hadn't cut my nails yet, it broke away easily. I looked at the tiny black velvet box, then opened it slowly. "Drew." It was a diamond ring. "I don't know what to say." He had taken me completely by surprise.

"I don't know what to say, either, Kate. Not anymore. The spirit of Christmas overwhelmed me, and I bought something I never thought I'd buy for anyone. I must have been out of my mind. For now, let's just not say anything."

I placed the ring on my nightstand, and as we walked upstairs, I tried to push the significance of a gift like that out of my mind. For a moment, Drew had actually wanted to belong to me, even if he never would again.

We reached the living room. I pushed the control box, and my security system lifted and let the night back in. It was clear, and the stars were shining.

"What about your toe, Kate? I forgot to even ask. Part of it burned away. Will it ever grow back? Are you in pain?"

I looked at the Christmas lights strung on the building next door. "I don't feel anything now, except its absence," I said. "And somehow I know it's gone forever."

I reached out for Drew, to pull him close. But I suppose I knew even then that he was gone forever, too. And before I could tell him I loved him one more time, he had slipped away.

It was cold. And it was dark. And it was Christmas Eve.

And then it was Christmas. I don't remember flying because it happened so fast. I surprised even myself with my speed, with my ever-increasing power.

One minute I was in L.A., the next I was hovering over Manhattan. Looking at the frosted landscape that rose to one hundred stories and beyond. Stretching upward where L.A. ran wide. The castles and towers of an empire.

I had awakened that evening wondering whether I was really engaged, then remembered I was missing part of my toe. I dialed Drew's number, but the only answer was his machine. The metallic click of his recorded voice. I left no message. What could I say? The only thing left to do was go home. And home was east. Where the sun always rose.

Every year, when I was young, my parents would take Kevin and me to Rockefeller Plaza to see the Christmas tree. It was the largest in the world. It always looked bigger than life, like a scene from a movie unfolding before your very eyes. And you were part of it, an extra in a star-studded cast of thousands.

And later, we would watch the ice skaters and look at the windows of Saks and Bonwit Teller. And pass by Santas ringing their bells, stopping to eat at Chock Full O'Nuts. And if we were really lucky, when it got to be night, a few snowflakes would fall, and Kevin and I would know, right then and there, it was going to be a white Christmas.

I stood in Rockefeller Center and looked at the Christmas tree, a million miles away from southern California. A million miles away from the band and the record company. A million miles away from graveyards and coffins. And I thought if I tried hard enough, I could go back in time and recapture the awe I once felt for Christmas. That childlike feeling of wonder for a holiday with a look, smell, and feel all its own. When the world became a red, green, and silver place filled with evergreens, peppermints, reindeer that flew, and boxes that were always filled with surprises.

But New York looked different after four years. Things were not exactly where they used to be. People's faces had changed. The hot dog and chestnut cart had disappeared. Chock Full O'Nuts had gone out of business. And some of the stores surrounding the skating rink were gone. The skaters on the ice seemed unfamiliar. And there was no snow on the ground or in the air.

"Excuse me, miss," a man said to me.

I turned to look at his unshaven face, his dirty clothes layered against the cold, and his red high tops with holes in the toes.

"Could you spare a little change? It's for a really worthy cause."

"And what cause is that?" I asked, wondering if I had remembered to take any money with me.

"I'm trying to get up the bus fare so I can go to L.A. It's real warm there in the winter. The sun always shines. So it don't matter if you don't have a home. You can sit on the beach all day and bother nobody. You don't freeze your ass off like here."

"L.A.?" I said.

"Yeah, man, L.A. Though I don't think it would make

much difference to you. It's twenty degrees outside, and you ain't even wearing a jacket or shoes. Maybe you need the money worse than me. Sorry I bothered you."

"Wait!" My hands closed on the bills I had stuffed in the pocket of my jeans. I took them out and counted them.

"Eighty dollars," I said. "Here, take it. But I gotta tell you, mister, the sun doesn't always shine in L.A. It can get pretty damn cold there sometimes. Cold enough to freeze your heart. And once you take away the swimming pools and movie stars, it's just a city like any other city, that shows no mercy at the time you need it most."

The man looked at the four twenties, not believing his luck. "Thank you, miss," he said, not even hearing my words of warning. "Really, thank you. I've almost got enough right here. Heaven must have sent you. Merry Christmas."

He ran off into the darkness of Sixth Avenue and I wondered if he'd ever make it to L.A. and if he did, if he'd ever find the beach.

I turned and looked at the tree again, but that wasn't the real reason I had flown three thousand miles. I had seen the past in the sparkle of a diamond ring, and it had pulled me like a magnet across the country. Calling me home.

A little humanity surfaced for a moment and I wanted to tell my mother: I think I'm engaged again. Unfortunately it hardly read like a story from *Bride's* magazine. It was really more suited to *Fantastic Stories* or *Tales from the Grave*.

So even though I wanted to cruise to Long Island, knock on my parents' door, have them take me in their arms to celebrate the fact that I was not only alive but that someone wanted to marry me again, I couldn't do it. When it came time to move, my feet had no feeling. They were frozen to the ice that was spreading out from the skating rink and circling around my ankles. Hardening me, keeping me from flight. Keeping me from the warm land that lay like another country on the other side of my parents' door.

And it was better to keep that door locked and frozen after all. Better to lose the key. Better to let them think whatever they thought than see me like this. A soul lost in the land of sunshine, who no longer needed a jacket even when the temperature dropped and water froze, snow fell and icicles formed on windows. Because, where I lived, it was always cold when the coffin was closed, and I was used to it.

"Kevin," I said softly, touching his shoulder. He had fallen asleep in his reading chair, a mystery story lying in his lap. From the bedroom I could hear the quiet breathing of Maddie, his wife.

"Kevin," I said again. Christmas gifts lay under the tree that touched the ceiling of his tiny Soho apartment. The point of the angel's head had scraped a bit of the paint away and some of the tinsel had fallen on the ground.

"Kevin." I almost shouted. He had always been impossible to wake. And now at thirty-six he had started to take on the look of our grandfather who could never wake up, either, no matter how loud my grandmother screamed in his ear. "Kevin!"

He stirred, and his gray eyes opened sleepily. It took a moment for them to focus and another for the impact of the situation to register.

"Kate?" His mouth formed the word but no sound came out. He started to get up out of his chair, but I pushed him back gently and put my finger to my lips.

He stared at me while the red and green Christmas lights flickered on his face. And I noticed his auburn hair was now streaked with a tiny bit of gray. Somehow I had not expected him to change.

"I must be dreaming," he said to himself.

"In a way you are," I whispered. "If ghosts are only dreams and dreams are the way the living speak to the dead."

"Kate," he said. "Kate, is that you? I mean, are you a ghost? Is that what you're saying?" He reached out to touch my arm and was surprised to feel solid, warm flesh. He had expected nothing. "But I can touch you. You're standing right here in front of me. You're alive, you've come back."

"No, Kevin," I said. "For all intents and purposes, I am dead. But I had to see you one last time."

He stood up and put his arms around me, pulling me against his chest. "Oh, Kate, no. Not dead. I hoped all these years that somehow you would come back. That it would be like the police thought at first, that you had run away with another man. Not dead. I refuse to believe it."

I pulled away from his arms and looked at his face. It was still kind and boyish, but there were lines there I had never seen. He would grow old. He would die. "Kevin, look at me. Do I look the same to you? Do I look like I belong in this world anymore?"

He stared into my eyes for a moment, and then he blinked.

"Your hair." He reached out and touched it. "Your skin and your eyes. Something's not the same. You look more . . . I don't know if *beautiful* is the word. But not dead, please, not dead."

"Kevin," I said, "a man killed me. It doesn't matter who or why. It just happened, and I never really even felt it at the time. It was quick, like going in your sleep."

I saw the tears come into his eyes, and he looked away.

"But I wanted to see you again, Kevin, one last time,

one last Christmas." I walked over to the tree and looked at the presents. Shirts, ties, and CDs. A pair of earrings, a bottle of perfume. I sat down, opened the bottle, and breathed in a little of the cologne. It smelled much too sweet. "Remember the year Dad bought Mom that awful pink sweater, and she had to wear it anyway?"

"Oh, God, yeah." Kevin sat down beside me. He picked up a book that featured a child's face and traced it with his finger. "And remember when you got the Barbie playhouse you always wanted, and I fell on top of it and broke it before Christmas was even over?"

"I was so mad at you then. Dad had to go out the next day and buy a new one."

"You know," Kevin said, sitting down again and touching his hand to his face, "it almost killed Mom and Dad, not knowing, hoping every day that you would turn up. And then finally hoping that they would at least find your body. For a long time they secretly blamed Ben for moving you to L.A. in the first place. For letting you take acting classes. For letting you drive alone there. It's only recently that they've been able to forgive him a little. You know, he's already married again."

"No. But I kind of figured that would happen."

"Mom and Dad went out to L.A. so many times themselves. Long after the police gave up. Long after Ben gave up. They tried to investigate themselves. But it was pointless. All they did was waste money and drive themselves crazy. I used all my connections as a writer to track you down. I contacted a couple of friends I have on the L.A. *Times*. But thousands of people disappear in L.A., and no one ever hears about them again."

Kevin reached out and touched my hand again. "But you feel so real, Kate, even if you don't look the same. Is this what heaven does to a person? I thought angels were supposed to wear white, not black. I know you couldn't possibly have ended up in the other place."

"It's not as simple as heaven or hell," I said.

"No, I guess it's not." Kevin turned and looked toward the bedroom. Maddie had moaned in her sleep.

"I've got to get Maddie up," he moved and knocked an ornament off the tree. It broke into tiny glittering pieces. "You don't know how much she's missed you. She'll need to see you. To know you're all right."

"Kevin." I rested my hand on his leg and held him there. He was surprised by the strength of my grip. "This is only between you and me. And only for a little while longer. I came back to tell you because I knew you would understand. There's no need to mourn anymore. I'm all right. If nothing else, I've got my wings and I can move through the night 'faster than a speeding bullet.' I'm able to 'leap tall buildings in a single bound.' And now, disguised as the ghost of Christmas Past, I've come back to tell you: I miss you, Kevin, the jokes you tell, the stories you write, the memories we have in common. I miss you, Kevin, but you're part of another world, the world I had to see one last time, but I can never see again."

He grabbed onto my hand that was holding his leg as if he thought he was stronger than me. "Please, Kate, don't go. Mom and Dad need you. Please stay. Maddie's pregnant—you're going to be an aunt. They never found your body. Please stay."

"But this is only a dream, Kevin, and I know you don't believe in ghosts." I gently pushed his hand aside, lay down, and rested my head on his knee. It reminded me of when we were children a long time ago. "And I don't believe in anything anymore."

He stroked my hair, because there was nothing else he could do, and we stayed that way for a long time as I tried to memorize his touch, and he tried to hold on to mine.

Outside, a few tiny snowflakes began to fall. Building into a storm that would cover the city and leave it white and tall. A day late but still within the boundaries of Christmas.

"Stay," he said again.

But by then I was a ghost, dissolving before his very eyes. Formless. Soulless. Drifting like the snow. And Kevin was only talking to a dream.

"Drew"—I put the menu down on the table—"I don't see why we had to meet here."

"Don't you," he said a little too loudly, and several people in the diner turned around to look at us.

After five nights of only getting his answering machine, I had finally left a message: either call me or I would come over with or without an invitation. Ten minutes later he had returned my call and agreed that we should talk in person but not at his place or mine. Instead, he gave me directions to the Dennys in Hollywood, only blocks from his apartment building.

"You don't have to shout," I said, touching his hand across the table. He flinched slightly but didn't move away.

"I thought I'd feel a little better in a public place, where there were people and a lot of lights. A lot of noise. A lot of activity."

He looked up at the waitress standing over us, her pen in hand. "I'll have the Big Breakfast, and a side of hash browns and an extra side of sausage, and a blueberry muffin, and a large orange juice and a cup of coffee, and maybe a couple of biscuits, too."

The waitress shook her head slightly and turned to me.

"Just coffee, thanks."

"Right," Drew said. "As you may have noticed, I do the eating for both of us."

The waitress didn't smile as she picked up our menus and walked away.

"I always eat a lot when I'm nervous, Kate."

"There's nothing to be nervous about," I said, leaning across the table. He seemed so far away. "Nothing's changed. It's still me. It's still Kate. Only now you know that I'll never get fat, and that we probably won't be spending a lot of time at the beach together. So big deal. Every relationship has its problems."

"But you don't exactly qualify as a human being anymore. I think that's a lot bigger problem than religion, race, morality, or even sexual preference."

He looked anxiously around the room. "You've got to admit, Kate, this is all pretty weird. How do you expect me to react? Should I be all smiles about the fact that my girlfriend has a coffin in her apartment? That when she sleeps she looks like someone's idea of a practical joke at a wake? That she has a set of fangs that would make the Big, Bad Wolf nervous? I've thought about this for days, Kate, or in your case, nights, and I still can't come to terms with it. On top of that we're playing our biggest gig yet tomorrow, on New Year's Eve, and I haven't been able to get Matt on the phone all week. Not to mention the fact that I paid two thousand dollars for an engagement ring I can't afford and I'm not sure exactly who or what I asked to marry me."

"That reminds me," I said, reaching under the table, "I forgot to give you your Christmas present."

Drew stared down at the perfectly wrapped gift in surprise.

"Go ahead," I said. "Open it, before all your food arrives."

He undid the wrapping carefully and lifted the black shirt up over our table. A man in another booth smiled in appreciation.

"It's beautiful, Kate," Drew said.

"You may not be able to fit into it, after you eat all this," the waitress said as she held the heavy tray, waiting for Drew to clear the table.

He folded the shirt back up and placed it on the seat beside him. I watched with an ever-growing feeling of disgust as she set down the plates of food. I was particularly alienated by the extra sausage.

"Enjoy!" the waitress said, and wandered away.

"Drew"—I tried not to look at the way his fork was stabbing at the hash browns—"can't things be the way they were? I love you, and I know somewhere under all this extra appetite you still love me, too. Besides that, we're about to get a record deal together."

"What about the record deal?" Drew said. "How can you go on tour when you can't go out in the sunlight? Am I going to have to transport a coffin along with all of our equipment so my bass player doesn't explode in the tour bus?"

"There are ways around everything," I said, though I had to admit traveling was something I hadn't considered. All my safety precautions were based on my residing in the condo. Being on the road would mean I would have to trust someone completely during the day, to place my life in their hands. And I would need a lot of aluminum foil for those bright hotel windows.

"Kate," Drew said, "I've got to ask you this." There was very little food left on his plate, half a biscuit at most. "If you're a vampire or whatever and you may possibly live forever . . . exactly how old are you? I mean, you haven't existed since Egyptian times or something, have you, like the mummy? I mean, am I sitting across from someone who's as old as the hills?"

"I would be four years older than twenty-seven," I said,

smiling a little, "if this hadn't happened to me. That's all."

Drew gulped down his coffee and looked around the room for the waitress. I quickly exchanged my cup for his to keep him happy.

"So you'd be thirty-one," he said. "Well, that's not too bad for the moment. You look twenty-seven, but you're thirty-one. But what about when you're sixty-five, and I'm sixty, and you still look like you're twenty-seven and I look like shit? How do you think you can keep on fooling people forever? Eventually someone's going to notice. To say nothing of what it will do to my ego."

"People don't stay together forever anymore. It's amazing if a relationship can even last five years. Why do you have to worry about old age at this point in your life? Why can't we take it one step at a time? Why can't we go back to your place?"

Drew shut his eyes for a moment, then opened them again.

"I hate to sound like Charly," he said, "but I'm afraid. What if you're lying to me? What if you're more of a vampire than you want me to believe? What if you want to change me into one of the living dead? What if you really do drink blood?"

"First of all," I said, a touch of anger in my voice, "I have no idea how to change you into the night-loving, ageless person that I am. Second of all, and I'm not going to say it again: I don't drink blood. I don't even like the way it tastes."

Drew picked up his knife from the side of his plate. A tiny bit of syrup clung to its teeth. He dragged it roughly across his wrist and cut a small hole into his skin, close to the vein. Blood began to seep out onto his plate.

"Prove it," he said, holding his wrist up to my lips.

A tiny drop fell onto my tongue, then slowly slid down

my throat. His blood tasted sweeter than any I had ever tasted. And I realized with a sudden feeling of panic and longing that it had been almost four months since I had made my last kill. My quarterly need was almost upon me.

"Prove it," he said again, pushing his wrist into my mouth.

More than anything I wanted to open my mouth wide and bite down on the soft skin of Drew's wrist. I wanted to grab his vein with my teeth, cut it open, and suck all the sweet-tasting life out of him. And I wanted to do it in the bright lights of Dennys while the rest of the world ordered their Big Breakfasts and ate them.

"Stop it," I said to Drew, summoning all of my self-control. "Stop it." And I grabbed his wrist and pushed it away. His arm hit the table with a thud and spilled the little bit of orange juice left in his glass.

"Is our food so bad it makes you want to commit suicide?" the waitress asked, standing over us again with the check. "Or are you ashamed of how much you've eaten and can't live with yourself anymore?"

"A little accident," Drew said, grabbing the check from her. He took a napkin and tied it around his wrist. I watched it go from white to red in seconds.

"I'm sorry, Kate," he said, turning to look at the half of the restaurant that was still watching us. "I apologize for being so melodramatic. For not believing you. I guess I'm being a little weird. As a matter of fact, that is probably the weirdest thing I've ever done, to say nothing of how embarrassing it is. I come into this Dennys all the time." He looked down at the pool of blood on his plate. "Shit," he said, "I feel like I'm going to get sick. Come on, let's go back to my place and get a big bandage. The bigger the better."

He threw a five-dollar tip on the table, hoping some-how to placate the waitress.

"All right, Drew," I said. "Apology accepted." But I still had the taste of his blood in my mouth, and my teeth were aching.

"What was that?" Drew said, sitting up in bed.

"What?" I asked, raising my arm to rub his back. His skin felt so warm.

"That noise. It sounded like a wolf or something."

"I didn't hear anything." I pulled him back down on top of me. He began to kiss my neck, then lifted his head to kiss my lips.

"Kate," he said, stopping for a moment, "those teeth. Where do they go when you're not sleeping? I can't feel them now."

"I don't know exactly," I said. "They just kind of re-tract or something into my gums. I don't feel them, ei-ther. Don't worry about them."

"All right," Drew said, "I'll try. To take it all day by day. To somehow deal with this uniqueness of yours. Did you know I fell in love with you the first time I saw you? The minute you first walked in the door for the audition? I would have killed Charly and Nathan if they hadn't wanted you in the band. I thought there was something so unique about you then. I had no idea how right I was."

Outside a howl sounded and echoed through the Hol-lywood streets. Something about it chilled me to the bone.

"You must have heard it that time," Drew said, and I nodded. "It's probably one of those damn coyotes that's come down from the hills. . . . Oh, well, we're safe in here."

And he pressed himself hard against me, and I held on tight. While through the window, the full moon shone.

*   *   *

Later, I sat on my own bed and wondered why it didn't
feel as comfortable as the coffin anymore. Then I reached
over and picked up the diamond ring from the nightstand. I looked closely at the tiny engravings on the gold
band and realized there was a musical note on either side.
Drew must have had it made as a special order.

Carefully I placed it on my finger. But it felt awkward
and heavy to have jewelry there again. So I quickly took it
off and set it back on the nightstand, where it belonged.

It was almost midnight. Nathan sat with a bottle of
champagne on one knee and Sherrie on the other while
his eyes focused on his watch, counting the seconds till
the next year.

Drew and I sat with them on the ripped couch in our
dressing room with plastic champagne glasses in our
hands. Drew was wearing the black shirt I had given him.

The band was not due to go on stage until 1:00 A.M. as
we were the headliners and it was New Year's Eve. This
was the largest show we had ever played, at a venue
called The Wall, which looked like an opera house without the rows of seats. They had been torn away to leave
plenty of room to dance. But the stage was still standing
with its wooden floor and its velvet curtains, and it was
raised high above the audience.

We had two other bands opening for us that did not
fare too well. The audience barely paid attention to the
first band, and the second, which was still on, had to deal
with a lot of friction from the paying customers.

The Wall had been completely sold out for a week now,
and every one of those people was waiting to see us. It
was so crowded out in the club that people could hardly
move, let alone dance, and every few minutes we would
hear them shout almost as one: "The Uninvited!"

"Where the hell did Charly go?" Drew asked. "I thought the band was going to celebrate New Year's Eve together."

"He said he had to get something from his car," I answered, brushing a piece of lint from his shirt.

"Thirty seconds," Nathan chimed in. He was already working at removing the cork.

At that moment Charly burst into the room, carrying the largest panda bear I had ever seen and two wrapped Christmas presents.

"Did I make it?" he asked.

"Ten, nine . . ."

"I thought I'd save your gifts till next year . . ."

"Five, four . . ."

"'Cause that's the year we're gonna make it big!"

"One. . . . Happy New Year!"

The cork popped out of the bottle and sprayed the dressing room walls as Nathan kissed Sherrie. Outside, the club sounded like a riot was taking place. People were screaming, and I thought I heard something fall. Drew turned to me and wiped the champagne from my eyelashes.

"Happy New Year, Kate," he said, and his lips moved against mine.

"Well, I guess that only leaves me and the bear," Charly said, putting the other presents down. And he kissed the panda that was almost as tall as him, hard and loud.

"Hey," Nathan said, "have some bubbly." And he started pouring the champagne as Charly got control of himself and handed a present to Drew and Nathan.

"Of course," Charly said, "the bear is for you."

He came over and sat beside me on the arm of the tattered couch. It had been a long time since anyone gave me a stuffed animal, probably not since I was a little girl, still harmless and sweet and human. When the idea of killing someone still seemed unthinkable to me, and marriage was still an ideal state of mind. I smiled at Charly for still seeing me that way.

"How do you like it?" he asked. "I saw him in the store, and he started yelling at me, 'Buy me for Kate, buy me for Kate,' so what could I do? Besides," he said, leaning to whisper in my ear, "I really owe you. I feel so much better since I tried to drown Drew. You know, the doctor called me just yesterday. He's back in L.A. again, and I told him to take a hike. Any man that downgrades my friends doesn't deserve to live."

"I'll drink to that," Nathan said, "but can Kate even fit that bear in her Porsche?"

"If not, I know Drew's car can carry him, or I'll hire a limo to take the panda right to her door."

"Thanks, Charly," Drew said. He had opened his gift, and it was a video of *The Beast from 20,000 Fathoms.*

"I wanted to remind you of the night I learned monsters only exist in the movies, and not in your own band."

Drew started to smile, then looked away.

"Well, I'm glad I missed the night Drew got all wet," Nathan said, "but I sure appreciate this new drumstick bag. Thanks, Charly."

Charly stood up and took a bow. Then he raised his glass in a toast.

"To the best friends I've ever had, and the best Christmas there ever was, and to all the billions of dollars we're going to make this year."

"Amen," Nathan yelled, and kissed Sherrie again.

Drew pulled on my sleeve. "Can I talk to you alone for a second outside? There's no one but a couple of bouncers on the stage wings, and we can have some peace for a second."

We got up and walked to the door.

"Uh oh," Sherrie said, "I guess they want to sing 'Auld Lang Syne' by themselves." And Nathan and Charly laughed as we left them behind.

We found a place in the long purple draperies that had been drawn aside for the show. The second band had finished, and our road crew was rushing around, setting up our equipment. The only noise we had to contend with was the DJ's music, which was nowhere near as loud as any band's.

"I'm worried about something, Kate," Drew said.

"What?" I prepared myself for the fact that the subject of my teeth was going to come up once more, or some other question about vampires. But I was wrong again.

"I haven't heard from Matt all week, and now none of us has seen him tonight, our biggest gig. I expected an answer by now. I thought he was bringing all of CMD to hear us."

"What about Lisa?" I asked.

"What about her?" Drew looked uncomfortable.

"Have you seen her? She's supposed to be in on this project, too."

"No, I haven't seen her tonight," Drew said. He looked over his shoulder as if he were expecting someone to be right behind him, but there was only empty space. "Oh, well, let's just give a great show and worry about the record company later. Do you realize that all those people screaming and stomping out there are here to see us?"

"Yes," I said. "Us."

He grabbed me and pulled me toward him. "Happy New Year again."

And we began to kiss as we lost ourselves in the curves of the velvet draperies. They felt soft and old and smelled familiar.

"Drew!" Nathan shouted from somewhere below.

"Drew, we need you, now. Jeff needs to know which microphone you want to use."

"Shit," Drew muttered. "Just when I was getting used to the New Year." And he pulled himself away and walked toward the stage, which was now hidden from the audience by another set of purple curtains.

I started to follow him, but a hand reached out, grabbed my arm, and held me in place.

"When you can't be with the one you love, love the one you're with," Justin said, and I whirled around to face him. He didn't let go of my arm, and I found myself almost face-to-face with his leather jacket. I looked up into his green eyes. "Not the most romantic lyrics, are they?"

"I'm getting real sick of these surprise visits," I said. "The mysterious vampire appears again. Do you always have to be so melodramatic?"

"I just came to say good-bye," Justin said, and he smiled a little.

"Really?" I said. "Well, I guess I won't see you for another four years. Where are you going this time? The moon or maybe beyond?"

"Denise is doing a play in Europe, so I thought I'd join her," Justin said. "L.A. is getting to be annoying again. There's nothing for me here anymore."

"And I suppose you've got a condo ready and waiting for you there?"

"Of course, but I do need a few things from my Santa Monica one. I'll stop there tomorrow night if you don't mind and pick them up. As far as I'm concerned that condo is now yours."

"Gee, thanks," I said. "Can I keep the coffin, too?"

"It's been mine for a long time, but I don't see why you can't keep on using it, if that's what you need." He stopped smiling and looked at me seriously. "Kate," he said, "are you all right? I've had a funny feeling for the last week that something was wrong. I can't quite put my finger on it. No one knows about you, do they?"

"Of course not, Justin," I said. "Everything is hunky-dory. I feel like a million bucks. As a matter of fact, I feel like I could live forever."

"Careful, Kate," Justin said. "You never know what will happen. I wouldn't tempt the fates if I were you."

"Whoa, I'm shaking in my shoes. Justin, the almighty vampire, my exalted maker, has warned me. Pride goeth before a fall."

"You know," Justin said, "I'm finding it really hard to remember what attracted me to you, too. Maybe it was only a dream, dreamt one dark night a long time ago. A dream that became a nightmare, that became a monster, that took away the Kate I used to know. I may have killed your body, but you've destroyed your soul. There was a time when I thought you needed me the same way I did you."

"Wrong again, pal," I said. "The enigmatic and elusive Justin is wrong again. But don't worry, maybe you can still fool Denise with all your deadly charm. Are you planning on changing her, too, and giving her the thrill of a lifetime? And by the way, I've been meaning to ask you —are you as old as the hills, by any chance?"

"When will you ever learn," Justin said, "I'm not your enemy. But I guess our time has come and gone without a second thought."

"Nathan!" Jeff's voice boomed from the stage beyond. "Where's your fucking snare drum?"

"Where do you think?"

And then Drew's voice, even louder. "What about my God damn Evian bottle? And where the hell has Kate disappeared to?"

Justin turned his head, but the band members still

couldn't see us behind the curtains. In the background I could hear the crowd shouting, bottles breaking, music playing. The old wooden floor creaked as he moved toward me. "The hell with everyone." Justin grabbed me tight around the waist and pulled me close until our lips were almost touching. I could feel his body pressing against mine, and I could feel his breath on my face and neck. And then he moved even closer, and our lips touched, softly at first, then harder. I was captured again as I held on tight to his leather jacket. And I remembered the way he felt, the way he smelled, the way he tasted. My tongue touched his teeth, and I felt the points caress me in return. For a moment I forgot about the club, the record contract, and all of the band members, including Drew. Justin held me harder, and then suddenly he let me go. I looked at him too dazed to speak, already missing his mouth against mine.

He reached out and touched my face with his finger. "I'm not your enemy. . . . Take care of yourself, Kate."

"Kate, Kate!" Jeff was yelling to me. "What are you doing? All of your equipment is on stage and ready to go. It's time to go on!"

I stared at the space where Justin had been, almost expecting him to appear again. But there was no one there. I raised my fist tentatively and hit the curtain. Then I hit it again until I was beating it so hard the vibrations extended across the stage.

"Kate!" Jeff grabbed my arm. But I was not in the mood to be stopped, and I sent him flying backward onto the floor. I heard the crash and turned around. It broke my current of anger to see him lying there in confusion. I reached down and picked him up in one motion and set him in a safe place. "Jesus Christ!" he said, shaking his head. Then I hurried out to meet the rest of the band, who were now in place behind the cover of the curtain. I could hear the crowd clapping already, just knowing our show was about to begin.

"Where have you been?" Drew touched my shoulder, but I pulled away and I slipped on my bass.

"Saying good-bye to the past," I said. "Happy New Year, Drew. Let's give them the show of a lifetime."

And he smiled and turned to Nathan to start the song.

It was not only the largest but the best gig we had ever played together. The band was tight, the sound of the PA was perfect, and the crowd was more than enthusiastic. We had picked up such a large following in the last year that I had trouble even believing it. The fans knew all our songs and most of the lyrics and knew each musician by name.

During the show several girls threw themselves on stage at Drew, and the bouncer had to remove them bodily. One ardent fan got hold of his ankle and refused to let go. This inadvertently brought Drew to his knees but he kept on singing in spite of it until the girl was pried loose. He laughed to me and shook his head at the fervor he had inspired. It was intoxicating.

It took four encores before we could leave the stage, and by then everyone in the band but me was exhausted but happy. I realized this was the first gig we had ever played without Charly believing Drew was a demon who had to be destroyed. It was the first gig where all the band members could look at each other and smile. Where no one was haunted by fear or regret.

"Come on," Drew said to me in the dressing room, "let's go put the panda in your car and get some air. I need a minute before everyone starts driving us nuts."

I grabbed the bear, and we headed out the back door to the fenced-in parking lot, where only the band and club employees were allowed to leave their cars.

Drew was sweating so badly that he shivered in the

glow of the moon that was just beginning to wane. The two of us pushed and pulled until the panda barely fit into the Porsche, its head lodged in the passenger seat while the rest of its body was squashed into the back. I shut the door to keep it from falling back out, and I forgot to lock it and set the alarm when Drew grabbed me and lifted me into the air.

"God, Kate," he said, "this is the best I've ever felt in my whole life. I think I'll be addicted forever to the sound a crowd of people make when they love you."

He spun me around in the moonlight, and I laughed out loud.

"Hey, guys," a voice said in the darkness, "I hate to spoil your fun, but I thought I'd have one more beer for the road away from the yammering masses inside."

"Matt." Drew put me down on the ground. "Where the fuck have you been? Did you see the show? It was great."

Matt walked a few paces toward us, then swayed a little in a drunken haze, and pitched forward to land on the front of the Porsche face first.

"Nice car, Kate," he said, straightening up. "Who's the black and white guy inside?"

"I've been trying to call you all week, Matt," Drew said. "What's the story? Did they give you an answer on the tape?"

"The tape?" he said, laughing. "The tape? Who can think of a tape when your life vanishes right before your very eyes?" He took the last swig of beer, then threw the can across the parking lot. "Hell, I've been sitting on the beach for the last few days contemplating the meaning of life. Do you realize I owe probably thirty thousand bucks, to say nothing of the car I'm leasing and the house I'm renting in Toluca Lake?"

"What are you talking about, Matt?" I said. "What about our tape? The one we've been killing ourselves to make for the last two months? The one our lives depend on!"

"It's gone, just like me." Matt brought his fist down and hit the sideview mirror hard. "One day you're the head of A and R, the next day you're thinking of what you can sell to be able to eat. They fired me, and everything that had to do with me, the day before Christmas. Sure, your show was great, but what does that matter now? You've got my blacklisted name all over you."

"I don't believe it," Drew said. "That tape's still good. Somebody's gotta listen to it. We were counting on it. You said it was in the bag."

"Grow up, Drew," Matt said. "What makes you think talent ever counted for anything? It's all about making money and the politics behind that money. And the politicians don't like me anymore, so now they don't like you."

He started to stagger back to the door of the club. We watched him climb the cement stairs, too shocked to believe what we had heard. When he got to the top, he turned around. I noticed there was sand still clinging to his Hawaiian shirt.

"Of course," Matt called to Drew, "there's still Lisa—if you know what I mean, buddy. A little more personal contact might just put you into a new ball game. Or are you smarter than you look? Were you covering your bases a few weeks ago, in case I fell by the wayside, huh, Mr. Blond Rock Star?"

Drew moved as if he wanted to punch Matt into the wall, but Matt gave a little wave and disappeared into the door. Drew looked down at his fist as if he wasn't sure if that was real, either.

"It's gone, Kate," he said. "We've lost it. Everything we've been working for. We've got to start all over again from square one. I don't believe it. Everything seemed so sure. . . . How can he be fired? He's the fucking head of A and R. Why didn't he call and let us know? Why did he leave us in the dark? Damn it!" Drew ran over and kicked Matt's beer can as hard as he could. "And damn him. Damn everybody. And fuck everybody, too."

I watched him turn in circles, unsure of what to do next. I couldn't believe it had happened to us, either. But there was something else bothering me—the memory of Lisa's hand on Drew's leg.

"What did he mean about Lisa?" I said, walking over to Drew.

Drew stopped cursing and looked at me. "That's been something I wanted to talk to you about, Kate."

He pushed his hair out of his face and looked at the moon for a moment. "When we had broken up around Thanksgiving . . . I wanted to tell you, but then the whole thing happened with your toe, and you know the rest."

"Tell me now, Drew," I said.

"Let's go inside." He grabbed my arm and walked me toward the door. "I'll tell you inside."

Before we ever reached the door, I heard a low growl echoing between the cars. The growl of an animal in pain that was ready to strike out at anything that came near it. And a familiar bad smell tickled my nose and made me want to pick up Drew and drag him inside before it was too late.

"Come on," I said, now leading the way.

And then a dark figure jumped out of nowhere and blocked our entrance to the club. He had on a different flannel shirt but that same dirty pair of jeans and those same dirty work boots. And everything about him seemed hairy.

"Hello, vampire," Henry said, and he smiled. Even in

the darkness, I could see what looked to be pieces of meat caught between his teeth. "Long time no see."

"What are you doing here?" I said, as anger began to replace every other feeling inside of me. All the memories of my downtown existence that I had suppressed for so long were beginning to flood my brain. I remembered the moonlight and Lil and all the nights we spent filling up the emptiness in each other's lives. I remembered the panic I felt when I couldn't find her that night, and the pain I felt when I heard she was dead, killed by a monster. And most of all I remembered the desire for revenge that had torn me apart, and the vow I'd made to find Henry one day and make him pay. God, how I wanted to make him pay. "What the hell are you doing here?"

"Oh, I came to hear a concert and to get a better look at your little boyfriend before the next full moon. You know I missed him last time."

"Who is this asshole?" Drew shouted, but I held him back.

"Hey, pretty boy," Henry said, and he spit in Drew's direction, "I've known your lover since way back when she lived in a godforsaken dump downtown and used to pal around with this good-for-nothing little old lady."

I hadn't realized how much I still missed Lil until this very moment, but just hearing Henry speak about my former companion made me see red. Lil had been my only friend at a time when "lost" was my middle name, when I slept on a dirt floor, when I still believed a werewolf could help me find some answers, when I still cared if there were any.

Suddenly I felt as if I was back downtown and had just heard that Lil had been ripped apart by a wild animal. My only friend—gone. And this was the werewolf that had taken her away.

"Why don't you ask the vampire what happens to anyone that calls himself her friend? As soon as the moon is full, they're history, just like you're going to be, blondie. I know where you live, and I can take down anybody, even Miss High and Mighty, if I feel like it. But somehow I've been driven to show her some professional courtesy. Kind of like one monster to another."

Henry looked up at the moon and laughed.

"Only thirty more days, and I get to tear you limb from limb, pretty boy, and watch you scream in horror while I do. That fucking little old lady screamed like there was no tomorrow."

Suddenly a cloud crossed the moon, and in that second of complete darkness, I totally lost any grounding I might have had in reality. I forgot about Drew and the other humans inside. All I wanted to do was take Henry's face off before he was able to spit out another word.

I jumped up on the steps to the doorway, grabbed him by the front of his greasy shirt, and threw him onto the cement. As he started to rise up on his knees, I jumped down and flung him flat against the brick of the building. Then I held him in place with one hand wrapped around his neck. As he struggled, I looked down at the tiny hairs that connected his eyebrows together, making them one dark line.

"You bastard," I said, "if anyone deserves to scream in horror, it's you."

He lifted his eyes and smiled, as a trickle of blood eased its way down his dirty, greasy forehead. For a moment the only sound I heard was his breathing, which began to come faster and faster, and all I could feel was the pulse in his neck, drawing me further and further into his dark world.

"Then do it," he said, mocking me. "Drink my blood if you've got the nerve. But I bet you're a wimp, just like that old lady friend of yours."

"Like hell I am," I shouted, and with my free hand I grabbed one of his ears and pulled on it a little. "Haven't you heard, Henry," I said, "vampires are a lot of things, but they're not wimps." And then I ripped his ear right off the side of his head. I looked at it for a moment, then I let it fall to the ground. Blood began to stream down the side of his neck as Henry stared at his ear in the dirt.

"What are you doing?" he moaned.

"Making you pay." I tugged on the left one, feeling skin and muscle separate, until blood ran down my fingers. And then I ripped it off and dropped it beside its mate. He fell back against the wall and began to sink to the ground, as his hands rose to feel the place where his ears used to be.

"Not so fast," I said, grabbing his arm to drag him back up to eye level. As I lifted him, I felt the snap of his arm breaking and the tiny click my teeth made as they descended from hiding.

"No!" he said. "No, wait! My ears! My ears!"

"You shouldn't even be allowed to exist," I whispered to him, and pushed the bottom of my hand into his face, breaking his nose. It crumpled like a piece of paper. At the full moon Henry was a werewolf, but right now he was as frail and harmless as any other human. He was mine for the taking. He screamed in agony, his good arm flailing in the air, his head so covered in blood, he could barely see. His mouth was wide-open, gasping for air.

"Go to hell, Henry," I said, and I reached in and grabbed his tongue and ripped it from the back of his throat. It fell down beside his ears, along with a few of his teeth I had knocked out with my hand.

He began to choke on the blood rising over the teeth he had left. His eyes had rolled to the top of his head, and at that point I don't think he knew who or what I was anymore. He crumpled to the ground, and I stood over him and watched him bleed.

But suddenly the scent of blood became overpowering, and it turned my anger into need. His throat was there waiting, and there was still enough life in him to make it worthwhile. I knelt down beside Henry and pushed his head to one side.

"You're going to get your wish," I said, as I bit down on his neck, feeling his body convulse violently and then give up. And I sucked Henry dry until the only blood left were splattered on his body and the wall.

I heard a moan behind me, and suddenly remembered Drew, who had witnessed the entire spectacle. I turned to him, wiping the blood from my lips, unsure of what to say. But he was already running, and he reached the iron link fence surrounding the parking lot and began to scale it.

"Drew!" I shouted. "Wait! Let me explain!"

But then I heard another noise from my right, and I looked up to see Charly's red hair and the tears in his eyes. He had come outside looking for Drew and me, but I never heard the door open because I was so lost in sending Henry to hell. "Not you!" Charly made the sign of the cross, jumped behind the door, and slammed it shut. I heard the bolt of the lock being drawn.

But I didn't have time for Charly now. I stood up to look for Drew, but he was already gone. But I could still hear the sound of his running feet.

I left Henry a bloody and lifeless mess. I could worry about his disposal later. It was much easier to look for someone on foot by air, so I dissolved into dust and floated toward the sound of his black boots scraping.

He made it as far as five blocks, and then he collapsed on the sidewalk and vomited over and over again.

I materialized beside him and began to rub the back of

his head. He jerked around and looked at me, tears streaming down his face.

"Oh, shit, oh, shit," he muttered. "You can fly, too." And he threw up one last time.

"Listen, Drew," I said, as he laid his head down on his arm, exhausted, "I had to do that. He would have killed you next."

But Drew wasn't listening.

"You tore a man's ears off and his tongue. It was the most disgusting thing I've ever seen and then, oh, God . . . then you bit him with those God damn teeth and sucked out his blood. I saw the whole thing. You can't lie to me anymore. You kill people and drink their blood."

He began to tear at the shirt I gave him, trying to rip it off.

"Henry wasn't a man," I said, trying to stop him from ruining the shirt. "He was a monster. A werewolf. He would have tracked you down next month and ripped your body apart."

"Oh, yeah, right," Drew said, starting to cry again. "Now you're gonna tell me werewolves exist. . . . What the hell is happening to me? What did I do wrong in a past life that I lose my record contract and watch my girlfriend rip some lowlife into a million pieces all in one night? He's not the monster—you are. And I almost married a monster. It sounds like one of Charly's movies. Oh, God, there was so much blood."

He dry-heaved a little, but there was nothing left.

"I'm sorry, Drew." I stroked his hair. I wanted to placate him, to calm him down, until I had time to think. There was no way I was going to let Henry ruin everything for me again. "I'm sorry you had to see that. He killed a very good friend of mine a long time ago, and now he was going to kill you. Please, I'm sorry, I do need blood. But not that often. I couldn't tell you before, you'd

never have understood. Really, Drew, it's not that bad.
It's no worse than people eating animals to survive. Try to
understand. I only do what I have to do, when I have to
do it. I love you, Drew. I'd never hurt you. And I couldn't
let Henry hurt you, either."

Drew's pale face turned even paler, and he made an
attempt to stand, to regain some of his control. But the
world was spinning before him.

"Oh, no," was all he said, and then he passed out cold.

I looked at Drew lying on his bed. His arm thrown
carelessly to one side. His eyes shut in the denial of sleep.
His face felt cold and his feet even colder. So I took off
his socks and rubbed his toes, wondering if he would
come to before the dawn broke again.

After he had collapsed on the street, I had carried him
the other three blocks to his apartment, which was lo-
cated only minutes from The Wall. Drew had been running there all along. It's amazing how even when we are
blinded by terror, we can always find the direction home.
Even if we never reach it.

After making sure he was all right and tucking him into
bed, I had headed back to the club to assess the damage
done. The Wall was almost empty, and Charly was nowhere to be seen, but I found Nathan in the dressing
room, looking confused.

"Where have you been?" he said. "And where's
Drew?"

"We went back to the apartment to celebrate with
some more champagne," I said. "Drew got completely
bombed and is now asleep. I came back to get my bass
and the Porsche before everything closed."

"Gee," Nathan said, "I was afraid something was
wrong. Charly took off like a bat out of hell after the

show, and then you two were missing. And as far as I can tell, no one from CMD was here either."

"It's New Year's," I said. "You know how record people are. All they ever want to do is party. And Charly's probably off on a tangent again. Why don't you and Sherrie go home, and we'll worry about everything tomorrow. I'll be over at Drew's in the evening. . . . Give us a call."

Outside, in the parking lot, shadows engulfed the area where the pieces of Henry were left, and the blood was splattered on the wall. He had become one with the darkness, and apparently no one else had seen his remains as they got in their cars and left.

I took out my pack of matches and lit the fire that would burn the evidence away. When only the bones were left, I pulverized them with my foot until they were like particles of sand mixed with the dirt. Even if someone noticed the debris and the dried bloodstains on the wall, it would make very little sense.

While I watched Henry burn, as he should burn in hell, I thought about checking on Charly, but I decided to wait another night. Maybe I could reason with him. Buy a little time. Appeal to that part of Charly that liked to watch monster movies. The part that wanted to be my friend.

But now the sun was inching its way across the continent, and I wanted to spend what little time was left with Drew.

Drew stirred a little and kicked his foot in a reflex action. I held on to the warmth I had generated in his big toe, but it was fading fast.

His eyes opened, and he jumped into a sitting position, as if someone had lit a fire under the bed.

"You!" he said. "What are you doing? What's going on?"

"I took you home," I said, barely moving on the bed. "It's okay."

"Kate, it's not okay." He drew his knees to his chin. "It's not okay." His hand flew out as if indicating the entire world was not okay. "I've never seen so much blood, and I've never actually seen someone die except on TV."

"He was a killer," I said.

"Oh, you mean, just like you?" Drew laughed a little. "Don't you think someone's going to notice the body?"

"I took care of it," I said, and I moved a little closer.

"Don't touch me," Drew said. "Whatever you do, don't touch me." The shadows were getting longer in the room. "I can't stand it anymore. If you're going to kill me, then get it over with. If not, don't touch me again."

I moved closer, reaching out my hand. But he looked at the window triumphantly.

"Look," he said, "it's almost time. You don't want to blow up, do you? Like the fucking A-bomb? Better hurry back to that coffin of yours. Better play dead."

I turned my eyes to the curtains and could see the night beginning to evaporate. Black becomes gray becomes white. There really wasn't any time left. But I knew Drew would come around. He had to. He loved me. He had bought me an engagement ring. It would just be harder this time. I would have to overcome the visual spectacle, the smell and feel of violent death. But I would do whatever I had to do to win him back. There was always tomorrow.

I withdrew my hand and walked to the window. There was no need for pretense anymore. And with one last look at Drew, I melted away, hearing him say, as I escaped the sun again: "I've always hated things that fly."

* * *

I was dreaming. And even in my dream, I was surprised that I was dreaming again. There was something so alien, so human about it.

And even more surprising was that it was daytime. The sun was shining down on my hair and on my legs, as I sat on the beach reading a book about vampires.

How silly, I thought, turning the page.

The king of all vampires had just gorged himself on a young girl's blood and had thoroughly enjoyed himself. Blood dripped down the sides of his mouth as his stark white face took on the mask of a human.

How silly, I thought again. Yet there was something horribly familiar about the whole thing. As if I had read this book before. I shifted uncomfortably and shielded my eyes from the rays.

And as my memory began to return, so did the power of the sun. The gentle warmth that had been tanning my body now began to set my skin on fire. Why had I ever come to the beach? I couldn't remember. What had I been thinking about? I began to run as the skin on my back began to blister and burn. And then I screamed. And as I screamed, I heard a man laughing. Soft and restrained.

It's the king of the vampires, I thought, *and I'm only dreaming. If I open my eyes, I will wake up.*

But then the laughing continued, and I realized I was awake. And the man laughing wasn't part of my dream. And I was tied up again. Like I had been so many years ago. I was bound by my hands and feet to the bed that I never slept in anymore. And my naked body was covered by a sheet that also covered my face. Just like a morgue.

"Careful," the laughing man said, "or you'll wake up the dead."

And I struggled to see and breathe under the sheet. Struggled to establish what exactly had happened. How could this be happening to me? My wrists twisted and turned in the metal cuffs, but I couldn't break free. I was helpless against them. I tried to dissolve into nothing, to will myself into flight. But no matter how hard I thought, my body remained. I was captured and my power was somehow gone. And the pain from the metal handcuffs was as real as the fear that was starting to seep into my brain.

"Who are you?" I shouted.

But he laughed again.

"You don't know who you're dealing with," I threatened. But I wasn't that sure of myself, and my voice broke.

He laughed even harder. "But I do know what I'm dealing with. I really do. That's what makes it so funny. My plan finally worked. Finally I found you and my ingenious idea worked. I can't believe how lucky I am. God is truly on my side. I'm sure now, he'll forgive me my mistakes. Now that I can send one of the devil's own back to hell. . . . You'll like hell," he said. "It's hot, and the fire burns all the time. It's a regular Dante's Inferno."

"What are you talking about?" I said, trying to keep my mind under control. "Let me go."

But the only answer I heard was the clink of metal. The sound of tools being removed from a little black bag.

"I've sent Charly away," he said, as if I had asked. "He's too much of a child to see this. He's afraid of blood. He really is, but I'm not. I'm used to it. I almost like it in a certain way. . . . Everyone bleeds, you know; it's a universal thing. God gave us blood so we can bleed."

I twisted my head wildly to remove the sheet, but it held on with a life of its own.

"It's too bad about all the deaths it took for me to find the real thing. But I'm not to blame. I did it in the name of God. He knows I did, and he'll forgive me. . . . But I was smart this time. Age gives you wisdom. No stake through the heart for you. It's unfortunate those other people had to suffer, especially that woman who was with child. But I had been so sure they were the devil's disciples, that all of them flew through the night and drank the blood of the living. . . . How could I have known they were only human until I drove the stake deep into their bodies, and they just died . . . and did not burn away?"

God, I thought. *God, please, why can't I move? What is happening to me? I should be able to break these handcuffs and send this madman to the moon.*

"But the wonder drug did it," he continued, giggling along the way. "It took away your powers, made you as helpless as any human being. I gave it to you while you slept. Dissolved it in your mouth, which was still wet in your sleep, even when your heart did not beat or your lungs take in air. Your teeth. They were the final proof. Even though Charly saw you rip that poor man apart and drink his blood, it took seeing you lying there in that hideous coffin to really make him scream. So I sent him away. I couldn't be sure if my plan would work. And if it did, Charly would probably faint or throw up when he saw what I planned to do to you. . . . So I lied to him. A white lie, really. The kind of lie you tell a child who cannot take the truth."

"Who are you?" I screamed, the sheet filling my mouth.

"I'm a doctor." He pulled the sheet down from my face. "A coroner, really, a medical examiner, Dr. Reeves —and I regret to inform you that you've died, and it's absolutely necessary that we do an autopsy."

I looked with horror at his grinning face, his white hair sticking up every which way, his one blue eye, his one brown, and then I saw the glint of steel laid out carefully on the nightstand next to my diamond ring, ready for the operation. A scalpel, a bone cutter, and more scalpels. Razor sharp. Ready to cut a person apart.

"No!" I screamed, struggling even though I knew it was useless. "No!" Because it was starting to become clear what he intended to do. I hadn't felt fear like this in such a long time. The tables were turned, and I wasn't in control of the situation. The tables were turned, and I was the victim. I found it overwhelming. "No!"

"Yes," he said, leaning in toward my face. "My wonder drug had rendered you powerless. Made you as weak as a kitten. Made you able to feel pain again."

"What drug?" I whispered. "What drug?"

"Why, aspirin, my dear," he said, his eyes crossing for a moment. "Something so simple, I should have thought of it a long time ago. It thinned your blood out. Neutralized your skin. The drug that has helped humanity for so long, that takes away fever and pain, has had the reverse effect on you. Your power is gone. Now you're not so strong and scary, are you?"

"But why?" I said. "I've never done anything to you . . . or Charly, either." I started to cry and was surprised at how tears felt again as they fell down my face. It had been so long since I was able to cry.

"Not you, but someone like you, same difference. My brother was taken away by a monster like you. Maybe he wasn't perfect. Maybe he did some bad things. But that's no reason for him to die such an un-Christian death. You are smart but not smart enough. We found your address on the registration inside that black horror of a Porsche, and we cut through your security system like scissors through paper. And now it's like rock against water. I'm going to cut you open . . . while you're still alive. I'm going to make you pay for my brother's death. Someone has to. It's taken me twenty-five years, but it will be worth it. You won't die right away. You'll live for a little while. As I get to see just what it is inside that makes a vampire tick, that makes a vampire breathe, that makes a vampire have to drink another living soul's blood. And all the while you'll scream in agony as you watch yourself being ripped apart. To have all your internal organs, which no one is ever meant to see, exposed and bleeding."

At that point I started to scream, and I really could not stop, as his old and shaking hands picked up the first available scalpel. He pulled the sheet down around my feet, and I was left with no protection.

"Vampire," he said, making the sign of the cross, "get ready to be sent to hell."

For a moment all I could think of was Drew. The way he looked when he slept—innocent, angelic, with the suggestion of a smile on his face. And of how I would never have the chance to explain to him, to make him understand. That there were worse things in this world than me. That I wasn't the monster he thought I was.

I looked at the white walls that had protected me for so long, at the black clothes that hung so neatly in the closet. I had pushed Justin's aside, but mine were identical—dry-cleaned and pressed without the taint of human life. I looked toward the coffin, but the doctor had seen fit to close that door. To leave my final resting place hidden.

And then I thought of Justin, sitting next to me after my acting debut and looking at me with those green eyes. I had really loved him back in that lifetime. I had risked my marriage, everything I had, just to be close to him for one night. Why had I been so hard on him when I found out the truth? Always sending him away? When I had called out his name in my sleep, praying he would take me away? He had answered my prayers, but not in a way I could understand. And just like Drew and all of human-

ity, I had only shown fear when confronted with something strange and new.

The doctor lowered the scalpel and positioned it at the
center of my chest. He wet his lips with his tongue, as if
he were about to carve the Thanksgiving turkey. And
then he began to cut.

But as I felt the first shock of pain, so unfamiliar but so
easily recognizable, I also heard someone else in the
house. Someone coming down the stairs. Someone, *please
God,* someone to save me.

"What are you doing?" Charly asked, staring at my
naked body and the trickle of blood that had now reached
my waist. He looked as if he hadn't slept in days. His eyes
were swollen and his white tee shirt a wrinkled mess.
"You said you were only going to neutralize her. To take
those awful powers away. So she wouldn't have to drink
blood. So she could be Kate again."

Charly averted his eyes, as if he were at a peep show
he'd been forced to attend. He stared, instead, at the
perfect symmetry of my clothes hanging in the closet.
"Doctor, please, you can't hurt her like that!"

"Charly." The Doctor brandished the scalpel in the air.
"You're a fool and a baby. You know all vampires must
be killed. Go back outside. I told you to wait. This is not
something you want to see. I've examined dead bodies a
million times, so I'm prepared for how revolting it can be.
It's my job."

With a look of satisfaction, the doctor turned away
from Charly and began to cut again. "It hurts, doesn't
it?" he said to me.

Charly stood at the foot of the bed, unsure of what to
do next, as tears streamed down my face and I choked in
pain. His eyes met mine. "Please," was all I got out, and
then I jerked in the involuntary reflex of agony.

"Stop!" Charly's fist hit the footboard of the bed. "Please stop!"

"I can't stop, Charly." The doctor sighed impatiently but didn't falter. "She deserves to die. As a matter of fact, she's already dead. She's evil, and it will serve God if we know how she works. If you're going to stay, then learn from this. Watch how a vampire's blood may circulate differently from a human being's. If any of the vital organs have changed. Watch how she reacts to pain."

"This is horrible!" Charly moved to the side of the bed and grabbed the doctor's hand. For a moment their fingers locked across the bed. "I never meant for you to cut her up. She's been my friend. I have feelings for her. If it weren't for Drew—"

"Idiot." The doctor's free hand pushed him aside into the nightstand. The clock fell onto the floor. "If I don't make her suffer, then all the innocent people I've killed to find a true vampire will have died in vain. God, I had to bury that unborn child, too. It's all her fault! Now I have to make her pay, to find out what makes her body work even after death. So I can wipe all the other vampires off the face of the earth. Then this planet will be clean and safe, and my brother will be proud and God will make me a saint, and I will sit at his left hand with all the other angels."

He lowered the scalpel and cut a little further toward my stomach.

"First," he said, "I will pull back the layers of skin to reveal the heart and the lungs—"

I screamed in a pain that I never thought possible. And that scream turned into a word, turned into a name. "Charly!"

Charly rushed to the other side of the bed and threw his arms around the doctor in an attempt to stop him. They struggled frantically. "Damn it, Charly, I'm warning you!" The doctor broke free, turned, and sliced Charly's shoulder with the scalpel.

"What are you doing?" Charly touched his shirt, then looked in disbelief at the blood on his hand.

"You're bewitched, Charly. Get out of my way, or I'll kill you, too, if I have to. You're the one that helped me find this thing, this monster. So sit back and watch the fun."

Charly's disbelief turned into anger, and he lunged at the doctor again. "You fucking bastard!"

I screamed as the doctor, true to his words, drove the scalpel directly into Charly's stomach. It twisted and ravaged him inside. As the doctor pulled the scalpel back, it dripped blood onto my clean bedroom carpet.

Charly staggered back a few steps, and his white tee shirt turned red. He looked around the room, unsure of what had just happened, then collapsed into a kneeling position at the side of the bed. He looked as if he was about to pray, but instead grabbed my leg and tried to pull himself back up. "Kate." But the life was draining out of him, and he was too weak to fight anymore. "I'm sorry, Kate, I tried." His grip weakened. "Now you owe me."

I struggled with the handcuffs, wanting to do something, anything to help him, but I was powerless. Charly turned his head for a moment to look at my face, and I was reminded once again of the Phantom Zone where monsters were real. Then his eyes flew to the top his head. His hand released my leg, and he slid to the floor.

"I'm sorry too, Charly," the doctor said, standing over him. "But you're just another victim. An innocent in the way of my obliterating true evil. A martyr for the cause."

"Charly," I moaned. I could see the side of his head and his arm, but I couldn't see his face. And then I screamed as loud as possible, "Help him! Help him!"

over and over again to the doctor, begging him to save Charly even if he was dead set on putting an end to me. But the doctor laughed, instead.

"God knows," he said, picking up a pair of retractors, "I'm only doing my job."

But then there was another noise upstairs. Someone else in the house. Someone running down the stairs. Footsteps quiet but heavy. The sound of sneakers on the carpet.

The doctor grabbed a piece of my flesh with his retractors and began to pull it aside. I could feel the metal tearing at my skin.

I heard a voice say, "Police! Hold it!" But the doctor only laughed again, as Charly and I moaned in unison.

"This is a vampire," he said. "She must be taught a lesson and then be sent to the hell that created her."

He picked up the scalpel again to cut at some resistant skin. I heard the sound of the safety of a gun being released. The doctor heard it, too, and he turned with his weapon to lunge at whoever had dared to interrupt his holy mission. I heard the shot fired and I saw the look on the doctor's face as it hit his forehead. And then his forehead blew away. It was a look of disbelief, as he met his Maker and found that he was bound for hell, too.

I looked up gratefully into the face of Detective Warren, my guardian angel, who was now carefully lowering his gun and then speaking into a walkie-talkie.

"Call an ambulance. Two people injured, one dead. Jamie, come down and give me a hand." Warren pulled the sheet over my body, then noticed the keys to the handcuffs on the nightstand. "Take it easy," he said, as he released me from my chains. "Don't move." He sat down on the bed beside me.

I heard the clump of shoes as Jamie joined his partner and surveyed the scene before him. "Oh, Christ!" My

clean white bedroom looked like a torture chamber to
him. Jamie knelt down by Charly's side and held his head
in his arms. He pulled the blanket off the bed and used it
to try to stop the bleeding, but it was useless. "It's all
right," he said to Charly over and over again.

I tried to move, but Warren insisted I lie still. He
pressed his hand against the sheet but the bleeding had
almost stopped. It hadn't really been that bad, after all.
Or maybe I still had some healing powers left. I could
almost feel my body repairing the wound the doctor had
made only inches away from my heart. I tried to speak
but it sounded like I was gasping for air, instead. I
couldn't find the words for what I wanted to say. Warren
raised my head and held me in his arms like a baby. "He's
dead. He can't hurt you or anyone else again. Thank
God, I got to you in time, before he drained you of blood,
too. I hate these religious psychos. I'm so glad I've been
following your guitar player. What is this world coming
to?" He looked toward the stairs, but no one was there.
"Hold on. You'll be okay."

"Charly?" I said, looking into the detective's eyes.
"Charly?"

Detective Warren looked down to Charly's bleeding
body that was staining my white carpet forever. It was an
image that would never leave me. Jamie, who was still
sitting on the floor and holding him, shook his head. I
heard Charly's voice float up from the floor.

"Kate." He sounded as if he were speaking from far
away. "I'm so sorry, Kate. He was crazy. I can see that
now. I never meant for you to suffer, believe me. I only
did what I had to do . . . what I thought I had to do."
He coughed and wheezed in pain.

"Hush," Jamie said, but it was no use.

"If only things had been different . . . if only I had
never walked out in the parking lot last night . . . if only

I had never wanted to play music . . . if only someone had made the rules clear, showed us right from wrong, good from evil, men from monsters, girls from boys. . . . If only you had loved me, instead of Drew. . . . If only, if only, if only . . . I will use my last breath to tell you . . . if only I had never been born, and you had never been made. . . ."

I heard a funny noise, a rattle, and Charly was gone. And Jamie was laying his head back down on the carpet, as the paramedics rushed into the room. And one of them began to tape me back together again.

"If only," Detective Warren said, as he held my hand. I had a final image of Charly shouting in amazement as the Beast from 20,000 Fathoms met its death in an amusement park sometime in 1953. "If only . . ."

When, I thought, *will God ever hear our prayers?*

"You're taking this really well," Detective Warren said, his eyes leaving the road for a second. "You're a very brave woman. A lot of people would have just fallen apart after something like that."

"Thanks," I said from the passenger seat, "but at least it's over now." Though I could still feel the pain from the cut in my chest.

They had insisted on taking me to the hospital, even though I had protested over and over again that I was all right. Lucky for me the emergency room was very crowded that night, and my injuries appeared so minimal the doctor on call barely examined me. In his eyes, I was alive and able to walk and talk, which was a lot better than the three accident victims who arrived right behind me, along with two teenage boys that had been shot by their own father.

Whether I was human or vampire anymore, I didn't know, but the last place I wanted to stay was a hospital.

Even though my powers were gone, I didn't need anyone doing elaborate tests and finding something strange. Besides, I wasn't feeling that well. Not like myself at all. I didn't want to be alone, but I didn't want to deal with hospital nurses, either. What I wanted was to have Drew hold me and help me forget what had just happened. So when Detective Warren, who had waited at the hospital to make sure I was all right, offered to drive me somewhere, I asked him to take me to Drew's, where I knew I would be cared for.

"Yes, it's over." The detective turned his car onto Santa Monica Boulevard. "God knows how many people that maniac killed, believing they were vampires or whatever. Apparently he got that guy Mitch, your predecessor, and maybe Thomas Hyden—"

"And a lot of others," I said. "He was ranting and raving about killing people in New York, Florida, and Vegas. He even said he had murdered a pregnant woman." I started to cry a little, as the image of the scalpel reaching my stomach came into my mind again.

Detective Warren reached over and patted my hand. "Are you sure you'll be all right? I would have preferred you'd stayed at the hospital, let them check you out, maybe talk to a counselor."

"I'll be okay. I'll be better off with my boyfriend than anywhere else." I twisted the diamond ring I had placed on my finger. I wanted Drew to hold me and help me forget what had just happened.

"Well," the detective said, "like I mentioned, you can come down to the station or I can come to you in a few days to take your statement. Forensics will be poking around your house all night, so I wouldn't go back there right away. And you'll want to hire someone to clean a little, if you know what I mean."

"Yes," I said, "the rug is ruined." And I thought of all

the people who were now scouring my apartment for evidence. There was nothing I could do to keep the police from investigating the scene of a crime, but with my secret door closed and locked, there wasn't much I had to worry about.

Except for Charly, who was still lying there, waiting for chalk marks to be drawn around his body. Charly, who had been afraid of the dark and the cold. Charly, who had tried to save me in the end, even though he knew exactly what I was. Just like Lil, he had seen what I was capable of but wanted to be my friend anyway. If only I had been able to save him. If only.

"You know"—I brushed the tears from my face—"Charly never killed anyone. He was just mesmerized for a short time by the doctor. Caught under his spell. First, he thought Drew was a vampire. Then, it was me. But when he saw what that madman intended to do, he risked his life to stop him. He risked his life for me."

"I know," the detective said. "Charly saved your life in more ways than you know. I had been following him, convinced he was linked to the murders. He certainly seemed weird enough. I was at your gig last night, and afterward he seemed very agitated, so I decided to follow a hunch and stay on his tail. If he hadn't run back into your condo and left the door wide-open, I wouldn't have heard you scream. . . . God!" He shook his head as we pulled up to Drew's apartment. "At least I had just cause to enter without a warrant."

He parked the car, and together we walked up toward the door as the first few raindrops began to fall. A storm was setting in, gathering its forces and preparing to assault L.A. with the fiercest bout of rain it had felt for the last four years.

Detective Warren had called Drew earlier, only saying there had been an accident, that I was all right but couldn't be alone and that he was bringing me over. What could Drew say to that but yes? He had no idea what was going on, but I'm sure he knew it was something bad. Maybe fatal.

As we walked the familiar path to the entrance of Drew's apartment building, I saw the first flash of lightning illuminating the western sky with a sinister clarity. And several long seconds later I heard the crack of thunder, which startled me even though I'd been expecting it all along.

It was then I realized how much I needed to have Drew's arms around me, to hold me close against his body and tell me everything would be all right. I needed his humanity, his compassion, and his understanding. I started to cry. The sky became darker. The rain began to fall. Thick drops of water, chilled from the night air. Perhaps there was a part of me that was still human after all, the part that missed Lil, regretted Charly, and reached out to Drew. Perhaps the aspirin that took away my vampire strength and gave me back my tears might also resurrect my soul and allow me to live in sunlight again. I would wait and see, but for now all I wanted was for Drew to touch me again. The world suddenly seemed like a very bad place and there were more monsters out there than I'd ever dreamed of.

Detective Warren knocked on Drew's door as a wave of weakness overcame me, and I realized I was now sweating, a habit I had given up years ago. Drew opened the door a crack as if he was expecting to be doused with water again, but he finally gave in. "Come in," he said stiffly and threw me a suspicious look.

The detective helped me to the sofa, almost stumbling over a half-filled bag of cheese puffs and a full bag of potato chips. Drew was on an eating spree again, and the empty containers of Chinese food on his reclining chair made me feel slightly queasy.

Warren stood in the center of the room and prepared to give Drew the bad news. I laid my head down on the sofa arm, and I felt my stomach begin to harden, as if something bad had found its way there and was forming a permanent fixture.

"I'm sorry to have to tell you this," he said, "but your friend Charly is dead." Drew shot a quick look at me, but I was too weak to even appear guilty.

"This doctor he's been associating with—a serial killer, really—has been murdering people all over the country for years believing they are vampires. He apparently convinced Charly that first you and then Kate were also vampires. Tonight the two of them broke into her house, tied her up, and the doctor was planning to . . . Excuse me, Kate," he said and pulled Drew into the kitchen.

I could hear only the low hush of the detective's voice, but I knew he was giving Drew the gory details. There was only stunned silence on Drew's part until I heard him say, "And Charly died trying to save her?" And then the detective was walking to the door. He smiled at me across the room.

"Get some rest. I'll see you in a few days. Drew, take care of that girl, she's very special."

Drew shut the door quietly behind him and then leaned back against it. His face was very pale, and when he closed his eyes, there was no color at all.

"Charly," he said, then lifted his head. "That fucking doctor killed him . . . and for what?"

"Drew," I said, "I'm sorry about Charly, more than you'll ever know, but I don't feel good. I need to go to bed."

"What are you talking about?" he said. "It's nowhere near daylight yet."

"I know, but the doctor took away everything that makes me what I am, at least for tonight. He gave me aspirin, of all things, and it somehow negated my powers . . . and now I really don't feel well. I thought maybe it had cured me, but instead I feel like something bad is happening. . . . Drew, please." I reached out my hand. "He was going to cut me up. Please, help me get to bed."

Drew didn't move from the door.

"Why would Charly change his mind at the last moment? Why would he care what happened to you once he saw what you were? You ripped a man to pieces. . . . So what, if that guy tried to hurt you?"

"Drew," I said, crying again. "Please . . . I think maybe I'm poisoned. Help me. Please." I got up from the sofa, walked a few paces, then collapsed on my knees. The hardening pain in my stomach was beginning to extend outward through my veins. A chemical reaction. Nuclear fallout. The first touch of death. "Drew."

He walked over and stood beside me. "So what am I supposed to do now? Someone gave you a couple of aspirin, and you don't feel right. Meanwhile Charly's dead. You say your power's gone. What does that mean? Do you still need blood to survive?"

"Drew," I said, crying, my face against the floor, "I don't know. I don't know anymore. You said you loved me. Can't you help me now? I'm in pain. And I feel cold and I'm having trouble breathing . . . and I'm afraid."

He reached down and picked me up, his hands hot against my skin. Outside, the rain pounded as if it meant to wear the roof away. Drew carried me to the bed that we had spent so many nights in. I wanted him to never let me go, but he set me down on the mattress and pulled away. And lying there, even with the blanket drawn against my chin, I could not get warm.

Drew sat down on the edge of the bed and looked at me.

"What can I do, Kate?" he said, shaking his head. "What can I do? You're not even human."

I shivered beneath the sheets as sweat rolled down my face and mixed with my tears. I began to twist and turn from the pain but could find no relief. I tried to focus on Drew's face, but instead my eyes were drawn to the window where the rain was reflected. The reflection formed shadows on the wall and the shadows began to take shape. They began to twist and turn, too, as if they were part of my pain. Pain. Pain. Pain. I was sure of it now. Somehow the aspirin was poisoning me.

I heard the phone ring, and Drew got up to walk into the living room to answer it.

"Don't go," I said, but he was already gone.

His voice floated back to me in the darkness, but the words were lost as I moaned from being tortured. "We cannot suffer the witch to live," someone said, but it was only a shadow in the corner.

"I have to go," Drew said, standing over me again.

"No." I tried to touch him. It looked like Drew, but I wasn't really sure. Maybe it was only someone pretending to be Drew, an impostor. I did not remember him being so cold.

"It's important. It's Lisa. It's about maybe still getting a record contract."

"No, don't leave me. Something's wrong. . . . I'm afraid." Two shadows were dancing in the moonlight.

"Look, Kate, there's nothing I could do for you anyway. It's not like I could get you to a hospital or something. You'll be fine. Remember how fast you got over your toe? Vampires are always fine. Vampires live forever. Lisa can't wait. If there's even a slim chance that CMD might still want me, I have to find out. Just stay in bed and rest. I won't be long. By the time I get back, you'll probably be up and flying."

I grabbed Drew's wrist, but I had lost all of my strength. Paper against pain. Pain against shadows. "It hurts, doesn't it?" the doctor had said. And I had forgotten how much some things can hurt.

"I'm afraid to be alone," I said. "Please don't leave me here alone."

But he shook free of me, grabbed his jacket from the closet, looked in the mirror, and combed his hair.

"I'll be back in a little while," he said. "You'll be all right." I lifted my head in agony, looking for Drew in the darkness. "Drew, I'm afraid I'm dying." The lightning lit up the room, showing me there was no one there. Only ghosts and shadows and memories and the thunder that seemed to be getting closer all the time.

It was ironic that the doctor had died without ever knowing just how far-reaching the damage of his wonder drug could be. A modern-day vampire cure. As long as it was absorbed by the vampire herself and not distilled through anyone else's blood.

Aspirin was a lot less messy than a stake through the heart or exposure to sunlight. What cured humans of fever and pain was to a vampire poison, slow and painful. Sharp and cold. I was dying, and there was nothing I could do about it. I just didn't want to die alone.

"Drew," I said out loud, "I'm afraid. I'm afraid of spiders and rats, and I'm afraid of being alone for too long, and I'm afraid of serial killers, rapists, and the possibility of aliens. And I'm afraid of going crazy and never accomplishing anything . . ."

Someone had said those words, a long time ago on a stage. It must have been another lifetime. So much had happened since I'd found myself standing before Sandy Klein's acting group. I didn't even know the meaning of the word *fear* then. But I knew real fear when I woke up in Justin's bedroom that first time, and later when I realized what I really had become, a monster forced to feed on other people to survive. And I knew fear when I watched the doctor's face fill with a holy purpose, and heard Charly's words as he died, and saw Drew's eyes as I reached out to him and he combed his hair and walked away.

I turned to look at Drew's alarm clock, its red numbers burning in the darkness. It had already been an hour since he'd left. *He'll come back for me,* I thought. *He has to come back to me.* I looked at the clock again. Another hour had passed and I didn't remember it going by.

"And I'm afraid that there is no heaven or hell, only nothingness."

How wrong I had been. As I lay dying, I realized that nothingness might have been a welcome relief. A one-way trip to oblivion. Instead, I could see quite clearly that there was another world after this, another place. And it wasn't heaven or hell. And it wasn't reincarnation. It was just another place, a different world, where nothing was familiar, and where you had to learn everything all over again, and you could take nothing there with you and you wouldn't know anyone. And all the people you had loved in this world, you would never find again.

"And I'm afraid of dying, because I know it will hurt and because there are so many things I won't have done and will never have the opportunity to do again . . ."

I turned to check the time again, but Drew's bedroom was starting to fade. There was only me and the darkness and pain. And soon I would leave, and there would only be darkness. And the pain would have to find another home.

I heard a noise somewhere in the room, and it brought

me back. I was filled with joy. He had come back for me. Drew *had* come back. I could hear his soft breathing.

"Drew," I said, and I strained to see his face.

"No," said a voice that sounded as cool and distant as Drew's had hours ago. "It's Justin."

"Justin?" I fought the pain that threatened to take me under. I didn't want him to see me like this—helpless and afraid. "How did you find me?"

"I know where to look," his voice answered somewhere across the room. "Where is that idiot boyfriend of yours?"

"He'll be right back," I said, trying to find him in the darkness. I could see the shape of something moving by the window. But it blurred into a liquid line. "Why don't you run along to Europe before you miss the dramatic event of the century?"

"I'm going," Justin said, "but first I want to know what's going on." He moved to stand at the foot of the bed. "Are you all right? You look ill, tired." He hesitated. "Almost human."

I summoned all of my strength and self-control and leaned up on my arm. "I'm fine. I just had a wild night, and I capped it off with a little too much physical enjoyment, if you know what I mean." A wave of dizziness hit me, but I ignored it as best as I could. "Any more personal questions?"

Justin sighed. "Just one. Why are there police all over my condo and blood all over my bedroom?"

"I thought it was my condo, my bedroom," I said, trying to keep from crying out in pain. I wouldn't be able to keep this act up much longer. "Don't worry about the police, Justin. They'll be gone by tomorrow night. They don't know a damn thing about me or you or your coffin or your videotapes. Almost anybody that knew anything is now dead. You can get your little mementos tomorrow and then fly to your lover's stage debut and live forever. Isn't that what vampires are supposed to do? To live forever? And forever is a long time. A long, long time. How long is it? It's so long that—"

"Okay," Justin said, "since you seem to be your usual charming self and—you're sure you're all right?"

"I'm fine, I'm fine." I smiled, but it felt unnatural.

"Then I have nothing to worry about. I guess you can take care of yourself, after all. So I'll give you your wish, Kate, and disappear from your life forever."

"That's fine with me," I said, as shadows fell across his eyes, making the green seem black.

And from the way the pain had now settled into a numbness that was overpowering, I knew forever wasn't really that long at all.

I watched as the outline of Justin's body became less distinct. As uncertainty replaced form. As fog replaced matter. And as he left, the shadows that had been distracted by his appearance moved in for the kill. I fell back onto the bed in a spiral of blackness, as all of my senses surrendered to sleep.

"Justin," I said to an empty room, "you were right. I am afraid to be alone. I just never want to admit it anymore. I remember that now, just like I remember why I loved you. And it wasn't just your eyes . . . it was your thoughts, your words, your touch. But I can't remember calling your name out in my sleep. I want to remember, but I can't. Justin, Justin, Justin. I'm dying, and I can't remember."

"But I remember, Kate," he said, "and that's enough."

I could hear his breathing again at the edge of the bed. He had come back for me.

"What have they done to you, Kate?"

"Poison," was all I could whisper, and I felt him kiss my forehead.

"Why couldn't you just tell me in the first place?" Justin shook his head and touched first my wrist, then my neck. "It's gone too far. There's only one thing I can do and I don't know if it's possible for me to do it again," Justin said. "I don't think anyone has ever done the impossible twice—resurrect someone from the dead—but I will try, if you tell me that's what you really want. If you don't want to go on to what's next. If you want to stay here. But if I roll away the stone, it has to be your choice this time. So tell me. . . ."

I couldn't find the words, so I reached out for his hand, and he grabbed it and held on.

"All right, Kate," he said. "I'll try." And the shadows moved aside, and I felt his hands pull away my clothes. And then pull away his. And as he lay down beside me on the bed, I realized how wonderful he looked without them. Something else I hadn't remembered.

"Creation is always sexual," Justin said, and I saw his teeth, four sharp points, beneath his lips.

"I can't sedate you this time, Kate, so there's going to be some pain. Just hold on to me, and I won't let you go."

And then he was inside me and I felt his teeth begin to caress my neck. I held my breath, and he bit down. Cold, hard steel invading my throat.

"Oh," I cried out, and he sucked for a moment, then lifted his head, and spit the contaminated blood aside.

"It's turned your blood to poison, too," he whispered. "I'll have to let it drain away." And he held my head as the blood rushed away from me onto Drew's blue and gray sheets. "I'm here, Kate. Just follow my words, and you won't get lost."

"Tell me a story, then," I whispered as he lay against me. "A fairy tale."

"There are no real fairy tales," he said, "only anti-fairy tales like this one my mother used to tell me. I think it was by Hans Christian Andersen. . . . Once upon a time there was a demon who had invented a mirror in which everything good and pretty reflected in it shrank away to nothing, and every bad thing stood out. And the demon was so proud of this mirror, he wanted to fly up to heaven and mock the angels with it. But as he flew higher, the mirror became heavier and heavier until it slipped out of his hands, fell to earth, and broke into a million pieces. Even then, it did more harm than ever, for even the tiniest grain of glass had the power of the whole mirror. Some people even got a bit of glass into their hearts, and that was terrible, for their heart became like a lump of ice . . . and that was how the Snow Queen was able to steal the little boy away from his girlfriend. She put a sliver of the mirror in his eye, so the only things he loved were ones that were cold . . ."

A lot of blood had left my body, and I felt cold even with Justin's body against mine. I could feel my empty veins and arteries. The lightness of a body losing life.

"Justin," I whispered, "I need a better story than that."

"Then I'll tell you a love story, Kate, because they're a lot better than fairy tales, even if this one doesn't have a happy ending. Once there was a prince who had lost everything in his life. His wife had died from pneumonia, his daughter had died of old age. And he had spent so many years alone that he thought he would probably stay that way forever.

"And then he met this princess who was beautiful and smart and funny, and he could talk to her as easily as he could talk to himself. And he thought she needed him too.

"For a long time all he did was talk to her and watch her sleep. He'd fly into the tower where she was being held prisoner and watch her dream. And she'd whisper his name, and he'd whisper back to her.

"And because this prince had been alone for too long and had forgotten that fairy tales were only for children, he made a mistake. He rescued her from the tower, when she really didn't want to be rescued at all. And instead of loving him, she hated him for it.

"So the prince was forced into exile, because he couldn't bear to face her anymore. But while the prince was away, all he did was think of the princess and wish he could watch her dream one more time. So he returned to the land she was living in, but by then she had already fallen in love with another man . . ."

I felt my heart slowing down, coming to a standstill.

"There," Justin said, "you're only a beat away." And I hung at the edge between life and death.

"Now," he said, "you'll have to take me." And he reached up to his neck and ripped a hole with his nails. And then he leaned his head down so my mouth could reach him, and his arms circled around my back.

"Take me now," he said, as the first drops reached my lips. And with all of the tiny bit of energy I still had left, I swallowed his blood, which tasted sweeter than anyone else's, remembering I had done this same thing, the same way, with this same man in another bed, where the sheets were white, a long time ago.

Justin, I thought, *I'm the one who made the mistake. Why don't you rescue me again?*

And I began to drink harder as my strength returned, throwing my arms around him and holding him tight. And we made love all night, and it brought me back to life again.

I opened my eyes and took in the white walls, which weren't the walls of my bedroom. I was lying in the coffin, but I wasn't in the small red chamber. I moved my hand a little, and I heard someone else in the room.

"Hi," Justin said. He was sitting in a rocking chair next to the coffin. The coffin seemed to be on some kind of platform, as I was level with his knees. He was wearing a black sweatshirt and jeans, and his hair was uncut and hung below his shoulders. His fingernails were ten sharp points, circled around the arms of the chair. He leaned over, and I saw he was a little paler than usual, but still perfect, untouched by any weakness or decay. "How do you feel?"

"Where are we?" I lifted my head, but it fell back against the velvet. "I'm a little weak."

"We're in Malibu, and you're all right." Justin touched my hair. "This can be your house now. I'm having my financial manager get rid of the Santa Monica condo as soon as the police are satisfied. Too many bad things. Too many memories. You need to live somewhere that isn't tainted by tragedy."

He sat back and rocked in the chair for a moment. It looked and sounded like an antique.

"And don't worry about your fiancé. When I saw your ring, I figured I'd better leave him a note that you're okay. I couldn't wait for him to come back; I had to do something right away. I moved you to a place that's safer for both of us. You've slept for three nights. I wasn't totally sure you'd survive. You didn't move. You didn't breathe. So I watched and waited. I postponed my trip. . . . I explained to Denise, I had some pressing family matters, that I had to miss the opening of her play, but I'd be there soon. Now that I've seen you wake and take your first breath, I know you'll be okay."

"Oh." I tried to sit up. "There are so many things I want to tell you. . . . Can't you wait just a little more?" I fell back, truly unable to move under my own power yet. I was completely exhausted. It was an effort just to speak, and probably a miracle I still existed. I felt the urge to cry, but no tears fell.

Justin stood. He looked handsome and elegant even in jeans. "I think your boyfriend's waited long enough without any word from you," he said. "Here, let me help you." He reached in and picked me up, and I circled my arm around his neck and rested my head against his shoulder. He carried me up two long flights of stairs that hid the secured bedroom below. We reached a trapdoor that opened into the living room, where the metal window gratings like those in the condo had been raised to reveal the night outside and the waves crashing on the beach only a few feet from the front door.

He set me down again on the white sofa, put a pillow carefully under my head, and went to stand at the window. I noticed the room was as spotless as those in the Santa Monica condo. The walls were pale gray, without a hint of dirt or abuse, and they held no pictures or photographs, no indication of life. Besides the sofa, the only furniture in the room were a matching white chair and two empty white bookcases, which reached the ceiling. But there was a small fireplace, with a huge fire burning noisily, near the entrance to the dining room. The dining room was empty, no table or chairs. It was designed for someone who did not have to eat or watch anyone else eat anymore. Not a human home, but perfect for me.

"There are no other houses around here for a quarter mile on either side, so it's very safe." Justin looked out at the night. "And an outsider has to get past a security guard to even reach this part of Malibu, and they patrol the area constantly. I've already told them you'll be living here, that you're a writer who wants complete privacy and not to disturb you unless it's an emergency. In Malibu that kind of behavior is par for the course, so I know they will leave you alone.

"You may also have noticed that there are two metal doors that lock between the bedroom below and the rest of the house. The trapdoor when closed from the inside cannot be opened by anyone above. I've moved all of your things from the other place; your clothes, your stereo, your musical equipment, and, of course, the coffin. I've also left you plenty of money, and the Porsche is parked in the garage."

"As always, you've taken care of everything," I said. "All the little details that make lives like ours work."

"Everything except your explanation to your fiancé." I saw Justin's profile harden for a moment, then relax. "I don't know how much he knows, and I don't want to know. You've made it quite clear that it's none of my business. I've only written a note that you were ill, and you're with a friend. . . . And then there's one more thing before I go. . . ."

He turned from the window and seemed to hesitate. "It's your first night again, and you need blood."

"Don't worry about it," I tried to stand up, but my legs wouldn't obey me. "I'll take care of it."

"No," he said decisively. "I will." And he sat down on the sofa beside me, the moon highlighting his face, and offered up his wrist. "Here," he said. "This is what you need."

I hesitated for a moment, but my need was overpowering. I gently took his arm and pushed up the black sleeve of his sweatshirt. Justin leaned back in the sofa and closed his eyes. I began to kiss his wrist, my tongue touching his skin, and then I suddenly stopped and gazed at his face. He looked like a beautiful statue, perfectly composed, that could be awakened with the magic of a kiss. On impulse I leaned up and kissed him on his forehead. His eyes opened for a moment in surprise, but he closed them again as I worked my way down his arm and back to his wrist.

"Justin," I said, and I bit down on his vein and began to suck as he rubbed the back of my head. And I thought of how much I had missed him in the last four years without ever knowing it. Until finally he gently pulled his arm away.

"Too much," he said, rubbing his wrist until the cut disappeared, "and you'll have to bring me back from the dead, too."

"Stay with me, Justin," I said, the taste of his blood still in my mouth. And I reached out and touched his face. "Why don't we pretend the last four years never happened? That I've just woken up in your bedroom, and you've explained to me what I am, what we both are, and that I never told you to go away, and you never left. . . ."

"Oh, Kate." Justin grabbed my hand and held it tightly. "If only it were that easy to change the past. But the past exists no matter how much we may want to forget it. It's too late now." He kissed my fingertips and got up and walked toward the door. "Too much has happened between us."

"Wait," I whispered, but he didn't hear me. I wanted to stand up and shout, "Stay with me forever," but I couldn't move.

"I have to go, Kate," Justin said, as he stood in the doorway. "You're in love with someone else and about to be married again, and I'm committed to someone, too. The last four years did happen, and nothing can change that. I have to go. I have to leave for Europe tonight. I've already stayed here too long. I'm sorry. I wish it could have been another way."

"Right," I said, feeling the cold from the ocean moving in. "I forgot. The play's the thing. Actresses are your game. And I'm just a musician without a record contract. Better not keep the young starlet waiting. You've already stayed too long."

"Kate." Justin smiled. The same smile that had captured me years ago. "I've got to admit, you've got an answer for everything. That and your will to survive—and you do want to survive, Kate—will insure you live forever. I don't think I have to worry about you anymore."

And then he opened the front door, disappeared into the night, and was gone. "I love you," I said to no one, and no one answered. And I was left with a new house, an old coffin, a lot of money, and some people I needed to see.

V

Fame

I took care of Detective Warren first, and that was easy.

Dr. Harrison Reeves was linked to a possible twenty murders—three of which were mine—and one attempted murder, which was me. He had originally been a coroner in upstate New York, but after his brother's death twenty-five years ago, he had resigned to pursue other interests, namely, vampire hunting.

His brother, a veterinarian in Manhattan, was no saint either. He had moonlighted by performing illegal abortions that often resulted in tragedy. He had disappeared mysteriously one June night, and was found on Wall Street the next morning, completely drained of blood. The doctor had decided it was the work of a vampire. And if it hadn't been for Charly, he would have finally been able to kill the genuine article.

Detective Warren thanked me for coming in to the station that night, for filling in the missing details, and for finally helping to close the case of the serial killer who drained blood and/or stabbed his victims through the heart, thereby being both vampire and vampire killer.

The detective understood why I wouldn't be living in Santa Monica anymore. He told me to keep his card in

case I ever needed help again, and he wished me luck
with my music. I gave him the new pair of Reeboks I had
bought him as a present, kissed him good-bye on the
cheek, and left.

"Kate," Nathan said, standing up at the table in Burger
World. "God, I'm so glad to see you. I've been asking
Drew about you, leaving messages, but, of course, no one
can get to Drew nowadays."

I sat down in the seat across from him. He ran his hand
along the yellow table, moving the straw in his soda from
side to side. He looked so much older than the night I
first met him at the audition.

"After Charly died, and knowing what that doctor tried
to do to you, I didn't even care about the band anymore. I
didn't think Drew would, either. I mean, CMD supposedly turned us down after they fired Matt. Now all of a
sudden, they're hot again but only for Drew?"

I nodded at Nathan as if I knew what he was talking
about.

"Of course you know and I know, it's only due to Lisa
and the thing she's got going with Drew that has him in
the door at all. It's funny, but I never figured Drew for
that kind of guy. Sherrie can't believe he'd dump both
you and me just to have a record deal. . . . It's amazing
what some people will do for fame. It turns them into
raving lunatics, complete monsters. Hell, I don't care anymore, anyway. I've got Sherrie, and that's all that matters.
I just worry about you."

"I'll be all right," I said. "I'm a survivor."

Nathan took a sip of his soda and smiled. "Hey," he
said, "did I tell you I've got a job with a Top Forty band in
Vegas for three weeks? It's money, there's no pressure,
and I'm still playing music. It's a lot better than selling my
soul like Drew, just to hear myself on the radio."

"Well," I said to Nathan, "what does it profit a man if he gains the whole world but loses his soul? Eventually, one way or the other, he's going straight to hell."

And Nathan laughed and took another sip of soda.

For weeks I sat at night on the beach in Malibu, looking at the lights that made up Santa Monica and wondering if anyone was looking back at me.

Soon, I thought. *Soon I'll have to pay a visit to Drew.* I twisted the diamond ring round and round my finger, imagining all the brutal ways one man could die. *Soon,* I thought, *I'll see my fiancé.*

I had read in the local music paper that he was definitely signed to CMD. And before his record even began production, there was a buzz circulating around L.A. about the only real surviving member of The Uninvited, a band cloaked in mystery, mayhem, and death. As far as CMD Records and the public were concerned, Nathan and I no longer existed.

The vampire stories, the serial killings, the blood, the violence, the death served only to make Drew a bigger star, the latest fad in a town that lived for them.

Already, *Music Connection* had featured him on the cover with the title article: "The Man Without a Country —Is He Vampire, Devil, or the Next Big Thing?"

I took the diamond ring off and let my tongue caress the stone. I wondered if my teeth could tear through one of the hardest materials known to man, but I decided to keep my symbol of love intact for the time being.

Soon, I thought, *Drew will see just how big the next thing can be, and that the old saying is true—you're more famous when you're dead than alive.*

And the waves kept rolling up and down the beach that now belonged to me, in Malibu.

* * *

I sat outside the window of Drew's bedroom and watched him make love to Lisa. He had changed the sheets he'd left me to die on. They were green now, instead of blue. I watched as his eyes closed, and his hands moved, and his blond hair fell across his face.

And at the height of the whole thing, he called out my name. Not once, not twice, but three times. Kate. . . . He called my name as if he'd always meant to come back for me. *Kate.* . . . *Kate.* . . .

Lisa pretended not to notice. Or maybe she was thinking of someone else, too. You never know what someone's thinking when they're making love to you. And you never know what they'll do when you really need them. Just as you never know who your friends are in L.A. until it's too late.

I watched as Lisa put on Drew's shirt and padded off to the bathroom. "I'm going to take a shower," she said. "When I come back, we'll talk about producers again."

Drew rolled over onto his stomach, closed his eyes, and began to fall asleep. I could see his back, falling and rising as relaxation set in.

Perfect time for a little dramatics. And I floated into the room and materialized at the side of the bed.

"Drew," I whispered, sitting down on his side of the mattress, "I think it's time we set a date."

"What?" Drew said sleepily.

"I think it's time we set a date for our wedding."

"Shit," Drew said, turning his head in my direction. "What the hell?"

He started to get up, but I put my hand on his back and held him in place. The muscles of his back strained against me, but I was strong again.

"Kate?" he asked. "Kate? Is that you?" He turned his head to the side so he could breathe a little more easily. "Kate?"

"What's the matter, Drew? Having second thoughts after leaving me to die? Not sure if you want to spend a lifetime with me? Not sure who you want to be your best man now that Charly's gone?"

"Kate," he said, "let me up. Let me see your face. You don't understand."

"All right." I released him, and he pulled himself up and crawled to the end of the bed.

"What's going on? What are you doing here? I only got this note that you were okay and at a friend's. I didn't know what to think." Drew pulled the sheet up to his waist as if there was some need for modesty.

"You didn't know what to think." I realized I was shouting, but I didn't care anymore. "Lisa calls you at three in the morning when I'm doubled over in pain and begging you not to leave, and you just go running off without a second thought, telling me vampires are always all right. You didn't know what to think?"

I slammed my hand against the bed frame, and it shook violently. Then I stood up and walked to the end of the bed, where Drew was sitting. His eyes stared back at me, empty and afraid. He looked like a mouse caught in a trap, knowing doom was on the way but hoping, always hoping.

"I told you I was poisoned, Drew, but you didn't really care. When it came right down to it, you didn't really care. Do you realize, Drew, that you left me alone to die only a week after you asked me to marry you?"

Drew looked in the direction of the bathroom, then back at me again.

"Worried about Lisa?" I asked. "No problem." I smiled and went to Drew's oversize dresser, pulled it out into the hallway, and pushed it up against the bathroom door. "There'll be no further interruptions." I smiled at Drew as if I only meant to seduce him. He had pulled on his jeans and was standing beside the bed, unsure of what to do next. He glanced at the door and then the window. His hands were shaking.

I walked back to face him. "So tell me, are you happy now? You've got a record deal, and you're the hottest thing in town. A man without a country—and a man without a band to worry about. Charly's dead. Nathan might as well be, and I've always been. And to top it all off, you're sleeping with the power that got you that deal in the first place. And you were sleeping with her even before you gave me this stupid, two thousand-dollar engagement ring."

I took the ring off and threw it on the floor.

"I'm calling the engagement off," I said, "and you may be looking at a breach of promise suit, a copyright suit, and a real, honest-to-God death threat!"

"Look, Kate"—Drew extended his hands in a plea for mercy—"I know damn well you could kill me right now. Rip me limb from limb. I've seen you do it. Maybe that's what you're here to do. Maybe that's what you've waited for. I don't know. And I don't know what you expect from me—what you ever expected from me. I'm just a regular guy who likes to play music and who wants it to make him famous. I need this record deal. I can't live without it anymore. I've got to have it. When Lisa called, what did you expect me to do that night? I felt like dying after Matt's whole thing fell through. And what could I have ever done for you? I'm just a regular guy. What do I know about vampires? I don't have the kind of open mind it would take to live with that kind of thing. I just want the fucking American dream. I want to be rich and famous. And I want somebody to love. And Lisa, even if she's not all that lovable, at least she's human." Drew's hands fell limply at his sides.

I heard a noise behind me. It was Lisa, turning the knob of the bathroom door and finding herself trapped.

"Drew," I heard her call out anxiously. "Drew, I can't get out."

"Drew," I said, "you can't get out, either." And as he started to move to the door, I jumped in his way, and he fell back onto the bed. And I fell on top of him.

My hands held his against the new green sheets. There were bits of corn chips in the creases. "When I saw the doctor's eyes as he took the scalpel and began to cut my stomach open, I asked myself, what kind of man could be driven to torture someone like this and enjoy doing it? Now, you may think I'm a monster for single handedly tearing up a man who has eaten children and destroyed an old lady who was my only friend. A man who intended to kill you when the moon was full again. But there are all kinds of monsters in this world, and I was never a monster to you."

I moved closer to Drew's face so I could feel his breath against my lips. It was hot and frightened, and it became shorter with every second.

"But the question that is really plaguing me now, the sixty-four thousand-dollar one, is what kind of monster would leave the woman he loves—no matter what kind of woman she really is—all alone in the darkness to die?"

Drew closed his eyes as if he expected me to bite down any second, and I heard Lisa call out again.

"Drew, God damn it, are you awake? Get your ass out of bed, you idiot, and open this door!"

I looked around Drew's bedroom one last time, but it no longer felt safe and forgiving. It was haunted by shadows that would never leave. It reminded me of pain.

"The answer," I said, releasing his hands, "is a human one. Someone who would do what any ordinary guy would do when confronted with the supernatural. And that's not what I expected, and that's not what I need. Because even though I've tried very hard to disguise it by leading something of a normal life and believing I loved a normal guy, I'm not ordinary anymore, and I'm just beginning to learn to live with it."

Drew opened his eyes. The blue did not match the green. There was a coldness there I had never seen. He was not the same person I had wanted a long time ago, when we danced under the moonlight.

"The funny part," I said quietly, "is that all of this has made you harden your heart, and all it did for me was soften mine. I said I'd never hurt you, and I meant what I said. But at least give me half of the credit for our song on your album, even if nothing else is the same."

I slid off his body and stood again at the side of the bed. Drew lay still, not sure if his life would end at any moment. Afraid I would pounce if I noticed any motion on his part. I smiled because I had put the fear of God or the devil back in his life again. At least that was worth something.

"And remember this: Don't be so quick to tell someone good-bye, to write them out of your life, until you're really sure that they didn't watch you when you were sleeping, talk to you when you were dreaming. Or you may find yourself calling out their name when you try to make love to someone else."

I blew Drew a kiss.

"Kate . . ." he said, but I was already merging with the shadows on the wall, and Lisa's voice took precedence over every other sound in the room.

"Drew! Can you hear me? Drew! Wake up, you asshole! Get me out of this bathroom, now! Or you'll be sorry. And I know just how to make you sorry! Drew!"

* * *

Water and paper and stone all rolled into one. Ashes to ashes. Dust to dust. How many times can we mistake lust for love? And how many mistakes can one person make in one lifetime?

I look up at the moon, which is full again, and shake my head at the stars.

"And what is life," I whisper to the dirt that covers Charly's body, "but a series of little deaths, parts of us dying, both good and bad, until we finally hit the big one? Then all mistakes are canceled, and everything we ever loved or lusted for is translated into dust.

"You were right, Charly," I say, lying down flat on his grave, "you were right about Drew. It was supernatural the way he claimed me as his own and the way I pretended to be the woman he wanted to claim.

"And even though I now know Drew was only a human stand-in for the person I was trying to replace, my pathetic attempt to find love and be part of a world I was no longer welcome in—my last human weakness—I'm still mad at Drew. I'm disappointed in Drew. I hate Drew. But that's the easy part.

"What's hard is the emptiness I cannot fill by having him in bed beside me. By having him hold me till dawn. I cannot even long for him, because the Drew I once thought I loved no longer exists. Just as the human Kate no longer exists, and pretending she does isn't worth it. Just like you no longer exist.

"And if there was a way I could reach down through the ground and grab your hand and pull you back up into this world, I would, because if there was ever a time I really needed a friend it's now.

"I think we could have been good friends, Charly. If only. And there are always those two words. Sliding in between everything we remember as good and everything that we cannot do over again because it only happens once. If only."

I get up from Charly's grave and brush off the dirt still clinging to my black leather jacket. I had hoped that he would have an angel watching over him, but instead, it's just a little square of a tombstone with a name and some dates. So I leave the panda there to mark that square different from all the others. If only. If only.

I walk back to the limousine that is waiting for me. The one I hired for the night. To be in keeping with the lifestyle of the rich, if not the famous, that I was now leading.

James, the driver, nods at me, but no expression reaches his face. He knows better than to ask any of his customers what they've been doing. After all, it's L.A., and he's probably already driven plenty of people to plenty of places stranger than a graveyard on a Saturday night.

"Where to now?" James asks as I settle back in the seat, the black leather caressing the back of my neck.

"Let's just ride around till dawn," I say, and he puts the car in drive and heads to the highway.

"James," I say, as we coast down Interstate 405, the tinted window shielding me from any human stares, "are you an actor, by any chance?"

"Yes," he says, brightening, the possibility of a part entering his head.

"I'm not a producer, director, or anything like that," I say, "so don't get too excited. I'm just curious. . . ." And I see him fall back into his seat. "If you were going to do a play anywhere in Europe, where do you think you'd go?"

James looks in the rearview mirror, and I smile encouragingly.

"Well," he says, "it would probably be England. Where

else could I go? I'd have to know the language. . . . London would be the likely place."

"London," I say a little too intensely, and I see the hairs stand up on the back of James's neck. A reflex. An animal instinct. I'm not as controlled as I was when I had the band and Drew around me all the time. In three months I've forgotten how nervous I can make some people.

"London," I whisper again. Of course, London would be the place. I could hire a real estate agent first, to find a safe place to stay, then ship the coffin there so it would be waiting for me when I arrived. I could have all the comforts of home.

I might like London, a city of fog and mists. Where the sun hardly ever shines. Where history extends so far back in time, the modern world cannot totally erase it.

London—a lifetime away from L.A., which is getting annoying again. There is nothing for me here now, and music can wait.

Because I have forever again. And forever is a long time to waste on regret.

SCIENCE FICTION / FANTASY